COLD WALLET

ROSY FENWICKE

Wonderful World

Published by Wonderful World Ltd

Author website: rosyfenwickeauthor.com

Facebook: facebook.com/rosyfenwickeauthor/

Please follow Rosy on Facebook for news, posts and offers.

This is a work of fiction inspired by events at Quadriga, a Canadian cryptocurrency exchange, as reported in the public domain.

The names, characters, places and incidents are the product of the author's imagination or are used fictitiously and any resemblance to actual persons ,living or dead, events or locales is entirely coincidental.

A catalogue record for this book is available from the National Library of New Zealand.

To Josie without whom this book would not have seen the light of day.

PROLOGUE

THE RIGHT THING TO do would have been to walk across the road and stop the wedding. The right thing to do would have been to tell Andrew to run — to run as far and as fast as he could, to a place where no one could find him. No one. Not even me. When did I ever do the right thing?

I figured it was easier to stay in the café and finish my coffee than tell him the truth. Easier — and kinder. Why should I ruin the happy day? I'd read the etiquette sheet Jess had provided — specifically points five through seven, underlined and detailing my responsibilities as his best man. Not one included me telling the groom to run for his life.

Andrew was to be at the appointed place ten minutes before the appointed time, preferably sober and wearing clean underwear. I was to bring the ring and hand it over when asked. Afterwards, at lunch, I was to make a speech — amusing and short. Smut verboten. Simple.

I was late, yet still I waited. I nursed my coffee and stared across the street at the bridal party standing in the driveway of the hotel. Late December, it was a perfect summer's day in Auckland. The sun was shining. What little breeze there was, gentle and cooling. Jess, the epitome of elegance stood to one side — her white satin sheath fluttering against slim curves. She looked serene. In contrast, Carole, her bridesmaid was pacing up and down, examining the faces of passers-by, searching for me, swearing under her breath. Shorter and plumper than Jess, her navy dress was wrinkling in the heat.

Andrew leant against the veranda watching them from behind his sunglasses. I was still getting used to his haircut. Gone were the random shoulder length curls and in their place slicked-back brown hair with fades on either side. Clean-shaven, and wearing his new suit and shoes he looked for the first time, like the wealthy thirty-two-year-old man that he was. He caught Jess's eye and shrugged, smiling. I know that what-can-you-do smile. I'm his best friend. I'm the person he told that he was in love, and later that he was getting married. I know what he's going to do before Jess does. He talks, I listen. At least that's the way it used to be. Until she came along. I said nothing when he told me he'd proposed. It was too late to say anything now.

I finished my coffee, went to the bathroom took a leak and washed and dried my hands. Ducking down to check my hair in the mirror, I paused. People — women and men — tell me I'm good looking. I believe them. Brown eyes, dark hair, good teeth and built like the rugby player I used to be, what's not to like? I eat well and work out three times a week. I have a stylist who organises my wardrobe — I take care of myself — I have to. No one else will do it. Not now. With a nod at the barista, I left the café and sauntered across the road. Carole stopped pacing and put away her phone. With my best smile, I greeted the wedding party, told the women how beautiful they looked, shook Andrew's hand, clapped him on the back and muttered about a late taxi.

The venue, chosen by the bride, was a boutique hotel — expensive, discrete, small and to give Jess credit, tasteful. Inside, it was all French flea-market elegance — chandeliers and white-upholstered Louis XIV chairs. Outside, white gravel paths lined with box hedges marshalled us to an archway brought twelve thousand miles from a decrepit French chateau to this garden in New Zealand.

I stood beside Andrew under the archway and handed him the ring at the appropriate time. I didn't ruin their day.

We risk everything when we love. Andrew knew that. He committed to love Jess in good times and bad, until death parted them. On the happiest day of his life Andrew wasn't thinking about death. It was not my place to remind him. Not when there was a chance of happily ever after. That chance was my present to my friend.

Keeping quiet saved a whole lot of trouble — it saved me — for a while. What did that philosopher say? Life is nasty, brutish and short. Terrifying, he forgot terrifying. Images of retractable baseball bats wielded by Murray's mates loomed large when I considered telling Andrew the truth. I feared losing my friend. Even more, I feared what would happen to me.

It was done. I slapped him on the back and kissed the bride — and Carole. I smiled, I laughed, and I posed for photos. At lunch, I made a short but amusing speech with only a smidgen of smut. I did what a best man does — as ordered — as per the etiquette sheet.

ONE

JESS STRETCHED and sat up wincing when the straps of her bikini bit into her sunburnt shoulders. The immunology text she'd been reading tumbled on to the sand beside the sun lounger. A staff member leapt forward to retrieve it, but she waved him away and picked it up, shaking the sand from its pages before lying it face down on the table beside her.

As she leant forward she adjusted her sunglasses against the glare from the water and searched the lagoon for her husband. A moment later she spotted a waterspout and a flurry of fins in the distance near the reef. Reassured, she took up the book, found her page and started to read about T cell development in adolescence. She'd never felt happier or more at peace. She was in love with a man who loved her in return. She was staying at Sea Change — one of the world's most exclusive resorts built on a volcanic atoll in the Yasawa chain, west of the two main Fijian islands.

A year ago, the thought of falling in love and throwing caution to the wind to marry so quickly would have made her scoff. At thirty, she'd had the next ten years mapped out. Ward work, research and a doctorate in immunology, followed by post-doc research overseas —

enter Andrew Cullinane. She fell in love and within weeks her plan had been shot to hell.

With her concentration gone the words on the page jumbled into a meaningless mess. She closed the book and put it down. Who was she kidding? Immunology could wait. This place was too gorgeous for words. The white sandy beach overhung with coconut palms, the blue of the sea, the line of jungle-covered hills behind the bay — it was exactly how a tropical paradise was supposed to look. The smell of freshly squeezed lime heralded the arrival of the gin and tonic she'd ordered earlier — Jonah their valet, put the glass down on the table next to her book.

Andrew had suggested the Sea Change resort as a possible honeymoon destination when they were out at dinner one evening. It was Henry, his friend and business colleague, who had insisted it was perfect and that they must go. 'No Internet, Jess. It's the only way you'll get him to switch off,' he'd said. 'I'd come with you if I could afford it,' he added half-jokingly. Jess remembered tensing. Given the slightest encouragement, Henry Turner would have had no compunction playing the third wheel. He followed them most places — a volcanic atoll in the middle of the Pacific ocean would be nothing to him.

Before their wedding, Andrew checked out the resort online and showed her the photos. Sea Change looked amazing — and exclusive — and hideously expensive. She couldn't imagine being able to relax in such a place. Unused to people waiting on her, worried she would appear gauche and unsophisticated, she didn't want to embarrass Andrew. The only time she'd left New Zealand was the year before, when she'd travelled to Sydney to sit her final exams. Carole had come with her for support, and after Jess was told she'd passed, they had relaxed and enjoyed three glorious days of sun, surf, shopping and dining out. It was Jess's first proper holiday as an adult.

'Let's go somewhere closer. This place is over the top,' she whispered to Andrew as they were sitting in the travel agent's office in downtown Auckland. 'We're away for such a short time and it's so expensive.'

Andrew ignored her, and turned to Sophie, the agent, to ask more questions. Sophie, a buxom woman in her fifties, successful judging by her clothes and the office, focused her attention on Andrew, leaning into their conversation across her desk. Jess didn't take offence. Sophie was only doing her job and Andrew was often like this. She was used to him. Dismissive at times, he was also blunt. She'd heard him referred to as arrogant, but she preferred to think of him as a man who knew what he wanted. Many of the senior consultants at the hospital were just like him. Usually men, they expected to be heard the first time they said anything. She found it easier to go along with them, only interrupting or asking questions when she considered a patient was at risk, and only after double checking her facts.

Jess had found out very quickly that when Andrew wanted something, he got it. Straightaway or later, the timing was irrelevant. He got what he wanted. One way or another.

'As you know,' Sophie said turning her screen so they could both see it. 'Sea Change is one of the most exclusive resorts in the world. You arrive by helicopter, plane, boat, whichever you prefer. There are four villas. No more.' She clicked a key and photos of their destination tracked across the screen. 'Because each one is set in its own bay, you won't be aware of the other guests on island. Children are strenuously discouraged. The beach is pristine, the reef untouched; it's a marine reserve actually, so the snorkelling is spectacular. Do either of you dive? Snorkel?'

Andrew had looked at Jess, eyebrows raised. 'I can't dive, but I'd like to learn,' he said. 'You?'

'I swam at school,' she said. 'We can learn to dive together, that would be fun.'

Sophie continued. 'The island is covered in virgin tropical jungle and there are tracks which take you to lookouts where you can see the most delicious sunsets. I'm guessing being newlyweds, you may not be so interested in sunrises.' She paused for a reaction. None was forthcoming.

'The chef is new,' she continued. 'He's Japanese and specializes in seafood and Pacific fusion. A lot of produce is grown onsite and every effort is made to be self-sustaining. Imagine the Garden of Eden but with a beach, a warm sea, a gourmet restaurant, and enough staff to attend to your every need.'

Jess reached over and squeezed Andrew's hand.

'I'm thinking we leave straight after the ceremony,' he said.

'But what about Carole and Henry?' she asked.

'What about them?' Andrew asked.

'We can't ask them to be our witnesses and then walk out.'

'Why not?'

'Because it's rude. It's also the only time we'll ever get married. I'd like to celebrate. Lunch at least. We can't say I do, tell them to sign here, and jump in a car and go straight to the airport.'

'You're having a small wedding?' Sophie asked. 'You're so lucky. Big weddings are a lot of work. My husband and I spent months organizing our daughter's big day. I can't tell you how exhausted I was by the end of it.'

'We're orphans,' Andrew said.

Sophie swivelled back to her keyboard and started typing.

'We're keeping it low key,' Jess explained. 'No family, no fuss.' She reached out and took his hand again, gently this time. 'Lunch wouldn't be making a fuss would it?'

He smiled, leant over and kissed her lightly on the lips. 'Whatever my bride wants.'

Sophie, sensing peace turned back to them. 'Fabulous ring,' she breathed, pointing at Jess's engagement ring.

Jess was still not used to the weight of the four carat white diamond set in rose gold and flexed her fingers. 'My fiancé is a very generous man,' she replied.

She looked at the ring now, the brilliant white of the stone nestled beside a simple gold band. She was a married woman. Dr Jess Cullinane. She hadn't hesitated when Andrew asked her to change her name. Such a small price to pay for love — besides she believed in tradition. Jess Gordon had served her well in recent years, but Jess Cullinane sounded better.

'You may well have the resort to yourselves,' Sophie told them after more keystrokes.

'Keep it that way,' Andrew said sliding his credit card across the desk. 'Book all four villas.'

Sophie checked, and when she saw that he wasn't joking, typed quickly. 'Confirmed. Your email address?'

'Print everything out if you don't mind,' he said. 'I don't want to take any risks with the Internet. One less thing to worry about.'

Sophie called her assistant over to take their coffee orders while she leapt into action and completed the documentation. Jess had never seen a woman look as happy in her work as Sophie had that afternoon.

Now in the late afternoon, the sun was on its downward slide towards the horizon. Andrew had been in the water for two hours. He must be getting tired. She got up and looked out to the reef, spotting him easily this time, his fins kicking up a froth of water behind him as he swam towards the beach — slowly. More slowly than he had swum out. She put up a hand to shade her eyes and assessed his progress. Behind her in the bar, the men stopped what they were doing, and one came down the beach towards her. They could both see it. Andrew was struggling. After pulling on her reef shoes, Jess sprinted down the beach, calling to the men to get help. As she splashed into the water, she took no notice of the warmth of the sea. She ignored the little fish scattering beneath her and the turtle who turned in alarm and swam off to her right. Her sole focus was to reach Andrew — quickly.

She dived in and struck out towards him, grateful for the pull of the outgoing tide. Every time she stopped to get her bearings, she was terrified she wouldn't see him, that he would be lost from view. She was a strong swimmer, much stronger than he was, but even with the tide, it took forever to narrow the distance between them. She heard yelling from the beach, and a boat, its engine whining with the throttle open to maximum, came speeding towards her. She waved it on. The boat overshot Andrew, slowed, then circled back and reached him just as she did, just as he was sinking. She put her arms around him and supported his head, treading water to keep them both afloat, while the men leant over and pulled his limp body towards them. He slithered into the bottom of the boat and lay still while they pulled Jess out of the sea.

'Go! Go!' she told them as she moved forward and cradled Andrew's head in her lap. She felt for a pulse on the side of his neck, and was relieved when she found it — fast and strong.

Andrew opened his eyes and took a long shuddering breath. 'I knew you'd save me,' he gasped. 'Has anyone told you that you have kind eyes?' Then he winked.

'You are a rat, Andrew Cullinane,' she said, slapping his chest. But she bent down and gave him the kiss of life anyway ignoring the look which passed between the men in the back of the boat.

They dined, as they had every evening, at the table on the veranda at the front of their villa. Someone had placed bowls of creamy white frangipani on the steps leading down to the sea, the heady perfume scented the air. Candles in glass holders provided the only light, so as not to distract from the glory of the Milky Way and the dark sky above.

Sophie had been right about the chef. The food was fabulous. Because the island was a marine reserve, everything except the vegetables had to be brought in daily by boat, the chef selecting the best ingredients the South Pacific had to offer. That night they ate crayfish from New Zealand, prepared in a Fijian Suruwa, a lightly spiced coconut milk curry, followed by a peach sorbet served with Central Otago cherries the size of plums, each one bursting with flavour at the first bite. They finished their wine while they stared out to sea; the only sound was the gentle slap of the waves against the steps of the veranda.

'Will it always be like this?' Jess asked.

'Our life, you mean? It could be, if that's what you want.'

'I want,' she said getting up and walking around the table to sit in his lap. He looked into her eyes and smiled that smile. The one she could never resist, the one she'd fallen instantly in love with, months before. She cradled his head against her, his breath warm on her breasts, before his lips moved, barely grazing her skin. She could feel his erection harden beneath her. She thought about straddling him at the table, but she wanted more, much more. Jess stood up, took his hand and led him towards the bedroom.

Afterwards, they slept tangled together in the sheets with the fan beating overhead in the darkness. Meanwhile the staff tiptoed on to the veranda and took away the remains of their meal — and made everything perfect again.

TWO

SOMETIME DURING THE NIGHT, Jess was half-asleep when she backed into the curve of Andrew's body, and expected him to wrap his arms around her. He didn't move. He was hot — burning hot. Sweat had pooled on the sheet, soaking through to the mattress beneath him. He was breathing fast and shallow and he barely moved when she sat up and turned on the light. He groaned when she shook him gently and then rolled away. She felt his wrist for his pulse and when she couldn't find it, she gave up. She felt it more easily in his neck. No longer steady and even, the beats were all over the place, and way too fast.

'Andrew?' She shook him again, firmly this time — he opened his eyes. He seemed to barely focus before they closed again. Licking his lips, he tried to swallow, but he only succeeded in rolling his sticky tongue around his dry lips.

'You're burning up. Did you take your meds today?'

'This morning.' His words caught in his mouth behind tacky saliva.

'Does it hurt?'

'Here, Dr Jess,' he said and flopped a hand on to his stomach. 'Here and here.'

She pressed where he indicated, and he let out a soft groan, his abdomen contracting under her hand. It wasn't soft as it should be.

She pushed his hand out of the way and put her ear to his stomach and listened. His gut was going crazy. It was as if he was boiling on the inside.

'Oh God, I gotta go.' He groaned, his eyes opened wide as he rolled over, hauled himself to his feet and using the wall for support, staggered to the bathroom. Jess heard an eruption of wind then liquid hitting porcelain — then silence.

She was already up and when she ran to his side, she ignored the terrible smell, the blood and shit spattering the toilet and the surrounding tiles, only seeing the pale face of the man she loved, looking at her helplessly from where he leant against the wall. She flushed the loo under him, then soaked a towel and used it to wipe him clean, hurling it behind her into the bath. She grabbed another towel from the pile and used it to wipe up the surrounding area and dumped that one in the bath too.

'Can you stand?' she asked.

'I'll try.'

Jess bent down in front of him and hooked her arms under his to help him upright. 'I'm going to swing you over to the bidet to clean you up. Can you take any weight?'

'Only if you don't let go.' His voice was hoarse. With a combination of lifting and pushing his feet, followed by a final twist, Jess manoeuvred him on to the bidet and turned the tap on full.

'Feels good,' he whispered and tried to smile.

'Stay there, don't move,' she said as she ran into the bedroom and grabbed the phone. As she sat on the floor beside him, she called reception.

'Please, we need help,' she said without waiting for a reply, before she hung up. Once she'd made sure he wasn't going to slide off the bidet, she ducked back to the bedroom and pulled on a t-shirt and track pants. When she returned, it was to find Andrew bent double clutching his stomach, teeth clenched, groaning in pain. She squatted down in front of him, took his hand, and squeezed it hard while she waited, counting the seconds waiting for whatever it was, to happen. All the while, praying that help was coming. Half a minute passed. It seemed like a century, then she felt him relax and he opened his eyes and this time he focused.

'You have such kind eyes. Has anyone ever told you that?'

'You have Andrew. You have.'

'You have the kindest eyes in the world,' he murmured before he shuddered against her, and as he was wracked by a bout of pain, he let go another burst of diarrhoea. The bidet was full. Not such a good idea after all.

'Listen,' she said, 'Can you stand up? I need to get you back to the loo.'

Andrew was worse if that was possible. Sweating and grey, he had lost all his strength, and as he leant on her he tried to manage the few steps to their destination.

She grabbed more towels, threw one over the mess in the bidet and used the others to wedge him into a safe position while she searched through her bag of medicines. Her hands were shaking so much she spilt tablets on to the floor in her desperation to find anything which might help. If only she'd prepared a better kit, thought it through, instead of assuming he was better. *Damn it, damn me.* She found two tablets, codeine and loperamide. Worth a try if he could swallow them and keep them down. She filled a glass with water. Supporting his head, she placed one tablet on his tongue, held the glass to his lips, poured water into his mouth, and tipped his head back. The water dribbled out the sides of his mouth and with it the tablet.

'Please, please try,' she said. 'It's the best I can do until you get to hospital. You need help, proper help.' She placed another tablet on his tongue and poured water in again. This time he swallowed and then managed to down two more tablets before another spasm of pain hit him and he bent double, crying this time.

'Do you understand what I'm saying? You need hospital.'

Andrew sat up and without opening his eyes, shook his head. 'I've been worse, Truly. Not hospital. Not here. I don't trust them. You help me. You do what you need to, and we can wait it out. Organize a plane tomorrow. Take me home.'

He was panting by the time he finished, his breath foul smelling and hot. Drained of energy, he leant back, eyes closed again, sweat running off him and dripping audibly on to the floor. Jess was about to tell him again that she couldn't look after him. That she didn't have the equipment, when he doubled over and fell against her. Caught by surprise she wasn't ready for his dead weight and he ended up sprawled face down on the floor. Blood spurted from his bottom; the towels turning bright red around him.

I'm not going to panic. I can't panic. I'm a doctor. I don't panic. She felt his neck for a pulse. It was still there — faint — but there. All she wanted to do was scream for someone, anyone to come and help. She couldn't do this alone. She checked her phone. Three minutes had passed since she'd called reception. It seemed like hours. Cradling his head in her lap for the second time that day, she rocked back and forth, stroking his forehead and whispering that it would be all right, and to hang on, help was coming.

Then thankfully, there was a discreet knock. 'In here. Hurry,' she called out.

Three men in neatly pressed Hawaiian shirts, warily pushed open the door to the bathroom and stood transfixed staring open mouthed at the chaos. Then the smell reached them, and their faces exhibited looks of disgust. One gagged and backed away, holding his hand over his nose and mouth — the others were desperate to do the same, but thankfully they stayed put.

'You! Get more towels,' Jess said pointing at one nearest to her. 'You!' she said, 'get the manager. Tell him to bring whatever first aid equipment there is.'

They didn't move, and she repeated herself, yelling this time.

'Go! Move! Please! He's sick. Really, really sick.' They didn't need to be told a third time. To Jess's relief, when the first man reappeared wiping his mouth, he set about tidying up the mess.

'How far away is the hospital? How long does it take to get there?' she asked as he ferried the filthy towels away. He didn't answer, just shook his head. She made herself take a deep breath and breathe out slowly. She had to stay calm or she would be no help to Andrew.

'We need to go to hospital,' she repeated as if this would make it happen. The man smiled weakly and shrugged. He might not understand, but she appreciated he was trying to help and for that Jess was grateful. The second man arrived with a stack of fresh towels and the three of them worked together to wedge them around Andrew, fixing him on his side, in the recovery position. He barely reacted. The blood seeping on to the floor had slowed to a trickle, but it was still bright red.

Jess didn't know how much longer she could keep it together. She felt like screaming, grabbing the men and shaking them, yelling at them to do more, to help her carry Andrew to hospital, to make it all stop, make him wake up and be normal again.

Thankfully, a second before she descended into full-blown panic, Simon, the manager arrived. He took one look at Andrew, at Jess, the towels and acted. 'James! Go! Help Paulo bring the first aid kit. Hurry!' He crouched beside Jess and got her to tell him what had happened.

'Andrew has inflammatory bowel disease, a disease in his gut,' Jess said trying but not managing to keep the stammer out of her voice. 'He was doing well. We thought he was in remission, but this ... I'm a doctor. He's worse than I've ever seen him. He has to go to hospital — now,' she said. 'How far away is it? Can you call them please? I can put up an IV if you have the gear, but it's not enough. It won't be enough. He'll need surgery to stop the bleeding.'

Simon checked his watch. He appeared to be thinking through the options, but why was he so slow? Just then Andrew groaned. Another explosion soiled the towels with blood mixed with the foulest of watery diarrhoea. This time though, Andrew arched his back and screamed, long and loud.

'We don't have much time,' Jess pleaded. 'Please help us.'

Simon stood up and walked through to the bedroom. She could hear him talking so, so, slowly. She forced herself to stay silent, to breathe and let him speak to whoever he'd called. She had to hold it together and keep people on side, if Andrew was to get help.

She knelt over her husband, hugging his head, stroking his face, whispering that it would be all right, and that she was here and wouldn't let anything happen to him, and to hold on, stay with her, to keep listening to her voice. Tears were rolling down her face. 'Please Andrew, please just hold on.'

Simon was speaking more loudly as she heard him call a helicopter insisting three paramedics were to come with it. She heard him yell at the operator that they were to come now, and that he didn't care if it was the middle of the night, the pad would be lit.

Paulo arrived with the first aid box. At last, Jess had something to do. She wrapped a tourniquet around Andrew's arm, then she got the IV and a bag of saline ready. His elbow vein was barely there, but she'd got lines into worse. She pushed the IV in, taped it in place and hooked up the bag of fluid, opening it to run full bore. After finding an ampule of tranexamic acid, she injected a bolus praying it would be enough to stop the bleeding until they got to the hospital.

Meanwhile, Simon was still talking to an operator, demanding to be put through to a doctor. He must have known the person because when he was put through, she heard him call him by name. He listed Andrew's symptoms, then spoke to her. 'Tim wants to know what medication your husband is taking. You speak to him.' He handed the phone to her and left the room to organize men to light up the landing pad for the helicopter.

It was a relief to talk to someone medical. Someone who asked the right questions and who understood the seriousness of the situation. It was as if she was reporting on a ward round and the familiarity of the words helped calm her.

'Andrew is thirty-two. He's got ulcerative colitis. He's had it for six years. Professor David Robinson in Auckland is his usual doctor. He won't mind if you call him — any time.' She recited the professor's cell phone details from her phone. 'Andrew takes Humira. Gives it to himself every two weeks. No, I can't be certain when he last had it. It was before we left. No, he didn't bring any with him. But we wouldn't have come if he wasn't stable. We couldn't have.' She listened as the doctor asked her about Andrew's temperature and other signs. She was able to tell him what he needed to know, feeling better to be of use. Then Andrew tensed and moaned. She dropped the phone. As another spasm of pain gripped him, he looked up at her. 'Kind eyes,' he said, then he lost consciousness.

It took twenty minutes for the helicopter to arrive in a flurry of wind. It took another ten minutes for three paramedics to stabilize Andrew, get him on to a stretcher and strapped in. Meanwhile Jess grabbed clothes, laptops, phones and passports, stuffed them into her tote, and ducking low beneath the blades she climbed in beside her still unconscious husband. One of the paramedics pointed to a seat, out of the way. He was the only one who spoke English, but he didn't have time to translate for her, as she watched them work to save her husband.

Five minutes before they landed, Andrew's heart stopped. Jess had seen people defibrillated many times. She'd done it herself often, but then it had been in a professional capacity. It was different when it happened to someone you loved. Your heart stopped with theirs as you waited to see if the white line would leap across the screen again. Disbelief overtook her that this could be happening at all. She was in a country where she didn't speak the language and didn't know if she could trust the hospital. Tim, the doctor, had seemed okay on the phone, but that was it. She had no idea who he was or what his qualifications were.

She couldn't hear the monitor's beep-beep above the noise of the helicopter as Andrew's heart started beating again, but she breathed a sigh of relief when the line saw-toothed into action. She thanked a God she didn't believe in and promised she would change, be good, do whatever was asked of her, sacrifice anything, if only he or she would keep Andrew alive.

Jess wasn't allowed in the ambulance. She had to follow behind in a car, the flashing lights reflected off the driver's face as dawn seeped light into the new day. She had to sit in the car and wait, watching the shadowy movements behind the glass panels in the doors of the ambulance when it suddenly stopped for five minutes, praying again to her non-existent God that Andrew was okay. She breathed again when the ambulance set off, lights on, sirens blaring, as it sped towards the hospital.

The minutes turned into hours. A nurse gave her a glass of water. At first, she was the only person in the waiting room. There was no air-conditioning, the humid air was rich with the perfume of frangipani mixed with disinfectant. She followed the progress of several cockroaches as they scooted under chairs and climbed into cracks in the corners, searching for places to hide. She stared at the walls, grimy with marks from hands long gone. Dust was embedded in the windowsills and several panes of glass were missing from the open louvres. As daylight sidled into the room, she watched people dripping blood, others holding broken limbs, people on stretchers, old people in wheelchairs, terrified children carried by worried parents, arriving in dribs and drabs, and being shepherded through closing doors by nursing staff.

Jess was bent forward in her chair, exhausted, eyelids drooping when she saw a tall man in a white coat, which was covering blood-stained scrubs walking towards her.

Jess didn't need to hear what she was about to be told.

It was writ large in the doctor's eyes.

THREE

THE ROOM WAS HALF full by the time Jess arrived. Pale beneath her tan, her once fitting black dress hung loosely from her shoulders. She was just grateful to have found the energy to shower and wash her hair. It had been a whole other exercise to apply her makeup and she had given up after putting on mascara. As long as she didn't smell, Jess didn't care what she looked like.

It was a plain room, white walls, wooden floor, no pictures, no windows, a long table at the front and rows of chairs separated by a central aisle, occupying the main area; it was the conference room next to Andrew's favourite café. Outside more people were milling around the entrance, unwilling to commit to going indoors on such a warm day. Most looked as if they hadn't seen the sun for a while. Predominantly male, young, wearing glasses and with carefully tended beards, some were vaping, others were chatting in small groups. A few wandered around alone, circling the groups unused to making eye contact with real human beings — the socially phobic. The last thing Jess felt like doing was making small talk with people she didn't know and who didn't know her.

It had been Henry's idea to have a memorial service. She'd been against it, telling him it was too soon, that she'd only just got back.

She tried to tell him she hadn't had time to process the nightmare her honeymoon had proved to be — let alone Andrew's death. She had pleaded with him to wait for a week, but he wouldn't budge. He said the sooner it was over and done with the sooner they could all move on. Andrew's death had been a shock to him too, but he had responsibilities to the business and more importantly to the clients, which transcended all feelings — hers included.

Vaultange, the cryptocurrency exchange which Andrew had founded and run with Henry's help, needed direction, he told her. The wedding and the honeymoon had created a hiatus not only in day-to-day operations but in leadership — as well as direction. A line had to be drawn. A memorial service where the crypto-community could come together, acknowledge Andrew and pay their respects was required and it couldn't wait. Her feelings were important, but so was the business. Why couldn't she understand?

Jess had stopped arguing then. Worn out and worn down, she gave in only to make him shut up and go away. She didn't have the strength to hold out against him. She hadn't slept for days. She still couldn't take in what had happened —let alone believe it. Maybe Henry was right. Maybe it couldn't wait.

Henry Turner, Andrew's oldest, closest friend and his best man, had worked at Vaultange as a business partner/associate/employee from the beginning. Jess had never figured out what he did. Andrew had never specified, other than to say, client liaison. What that meant, she had no idea.

Henry used to arrive at the penthouse apartment in a building on the Auckland waterfront every morning at eight o'clock. They either worked there or went downstairs to *their* table in *Café Pierre*, the first in a line of cafes and restaurants looking across the promenade to the marinas in the Viaduct Basin. They would flip open their laptops and go about their tasks, fuelled by a continuous stream of coffee. At twelve p.m., they had lunch, talked over the day's business and went their separate ways, staying in contact by phone, then meeting up again for dinner. After dinner they carried on working until nine or ten p.m. At least that's what they did on a typical day. Until Jess moved in. The routine changed when she arrived, and it didn't take long for her to find out Henry wasn't pleased.

She took the seat directly in front of Andrew's photo. She stared at it, remembering how happy she'd been on the day it was taken. They'd returned from a drive to Buckland's Beach to find Henry waiting for them in front of the apartment building. Andrew leapt out of the car before she turned off the engine; he was so eager to tell Henry where they'd been. Almost tripping over the curb then laughing at his clumsiness, before he embraced his friend. A day in the sunshine had bestowed a healthy glow to his natural pallor, and Andrew looked invigorated — alive. Henry had taken the photo of the two of them that afternoon, when all was well, when they were still getting to know each other. Today Jess had been cropped out. 'For the service,' Henry said.

Jess looked down at her hands as tears pricked her eyes and she hoped it would be over quickly. All she wanted to do was to escape back to the apartment and bed. Bed was the only place she felt safe. She could lie there, staring at the ceiling, pretending none of this was real. That any moment Andrew would walk through the door and take her in his arms and kiss her. In the silence, she could make believe he was in the other room, pouring them a glass of wine before he called out to her. Hearing his voice, she would get up and walk to the kitchen. There he would be, smiling when he saw her, and the world would be right again. In bed, she could close her eyes and hear him breathing beside her, she could feel his touch as he reached for her. In bed she could pretend he hadn't died, and that her world hadn't descended into nothingness.

When Henry came and sat beside her she jumped as his hand reached across to cover hers. 'Ready?' he asked.

She turned. The room was full. Every seat occupied by someone looking at her. 'Just a minute,' she whispered.

In the days following Andrew's death, in a country where she knew no one, Jess had coped with a bombardment of official forms in a language she didn't understand. For some odd reason she remembered Andrew telling her he wanted to be cremated, not buried. He'd said cremation was *better for the environment*. That was what he planned to do with his mother's body when she died. When it came to the actual decision Jess couldn't have cared less about the environment. All she wanted to do was to come home and bring her husband with her. Cremation was the best of the horrible options available. She saw no sense in transporting his body back to New Zealand, only for him to be cremated there. She had stood alone and watched his coffin being slid into the hole, jumping back when the furnace erupted ferociously in flames. She waited, unable to cry, barely able to move as the steel door descended in front of the roaring flames with a clang. Later at the hotel she had numbly accepted the wooden box containing his still warm ashes.

The cabin crew left her alone on the flight home. She hadn't told anyone she was coming. No one met her at the airport. She caught a taxi to the apartment, dumped her bags in their bedroom, went straight to bed and lay there staring at the wooden box on the pillow beside her. She hadn't slept, hadn't eaten for two days. She had only got up to shower and change when Henry informed her he was coming to talk to her.

Now, in this room filled with strangers, she had to force herself to stay put, force herself not to run. The mutterings of restless people grew louder behind her. The doors at the back were open, but it was a hot day and the air conditioner laboured noisily in the background. She knew she had to say something, explain, but her mouth was dry, and she didn't know if she could stand up. She looked across the row of seats at Andrew's mother in her wheelchair, staring around uncomprehendingly, tugging now and then at her nurse's sleeve, whispering loudly that she wanted to go back to school.

Andrew had introduced Jess to his mother after he proposed. Henry was with them — he was always with them. The meeting hadn't gone well. She was only fifty-eight and with the early onset Alzheimer's, his mother didn't recognize her only child. Worse, she'd accused him of taking her money and keeping her in *this prison against my will* — over and over again. They left. Andrew wished he'd never come and said there was no point in going back. He had arranged for his mother to go into care when his father had died, but Andrew, uncomfortable with old age, had barely visited her. No wonder she didn't know who he was, Jess thought and silently castigated herself for being uncharitable. She wondered whose bright idea it had been to bring her to the memorial service. The poor woman didn't even know she had a son, much less understand that he was dead.

As Jess's fists gripped the speech she had prepared, it turned into a mush of sweaty paper in her hands. She hoped the dampness under her armpits wasn't seeping through her dress. When she heard a woman cough she turned. Carole waved from the back of the room, nodding encouragement as she placed her hand across her heart.

Jess breathed out, releasing the tension she hadn't known was there from her ribcage. Carole, her old flatmate, her friend hadn't let her down. A research nurse at the hospital, they had lived together, with Jess moving into Carole's spare room two years before. The woman was crazy, fun, hardworking and kind. Knowing she was here today supporting her, gave Jess the courage to do what she had to do — speak about Andrew.

When she stood and faced the room Jess was grateful when she recognised a few familiar faces in the crowd. Ross Martin, Andrew's lawyer, was sitting in the row behind hers. Sitting beside him was Suzie, the manager from their apartment building. The Prof was there too, standing at the back wearing a suit, looking solemn, but he brightened when she caught his eye. He was so busy and yet he'd made the time to come.

The people in the room waited in silence for her to speak. At the back, with her hand still on her heart, Carole mouthed, 'You can do it.'

Abandoning the speech she'd prepared, Jess put the crumbled pages on the table next to Andrew's photo. She introduced herself, then thanked them for coming. 'Andrew proposed six weeks after we met,' Jess said. 'You knew him. I couldn't say no. He didn't understand the meaning of the word. And I didn't want to. The short time we had together was the happiest months of my life. He was the most intelligent man I have ever met and we spent every waking hour together talking about everything. We had so many plans. We were so in love.'

Jess looked across the room at Carole who nodded for her to go on. 'I felt so helpless when he got sick. There was no warning. One moment, he was well and the next, he was desperately ill. I'm a doctor. I couldn't do anything. We were far away from help, from the care he needed. We were alone and dependent on people I didn't know to save him. He was too sick.' Her voice faded. She twisted her hands in front of her, her fingers bending back on themselves, white where they were normally pink. No one moved, the room was quiet. After what seemed like hours, she looked up.

'It's been a shock,' she said. 'I am trying my best to make sense of it. I loved him. I miss him.'

Some rubbed tears from their eyes while others searched their pockets for tissues. There was a lot of nose blowing and shuffling in seats when she finished — with the exception of one man. Dressed formally in a black suit, white shirt and black tie, eyes half-closed and arms folded in front of him, he had taken off his sunglasses and his gaze remained fixed on her throughout her speech. He looked like a gangster from an old black and white movie except for one facet of his appearance. He had outrageous eyelashes — thick, black and long, they were incongruously gorgeous on an otherwise ugly man. Inexplicably, she felt nothing but relief when later she saw him leave.

Henry stood up next. An accomplished speaker and raconteur he spoke confidently about Andrew the businessman, the cryptocurrency entrepreneur, the tech visionary who in 2013 had been converted to the potential of digital currency.

'Andrew was one of the first certified Bitcoin professionals in New Zealand. When he started Vaultange five years ago, few people had even heard of Bitcoin — much less believed it had a future. The banks treated him as a maverick, an outlier. Typically, Andrew carried on regardless, backing himself to the hilt.'

Henry described how he met Andrew at school and how they stayed friends, meeting up again when Andrew returned from overseas in 2013, when the buzz around Bitcoin was starting to build.

He described being seduced by Andrew's devotion to the idea of a currency without geo-political boundaries and with the potential to be the digital equivalent of gold. There were murmurs and head nodding around the room. 'Andrew's enthusiasm was infectious,' Henry said. 'When he asked for my support to set up Vaultange I had nothing else to do. Of course, I said yes. No one said no — to Andrew.'

'Vaultange,' Henry continued, 'was never going to be a fly-by-night operation, set up to take people's money only to disappear as so many exchanges did back then. Andrew worked hard. We both worked hard. But Andrew was the key to gaining the trust of our clients. His brilliance meant client numbers have grown exponentially as has the total value of the crypto-assets under management. He had big plans for the world he could see coming. When I say Zuckerberg, and the Chinese, you'll know what I'm referring to.' More head nodding and murmurs took place around the room.

'Andrew was a genius in his field.' He paused. 'And a born klutz on any sports field — indoors and out.'

Jess laughed then. As did everyone else.

'He was a man with vision and integrity who worked hard to do his best, putting the needs of others before his own, despite his serious health issues. Things were on the up, Vaultange was doing well. He was on new medication, wasn't he professor?' Jess turned to look behind her and saw the Prof caught out, and nod without thinking.

'In remission for the first time in years,' Henry said, 'he had just married the woman he loved. His death, so unexpected, is a tragedy and he will be missed.'

With that Henry walked over to Jess and held out his hand. She had to take it. She stood up and was immediately wrapped in Henry's tight embrace. The room was quiet. A few people started clapping, others unsure if this was appropriate, checked themselves. Henry let her go, but still holding her hand, announced drinks and food would be served next door.

Chairs scraped the floor as people stood up, some coming forward to offer quiet condolences to Jess before moving across to shake

Henry's hand. Two men, both with beards introduced themselves to her, recounting stories of the hapless Andrew and his disastrous exploits on sports fields. One told her how much Andrew had given to charity, something Jess hadn't known but which didn't surprise her.

Carole appeared at her side wearing a black dress and jacket. Her dark hair caught up in her usual high ponytail, her trademark red lipstick carefully applied, the black which made her looked slimmer, suited her. 'I knew you could do it,' she said as she hugged her friend.

'Only because you were here,' Jess said grateful to her friend for giving her a reason to move away.

'Of course, I'm here.' As she held Jess by the shoulders Carole looked her up and down. 'When did you last eat? Or sleep?'

'No idea. I go to bed, but my mind keeps going. I can't stop thinking about him and if I try to eat, I feel sick.'

'If you don't eat, you will be.'

'Not now. I'm the hostess. I have to do the hostess thing and circulate.'

'Sure, but only after you've eaten. Sit down. Don't move.'

Jess knew when she was beaten. She sat down, closed her eyes and woke seconds later with a start to Carole standing beside her, a cup of coffee in one hand and a plate of food in the other.

'Eat,' Carole ordered.

Suddenly hungry, Jess wolfed down two sausage rolls, and a club sandwich. She finished the coffee and looked at Carole with a clear head for the first time in days. 'Thanks. You're a good friend.'

'Always,' Carole replied. 'Now, go next door and circulate. They want to meet the woman who won Andrew's heart.'

FOUR

THE REST of the afternoon passed in a blur as Jess circulated through the crowd trying to talk to as many people as possible. She was surprised that so many wanted to meet her. A few asked questions about what she planned to do with Vaultange, assuming as Andrew's widow she would be familiar with the workings of the exchange. Some asked about cryptocurrency and where she thought prices were heading. Others asked more technical questions — the people, the conversation — a messy confusion of words she didn't understand. Just as she was about to open her mouth to say she didn't know what they were talking about, Henry would appear at her side and answer for her. She appreciated his help, but Jess was used to answering questions for herself. She wasn't used to feeling stupid much less having someone speak for her.

One person she'd been hoping to talk to was the Prof but he had left early. Carole passed on his apologies saying he had to get back to the hospital for his afternoon ward round. Jess was disappointed. She had particularly wanted to talk to him because if anyone could explain why Andrew had deteriorated so quickly, he could. She wanted to go over every detail of what happened to Andrew to figure out if there was anything more she could have done. Part of her needed answers, but a larger part needed reassurance she'd done all she could to save him. The sequence of events leading up to his death and what she did and didn't do, played on a continuous loop in her mind — every time she closed her eyes. If she fell asleep, she'd wake in a cold sweat, hearing Andrew's voice calling to her, telling her she had kind eyes. All the while she was unable to get to him, unable to do anything — frozen in place, as she watched him slip away from her.

Empty paper plates, beer bottles and wine glasses littered the tables. Vape clouds floated into the room from a small group of stragglers gossiping outside, with most people having already left. Andrew's mother was still there slumped in her wheelchair staring vacantly at the wall, as her nurse stared up at Henry, entranced and hanging off his every syllable. *How did nurses get to be so young?* Black rimmed eyes, short-cropped hair, the young nurse looked as if she should still be in a classroom, not taking responsibility for a helpless old lady. Glimpsing movement, Jess watched in horror as a full catheter bag slid off the hook on the leg of the wheelchair, plopped on to the floor, and dark yellow urine spilt everywhere. Even as the smell permeated the room, the nurse couldn't tear her eyes away from Henry, until his nose wrinkled, and he looked down. Recoiling, he stopped in mid-sentence and walked away. It was Carole who came to the rescue, suggesting to the shocked young nurse that she take Mrs Cullinane home and that she would clean up the mess. The poor girl shot her a look of gratitude, picked up the bag, tucked it under the old lady's leg and wheeled her out of the café before Carole could reconsider.

'Jess, could I have a word?' Ross Martin appeared next to Jess still holding a glass of wine. Overweight, and sweating in the afternoon heat, his half-glasses perched midway down his nose, his dark suit well cut and made from fine wool — Ross was the embodiment of white privileged middle-aged men. He didn't wait for an answer and sat down, clearly expecting she would follow his lead which she did. 'I need to talk to you about the will. What happens to Vaultange. That sort of stuff,' he said.

'Not today. Surely?'

Ignoring her reluctance, Ross pushed on. 'I know, but it can't wait. Andrew left everything to you. All of it — lock stock and barrel. Business doesn't stop when someone dies. Especially not the business he was in and especially not now.'

'You must be joking.'

'I'm not. Henry's not happy, he thought he would inherit something. That's why we have to meet to settle this and get Vaultange back on track.' He stood up. 'Your apartment? Four o'clock?'

'This afternoon? Why not tomorrow?' Jess looked up. 'Please Ross, I'm so tired. I don't know if I'm in a fit state to understand anything.' She tried not to plead — it sounded so pathetic, but she wanted to appeal to his common sense.

'Sorry Jess.'

'Is Henry coming?'

'He suggested the time.'

'Do I have a choice?'

Ross had the good grace to at least look like he was thinking about it, but she knew what his answer would be. 'No, you don't.'

FIVE

As soon as she reached the apartment Jess kicked off her shoes to liberate her feet from high-heel hell and welcomed the return of blood to cramped toes as she cursed her earlier decision to wear such ridiculous shoes to the service. She padded barefoot on the cool-stone floor to the living room and pressed the remote. The curtains slid silently back to reveal Auckland city below. Across the harbour was Devonport and beyond that, past the Hilton Hotel and to her right was Rangitoto, the dormant volcano which dominates Auckland. Andrew lived in the penthouse of an apartment complex built on prime waterfront real estate on Customs Street West in the Viaduct Basin. The complex running the length of the block, overlooked two marinas, where the ultra-wealthy berth their leisure boats. She had moved in three months ago, barely long enough to call the place home.

Jess, who'd been born and bred in Auckland, New Zealand's largest city, had moved away when she was fifteen. Since her return ten years ago she'd noticed the impact of the huge population growth over the previous decade. City streets were more crowded, the shopping was more sophisticated, the traffic more congested and the buildings taller than when she'd been a girl. The Viaduct Basin development that began in the late 1990s had been part of the city's transformation.

Backing onto the CBD, the complex had been designed to be seen primarily from the sea, its façade built to resemble a ship with the penthouse *bridge* overlooking everything below. The living area featured floor to ceiling windows and doors designed to take full advantage of the view. These opened, folding concertina-like to reveal a wide balcony along which outdoor furniture had been arranged in different areas. Wooden boxes planted with standard bay trees, provided respite from the grey and white colour scheme. At the rear of the main living area, a marble topped island separated the kitchen from the rectangular dining table and twelve chairs. In the seating area to the right, dark blue sofas, a square glass coffee table, and occasional lamps completed the showroom feel to the place. When she moved in, Jess had tried to inject some vibrancy to the décor with cushions and flowers, but she had been fighting a design created in magazines, not real life and her additions looked amateurish. The cushions had been moved to the closet in the spare bedroom and the flowers were not replaced when they died.

Jess pushed open one of the doors. The fresh sea air felt good on her skin. Next, she checked the contents of the fridge — white wine, a shrivelled piece of brie, low-fat milk, Diet Coke. No wonder she hadn't eaten.

She was opening a bottle of chardonnay, when the remote buzzed letting her know Henry and Ross were downstairs. As she pressed the button to let them in she noticed her shoes on the floor by the elevator. Without looking she tossed them through the door into the bedroom, pulling it shut as the elevator opened. Henry strode straight past her not bothering to say hello. Ross who made regular trips to the South of France with his family, gave her a kiss on each cheek and then another for good luck. He seemed to think it was sophisticated, charming even, rather than the invasion of her personal space that she felt it to be. There had been no kissed cheeks at the hospital. On the one hand the habit spread disease and on the other it could be construed as sexual harassment. But Ross, secure in himself and his place in the world, would have thought it infinitely strange, PC gone mad even, if she had ducked away, or worse told him she didn't want the kiss. Better to politely proffer her cheek and let him get it over with.

'You'll miss this,' Henry said as he stood in the front of the windows.

'What will I miss?' she asked reaching into a cupboard for the wine glasses.

'The view, this apartment.'

'Why do you say that?'

Ross who was busy emptying his briefcase of folders and papers, and placing them on the table, spoke. 'For goodness sake Henry, wait until I'm ready. We have to do this properly.'

'What does he mean?' Jess asked.

'I'll explain when we're all sitting down. You pour the wine Jess.'

Henry pulled out a chair and sat down. 'Andrew didn't own the apartment,' he said. 'It's rented.' His tone was almost cheery, meant to annoy, or to punish? She couldn't decide. Gone was the public face of the solicitous best friend of her dead husband, the comforter of widows. Self-absorbed as always, he was no longer the approachable fellow oozing sympathy. Away from his audience, Henry was being himself.

Initially Jess had played along, accepting his over-bearing behaviour while Andrew was alive because they were friends. There'd been times though when she'd drawn blood biting her tongue hard, forcing herself not to call him out for his antiquated view of the world, and of women in particular. She'd never understood what Andrew liked about him. She knew they'd been to school together. Henry, the first-fifteen God worshipped by everyone. Andrew who had been mercilessly bullied, was grateful when Henry had taken him under his wing. No one could figure out why Henry had done this, least of all Andrew. With Henry's protection, the bullies backed off. Andrew told Jess he knew what he was like, but he owed him and that was that.

Henry was a misogynist, something Jess picked up on as soon as they were introduced. She saw the real man under his twenty-first-century veneer of manners and his pseudo-deference to women. To Henry no woman could ever be genuinely as smart, strong, competitive, or as intelligent as a man, but he couldn't say it, not aloud, and not to Andrew. He had been suspicious of her and her relationship with Andrew from the beginning.

His overbearing self-confidence combined with his distrust of women meant he gave himself permission to hit on her. His body language, his standing closer than necessary, his hips angled towards her, his eye contact for a microsecond too long, and raising an eyebrow when Andrew wasn't looking, made her sick, but she couldn't call him on it — not without hurting Andrew. The first time Henry did anything overt, they were out having dinner. Andrew had invited Henry. Jess had invited Carole. A getting to know each other occasion at a Chinese restaurant.

Henry completely ignored the women, dominating Andrew's attention by talking business so quietly that Jess and Carole couldn't hear what he was saying above the noise of the busy restaurant. Andrew, who was absorbed by what Henry was saying, didn't notice anything was wrong until Jess brushed his hand, indicating with her head that he should talk to Carole. Henry, deprived of Andrew's attention, had sighed loudly. He looked Jess up and down, stopping at her breasts, all the while talking in a voice so low, she could only hear him if she leant towards him. She felt his thigh against hers and moved her leg out of the way. He chuckled and moved closer. Jess excused herself. He was waiting when she emerged from the bathroom. His hands open, a cheeky *why-not* look on his face.

'Do you do this to all of Andrew's dates?' she asked.

'Only the good-looking ones. Come on, I'm fun. We'll have fun. I won't tell if you don't.'

'Really?' She had raised her voice. People were looking. 'You're really doing this?'

He stepped back. She stepped towards him.

'Let's get this clear, shall we. I love Andrew. He loves me. You don't figure anywhere in my life other than as Andrew's friend and after this, I'm not sure you're even that.' As Jess moved past, Henry caught her arm.

'You're not going to say anything?'

'No. I'm not. For his sake — not yours.' She shook her arm free. 'But if you do anything like this again, I will.'

'He wouldn't believe you.'

'Really?' She returned to the table and took Andrew's hand once she'd sat down. Then she told him about her day at the hospital. Several glasses of wine later, Henry was giving all his attention to Carole who seemed only too happy to reciprocate. When it became boring Jess and Andrew excused themselves and let them get on with it.

Over the next week she watched Henry as he tried to rationalise her rejection. He never missed a chance to make a snippy comment about her especially with regard to money, and in particular how little she had.

'It must be nice not to have to pay rent any more now that you're living here,' he'd muttered one morning while he was waiting for Andrew to get dressed. 'Any girl would be grateful to snag a man as rich as Andrew and I've seen more than a few come and go over the years.'

Andrew had walked into the kitchen wearing a t-shirt emblazoned with a Smashing Pumpkins logo, shorts and tattered All Birds. His appearance prevented her from replying as she would have liked. Without looking at Henry, she had kissed Andrew and excused herself, saying she was late for work.

Henry didn't stop. Whenever he thought he wouldn't be overhead he went out of his way to hurt her. Jess wasn't a tattle-tale. She had fought her own battles since she was fifteen against people worse than Henry could ever be and she'd won — eventually.

'Carole told me you've only just paid off your student loan,' he said one evening as the four of them waited for a table at a crowded bar and Andrew was seemingly absorbed in conversation with Carole. 'With no family to back you up, it was a lot of money. Why is that? No family? No support? Is that why you've latched onto Andrew? It is, isn't it? He's your ticket to the good life.'

'What ticket Henry?' asked Andrew.

'Nothing. I was talking rubbish to pass the time. I don't think we're ever going to get a table. Shall we go somewhere else?'

'No. Let's not,' Andrew said. 'I heard what you said. You're my best friend and on one level I understand you think you're looking out for me when you accuse her of being a gold digger. On the other hand I think you're being a prick. It's the other hand which I think is right. Let's clear this up once and for all. Jess is the woman I love. If I ever hear you disrespecting her again, we are done. Our friendship is over.'

'But ...'

Andrew leant over and grabbed Henry by his lapels pulling him down so their faces were level. 'Do I make myself clear?'

'Perfectly,' Henry said. Just then, the maître d' arrived, informing them their table was ready and apologising for their wait. Henry spent the rest of the evening talking to Carole.

As her relationship with Andrew deepened, Jess ended up spending more time than she would have liked in Henry's company. Having Carole there to attract his attention was helpful, even so it wasn't enough. She tried to nudge Andrew towards other people, but it was no good. The matter had been settled and as far as Andrew's was concerned, Henry having learnt his lesson, was still his best friend and he could do no wrong.

Now Andrew was gone. There was no buffer and the way Henry was speaking to her did not auger well for the coming weeks. She would be forced to spend time with him on his terms — not hers. She needed him to run the company and he knew it.

Henry leant back in his chair and smirked at her when Ross wasn't looking. Sickened, Jess took a gulp of wine, spluttering when tannin hit the back of her throat. She wiped her chin, then forced herself to smile. There was no way she was going to give him the satisfaction of seeing how shaken she was. She'd met bullies before, enough to know they were cowards who fed on weakness. She was on her own now and she had to be strong or he would grind her down at the first opportunity.

'How much do you know about Vaultange?' Ross asked, clearly keen to move on.

'Not much. Andrew wanted to keep the business separate from our relationship. He said he had Henry to talk to about Vaultange.'

'Do you know anything about cryptocurrency?'

'The bare minimum. I mean, I googled Bitcoin when I started seeing him. I didn't want to be a complete idiot. Assume I've got a basic level of understanding.'

'Fucking great,' Henry said as he refilled his glass and no one else's.

Ross flicked him a warning look and turned back to Jess. 'Andrew had me draw up a new will before your wedding, leaving you everything. Recently, he'd purchased a number of properties, all of them overseas. They belong to a company he called Gordon Holdings.'

'Gordon Holdings? That's my name,' Jess said. 'He didn't say.'

'Vaultange and Gordon Holdings are separate companies. For legal reasons each is independent of the other. Now you own both.'

Jess sat very still.

'He also left money in trust to take care of his mother, and he made you the trustee. Effectively, she's your responsibility now.'

Jess leant back. 'That's a lot to take in.'

'And you don't have much time,' Ross added.

'I'm not sure I understand?'

'Vaultange has been closed to trading since Andrew died. The clients have been patient considering the circumstances, but naturally they want to know what's happening to their money.'

'So, why can't we open?'

Henry got up and walked over to the fridge. Without asking he took out another bottle of wine and brought it back to the table where he unscrewed the cap and refilled his glass. 'There are a number of reasons. The first being that we can't access client records, and the other being we can't access the assets in the wallets.' He drained the contents of his glass and refilled it. Ross reached over and moved the bottle away from him.

Jess felt the enormity of his words bear down upon her. From the look on Ross's face, he already knew.

'What do you mean?' she asked looking first at Ross then Henry.

'All that was Andrew's side of the business. He kept it to himself, for security reasons, he told me. I looked after banking and exchange relationships. Sometimes I checked in with the contractors he sent the transactions to, but he handled the day-to-day stuff. The money in and out.' He paused. 'He maintained the client database. We were moving to a more modern system, but then you came along, and he lost focus.'

She put her hand on her chest and gasped. 'This isn't my fault.'

'Of course not. I'm just saying that after you came along, he stopped doing things. He stopped making the decisions he needed to make. He knew what he had to do, but he said he'd do everything after he got back.'

'Okay, okay.' Jess put her head in her hands and stared at the table for a moment before taking a deep breath and looking first at Ross then at Henry. 'Tell me what to do?'

'The money in the hot wallet is safe. I checked.'

'Hot wallet? That's online, isn't it?'

'Correct.'

'It can be hacked if it's online.'

'Technically, correct. So far it hasn't been.'

'But the vultures will be circling. I've read about this. Vaultange is vulnerable. Why is it still online? We need it off,' Jess said.

'You're the boss,' Henry said. 'I was going to do it, but he didn't leave the company to me.'

'Do it. I don't know how.'

Henry stared at her, a tiny curl of contempt escaped the side of his mouth, hostility in his eyes, as he waited.

'Help the girl, for chrissakes! Stop playing games.'

Ross had come to her rescue. She wasn't going to have to grovel.

Henry sighed and produced a USB stick from his inside jacket pocket and asked for Ross's laptop.

'Can I watch how you do it?' Jess asked.

'Be my guest, it's your company.'

She got up, walked around the table and stood behind his chair. He keyed in the Vaultange URL, then scrolled down to find what he was looking for, stopping at a page of files. He opened one and lists of numbers and letters appeared.

'Here,' he said pointing at the screen, 'these are the buys, and the private keys, these long numbers are different types and amounts of crypto-assets. See this,' he said pointing to another line. 'It's another digital key. Twenty-four randomly generated numbers and letters which open the wallet, or you could use this — a QR code.' He pointed to a black and white crazy square. 'If I open it, all you'll see will be more keys.'

'How much is in there?'

'Based on the money transacted through the current account since before you left there should be between fifteen to twenty million.'

'My God! That much in three weeks?'

'Bitcoin is low. People are buying. It's trading at around three and half thousand US at the moment.'

'Why is it low?'

'Andrew's department. I have no idea.'

Jess felt a band tighten above her eyes. 'Take the wallet offline and make it safe. I've read about hackers. A hot wallet is like an unlocked door with a sign saying all welcome, help yourself.'

Henry held up the USB so she could see a tiny screen on one side. Jess read the words, ledger Nano S beside the screen.

'This,' Henry said, 'is a hard wallet. It's more jargon, but you'll catch up.' He attached the ledger to the laptop with a cable, which he took out of another pocket, and keyed in another URL.

Out of yet another pocket, he extracted a tatty notebook, plastic covered and with a small pencil tucked into the spine. After flicking through the pages to find the one he wanted, he set it down, and clicked a PIN into the blinking spaces on the side of the Nano S. Turning to the next page, on which was a list of words next to the numbers one to twenty-four, he checked them off as he entered a series of Y or N clicks as requested next to words and numbers on the screen. When the picture of a wallet appeared on the laptop he pressed another button. 'Done. I've transferred the contents of the hot wallet into this,' he said holding up the USB. He exited the programme, unplugged the USB and took out the cable.

'That's all? So the money is safe?'

'Offline. Safe. As long you have the PIN and seed words. Lose those and you might as well throw the crypto into the bottom of a deep-dark hole and forget where the hole is.'

'Thank you,' Jess said as she held out her hand. He paused, sizing her up. It took a lot for him to give her the USB — but he did.

'The PIN and seed words?'

He ripped the pages from the notebook and left them on the table.

SIX

'THAT WENT BETTER THAN I THOUGHT,' Ross said after Henry had gone. 'I wasn't sure what he would do. He was furious when I told him about the will ... you should've heard his language.'

'Thankfully he seems willing to help. Without him, this would be a disaster.'

Ross gathered the papers on the table into a pile. 'Your copy of Andrew's will,' he said passing the document to her. 'Terrible thing to give you less than a month after your wedding. Judy — you haven't met my wife, have you? — sends her condolences. She said, you're very welcome to come and see us — any time. The door's always open.'

'Very kind. Please tell her how much that means to me.'

Ross nodded. They both knew she wasn't going to call.

'More documents for you to read,' he said adding more paper to the pile in front of her. 'These relate to Gordon Holdings. They're releases you need to sign for the bank. Can you read them, sign where I've marked next to the yellow stickers and get them back tomorrow?'

'I'll try,' Jess said as she collected the glasses and put them in the dishwasher. 'You've been very kind. It's hard for you too, isn't it?'

Ross stopped shuffling papers and looked at her. 'I've known

Andrew a long time. I was his father's lawyer. Same firm. His father was the senior partner when I joined. He was a patient teacher, and he must have seen something in me, because when he retired, he asked me to manage his affairs. Quite an honour.'

'I thought you specialized in the banking and commercial side, not family law?'

He shifted, settling back in the chair, his eyes bright behind his bifocals. 'You'd be surprised how often one leads to the other. Succession planning involves negotiating with families which can get tricky, especially if one member has been more involved in a business than another. The firm has grown since Fred left. We've taken on new partners. Had to. Not least because Andrew's work brought a different dimension to what we normally do.'

Jess closed the dishwasher carefully and leant against the bench.

'Don't look so petrified. I know there's a lot to get your head around, but it's short term. You're smart. You'll be up to speed in no time. My advice to you is learn everything you can about Vaultange. Do what needs to be done quickly — and get out.'

'You mean that?'

'This crypto business, it's not for the likes of you. You're a professional woman. You have your own career, an admirable one where you can do good for people. Crypto is a bit dodgy if you want my frank opinion. Any success is more to do with luck and timing, than anything else. My old school chums at the Northern Club, the ones who went into banking, they don't give it much chop. One giant Ponzi scheme according to them, which will come crashing down sooner or later.' He peered at her over his glasses and smiled. 'A few with family money bought Bitcoin in the early days as a bit of a lark. And they did very well. Typical isn't it? The rich getting richer? Bought at $100 and sold their positions the Christmas before last, in 2017, at $19,000. The exception rather than the rule.'

Jess had heard stories like this before. The Prof had said the same when Bitcoin started to get traction in the wider press. He didn't trust it — until he talked to Andrew. Then he became quite a fan. Jess was studying for her final exams and hadn't paid much attention. She was still paying off her student loan and had no spare money to invest anyway.

'Wind up Vaultange. Sell it. Give it away, I don't care, and neither would Andrew,' Ross said. 'You're not obligated to keep it as some sort of memorial. That's the last thing he would have wanted. Andrew was first and foremost a businessman. To him Vaultange was a means to an end. That's all. He wasn't sentimental. Neither should you be.'

Suddenly liberated from a prison of her own making, Jess felt better. Ross was right. Andrew had left her the exchange, but she didn't have to keep it going. Sort it out and move on. It was simple. No one would judge her, no one in the crypto-world even knew her. Now that she had a plan, all she wanted was for Ross to leave so she could go to bed, pull the duvet over her head and block out the world until morning.

Ross; however, was doing what he loved best. Giving advice. 'And another thing, about the apartment. Henry's right. It's not part of the estate and the lease comes up in three months. No one's going to throw you out, but you need to decide whether you move or renew. You might not feel like another upheaval. I wouldn't. Let me know and I'll negotiate an extension with the landlord for as long you like. The rent's a bit steep, but that's what these outfits are getting and once probate is granted money shouldn't be a problem. Think about it. No rush.'

'Thanks. You've been so helpful.' She put her hand over her mouth to cover her yawn, not once but twice. Finally, he seemed to get the hint.

'You're tired, I should go,' he said. He tidied the last of the papers into his briefcase, stood up and fumbled with the clips. 'We'll get this sorted, you have my word. Great view you have,' he said turning to the window. 'I can see why Andrew liked it. You feel as if you're on top of the world.'

Why was he taking so long? Why didn't he leave? She was feeling more and more irritated by his dithering.

'There's this,' Ross said at length. She heard a quiver in his voice.

'Andrew had me commission it before the wedding. He read it

before he set up Gordon Holdings and before he signed the will. Remember that.' He placed an A4 envelope on the table and pushed it towards her. She waited for an explanation, but Ross didn't look up — he didn't make eye contact. Instead, with his head down he moved his briefcase off the table and left.

When she heard the elevator doors close behind him, Jess opened the envelope and took out a manilla folder.

Jessica Davidson: DOB: 26: 03: 1987. She felt her heart still, then leap forward in her chest as if it wanted to escape. She picked up the half empty wine bottle and drank what was left.

SEVEN

JESS WOKE at three the next morning. Her head lay sideways on the table, her neck at an awkward angle, cramp gripping her muscles, and the empty bottle beside her. In the past, in the years between leaving the care home and university, it would have taken more than a half a bottle of chardonnay to knock her out.

Where was she the last time she'd drunk too much? It had to be that little town on the West Coast where she'd been working as a barmaid. She blushed even now when she remembered what happened with the German tourist. Good looking, blond, not much English. Gunter? Gandolf? It was his suggestion they do shots, but she had been the one who had insisted they buy the second bottle and take it back to his campervan. She'd woken up two days later, alone and in her underwear on the outskirts of a town she didn't recognise. That had been her low point. She had no one else to blame. No sleazy Mr Brown taking advantage of the girls in his care, to defray her guilt.

With her hands on the edge of the table she pushed herself upright, unwinding her head above her spine inch by painful inch until she was looking straight ahead. Squinting in the brightness of the overhead lights, her teeth chattering with the cold, she got up and shuffled to the fridge, took out a bottle of sparkling Evian, cracked the top and drained it. She opened the second bottle in her bathroom, where she found a bottle of aspirin, took three, finished the water, and went to bed.

At seven-thirty she was woken by the cheerful alarm on her phone. She took more aspirin, had a shower and washed her hair. She'd developed what she called her hangover management system in her drinking years — the years she'd pushed to the back of her mind. Not that she would have been able to remember much about them, even if she tried. Apart from the tourist. There were no words to describe what happened with him.

After towelling off, she walked naked into the kitchen, snapped a Diet Coke and gulped it down. While the coffee brewed, she did a number of stretches, shook her arms and legs, then indulged in several deep squats until the pills kicked in and she could forget about the pain.

Had Andrew ever seen her messy drunk? Not socially tipsy-drunk as she was after a couple of wines with dinner, or after an exotic cocktail on the beach, but completely pissed — staggering, blathering, sobbing then crashing into darkness — drunk. Jess had binged to such an extent that she was unable to stop drinking until she passed out. She rarely vomited, which was good in one way because it saved her teeth from stomach acid. Not good in another way because she had to wait for her liver to process the alcohol, one unit an hour until it was all gone, before she could function again.

In her late teens, with no future, nowhere to be, and no one to answer to — worse, no one to notice her mistakes and offer to help — binge drinking was her solution to loneliness. Meeting Gunter had been the slap in the face she needed to break free from the shadow-life she had fallen into after leaving the care home. Gunter and his cruelty forced her to become an adult, someone who was wholly responsible for all her mistakes. It hadn't been easy, but there on the roadside, she made the decision to stop drinking. She wanted to be the person her mother knew she could be.

Andrew would never have married her if he'd seen her messy-drunk. Fastidious about loss of control, he would have been disgusted by her self-induced chaos. And yet he'd read the file. Ross had made a point of saying he had. What had he read? She couldn't look — not yet. Seeing her past life written in black and white when she'd managed to put it behind her for so long — she wasn't ready. With her eyes shut, she rocked against the bench feeling the cold marble edge against her pelvis. She didn't want to know what he knew — not yet. She wanted him to only know the Jess in front of him, the Jess she was — Jess Gordon — the woman who was worthy to be his wife. Not Jessica Davidson.

The coffee pot bubbled on the stove, spitting hot water on to her bare skin. She jumped back, brushed it off her arm and filled her mug, carried it to the bathroom and sat down to pee. A moderately pretty brown-eyed blonde, her centrally parted straight hair tucked behind her ears, stared at her in the mirror above the basins. When she stood up, Jess saw that the woman in the mirror had lost weight, her shoulders seemed less broad, her normally pert breasts less full, her tummy hollow, the curve of her hips flattened. The white lines of her bikini blurred where her tan had faded, the burnt skin on her shoulders no longer flaking. *Who is this person? More to the point who had Andrew seen when he looked at her? Jess Cullinane, Jess Gordon, or Jessica Davidson? A rose by any other name is still a rose. Isn't it? If you pinch me, here, here and here, hard like this, I'm the same person. Almost. What's in the file didn't matter, can't have mattered. He wouldn't have married you, all three of you, if it had. But why did he never talk about it?*

Clean underwear, clean shirt, clean jeans and sneakers, no socks. Dressed. Make-up. The downside of being blonde, pale eyebrows. She pencilled over them, but they weren't even. She wiped them off and started again. Eyebrow pencil, eyeliner, mascara. None of it helped. Her eyes, bloodshot and squinty, her skin mottled and dehydrated, she looked as bad as she felt. But not as tragic as the bedroom. Five minutes tidying up wouldn't hurt. She opened the windows, reeling as a sudden blast of fresh air blew in. She pulled back the duvet, exposing the sheets to the sun. She'd read that UV light was as good as a wash. She put away yesterday's clothes and her evil shoes. The bags from her honeymoon, still unpacked, lay against a wall, where she'd dumped them. She dug through her backpack, and hauled out Andrew's laptop, his phone and keys. In the kitchen she grabbed another Diet Coke from the pantry and shoved it with his stuff into her satchel along with her stuff and the papers Ross had asked her to sign.

The file was still on the table — waiting — she wasn't ready. She grabbed it and pushed it out of sight under one of the sofa cushions, and slung her satchel over her shoulder. She needed to be outside in the sunshine and fresh air and among people who didn't know her. She craved the safety of strangers. She took the stairs rather than the lift, galloping two at a time, all the way to the bottom. As soon as she escaped the building she took a deep breath of sea air. Revived, she felt alive for the first time in days.

EIGHT

ANDREW WAS NOT the first man Jess had slept with. Far from it. He was; however, the first man she had slept with since Gunter. He was also the first man she'd fallen in love with. And more importantly, he was the first man she allowed to love her in return. Love at first sight was the stuff of romance novels — bad ones. When it happened to her, she'd been shocked by how visceral it was — from the thump in her chest, to being able to feel every beat of her heart whenever she saw him. Andrew was a patient of the Prof's and she had been introduced to him on one of her mentor's ward rounds. After that, this man who was sick enough to be in the high dependency unit, had a stupid grin on his face whenever she passed by. To be fair, so did she. They talked. Drawn to his bedside when her work was over for the day, she felt at ease with him. They chatted and laughed about all manner of things. She fell totally and deeply in love —*Truly Madly Deeply*, the movie — in love. 'Cupid's arrow,' she told Carole. 'No — yes.' She'd stopped pacing the rug in the living room. 'This is disastrous. We're not allowed to fall in love with patients. In my defence, he is the Prof's patient, not mine.'

Carole who was chopping onions for dinner, stopped and wiped away a tear with the back of her hand. 'That's all right then.'

'I've worked too hard to get where I am for this to happen. I can't fall in love.'

Carole tipped the macerated onion into the pan on the stove while Jess skirted around behind her and filled the kettle to make tea. Carole added meat and stock, put the lid on the pan, turned down the element and wiped the bench.

'I can't be in love with him. I'm going to do my doctorate next year. Travel, post-doc in the US. It's all planned. The Prof told me there's a good chance I might get all three of the scholarships that I've applied for.' She filled two mugs with hot water, fished out the teabags, added milk to both and took hers to the chair on the other side of the bench. 'Falling in love is not on the agenda. Oh God! Oh God! Oh God!'

'You don't believe in God,' Carole said. 'You're sure he feels the same? His pain meds aren't the reason he's making goo-goo eyes?'

Jess took a sip and considered the last statement. 'It's possible. No. He's not on them anymore.'

'Okay, you have to be careful. Technically he's not your patient, but it is a bit dodgy.' Carole cocked her head to one side. 'You don't want it to get out. You're not the only doc after those scholarships.'

'It's so unfair. I never planned it this way.'

'You wanted the truth. And while I'm at it,' Carole said. 'He's in the HDU for a reason. He might not be around for long. Have you thought of that? Slow down, take deep breaths, count to ten. Wait and see. But whatever you do, don't draw attention to yourself. That's my advice.'

Jess heard what Carole was saying. It made sense. She knew that. If only her heart agreed.

'Now,' Carole said sharply. 'My turn. Let's talk about me for a change. What should I do about Dad?'

'Why? What's happened?'

'He's sold the farm and wants to move into town.'

'Are you serious?'

'I told you ages ago, remember?' Carole shook her head. 'Hopeless. You're not even pretending to listen.' After gathering up the empty mugs, Carole put them in the dishwasher, stirred the casserole, and turned on the extractor fan, effectively ending all conversation.

Jess knew Carole was right to be cautious. Common sense told her to stay away. An inappropriate relationship made for gossip in the closed hospital environment even if it wasn't like that. What if someone reported her? If only her heart didn't race whenever she was in the unit and found him looking at her. She couldn't pass by his bed and not stop. Couldn't not say hello. She had to be polite if nothing else. And once their conversation started he had such a fascinating view of the world and he knew so much, it would have been rude to break off and walk away.

His condition improved, too slowly according to Andrew. He made no effort to hide his frustration from the professor, or from Jess. When the Prof suggested a new combination drug that an overseas pharmaceutical company had asked him to evaluate, Andrew didn't need to be asked twice. It proved to be the proverbial miracle cure. He was discharged a week after starting the combination therapy, but with the proviso he have regular blood work, and that he complied with the protocols of the study. This meant injecting the medication, which had to be stored in the fridge, fortnightly into his abdomen. As soon as he was given the all-clear Andrew literally ran out of the ward, but not before asking Jess for her phone number.

Jess didn't hesitate when he asked her out. She knew it went against the arcane rules in the ethics handbook, but she didn't care. After their first date, which morphed into their first night together, she moved out of the house she had shared with Carole. She went back once to pack her worldly possessions.

The next month disappeared in a blur of loving Andrew and work. Patients and colleagues alike commented on how radiant (sickening but true) she looked. The Prof took Carole aside to find out why Jess looked so happy.

'Glowing was the word he used,' Carole said when she was visiting Jess at the apartment for the first time.

Jess had burst out laughing, but felt chastened when Carole told her how he looked when she informed him Jess and Andrew were a couple.

'Downcast,' she said. 'How kids look when they don't get the birthday present they wanted, or worse, no birthday present at all. I mean he put on a brave face, but you could tell.'

'Did he mention the patient-doctor thing?'

'Andrew is his patient, not yours. He was happy for you both. As much as he could be.'

'That's so nice of him.'

'I thought so,' Carole said as she finished her wine. 'Maybe, I could help him get over you?'

It's possible, thought Jess. They had work in common, Carole was a few years older than the Prof, but not many. Was she bright enough for him though? Jess felt awful, but it was a fair question to ask. She didn't want Carole to fall in love with someone incapable of loving her back.

'You can only ask,' Jess said wishing she was a better friend and not such a coward.

Carole got up and walked along the windows and looked out to the balcony. 'Maybe not,' she said. 'It's very private up here, isn't it? Very, very private. Nice though. If you like not seeing people.'

Jess emptied the last of the wine from the bottle into Carole's glass and changed the subject.

NINE

IN THE WEEKS after his discharge Andrew, now pain free was able to eat normally again and began putting on weight for the first time in months. The Prof was amazed at the difference in him when he went for his first check-up. Jess didn't need blood tests or the Prof to tell her what she already knew. Andrew was full of life, his mind was busy, and he was thinking up new projects for the business. If anyone looked tired it was Henry.

'We've got the rest of our lives together,' Andrew said. It was late in the afternoon and they were in bed. Making love had seemed the best way to celebrate the news of his medically sanctioned recovery. 'We're young. We're gorgeous and we're rich. What else is there?'

She poked him in the ribs, and he scrunched into a ball beside her, pretending to whimper. 'I'm gorgeous. What about you?'

Jess climbed on top of him, grabbed him by the wrists and pinned his arms above his head. Andrew poked out his tongue and broke free, reaching up to cradle her head in his hands. He kissed her lightly on the mouth before lying back and staring into her eyes.

'We're both gorgeous. How's that?' he said. 'I'm serious about being rich. We're very rich. We can do anything we like — anything.' He repositioned himself and she felt him slip inside her.

'Tell me what you want to do for the rest of your life?' he whispered staying perfectly still, daring her with his eyes to do the same.

She knew it was going to sound trite and sentimental before she said it, but she said it anyway because it was the truth. 'I used to think I wanted to be the best doctor in the world. I wanted to find cures for diseases in poor countries. Eventually, I wanted to win the Nobel Prize for medicine. My discoveries were going to change the world. Now, I don't care anymore. I'm happy as long as I'm with you.' She lost his silent dare. She couldn't help it. His penis felt so good. She moved slowly at first, pleasuring herself with each stroke, keeping him inside her, moving faster and faster until, collapsing across his chest, she came. Seconds later, so did he.

That was when he proposed. He slid out from under her and reached over to the drawer in the bedside table. It jammed when he tried to open it. He swore, tugged at it then rattled it before it gave way. Naked, he knelt beside the bed, opened the lid of a small blue box and revealed the largest most sparkling diamond Jess had ever seen.

'Jess Gordon, will you be my wife?' he said. Tears welled up in his eyes and ran down his cheeks. 'Will you? Because if you don't say yes ...'

'Yes,' she said. 'Yes, yes, yes.'

He fumbled with the box and took out the ring and slid the diamond on to her finger. 'You can't change your mind, now.'

'I'm not planning to,' she said pulling him into her arms.

This memory, she played over and over as the most romantic moment she'd ever had, dammit — would ever experience. She remembered the love making which followed. How afterwards, they had to hunt for the ring because it had slipped off her finger and they'd eventually found it among the twisted mess of sheets and pillows on the floor where their heated bodies had ended up.

She missed Andrew so much. She missed making love. Not only the sheer physical pleasure, but the subsequent intimacy. She missed listening to the steady thump of his heart, his arm around her shoulder curling her protectively into his body, her head on his chest, as they talked. She was a good listener. She enjoyed the sound of his voice and hearing what he had to say. She felt safe with him. Andrew radiated certainty in uncertain times, and confidence in the stories he told about himself and his world. A world so different from her own. 'Sex and the blockchain are very similar,' he'd told her. 'I mean it. No. Wait. I take it back. It's not sex. It's making love. That's what's similar.' Lying on his side propped up on an elbow he looked at her. 'Both are a series of unique actions between two willing parties. And for that one transaction — only those parties. Each transaction can only happen after the authenticity of the other is established. Only then can a new transaction take place and be indelibly marked forever in the memories of both.'

She looked to see if he was joking. He wasn't.

'I thought that was rather good,' he said smugly.

'It wasn't. It was horrible. Worse than horrible. Now explain it properly so that a poor physician who knows next to nothing about finance can understand.' She rolled towards him matching the length of her body against his. He stroked her arm, his fingers barely touching her skin.

'Okay,' he said. 'Ready?'

'Go.'

'A blockchain is a decentralised ledger. Imagine a list — of anything — words, numbers, names of plants, drugs, anything, but the items are related. Put the list on a page. Each page now contains that information ... the page is the block. Imagine a digital copy of the block. Copies of the blocks are held by people all over the world on their different computers in a chain. DE ... centralised. See? No one person, company, bank, or government can ever own the chain. It owns itself. It's controlled by everyone.'

'Okay. What if someone wants to add a new page or block of information?'

'Okay. The rules are, they can only do that if everyone agrees that the pages or the blocks already on the computers are exactly the same. That was the beauty of Satoshi's system. For the first time it was possible to establish a proof of trust in the information which eliminated the double-spend problem which earlier digital systems had.'

'Okay who is Satoshi and what is double-spend?'

'The simplest way I can explain it is this. One dollar bill. Two people. Only one person owns that dollar bill and can spend it. Two people can't spend the same dollar. Satoshi Nakamoto wrote the paper in 2008 which solved the problem. His maths, mean the chain has to be checked off as true and accurate before anything can be added to it.'

'So it's like a book … all the pages have to be there … in the correct order. It could be a great way to store medical records.'

'You are smart, aren't you? Yes. It could be. You might like to take that idea further. I can put you in touch with some of my guys and you could be the entrepreneur in the family instead of me. You could make us really, really rich.' He tucked a strand of her hair behind her ear. 'Getting back to what you already know … after all the computers agree the record is true and accurate then and only then, can the new stuff be added. That verification stops all sorts of problems which would send you to sleep if I told you. Trust me.'

'We don't want that.' She ran her finger along the top of his shoulder and up the side of his neck behind his ear.

'We don't want that,' he replied before he kissed her again. 'Where was I?'

'That's a lot of data. Doesn't it get clumsy?'

'Okay smart one. Let me blind you with science. Unfortunately, I'm going to need a whiteboard so I can write out the mathematical proofs.' He heaved himself over her and pretended to look under the bed. 'What happened to my whiteboard? Did you take it?'

'You're an idiot,' she said hauling him back beside her and laughing. 'If this information is on lots of computers, then does that mean anyone can access it?'

'Correct. With the right software, complicated but not expensive. I could give it to you for Christmas.'

'You'd better not. I like my Christmas presents without instructions.'

'You'd pick it up in no time.'

'Are you calling me a nerd?'

'If the glasses fit ....'

Jess slid her hand up the inside of his thigh and cradled his testicles gently in her hand. 'Carry on ... tell me I'm a nerd. I dare you.'

'When you put it like that, your eyesight is perfect. However ... we both know how clever you are. The Prof told me.'

Jess took her hand away. 'I'm shocked. What happened to doctor-doctor-patient confidentiality?'

'What I'm trying to say is that you'd have no trouble learning how to use the programme which works the blockchain. Not all blockchains are the same, of course. Satoshi set up this one to run the Bitcoin system and it's not hard to understand, that's all I'm staying, if you ever decided it was something you wanted to do.'

'Why would I do that when I have you to do it for me?'

'But I might not always be here.'

'Stop, right there!' She pushed herself upright, knelt on the bed and looked down at him. 'I've just agreed to marry you and you're talking about leaving? What kind of engagement is this?'

'The till death do us part kind. Sorry, I didn't mean that the way it sounded. I'll be the nerd. Okay?'

'Okay.' She lay down beside him again. 'That's better. What I don't understand is how information on computers can be money? I mean I understand Internet banking. I understand that's information on a computer. But I can go to bank, they look up my records on their computer and they give me money — cash. I can spend it, save it, burn it if I want to. It's real.'

'Define money.'

'Money is dollars, yuans, pesos, pounds — money.'

'They're all currencies. What ... is ... money?'

Jess thought, started to say something, then stopped. She started again — slowly. 'Money is what I earn. Money pays for what I want to buy.'

'Exactly. Money represents value. Your work. Your time has value. Human beings, have bartered value forever. My firewood for your pig.

Then they figured out cash is easier to carry than a pig or a load of firewood. The cash that you're talking about was invented to make trading easier.' Andrew pulled Jess into the curve of his body wrapping his arms around her so he could circle the skin of her belly with his fingers. 'Centuries pass. Cards get invented. Suddenly cash is a pain to carry around. Banks love cards. They can track and charge fees on every transaction. Governments love cards. They can track and tax every transaction ... with the collusion of banks. Corporations love cards because they can track not only what people buy, but where and when. Information they use and sell on to grow businesses — Amazon, Facebook, Uber.'

'Granted. But normal money on cards works. The world goes around. Why do we need a digital currency like Bitcoin?'

'Maybe,' he paused. 'some people don't want banks, governments and corporations knowing what they earn, or what they spend their money on. Maybe they want to keep their finances private as it used to be.'

'If they have something to hide, you mean. I don't care if people know what I earn or what I spend it on.'

'No offence, but you don't earn enough to need to hide anything.'

'Oh. You're talking about drug dealers and criminals. They use Bitcoin. I've read about that. To fund buying and selling on the dark net.' She grabbed his hand, and squeezed it tightly. 'Tell me you don't do that Andrew. I'm serious. You have to tell me you're not a drug dealer.'

'Hand on my heart,' he said placing his hand over his heart. 'I'm not a drug dealer or a criminal.'

Jess lay still beside him. 'But drug dealers use Vaultange?'

'I don't know.'

'Is that because you don't ask?'

'Vaultange operates according to the regulations. We're legal. I can't interrogate everyone who wants to trade crypto. More importantly, Dr Gordon, and you have to know this about me. I wouldn't ask even if I could. What people do with their money is their business. In fact, what people do, full stop, is their business. I don't think you, me or the government has any right to decide what anyone does or does not do. Freedom to live freely, is the most important right any civilised society can uphold for its members.'

Jess rolled away so she could study his face. What was she hoping to see? That he was joking? He wasn't. She stared at the ceiling, thinking about what he'd said. If everyone was free to do exactly what they wanted, it would be chaos. Without mutual trust in laws binding people to do the right thing by others, then the suffering wrought by a few would be catastrophic. Some crimes were beyond all forgiveness. Drugs destroyed lives. She knew this first-hand. Most of the kids in the care homes where she spent her teens were there because they'd been abused or neglected by parents who cared more about getting their next high rather than about their children. She'd seen the fallout, the wasted potential, the misery. She'd seen how drugs took over people's lives and contaminated a family, or a community. She'd seen her patients suffer. Decontamination, if it was an option, could take generations. If Vaultange was involved in drugs then it went against everything she believed in. But, and it was a huge but — she loved Andrew. She had thrown caution to the wind when she moved in with him so quickly. She'd agreed to marry him because she could not conceive of a life without him.

'Criminals use traditional banks too,' Andrew said quietly. 'If that's what's worrying you. They have to. The financial centres of the world, New York, London, they turn a respectable blind eye. Lawyers, accountants, legions of them are involved in making dirty money look clean in ways you and I can't begin to imagine. I'm not saying that's a good thing. I'm stating facts and asking you not to judge Vaultange or what I do, against standards which don't exist.'

She knew he was right, but her mother's voice came back to her. "If someone else does something stupid or bad or wrong, is that a reason for you to do it too?" No but —yes — sometimes. *Shut up Mum. Go back to being dead.* Could she trust him? Suddenly she didn't know. She rolled back to him and put her arms around his neck. 'Tell me the good things about crypto. There must be some.'

'Thank you for asking. Imagine you're Venezuelan or Argentinian.

One night, you go to sleep with x amount of money that you have worked hard to save for your old age and in the morning, when you wake up it's worth less than half that amount. The government devalued the currency overnight without so much as a by-your-leave to cover their own arses. You have a miserable old age in front of you. Bitcoin; however, it can't be devalued. Not by a government.'

'Not by a government, sure, but it goes up and down in value all the time.'

'So does the share market. So does the oil price. So, do houses. Gold. Any asset you name. Buy any of them including Bitcoin and you accept volatility. Most do. Because the really smart investors understand that like gold, Bitcoin is a buy and hold investment.'

'Okay, you can't use it like you use money. You can't use it to buy stuff. If all you're buying is something to store value, why not buy gold instead?'

'Buy gold. Smart people have both. Wealth should be spread around different assets, put into different baskets as the saying goes. One goes up while the other goes down. Not a problem. You're wrong though, you can use crypto to buy stuff. There are ATMs in the States where you enter your Bitcoin key and get dollars out. It's a ginormous waste of computing power, but some people like it. Bitcoin should be held like gold, as a backup for when economic shit hits the fan. Especially now. Governments can't keep on printing money when their budgets don't balance. The only way out of that scenario is inflation — devaluation if you will. I'd rather my assets held their value and so would the millions of others holding crypto.' He swung his legs over the edge of the bed and sat up with his back to her. 'Are you hungry? I'm starving.'

'Ravenous,' she replied running her fingers down the vertebrae poking through the skin of his back. The sun had set while they were talking. It was nearly dark, and she couldn't remember when they'd last eaten.

'What do you feel like?' he asked, picking up his phone.

'Pizza from that new place we went to last week.'

'Perfect, then I'll tell you a story about Bitcoin and pizza.'

Jess rolled over to the other side of the bed. 'Order first. I'm famished.' She left him to it and went to the loo, detouring to the kitchen to collect a bottle of champagne and two glasses on her way back to bed.

'To us,' he said raising his glass. 'Forever and always.'

'Always and forever,' she replied as they clinked glasses. She realised she meant it. She loved him. If he was a so-called respectable banker, she'd love him regardless. Trust doesn't happen in an instant, she told herself. It has to be built up over time. At that moment she'd never been more content, knowing he loved her as much as she loved him. She felt safer with him than she had ever felt with anyone. His business had nothing to do with her. It was his company, his concern. He said it was legal and unless she went through every transaction line by line, understanding what she was seeing, how was she to know otherwise. She saw no point ruining what they had by demanding a level of honesty that was impossible for him to give. Jess had her own secrets and one day she would share them. Not now. For now she would grab happiness and love with both hands and never let go.

The pizzas arrived and they devoured them without talking, red spots of the tomato base marking the sheets around them. When she found a lost shrimp as she swept crumbs out of the bed, Jess popped it in her mouth while Andrew scrunched the boxes and dropped them on the floor. He refilled their glasses, and emptied the bottle.

'You're ready for the pizza Bitcoin story, then?' he asked. He had his arm around her, she was resting against his chest.

'Oooo goody, more Bitcoin stories.'

'Once upon a time in 2010, a man called Laszlo Hanyecz bought two pizzas. Guess how much he paid?'

'Can't.'

'Ten thousand Bitcoin.'

'Which is?' Jess asked.

'Today a Bitcoin is worth four thousand. So that's ….'.

'Thirty-eight million dollars,' Jess interrupted. She sat up and turned around to look at him. 'For two pizzas?'

'And a year ago when the price was twenty thousand ….'.

'Those pizzas would have cost ....'

'One hundred and ninety-eight million dollars.'

'That's ridiculous,' she said.

'Except it's not. There are seventeen and half million Bitcoin in circulation. Just over two hundred billion in US dollars. Think about that. Bitcoin didn't exist in 2007.'

'Okay,' she said settling back against him. 'Tell me, why did you start Vaultange?'

He slid down and kissed her neck. 'I think the less you know about my actual business, the better. You stick to medicine and I'll stick to keeping us in the style to which you have rapidly become accustomed. That way we can concentrate on other things. Like this for instance.' His tongue was moving lower, his fingers were gently tracing the lines of her collar bones. Jess suddenly didn't care about crypto-whatever it was, or Vaultange. She only cared that his fingers kept doing what they were doing.

TEN

ANDREW OPENED ONE EYE. 'How long have we been asleep?'

Jess picked up her phone and focused. 'It's seven a.m., so six hours.'

'It's Thursday, isn't it?'

Andrew opened his other eye and checked his phone. 'It says it's Thursday. My bladder on the other hand screams Saturday.' He leapt out of bed and ran to the bathroom.

Jess reached for her sarong. In the kitchen, she put the coffee beans in the grinder and opened the curtains. A blanket of grey cloud was rolling up the harbour, the cars on the bridge were just visible through the mist. Andrew was in the shower singing something she couldn't make out, his voice wildly off key. Dammit. Coffee could wait. She joined Andrew in the shower.

'You're not a bad cook,' he said later surveying the remains of an omelette on his plate.

'Thank my mother. One of the many things she taught me.'

'Tell me about her.'

'Now? Don't you have work?'

'Work can wait. Tell me about your parents.'

'Okay. Quick snapshot. Henry will be livid otherwise. You know he thinks you're spending too much time with me. He as good as told me so a few days ago.'

'Don't worry about him. I want to know about you.'

'Father — never met him. He left Mum when she was pregnant with me. And I mean left — left. She never heard from him again. She brought me up by herself until I was eleven. Then she married Bryan.'

'What sort of person was she?'

'Smart. Really clever, but she had no formal education. She never told me why. She was shorter than me and feisty to the point of being testy. Because she didn't tolerate fools; she didn't have many friends. Thinking about it, she had no close friends, she only had acquaintances. I was her friend, I guess. I know she loved me. Anything I did, was fine by her.' Jess refilled their cups. 'I suppose she got lonely. It's not much fun being a solo parent. Having to do everything, earn the money, pay the bills, run the house and bring up a daughter, all by yourself. I tried to help, but I was a kid. I guess she missed adult conversation. Not that Bryan provided much of that. After they got married, he spent all his time at the garage. He was a mechanic. She said she loved him and because he made her laugh in ways I couldn't, I didn't mind. I had my books. And swimming.'

Andrew took her hand and was about to speak when his phone rang. Henry's name came up on the screen.

'Answer it,' she said. 'He'll be furious if you don't.'

Andrew tapped accept and put the phone to his ear, his brow furrowing as he listened. 'Don't worry, it's one bank,' he said eventually. He stood up from the table and walked over to the windows with his back to her. 'Others will happily take our business. Order me a coffee. I'll be down in five.' All action, Andrew bundled his laptop into his backpack and kissed her on the top of her head on his way to the elevator.

'To be continued,' he called out. 'I like hearing about your life. It's different. I want to hear more, but Henry's panicking. I'll get it sorted in an hour, two, tops. I'll text re dinner. Mexican?'

'Sounds good.' When she heard the elevator doors close she picked up the dirty plates, stacked them in the dishwasher, washed the omelette pan and wiped the bench — the way her mother had taught her.

Showered, dressed, hair, and make-up done, she did a quick tidy-up. She had thought she was going to spend her day off with Andrew, but that wasn't going to happen now. By mid-morning, she had nothing to do. She could go to the hospital and catch up on correspondence, but dammit it was her day off. She called Carole and told her about the engagement. Whoops of congratulations, followed. 'Let's celebrate,' Carole said and the day suddenly had purpose.

Jess saw that Andrew wasn't happy as soon as she popped her head around the door of the café to tell him where she was going. He was absorbed by whatever was on his screen, frowning as he jabbed at the keyboard. Henry who had his back turned, was staring out of the window at the rain, refusing to engage, even when Andrew muttered something. She'd be back before he noticed she was gone, so she decided it was best not to interrupt.

But she wasn't. When Carole saw the ring, she insisted they celebrate properly at a restaurant she'd always wanted to go to, but couldn't remember the name of so they couldn't book ahead. The problem was, it was across the bridge in Devonport and even in late-morning traffic, it took an hour to get there. A bottle of champagne later and they were planning the wedding. Or rather Carole was planning the wedding having naturally assumed she would be bridesmaid.

'One of my duties is to ensure the bride and bridesmaid are adequately refreshed,' she said before she ordered another bottle of champagne. 'And I want it understood. No Pink. No pale pink, no bright pink and no shocking pink because that would be shocking.' Her elbow slipped off the table and the contents of her glass slopped on to the floor. Undeterred she carried on. 'Just in case you were thinking about pink. With my height, or lack of it,' she chortled. 'It has to be a short dress, above or on the knee — not below. Otherwise, I'll look like a munchkin standing beside a Vogue model.'

'You will not,' Jess said as she shook her head at the waiter as he moved to refill her glass with the last of the bottle. Carole pushed her glass into range. The waiter obliged with a sigh. Earlier, at one p.m., the restaurant had been humming with the noise of people eating and drinking. Now they were the only ones left, apart from the wait staff and it was quiet. The second bottle lay upended in the bucket beside the table. Behind the counter, the maître d' stared at them, an impatient look on his face. 'I think,' Jess whispered, 'we've overstayed our welcome. Let's walk down to the harbour. The fresh air will help sober us up before we go home.'

'Speak for yourself,' Carole said staggering as she rose from her chair.

Jess settled the bill and added a tip large enough to transform the stony-faced maître d' into someone only too happy to hold the door open for them.

While they were eating, the day had undergone a transformation. No longer cloudy and grey, bright sunshine necessitated searches for sunglasses in handbags before they set off down the hill towards the sea. One of a handful of Auckland suburbs which had not been redeveloped in the 1980s boom years, Devonport's shop fronts and shady verandas retained much of their 1950s charm. Plots of brightly coloured flowers set among towering Morton Bay fig trees planted during the nineteenth century added to the holiday atmosphere of the area. Arm in arm they strolled past boutiques, art galleries, delicatessens and second-hand bookshops, the warm smell of freshly baked cookies following them down to the promenade and the ferry building. Across the harbour, cranes straddled the wharves like giant insects, while behind them the glass towers of the CBD were a world away from the peace and quiet of the seaside.

'Dad says congratulations,' Carole said as she looked up from her phone.

'Tell him thanks.' Jess was feeling woozy after the champagne and she headed towards a park bench facing out to sea where she sat down.

Carole finished her text, put her phone in her bag and joined her. 'I was engaged once,' she said as she swung her legs backwards and forwards under the seat.

'I didn't know.'

'No reason you should. It was before I went nursing. Mum was furious when I broke it off. Dad understood. I was always closer to him than to Mum. He was the one who encouraged me to travel and see the world while I was young. If I'd listened to Mum, I would have married the farmer down the road and gone into production.'

Jess raised an eyebrow.

'Kids. Grandchildren.' Carole's legs stopped swinging and she sat still. 'He was a nice guy, perfect really. Sporty, funny, smart, good at his job and I know he loved me.'

'What happened?'

'He'd done his travelling before we met. He wanted to settle down and have kids. Not in the distant future, but right away. Me, on the other hand, I'd been promoted to manage a big project in Hong Kong. It would last for two years. He didn't want to come with me and he didn't want to wait.'

'Did you stay in touch?'

'Too hard. It had to be a clean break. He lives in Hamilton. Three kids, two boys and a girl. Nice wife. She works part-time. They've no idea I follow them on Facebook.'

'Do you regret it now?'

'For a while I did. More so when I had to leave Hong Kong to come back and look after Mum. Bloody cancer! After she died Dad was a mess, and by the time I was ready to go back, the job was gone. The company said they'd find me something, but after what Mum went through my heart wasn't in project management anymore. I decided to be a nurse. You know the rest, I took redundancy, used my savings plus the money Mum left me and bought the house.'

'Do you think you'll ever get married?'

'I'm not ruling it out. If I meet the right guy, but I don't want to spend the rest of my life looking. I'd rather do what we talked about. Work and travel. Travel and work. Like you, I want to help people, and if I get to see the world at the same time even better. Morocco, Kenya, Europe, America … everywhere.'

'What about your father?'

'He'll be fine. He's got the money from the farm and he's still in good nick. He's actually a townie, born and bred in Auckland. He only moved to the farm to be with Mum. I think he's relieved to be off the place. She was the farmer, not him. Her family left her the property on the condition she kept it going. Dad stayed because she got pregnant with me. Don't let on you know. Okay?'

'Okay.'

A blast from a ship's horn made them look up. The Devonport ferry was noisily backing away from the wharf at the end of the promenade, its wake a churn of white in the dark water.

Jess checked her phone. 'Hell! It's quarter to four.' She saw the missed calls and unanswered texts — all from Andrew — all in the last two hours. Each text shorter and angrier than the one before, each demanding to know where she was and when was she coming home. She didn't open the voice messages. 'We have to get back.'

'We'll be stuck in traffic if we get a taxi. Better to wait for the next ferry. Text and tell him to meet us at the terminal,' Carole said.

There was no reply, just the *seen* note below her message.

Andrew was literally tapping his foot when they walked down the gangplank after the short ride across the harbour. Eyes wide, he glared at Jess but said nothing until after he'd helped Carole into a waiting taxi and shut the door.

'We'll talk about this at home,' he muttered and without waiting he turned and left her standing in the middle of the pavement. The walk from the old Ferry Building to the apartment usually took five to ten minutes without stops. Jess was used to strolling along the wharves, past the boats and the restaurants, arm in arm with Andrew enjoying the crowds. She wasn't used to half running behind him, dodging pedestrians and bikes, struggling to keep up as he strode ahead. They reached the apartment in four minutes.

As soon as they were alone Andrew let rip. 'How dare you go off without telling me? What did you think you were doing? Why didn't you reply to my texts, or answer my calls? Didn't you think about me for a moment? That I might be worried something had happened to you? How could you be such a fucking bitch?' He spat the last words at her, fury blazing in his eyes.

Stunned, Jess couldn't move. She stood open-mouthed as he ranted at her, giving her no opportunity to interject, no chance to answer his questions or explain. Her work in the emergency department at the hospital had taught her the wisdom of not interrupting anyone who was so angry, so furious that an otherwise innocent comment would only trigger a complete meltdown. She waited, head down while Andrew marched up and down, enumerating her faults, her immaturity, and her stupidity.

'There may be people out there who want to pay me back for things you wouldn't understand,' he yelled. 'How was I to know one of them hadn't decided to hurt you? To get at me, or punish me? You don't understand there are bad people out there. You've lived too long coddled up in your ivory tower to know how the real world operates. There are nasty people who would do things you can't imagine if they thought it would get them my attention.' He was marching up and down beside the bed, spittle from his mouth flicking on to the sheets. 'You can't just wander off any time you like and not tell me. For fuck's sake, I'm too busy, I've got too much to do to have to worry about you. I have to know where you are every second of the day or this won't work. And if you don't understand then you might as well pack your bag and fuck off.'

She looked at him. *What was he talking about? What people? Why did they want to punish him? For what? What had he done to them? Every second of every day? What?* Jess didn't want to be there anymore. He was behaving irrationally, saying the cruellest things, and he was scaring her. Grown-ups weren't supposed to be like this. Was he really involved in drug dealing, was that what was making him so afraid of people coming after him? Was he a criminal after all? She thought she loved him but after this?

Shocked, Jess went to the bathroom, locked the door and sank to her knees. The huge diamond on her engagement ring twinkled merrily at her making her feel sick with fear about what she'd got herself mixed up in. She didn't cry, she had no tears, the hollow feeling of disappointment overrode any need to cry. Thirty years old, a responsible qualified physician, and here she was hiding in a bathroom from the man she had agreed to marry. Thankfully, he left her alone. At least he'd got that right. She could forgive an angry outburst, she could even understand the worry which had caused it, but she couldn't tolerate what had been a tantrum, a childish discharge of anger when things didn't work out exactly as he'd wanted them to. To be fair, in his place she would have been worried if he hadn't answered her texts. She could see that. But furious? Terrified? Abusive? Entirely different.

She soaked a flannel with cold water, wrung it out and wiped her face. Then she repeated the process, this time she folded it and draped it across the back of her neck. What was she going to do? She could walk out and never come back. She should do exactly that. It's what she would advise any woman in the same position to do. She should wait until she knew he was gone, pack her bags and go back to Carole's. It was tempting, but she also knew a grand gesture would solve nothing. Not when she loved him as much as she did.

Part of her knew his tirade wasn't about her. It had nothing to do with her being late per se, or even drinking. She'd left him alone while she was out with her best friend and he had built up a scenario in his mind that something had happened to her. He had let his fear overtake rational thought and built it into more than it was. He was right. There were nutcases out there who overreacted to anything and maybe one of them had threatened him in the past.

She remembered one of her hospital colleagues had spent a year knowing that a disgruntled patient had been driving around with a rifle in his car, waiting for an opportunity to take a shot at him. Her colleague had done nothing more than tell his patient to lose weight. Eventually the police had caught the man and the problem went away. People were strange and unpredictable. But Andrew had seriously overreacted and she didn't like seeing that aspect of his personality.

He didn't disturb her. He didn't beg, or cry, bang on the door or whine at her to come out. He waited and when she eventually emerged, her face washed, her teeth brushed and her hair pulled back into a spiky ponytail, he was sitting on the edge of the bed. She saw his wobbly look of contrition, the tears in his eyes as he stood up and took two steps towards her, his hands outstretched.

'I'm sorry,' he said and she could tell he meant it. 'I'll never do that again. Lose control, yell at you. I didn't mean any of it. I was worried. I panicked.'

Jess stood looking at him, saying nothing, thinking.

'Don't leave me Jess. Promise you won't. I can't live without you. You know that. Please, please, don't leave me. I've never felt this way about anyone before. I've never needed anyone like I need you. It takes a bit of getting used to, but I promise you, I'll learn. I'll do anything.' He waited for her to speak, but she couldn't. She could only stand there looking at him. Sensing he wasn't convincing her, Andrew dropped his arms and stepped back. He sagged on to the bed with his head in his hands.

Jess moved then. She sat down on the bed beside him and took the hand closest to her, lifting it to her cheek. 'I know you were upset,' she said. 'I'm sorry, I should have checked my phone and let you know where I was. I'm sorry for making you worry. I know you didn't mean the things you said, but ...' she added, the tone in her voice forcing him to look up and into her eyes. 'I'm a grown woman Andrew. I can look after myself. I've been looking after myself since I was fifteen. I go where I want, when I want, with whoever I want. I come back when I want. I don't need to check in with you and I don't need your permission to do anything. You know I love you. I really do, but if you ever, ever speak to me like that again, I'm gone.'

He knew she meant it. The next day, they set the date for the wedding.

ELEVEN

JESS WAS SITTING at an outside table at *Café Pierre*, her sunglasses on, people watching. Already the promenade was busy. Curious tourists and office workers sidestepped each other and detoured around trucks delivering supplies to the restaurants lining the waterfront. Runners, a few with children in pushchairs hustled for space, becoming visibly annoyed when they had to slow to a standing jog before they could break free. Her flat white was helping to clear the hangover that had ruined the first part of her morning. Soon, she would be ready to read the paperwork Ross had given her — but not yet. She wanted to enjoy the sunshine, the street-life, take in the world moving on with its day and pretend Andrew was sitting beside her, checking his phone, making calls, reaching out now and then to squeeze her hand and whisper, 'I love you,' as he used to.

'Sorry to hear about Andrew,' Pete, the owner and café's namesake, said as he bent over to take her cup away.

'Thanks.'

'Good bloke,' he added awkwardly. Pete wasn't the most talkative of hosts which was why Andrew and Henry said they preferred his café over the others on offer.

'He was.'

'Tough.'

'Yeah, it is.' She paused, biting her lip, determined not to cry. 'Any chance of another flat white? Large this time.'

She decided that when Pete put the fresh coffee on her table, that would be her signal to start work. She extracted the papers from her satchel, settling them on the chair beside her, out of the breeze, which curled around the corner, and fluttered the newspaper of the woman sitting at the next table.

Her coffee arrived. The first document she read was straightforward. A transfer of ownership — a hundred per cent of the shares in Vaultange to her. She signed the bottom of each page, beside the x and yellow sticker, provided by Ross. Then she signed and dated the last page where indicated. *Nothing to it. I now own a crypto currency exchange. Who would have thought?*

The next document was similarly straightforward. It listed the assets owned by Gordon Holdings. It took her a few moments to understand that the figures listed under the column with three 000s in brackets at the top, represented the value of each property in millions. She had to take a breath as she quickly worked out the total. Then she took a big gulp of coffee. Five properties with addresses she didn't recognise in countries — she did — Australia, Panama, Costa Rica, two in the South of France, one in Berlin and another in Athens. No — not five — seven properties. Together worth more than US$15 million.

Appendix II of the same document set out the chattels belonging to each property — cars, boats, yachts, motorboats, jet skis and motorbikes, as well as rugs, furniture, paintings and sculptures. The houses had been bought fully furnished. When was he going to tell her, show her what he'd done, what he'd bought? More to the point, she wondered, why hadn't he told her? What was the big secret?

The next document, five pages stapled together, was a spreadsheet of closely typed columns — small font numbers and letters, no headings, just dates at the top of each column — the last date — two months ago. It was difficult to read, harder to understand the meaning without reference points. She stared at each page until a pattern emerged, rising and falling in value like waves on the sea, each row represented a starting figure, which evolved over time. She could see it now. On the final page a column of the totals from each row, the end point, a number at the bottom totalling 37,000. She looked to the top of the column, more zeros in brackets. $37, 000, 000.

She started again, fitting the pages together, one starting where the other stopped, reviewing the columns, the dates. Thirty-seven million dollars. She was sure she'd got the total correct, but what did it mean? She would ask Ross to explain when she saw him later.

The woman with the newspaper got up and edged her way through the narrow gap between the tables. Pete quickly pocketed the tip she'd left, before collecting the dishes and giving the table a quick wipe down.

'Do you mind if I join you?'

Jess looked up. Henry, his bulk silhouetted against the sun was standing in front of her.

'I was just leaving,' she said quickly. 'I have to get these to Ross.' Her words were garbled. She caught herself, not sure why she had to explain anything to him.

'I was hoping we could talk,' he said sitting down in the chair opposite, effectively blocking her exit.

Pete appeared with his coffee and collected Jess's empty cup. 'More coffee? Wine? No? Nothing? Right. Enjoy,' he said, moving on to the next table.

Henry was sitting too close. Even in the breeze, his cologne made her nostrils itch. Jess found men who wore too much cologne creepy. Was it the smell itself or their assumption it made them attractive to women? She didn't know, but she wasn't the only woman who felt this way — perfumed men were a frequent subject at ward-round morning teas. She leant away, almost tipping off the side of her chair.

'I won't bite, I promise,' he said reaching out and catching her arm.

'You say that, but ....' Her attempt at humour didn't produce a smile.

'I mean it. Truly.' He adjusted his sunglasses.

'Sorry Henry. I'm jittery this morning, can't relax. I miss him.'

Pete arrived with a fresh apple Danish, cleared away debris from another table and left balancing dirty plates along his forearm. Henry sipped his coffee and took a bite of the Danish, the warm smell of the apple and butter pastry blending with his cologne. 'These are so good. Want some?' he asked holding it out.

She shook her head.

'I miss him too,' he said. 'A lot.' He took another bite of the Danish chewing methodically as he stared at her. She imagined him thinking, *I miss him more than you possibly could,* as if grief was a competition he was determined to win.

'I know it's hard for you,' she found herself saying. 'You'd known each other a long time. I'm sorry.'

'Sorry for what?' he asked sharply. 'It's not your fault he died. Not really.'

'There was nothing I could do. He was so sick.'

'It was the disease,' Henry said. 'That was it.'

'I didn't know he was going to leave everything to me. If it's any consolation, I would give it to you if I could.'

'Andrew didn't want me to have it. There's nothing more to say.' He finished the Danish and brushed the crumbs off his lap then leant across the table. 'He loved you. I accept that. Have done since before the wedding. He was different with you. You became the most important person in his life. But it happened so quickly, it was hard to take the fact that suddenly he had no room in his life for me.' His voice faded away and he sat staring at his empty plate. 'I can't believe he's not going to walk over, sit down, order coffee and open his laptop.'

'I know. Every time a door opens, I expect him to walk through it. My phone rings, I wait to hear his voice and when it's not him ... the emptiness gets worse.'

'How about we start again?' Henry took off his sunglasses and held out his hand. 'My name is Henry Turner. I'm not a bad person. My best friend, Andrew has just died. He would want me to help his wife run the company he left her.'

Jess cocked her head and looked at him. Did he mean it? Could they truly start again? Could she trust him to help her? Could she trust him not to hit on her? If he tried that again she would have to show him the door and then what? The simple fact was, she needed him more than he needed her. Without Henry to guide her through the workings of Vaultange, the business would fail, and Andrew's clients would lose all their money. Jess smiled a trembling smile. Henry made eye contact and smiled back, just as tentatively. He was trying. She could see that. Andrew had trusted him. Andrew would want them to make peace for the sake of Vaultange, if nothing else. She took his proffered hand. It was sticky with apple Danish. She shook it anyway.

'We're both hurting. I've said things I didn't mean. So have you, but we have to put that behind us, because if I don't help you and you don't take my help, he'll come back and haunt us.'

'I accept,' she replied, smiling.

TWELVE

Jess's MEETING with Ross was short and to the point. His firm, Martin Derbyshire, occupied the tenth and eleventh floors of a recently refurbished office tower at the upper end of Queen Street. She had expected something more traditional — wood panelling, English countryside prints on the walls with faded copies of House and Garden on offer in the waiting area. Instead she found glass walls, chrome furniture, and a young receptionist with a friendly smile, a nose piercing and a name badge identifying her as Petra.

'Mr Martin apologises he can't see you straight away,' Petra said. 'Can I get you anything to drink?'

'Thank-you, no.' Jess sunk into one of two chairs in the waiting area and flicked through a property magazine. She had learnt about tenant's rights and avenues for their redress by the time Ross appeared and guided her into his office. Three of the walls were frosted glass. The wall behind him was panelled in the same oak as his large antique desk. His degrees, framed, were arrayed on one side, an antique map of New Zealand with Stewart Island shown joined to the South Island, on the other. Two buttoned-leather chairs in front of his desk were for clients, a small table between them.

She gave him the signed documents and he promised to keep her up to date with developments. He advised her to think about what she wanted to do with the properties in Gordon Holdings. They were too valuable to be left empty for long. 'Unoccupied properties not only attract unwanted attention, but necessary maintenance is often missed, leading to a decline in value,' he told her in best lawyer-speak. 'Andrew has paid for three months upkeep and gardening, but after that the cost will have to borne by Gordon Holdings which has no source of income unless you want to rent them out. If not,' he said peering over the top of his glasses, 'you'll have to come up with the money yourself.'

'Let me think about it,' she replied.

Next, he informed her he'd spoken to her landlord. 'Six weeks and then he needs to know if you want to renew the lease at the same rental.' Jess was used to living on nothing, first as a student and then as a junior doctor paying back her loan. Being rich and feeling rich were entirely different states of mind. She was still absorbing the news that the furniture had been leased, and she would have to pay for that too if she decided to stay, when Ross cleared his throat.

'I'm obliged to tell you, I am prepared to act as your legal adviser Jess,' he said. She waited for the kicker. 'But you'll need to sign this.' He slid a sheet of paper across the desk. 'It's an agreement between you, me and the firm, appointing us to be your legal representatives and that you undertake to pay all costs.'

She looked at the sum written on the first line, then quickly skim-read the small print. The first figure was only a retainer. There were monthly expenses in addition to it. She gulped. What choice did she have? She could hardly find another lawyer. She signed the agreement.

Shell-shocked by her new reality, Jess left the office. So much to be paid to so many, and so soon. Ross had tried to soften the impact, but she noticed, he did that only after she signed the agreement.

'There are provisions in the will, money has been set aside by the estate, to take care of Vaultange and your expenses, for three months — same as the properties. There should be enough to tide you over until you get back on your feet, which all going well, won't be too long.' Ross bundled the papers together and stood up. The meeting was over.

She thought about the *provisions* in the elevator on the way down, but they were little comfort. She wasn't accustomed to the amounts of money Ross had been discussing so casually. They belonged to a world she'd read about in magazines, seen on TV. In her world, every dollar was accounted for twice, first coming in and then going out with little left over after she'd paid her student loan. There had been times when she'd only survived the week by eating noodles and getting up an hour earlier to walk to the hospital instead of taking the bus. Damn it. She'd forgotten to ask about the spreadsheet.

Ross talked so easily of thousands here, and tens of thousands there, unaware of the terror building inside her at the mention of such vast sums of money. And he hadn't been as sympathetic in the office as he had been last night. Much to her annoyance he repeated everything five times asking if she was sure she understood what he was saying each time. She'd read lawyers billed by the minute. It'd better not take five explanations every time she asked a question, or she really would run out of money.

The stress she felt about her personal finances was nothing in comparison to the stress she felt regarding Vaultange. She was now the owner and the buck stopped with her. Ross had repeated this five times too. She needed to be informed and be able to understand things as quickly as possible. The long list of her responsibilities rotated through her head, not stopping long enough for her to make sense of any of them. She had important decisions to make and soon. By the time the elevator got to the bottom, Jess was wishing she was working in the hospital where all she did was cure people and save lives.

As she walked up the steps of Carole's house in Point Chevalier, a trendy suburb to the west of the city, Jess heard two people laughing. Deep male laughter joined by Carole's raucous hoots, reverberated into the street. Jess climbed the steps at the front of the wooden villa, knocked and waited, but when there was no response she opened the door and walked through to the back. French doors led from the combined kitchen-living room to a sunny patio surrounded on all sides by high walls covered in ivy. Seated at the garden table, Johnny was regaling his daughter with one of his many stories. Fascinated, Carole hung off her father's every word before suddenly erupting in laughter. Job done, Johnny picked up his empty mug and stood up to come inside. Of average height Johnny appeared taller. He had the wiry bow-legged appearance of a man who has worked the land all his life. Making no allowance for the heat, he was wearing riding boots and his usual blue jeans whose slide down non-existent hips was only prevented by a thick leather belt fastened with an outsized silver buckle. A red-checked shirt, sleeves rolled to his elbows, completed his ensemble. Catching sight of Jess, he stopped, put down the mug and opened his arms.

'Girlie!' Jess walked into his embrace and he held her tight. After her session with Ross, a hug was exactly what she needed. 'No one deserves what you've been through,' Johnny said as he let her go. 'Sit down and talk to Carole. I'll make the tea.'

'Are you okay? You look very pale,' Carole said.

'Lawyers do that to you,' Jess said as she sat down. 'They're like vampires except they don't just take your blood, they drain you of the will to live.'

'Ross Martin?'

'Ah huh. I signed the documents this morning. You're now looking at the scared owner of an exchange, an owner who knows next to nothing about what the exchange exchanges. Ross; however, made it very clear my ignorance was irrelevant. I have to get Vaultange up and running again asap according to him. Oh, and by the way, the buck stops with me. Guess what else has happened? Andrew bought seven overseas properties before he died and put them in a company which I now also own lock stock and barrel.'

'You?' Carole gasped. 'You mean you're rich.'

'On paper.'

'Paper is good. I'd be happy with paper.'

'You'd be happy with paper what?' Johnny asked as he carried a tray with three mugs on it, each sitting in its own puddle of slopped tea. He put the tray down on the table and they helped themselves, wiping off the drips with their hands.

'Jess's inherited Vaultange and seven overseas properties. She's rich — on paper.'

'I bet you'd rather have Andrew back,' Johnny said.

'Don't say that, or I'll start crying and I can't. I have to keep control. I've got a business to run.'

'Is there anything I can do?' Carole asked.

'Do you know anything about cryptocurrency?'

Carole shook her head.

'The big problem is neither do I.'

Johnny spluttered in his tea and put his cup back on the tray so he could wipe his mouth.

'I know a bit. Just not enough to run Vaultange. Not by myself. I don't even know how to open the wallets or more importantly where to find them. Promise not to tell anyone I said that. This is between us. Right?'

'Why would he leave the exchange to you if you know nothing about crypto?' Johnny asked.

'I guess he wasn't planning on dying,' she replied.

Johnny ran a hand over what was left of his hair and ended up massaging the back of his neck. When he looked up, his face, tanned and wrinkled from years spent outdoors looked strained. A thin sheen of sweat had appeared on his top lip. 'His partner, Henry-what's-his-name. I thought he'd be running the show?'

'Henry Turner? He wasn't Andrew's partner. I've never figured out what he was, but he didn't own any of the business.'

'Dad, is something wrong?' Carole asked.

'Jess's news. It's caught me a bit left field, that's all. I'm not sure … I assumed Henry was managing … that Vaultange was in safe hands.'

'What's it to do with you?'

'The farm money. It … I … Vaultange. All of it.'

'You mean? You didn't … You couldn't,' Carole said as understanding crept over her face and she stopped speaking to stare at her father, her mouth open.

'Andrew ... he said it was safe. It is safe, isn't it Jess?' Johnny's laughter was forced. 'I'm panicking over nothing, aren't I? You'll figure it out. You're a smart girl. Mostly you're smart enough to get help, aren't you?'

Carole looked from Jess to her father and back again.

'He showed me the graphs,' Johnny said. 'He assured me it was the perfect time to buy because the price is so low.' His voice petered out as he looked anywhere but at his daughter. 'I wanted you to have more when I die. I didn't want you working your whole life. I did it for you.'

'You didn't do it for me at all Dad. Don't say that. I've never asked for money. You did this for you.'

Jess leant across, took Johnny's hand and squeezed it making him look at her. 'I know it sounds bad, but I wasn't serious. I'll figure this out. It's not brain surgery. Henry is going to help. I should have said that at the beginning. Vaultange hasn't gone anywhere. You'll get your money back, I promise. I learn quickly.' She turned to Carole who didn't look much happier than her father when she blurted out the next words. 'I do, don't I? Learn quickly? I do.'

'You're sure about that, Girlie? You can do this?'

'Of course. Not tomorrow or the next day. I'll need time to figure it out. But I will do it. You'll get your money back Johnny. Andrew would have kept it safe, every last cent.'

THIRTEEN

As SHE SAT in an Uber on the way back to the apartment, Jess wondered why a retired sheep and beef farmer would suddenly invest all his money in something he knew so little about. Not just some of his money — all of it. The money he and his wife had earnt over two lifetimes of hard work. Even Jess knew the maxim about not putting all your eggs in one basket. What would induce a man Johnny's age, at his stage of life to ignore the wisdom of age and do exactly that? Johnny was sensible. He'd welcomed her into his home when Carole brought her home for Christmas, he'd shown her how to ride a horse, how to lamb a sheep and how to drive the tractor. He was as much her friend as Carole and he had done something so out of character she couldn't believe it.

Carole and Johnny had been her invited guests at the ceremony when she was awarded her specialist qualification. They had gone out to dinner afterwards to celebrate. Johnny, kind and thoughtful, funny and entertaining, had kept them in fits of laughter regaling them with tales of life in the country — a life she had associated with common sense. The amount he'd got for the farm hadn't been a secret. Over four million dollars, more than enough to live on for the rest of his life and still leave Carole an inheritance. What had made him risk the lot?

A number of the children at the care home had talked about their parents gambling away the family grocery money, not just once, but week after week, year after year, losing not only their own money, but money they'd borrowed or worse, stolen. Eventually they lost their families. Johnny hadn't stolen or borrowed money, but what if she couldn't find it? What if she couldn't get it back for him? He'd taken a huge risk in the hope of an even bigger payout when he couldn't afford to do this, not at his stage of life. It was gambling — plain and simple. Now the onus was on her to make sure Vaultange returned every cent he'd entrusted to Andrew. And not only Johnny. There must be more like him, all of them depending on her to do the right thing and shoulder a burden she hadn't asked for, and didn't want.

Jess had been telling the truth when she told them she had no idea how the exchange worked. She would need to learn and learn fast. First though, she had to find out what she needed to know and second, hone down that information to a manageable load, prioritising some areas over others. It would be like studying for exams all over again. Time consuming and exhausting. The guilt she felt at taking so much leave from her job at the hospital was a luxury she couldn't afford to indulge. No one could begrudge her holiday leave, or the bereavement leave which followed. Her colleagues covering her share of the call roster might not like it, but they would understand. They would have to. As would the Prof when she explained what would happen to investors if she didn't get Vaultange sorted. She thought about doing both jobs at the same time, but the mindsets required were too different and her responsibilities too great to risk it. A request for a month's leave, without pay, surely wasn't too much to ask under the circumstances.

The realisation that she would have no time to grieve, not properly, was distressing. Under the circumstance she had no choice but to put her feelings aside. Her focus had to be on Johnny and the other clients. Once she had discharged her responsibilities, she promised herself, she would devote time to processing Andrew's loss, but until then her feelings were of no importance. Securing the contents of the hot wallet had been a relief, but it was the tip of the proverbial iceberg. She needed time to sit down and methodically work through the bank statements and figure out where things had got to before Andrew left her to carry on alone.

The car slowed to a crawl in the ever-present Auckland traffic, inching forwards as they approached the offramp to the waterfront. Idly she glanced at the driver's ID hanging from the dashboard — Ahmed Prakash. The face in the rear-view mirror was the same as the one in the photo. Always good to know. Their eyes met and held.

'Worst time to travel,' he said.

'You're right, it would have been quicker to walk. I didn't have the right shoes.'

'Good for me. It's been a slow day.'

She looked at him again, a flicker of recognition rippling across her mind. He was the same driver who had driven her home from the airport, or if he wasn't, he looked a lot like him. That driver had also been South Asian, clean shaven with his hair cut the same way. Or was she mistaking one person for another because they were the same ethnicity? She hoped not. Shrugging it off as a coincidence, she settled back in her seat and wrote a mental list detailing what she needed to do when she got home.

First, she needed to call the Prof and arrange the month off work. Second, she needed to check the website, hoping she could remember the steps Henry had used to get into the back end. Third, the website needed to come offline. A *Closed for Maintenance* sign would do for a few days, but after that the clients deserved more information. Hopefully in a couple of days she would have the answers and they could all relax.

The car jerked forward then stopped, jolting her against her seat belt. 'There's been an accident on the bridge,' Ahmed told her.

Fourth, find the client list and work out who owns what, then give them the option to cash out or take their assets offline. Fifth, sell or close the exchange. Get the hell out. Ross was right. She was under no obligation to keep it going. Only then would she be free to grieve for Andrew properly. In her own time — between patients.

Mentally she scratched out four and five, making them five and six instead. The fourth thing she had to do was to learn everything about cryptocurrency. Reassuring people meant being able to speak their language. How else could she convince them to trust her? If she didn't take the *Johnnys* with her, they might block her attempts to make things right.

Twenty minutes later the traffic started moving again and the car left the motorway and scooted across less congested streets towards the harbour and home. Ahmed pulled into the curb and before she opened the door, he instructed her to give him five stars. As soon as she said she would, he smiled and drove away. She saw him glancing back to check on her before he turned the corner at the end of the block. For a moment, she was tempted to run to the end of the street and make sure he hadn't parked out of sight, that he wasn't waiting. It was a moment, a silly moment. Why would he do that? He'd picked her up once. Maybe twice, if indeed it was him. Twice — a coincidence — that's all.

When she reached the apartment, Jess dumped her satchel on the table, peeled off her jacket and slid back the doors to the balcony. Fresh air felt so much better than air conditioning. The sound of people enjoying the evening rose up to greet her. She leant on the balustrade, her hair flickering around her face in the breeze. On the harbour, yachts skimmed past a container vessel sitting at anchor. Whatever happened on the bridge had been sorted, judging by the stream of cars travelling across it in both directions.

Her stomach rumbled — for good reason. Jess had not eaten anything all day. She considered ordering Uber Eats. Albeit the unlikely risk of seeing Ahmed again ruined that idea. She recognised her paranoia for what it was, the symptom of a hungry brain, but she didn't want to test fate and be proved either right or wrong. The rigmarole of ordering from another service didn't appeal. More passwords, reminder emails, too many offers and special deals — it wasn't worth the hassle. Luckily, she found a leftover casserole she'd put in the freezer before the wedding. Casserole or curry? She couldn't tell from the outside. No matter, the steady hum of the microwave promised food. Fifteen minutes and counting.

Jess had watched Andrew key his password into his laptop so often it was no problem to replay the letters and numbers in her mind. Luckily there was enough charge left on his phone for it to receive the six-digit code required by his double encryption system. She was in. Next, she replayed the steps Henry had used to access Vaultange's back end. It didn't take long for her to understand she had no idea what she was looking at, much less looking for. She shrunk the screen, pressed Sleep, then took out her own laptop, booted it up and searched Google.

Outside the sky darkened, the city lights came on. She heard rain sweep across the balcony, but it wasn't cold enough to make her get up and close the doors and it soon stopped. She read about Bitcoin, Ethereum and the myriads of other alt-currencies spawned, since Satoshi Nakamoto published his White Paper in 2008. She brought that up and read it, surprised to find it was a remarkably concise and readable document — considering. Nine pages to change the world — the blueprint for an *electronic payment system based on cryptographic proof instead of trust.* So few words needed to launch the digital revolution of the world's financial system. She brought up charts and tracked how each currency had progressed over time and matched the rises and falls with the events which had triggered them. Many of the alt-coins had disappeared into virtual limbo-land, as soon as they'd been released to a gullible market hungry for the next big thing. These were the ironically named Lamborghini cryptos, which sucked money out of punters, only to have their creators cash out and vanish into the sunset to squander ill-gotten gains on luxury lifestyles. Poof. The proverbial puff of smoke. There one minute. Gone the next.

Bitcoin, Ether, Litecoin, Ripple and a few others had persisted. Initially they followed a boom-bust pattern losing and gaining millions for investors. Commentaries in the financial press abounded with predictions regarding the imminent demise of crypto. And yet, thought Jess, a lot of people remain believers. To these people, crypto is the 21st century disrupter of a banking system weighed down by debts which are unlikely to be repaid. To others crypto was merely something fun to play with. She concluded that with seventeen million Bitcoin in circulation worth sixty-six billion dollars, it would be around for the foreseeable future.

Her phone pinged her back to the real world. *C u tomoro. 10 am yur place. H.*

He'd meant what he said. This morning's offer of help had been genuine. She couldn't help wondering why he was being so co-operative. There had to be a reason because a man like Henry doesn't become a nice guy overnight. She hadn't trusted him before Andrew died. Could she trust him now?

She stretched, sensing the coolness of the night for the first time. The rain had stopped, but her goosebumps let her know there was more on the way. She closed the doors and turned on the lights. The plastic lid had peeled back in the microwave revealing the shrivelled crusty top on the casserole. It was cold, and looked and smelt unappetising. No matter, she was hungry. She forked down the contents without stopping to work out whether it was a curry or a beef casserole. Carrots figured as did the odd pea. It was food. That was all that mattered. When she finished, she tossed the container down the rubbish chute and made a plunger of coffee. If she was going to get everything done tonight, she needed to be alert. Having to pull an all-nighter was something she had thought was behind her. With a business to run, she had no choice but to revert to old habits.

She opened another screen, www.vaultange.com. She wanted to see what clients saw when they visited. A pop-up box advised them to read the Vaultange terms and conditions, then click the box confirming they had done so, before using the exchange. Scrolling to the foot of the page, she pulled up the terms and conditions from the small print in the footer. Based on the number of licence agreements she'd agreed to over the years, she knew few people actually read that stuff. Tick the box. Move on. It was a totally different arrangement from the laborious informed consents to treatments she was ethically obliged to go through with her patients.

From the start, it was made clear that Vaultange did not provide a financial advisory service. Nor was it part of any country's deposit guarantee scheme. More importantly and explicitly set out in the small print of clause ii.5, Vaultange, its employees, owners and directors, accepted no responsibility for the protection or security of any currency, fiat or crypto, kept in its wallets. After reading these statements Jess concluded there could be no comeback on any person associated with the exchange, if money or crypto disappeared.

She pulled up the terms and conditions and legal sections on other exchanges. They all said the same thing. Vaultange was no different. With perhaps two exceptions. On closer inspection of the small print the security actually offered by these exchanges was laughable. A client might, and the emphasis was on might, get their money back, but only if they were prepared to wait. Wait — and — wait. Even then it was likely that only a fraction of the original investment would ever be returned. Not one exchange anywhere in the world took any responsibility for client funds held in their system. Jess was accustomed to being painstakingly accountable in the hospital setting. She was horrified that governments had been so slow to put laws in place to regulate cryptocurrency and to protect unwary investors.

Johnny had no comeback or claim against the exchange. Technically and legally if she couldn't find his assets, that was it. He got nothing and Jess was free of any and all responsibility to make good his losses. It wasn't fair and she felt guilty. At the same time she breathed a sigh of relief. No one was going to take her to court, no one was coming after her, hounding her to the end of her days for money she didn't have. No one was going to take away her freedom or stop her from going back to work and resuming life on her terms. She would do her best to rectify matters, but if her efforts came to naught, any guilt she might feel would be a wasted emotion. She had coped with worse and survived. She would again.

FOURTEEN

JESS CLOSED down her laptop and plugged it into the charger on the
bench. She had searched everywhere, but Andrew's charger was
missing. She figured it must still be on the island. Thirsty, she filled a
glass with cold water and drank it down in one go, then poured
another. The apartment looked the same as it had when she'd left that
morning — tidy. She was wide awake after the plunger of coffee and
knew she wouldn't sleep if she went to bed now, so she got busy and
wiped benches, grateful just to be moving after sitting and staring at a
screen for so long. With a damp cloth in one hand, a spray bottle in
the other, no surface was spared. Dining chairs were moved, first one
way then the other. Sofa cushions were plumped and lined up the
way Andrew always preferred — straight up and down — not on
their points. It felt good to deliver a single, efficient karate blow into
the top edge, to give definition, the way he'd told her to. As she
smoothed the seat cushions, her leg brushed against the corner of the
file. She stopped with the spray bottle still in her hand. Now? Was she
ready?

Part of her hoped the file would magically disappear. That a fairy
would sneak in and whisk it away to file-land where it would be
shredded into tiny pieces and used to light fires in hell. And part of

her was curious as to find out what Andrew knew. She sat down and opened it.

Jessica Davidson: DOB: 26: 03: 1987.

Page one: List of contents:

1. Summary of court proceedings.
2. Background
3. Neuropsychological assessment
4. Psychiatric report

Skipping the court proceedings and background stuff, Jess turned to Sections 3 and 4. No one had thought to tell her the results of these assessments at the time. In the months after her mother's death she was told nothing, unless it was considered absolutely necessary. In shock, she accepted whatever happened to her.

Background:

Marguerite Davidson (MD) — Deceased.

Jessica Davidson (JD) daughter of MD — defendant.

Bryan Randall (BR) — MD's husband: JD's stepfather.

The family had been living at (address supplied) for six months prior to the incident. They moved after MD was diagnosed with motor neurone disease — the family home, (address supplied) not being wheelchair accessible.

MD's condition deteriorated quickly and at the time of her death she was bedridden and in receipt of outpatient nursing services and palliative care four times a day. These included oxygen, and regular suctioning of the upper airways to facilitate breathing. A hospital bed, hoist, commode and other equipment was provided. Bedridden, MD had difficulties with breathing and swallowing. She was dependent on others for all care. Her life expectancy at the time of the incident was estimated to be days to two weeks.

BR worked full-time, as a self-employed mechanic.

JD (15) — only child of MD, biological father unknown, left school to look after her mother. Concern was expressed by nurses, and child welfare services, that it was inappropriate for a fifteen-year-old girl to assume this degree of responsibility. JD and MD stated they did not want to be separated at this time.

Nursing staff commented on JD's maturity, her ability to understand the changing situation and most importantly, the deep love she had for her mother and her wish to be with her until the end. JD learned to administer medication, use laryngeal suction, and attend to MD's needs, particularly as MD's speech became less intelligible to others.

Nursing staff also commented on BR's emotional distance from both MD and JD, the excessive time he spent at his business, and his indifference to MD's worsening condition. He had been overheard making jokes, and on one occasion was heard to say, he wished she would hurry up and die, so "I can get on with my life".

On the morning of MD's death, Nurse Jenny Morell, arrived as usual at 7.30 a.m. and found JD kneeling on the bed holding a pillow over her mother's face. Nurse Morell pulled JD away and started CPR but to no effect. At 7.37 a.m. she stopped resuscitation. Emergency services arrived soon after.

All credit to whoever had compiled the report. It neatly summarised what had been presented in court. The psychological and psychiatric reports included comments taken from social welfare reports and the court's final decision. She had been convicted of manslaughter and sentenced as a juvenile with automatic name suppression. Jess hadn't minded the sentence. She felt so guilty about what happened, she thought she deserved it. What she didn't accept was that Bryan, who should also have been held to account, got off scot-free.

After the judgement, her stepfather had gone to the press demanding justice. He played to perfection the sobbing widower deprived of his wife by the actions of his heartless and conniving stepdaughter. It didn't take long for Jess's name to be bandied about on social media, despite the suppression order. Facebook was in its infancy, but as a result of Jess's case the trolls smelt blood and started a relentless vilification of her in posts. A page was set up devoted to seeking justice for Bryan. Her name, Jessica Davidson soon became synonymous with the irresponsible and lenient sentencing by the youth justice system. Jess loathed and consequently avoided social media to this day.

Mr Coates, her solicitor at the time, had done his best. He arranged for her name to be changed and for her to be relocated to a different part of the country. Mr Coates, if she remembered correctly, had been balding and walked with a limp. His suits were covered in pet hair. Dogs, he told her, even though she hadn't asked. He had caught her staring and volunteered the information with a smile. Labradors? She couldn't remember. Mr Coates had been appointed by the court when Bryan told her at his one and only visit, she was on her own and wasn't getting a cent from either the sale of the family home or from him.

Mr Coates said he knew how she felt. How could he? She didn't know herself. Her world had stopped when her mother died. She had barely spoken since Nurse Morrell took the pillow. 'Talk when you're ready,' he said. 'In the meantime, I'll try and get what's due from your mother's estate.' He was unsuccessful.

Bryan went to court and had Jess legally disinherited on the basis she should not be allowed to profit from a crime she had committed. Public opinion was on his side.

The words started to blur as her eyelids drooped. Jess stopped reading and pinched the top of her nose between her fingers. Andrew married me. He read the file. He said nothing. I was convicted of the manslaughter of my mother and he still went ahead, married me and left me his estate in a will he had drawn up and signed. On our honeymoon, he gave me no clue that he knew. Not a look, not a question — nothing. *Wasn't he curious? Why didn't he ask me for my side of the story? It wasn't for lack of opportunity.*

Jess ran her hands through her hair, flexed and extended her neck, hearing the gristle crunch as her vertebrae moved. It was two a.m. She had to be up in less than six hours. She yawned again and scratch-rubbed her scalp to wake up. She had to keep reading. She had to finish it, read until the end and get the bloody thing out of the way. Done. Gone. Tempting as it was to construct different scenarios to explain why Andrew hadn't said anything, she knew it was futile. She could torture herself, but it wouldn't change anything, or answer her questions.

The press reports had been taken from the Internet. She had read them before; the vitriol seared into her brain — it still hurt. She turned the pages keen to get to the psychological report, one page of which detailed the story of her life. That's all it took, one page to set out her upbringing without a father, the early years with her mother and the closeness of their relationship, which had been interrupted by Bryan's arrival into the family when she was eleven. It was hard to keep her eyes open and focus, but she needed to get through it. She skipped the next pages setting out the results of tests she barely remembered taking, stopping when she got to the summary of results.

The Weschler Intelligence test: 137 — well above average results across all indices. Verbal, visuo-spatial, tests of executive function, all in the high to exceptional range.

On the Beck Depression Inventory-II: her score was low to average. On the Beck Anxiety Scale, she was in the normal range. TSI-2, Trauma symptoms: average to high. Hare Psychopathy testing was negative as were the results for a dissociative disorder.

Gobbledy-gook but good gobbledy-gook.

Summary: Jessica Davidson scores in the highest range for intelligence, with no symptoms of psychopathology on testing. She is psychologically minded and demonstrates good insight. It has not been possible to give an opinion as to what formed the basis of her rationalization for her actions. Further exploration will be required. Based on the psychometric testing and her presentation at this assessment, the most appropriate DSM 5 diagnosis is one of an adjustment disorder — mild. (Adjustment disorder is a stress-related, short-term, nonpsychotic disturbance characterised by low mood with some rumination of recent distress secondary to the death of her mother.)

Jess knew the rest. She had been sent for close observation in a restricted living environment where she was encouraged to continue her education. That was it. She wasn't insane, she wasn't a monster. At least not one with an official diagnosis.

I am normal. I always was. Reassured now, but it would have been nice for someone to tell me at the time that I was okay instead of treating me as if I was crazy. Especially in that first place I went to. Hushed voices, locked doors, no one looking me in the eye. I had no one on my side. Once the case was over, Mr Coates was gone. Job done.

What followed were years of mostly odd, occasionally abusive foster parents, concerned counsellors, and worst of all the teachers at the *special* school. The knowing looks, the slow careful way they expressed themselves around her, constantly alert for a reaction drove her to distraction. Worse was the faux concern bordering on smugness wrapped up in righteousness. The way they pretended to consult with her so they could take her wishes into consideration, when all along they had no intention of giving her any control over her life whatsoever. Quickly realising how pointless it was to speak up, Jess elected to say nothing and do what had to be done to survive. She gritted her teeth and hunkered down behind a façade of compliance.

The system was not geared up for an intellectual outlier, the teachers less so. After she passed every exam she was set with distinction, she was left her to her own devices. She read every book which came her way, used the Internet and watched people, studying and observing everything about everyone she came in contact with. All the while Jess was making plans. She turned to the last page of the file.

Jess Gordon absconded from the care home and school the day before her seventeenth birthday. The police were notified. She had been compliant in care, submitted to regular assessments, did not abuse substances and exhibited no antisocial or borderline traits. She did not come to the attention of the authorities and as there was no cause for concern, her file was closed a year later on her eighteenth birthday.

The report ended there. She flicked back over the pages she hadn't read, noticing standout irregularities in the punctuation in the text. It was unusual, but on first glance, they were probably typos. She was so tired she couldn't read another word, but what to do? Destroy it or keep it? Which? Ross said this was the only copy. He said no one else had read it apart from Andrew. She didn't believe him. What sort of person doesn't read something secret, if they have the chance? No, she decided. Ross would have read it. She assumed the same could be said for Henry. He and Ross seemed pretty pally the other day. She was too tired to think of a reason why it would matter.

She stood up, arched her body and broke the tension in her back muscles. With her eyelids drooping over scratchy eyeballs she shuffled through to her bedroom and shoved the file between the bed-base and valance. She stripped off, climbed naked under the duvet and went straight to sleep.

FIFTEEN

'WHENEVER YOU'RE READY, MR TURNER.'

I opened my eyes. I was lying on a bed, wider than a single bed with starched white sheets, a light-blue cotton blanket lay folded across the end. Glossy white walls, no windows and one door, no pictures, dimmed lights recessed into the ceiling. On the bedside cabinet stood a jug and glass — both plastic.

The pain in my arm was growing worse. I pressed the button on the pump, as the nurse had showed me then I counted twelve seconds, a Mississippi between each number. Relief.

'Speak normally, as if to a friend,' said the voice. 'You're being recorded so don't think you have to edit anything.'

I was driving Andrew home from the hospital — the second time — when he told me he had fallen in love. It was mid-morning, around ten, ten-thirty. It was October 2018, and summer had started early. The roads were still warm from the day before. We were stuck on the inside lane of an on-ramp, despite rush hour being officially over — heat was rising from the tarmac fused with the exhaust fumes of cars going nowhere. Bad disco music, interspersed with inane comments from the host, played against the background roar of the air con on full blast. I was concentrating on busting into the next lane, the driver in the car alongside, equally determined that wasn't going to happen. Inching forward, nudging towards the centre line, attention elsewhere, it took me a moment to take in what he was saying.

'I'm in love,' he said. Actually, he croaked, his voice was still hoarse from the tube shoved down his throat when he was in ICU. Take away the voice though and he was looking better than I'd seen him in ages.

Five years before, when I picked him up from hospital, he looked much worse. Back then he'd insisted he was perfectly capable of walking to the car. An hour later, he collapsed. We were on the Southern Motorway in rush hour and it was raining. Rather than take any risks negotiating traffic, I stopped the car and called an ambulance — sirens, lights and the paramedics who knew how to treat him. They called the rescue helicopter. Needless to say, Auckland traffic was grid-locked for the rest of the day. The professor had been suckered by Andrew into discharging him too soon. I'd tried to warn David (the professor) what he was like. He ignored me. What would I know? My opinion didn't count.

Andrew had walked out of arrivals after an eleven-hour flight and he looked like shit. Three weeks spent getting steadily sicker in the tropical shithole he'd been living in, can do that to a man. Even I could see he was undernourished, scrawny and sweating like a pig. I took him straight to the hospital. I couldn't believe it when they gave him a prescription and said he could go home. I saw the fake smile. I knew he didn't want to stay. I listened to his banter about not wasting the country's health resources. I made faces behind his back when he reassured the professor, he would come straight back if he got worse. Not a bad actor, Andrew has always been foolishly brave. He was determined not to spend a day in hospital if he could help it. The professor said to take the medication, rest and drink plenty of fluids. Andrew nodded, shook the professor's hand, climbed off the trolley and with his head high walked out of the main entrance — only to collapse an hour later — on the motorway — as I said.

How long have I known him? We met at school. We both went to

Auckland Grammar, the state school in the middle of town which harvested its pupils from the surrounding posh neighbourhoods. Parents literally fought to get their kids into the place, mortgaging themselves to the hilt to live in the intake zone. I was an exception. I didn't live in a posh suburb. I lived in Mangere, out by the airport, the part of town where people were too poor to pay rent let alone take out a mortgage. I was allowed in because I played rugby.

Everyone knew Andrew. He was the little guy with the big mouth. He should have had a target painted on his back. It would have made it easier for the bullies to keep score. Until I landed on him at the bottom of a rugby scrum we'd never spoken. He was struggling to breathe with both nostrils plugged with mud, and the poor guy was being pummelled by the class moron. I felt sorry for him, beat off the moron and hauled Andrew out of there by the scruff of his neck. The real moron was the teacher. Mr Davies who forced Andrew to play. "Kiwis play rugby. Now get out there Cullinane. You'll enjoy it." he'd said. The hell he did. We walked off the field together — in the middle of the game —straight to the changing rooms and into the showers.

I never played rugby again. Why perpetuate a cultural stereotype? Guys like Andrew should not have their faces ground into the mud in order to pass some ridiculous rite of passage. It's not sporting. I'm serious. Mr Davies was an excellent English teacher. He knew a lot about rugby, but he knew zip about leadership. I would have given anything to be a fly on the wall when he explained to the headmaster, precisely why the captain of the first fifteen (me) refused to play in the final of the inter-schools competition when for the first time in twenty years, our team might actually win.

After that, me and Andrew were mates. Our friendship was nourished by the scorn heaped upon my head by my erstwhile teammates, the rest of the school, and last but not least my girlfriend at the time. She not only dumped me; she made a show of going out with the guy who replaced me as captain. Later, she married the poor bastard. Last I heard she'd podded five strapping sons, rugby players the lot of them and each one as dumb as their hen-pecked father.

I was the first person other than his parents who Andrew trusted with his secret. A bona fide genius, he hated the idea of being marked out as exceptional, so he hid his intelligence. He made mistakes in exams, always scoring in the top-ten per cent but never scoring top overall. He never spoke in class, mostly because he never listened. He said it was too boring and that he'd rather do calculus in his head. Knowing he was different and having to live with it, didn't mean others had to know it too.

An only child, his parents were decent but ordinary people. His dad was a solicitor who had gone to boarding school. He hated his experience there enough never to want the same educational exile for his son. His mum stayed at home. She came from South Island farming stock, and had her own money. She spent her days pottering in the garden, reading books and playing Bridge with the girls. Neither parent believed in unseemly displays of intelligence or wealth. They were old-fashioned, but they gave Andrew love and the space to be whatever he wanted to be — whatever that was.

My family? Drunken, criminals — all of them — without exception. Mum and Dad died within a year of me leaving home. Tragic, if you believe that shit about socio-economic factors forcing people to make bad choices. Me, I know their premature demise was the inevitable result of a lifetime's inability to say no to drugs — especially the free stuff. They were felled past their prime by the same batch of tainted heroin which they willingly injected. My siblings (older sister and younger brother) have inherited the family genes. No doubt they will follow the same predictable life trajectory into early graves. I still say I was adopted. Andrew met my folks once. He earnt my eternal gratitude when he never spoke about them or where I'd come from again.

In our last six months at school, Andrew started following the horses. He preferred the gallops, telling me there were less things to go wrong than in harness racing. People say racing is a mug's game, that you can't win when you bet on the ponies. Too many unknowns, too many hidden variables, they say. Andrew didn't listen to people. He developed a system which worked. He won and he won big. 'It's the algorithms, Henry. Algorithms and having sufficient data to minimise error, while at the same building significance into the formula to arrive at a logical outcome.' Meaning? No idea.

I plodded on. First at school then at university — AUT. I was one of over three thousand students enrolled that year to study business management. Churn is too mild a word to describe the business model of my alma mater. I can only hope as this century's third decade approaches, students will see the light and realise it's better to learn a trade, one which can't be replaced by robots. It's downright foolish to go into debt to get a piece of paper which is outdated the moment it's printed.

Andrew saw the light before I did. He avoided university preferring to self-direct his learning into areas which seem obvious now, but which I didn't understand at the time. However, it didn't stop him piggy-backing on my social life, stalking me and my mates, going to our parties, or wafting through the café on the pretext of meeting me for lunch, but really he was only there to meet girls. He insisted his taste in women was eclectic. I said it was *take-anything-you-can-get*.

His technique with the fairer sex was more method than flare, but it reaped results. Eighteen — he was average height, not as big as me, but few people are. He'd eat his lunch pecking away at a salad while he surveyed the talent. Once he selected a table of girls, he would saunter over and introduce himself. He literally stood by the table until one girl (usually the least attractive) took pity on him and asked him to sit down. His success rate matched his confidence.

I had my own problem. Her name was Rachel. Too gorgeous to say no to, Rachel was one of the *it* girls on campus. She decided in the first year, I was to be her *it* boyfriend. I didn't stand a chance. I was young. My penis overrode my brain on every decision.

Study? Or fuck Rachel? Work longer hours, save money? Or fuck Rachel? Apply for the scholarship? Or fuck Rachel? Go to the gym? Write the essay? Train for the squash championship? Get a university "Blue"? I fucked Rachel. In the end, Rachel fucked me.

Scene — graduation parade through town, Queen Street, Auckland. Rachel dumped me just as we were about to enter the auditorium where the degrees were to be conferred. I'd met her parents the night before. Our relationship went downhill from there. For her graduation present they rustled up a first-class ticket to Paris and a year's tuition at the Sorbonne. 'Long-distance relationships don't work,' she told me, sounding exactly like her mother. 'You'll thank me later,' she whispered in my ear as we sat down. If this was her way to make me feel better, it didn't work. I walked on stage to get my worthless piece of paper, (B pass — an average degree) in shock and feeling like shit. After leaving the stage, I headed straight out of the fire-door and set off the alarm — and the sprinkler system — bugger. Rachel was about to have her big moment.

I ripped off my gown and stupid mortarboard and dumped them along with the cardboard-backed degree in its plain manila A3 envelope in the first rubbish bin I passed.

Andrew was waiting for me. He rescued the degree and followed me through the rubbish-strewn back streets off Karangahape Road, but at a manly distance. When he saw that I'd stopped sobbing, he took me to the nearest bar. We got right royally — damn it all to hell — life's too short — and all women are bitches — let's plot the downfall of the world — drunk. It was 2007.

SIXTEEN

We didn't see each other again for six years. Andrew left the country, travelling first to San Francisco and the Valley, where he met up with fellow geniuses. What is the correct name for a group of nerds? A chip of nerds? A quant of nerds? A circuit of bright sparks?

I had to get a job to pay the rent and service my share of the country's debt burden — my student loan.

We lost touch. Occasionally I'd run into his parents at the local supermarket. His father had retired early after a stroke. Physically, Pop was a write-off. Or one side of him was, but he was still on to it mentally. Mum on the other hand could have run a marathon, but she was vague, the category of vague which starts early and gets worse. Together, they almost made a whole person. His dad always recognised me and said hello, masking his dribbling with his good hand as he did so. It embarrassed him that he couldn't stand, look me in the eye, and shake hands as men were supposed to, but he did his best not to let it show.

'You remember Henry,' he'd say to his wife, louder than necessary. She would nod and smile with dead eyes and ask how I was, and did I know her son because we looked the same age, but her son was overseas. Then Pop would tell me Andrew had called last week. 'Or was it last month dear?' He'd look up at Mum from his wheelchair, eyebrows raised, and she'd smile at something she'd seen on the shelf. 'Doesn't matter,' he'd add. 'He's doing well in Japan', or wherever he was. He always ended with a hearty, 'We must have you over for a drink' line, but this never eventuated into an actual time or date. 'Come on old girl, giddy up,' he'd say, and they'd be off releasing the backlog of shopping trolleys and annoyed people, waiting in the aisle behind them, like water from a dam.

At this point, I have to say that Andrew making Jess his mother's trustee was hurtful — and a surprise. I knew the woman. I knew her when she could walk and talk and smile politely and was continent. Jess met her once. Or was it twice? Anyway, by then his mother was unresponsive to everything except food. The look on her face when she spotted a spoon approaching — the focus, the quivering anticipation, the greed in her eyes, the licking of shaky lips as she opened her mouth. It gave me faith in the survival instinct. I should have been her trustee. I would have looked after her. Andrew should have trusted me. I should have been a lot of things. Where was I?

Andrew returned to New Zealand in 2013 after he got sick. Years before his dad must have given him my number. He called me out of the blue to tell me the reason for his coming back and his arrival time. I met him at the airport and took him straight to the hospital. An hour later, I called the ambulance, and they took him back. I owed the guy — big time.

In 2010, when I was working at the bank I got into serious trouble. That's right, the business studies degree got me a job in finance. It didn't pay much, and I was at the bottom of the corporate heap, but I could pay my rent and put a dent in my student loan. I had enough money left over to go out on Friday night with the boys from accounting. On Saturdays I'd sleep late, tidy-up, change the sheets from the night before if I'd got lucky and do the washing. Sundays I spent dawdling the net on a cheap notebook I'd picked up in a New Year sale. It was a complete accident when I found myself on the dark web. I never planned to stay. I wanted to see what the fuss was about — that's all. I didn't go there intending to purchase. Not on my salary, but I looked. It didn't disappoint. I window-shopped, I snooped and sized up the options.

Before assuming the worst, let's throw the elephant out of the room — I'm not a pervert or a paedo. I'm kind to animals. I like my women (never men) unbound and free of substances. I prefer women who say, 'Yes please,' before sex.

I have no excuse, no explanation for visiting one particular site, not once, but many times. On reflection, I guess I did it for the same reason motorists slow down when they pass a car crash. To see the blood and gore, the bodies ripped asunder by metal, people torn limb from limb and when they do see, they can't look away. Not until the full import of horror rocks them to the core. And they thank their deity it's other people and not them. They drive on then, castigating the others who slow down to gawk, for being ghouls with no sense of decency.

The images I saw transfixed me. Was I addicted? Probably. I have no rational explanation for why I kept going back. It wasn't sexual. It wasn't anything. I don't know why, all right? Don't judge me. And that's what I told the police one Sunday afternoon when they busted down my door with a warrant for my arrest.

'Is it okay if I take a break now? I need to pee.'

They'd been tracking me for weeks. Okay, I admit it. I had paid to view, and they used my credit card to find me. I didn't buy the really, really bad stuff. No killings. I do have standards. Some dude in Arkansas was making home movies, using his girlfriend's kids. An arsehole, he didn't know the first thing about cyber-security. He and his girlfriend went to prison. The kids went to a care home. The FBI followed up the leads on his computer. One brought them straight to my door. They visited over a hundred guys around the world from that one bust. Weirdos most of them. Sickos, sickos, sicker than sick. Which was what one detective called me. I took exception. My indignation at him lumping me in with the sickos got the better of me. When I'd finished, the detective added *stupid* to the list of names he called me. And added another charge to my charge sheet — assaulting a police officer. It looked like I'd be locked up in maximum security for the best years of my life. I called the only person I knew outside of work. Andrew's dad.

To cut a long story short, his dad called Andrew, who called Ralph Logan, the country's top criminal lawyer and next minute, the next day actually, they released me. The police had been so keen to arrest me, they hadn't crossed the t-s and dotted the i-s correctly on the search warrant. They even had to give my notebook back. Not that I wanted it, since it was full of police cyber-trackers. It's the principle of the thing, I told the cop with the busted nose. Yeah, I got off that charge too. Ralph had turned an inevitable conviction into a warning with diversion. I didn't have to pay a cent. Andrew took care of his ginormous bill. I was a free man — sort of. By the time the cops had finished their informal chats with my employers and given my neighbours what they called a heads-up, sure I was a free man. With no job and no place to live.

Andrew rode to the rescue again. A dollop of money landed in my new bank account and I lived to fight another day. It happened without a word passing between us and to this day I have no idea where he got that much money. I don't think he ever found out why I was arrested. He never asked. It was 2010. Two years after Satoshi Nakamoto published his white paper — Bitcoin — *A Peer-to-Peer Electronic Cash System.* That paper would change the world and both our lives.

In 2013, as soon as Andrew was diagnosed with an inflammatory bowel condition, (he was living in the aforementioned tropical shithole at the time) he jumped on a plane and came home. He'd researched who were the experts in the field and David's name came up. Home-based — a pleasant surprise. Auckland Hospital, New Zealand. I used to think it was a happy coincidence because he would never have returned to the land of his birth otherwise.

An unsentimental son, he sent enough money to make sure his

parents were looked after, but he had no desperate need to be with them in their final years. He didn't come back for his father's funeral. He had Ross Martin, his lawyer, oversee the sale of the family home and then had his mother moved into care. When he did eventually visit her, she didn't recognise him. He turned up at the care home unannounced. She smiled. She thanked him for coming before asking again who he was, and did he know her son because he looked about the same age. He didn't go back for five years.

Who am I to judge? I don't even know where my parents are buried —hey they could even be cremated for all I know.

After my brush with the Arkansas arsehole, I learnt as much as I could about cyber-surveillance and security. I was never caught again. Interestingly, in the three years before he called me, I never managed to track Andrew down. Not once. I wanted to thank him for his assistance, but it didn't happen despite my best efforts. The lesson being if someone doesn't want to be found, they won't be — if they go about disappearing the right way.

During 2013, he was in hospital for weeks. When he was finally well enough to be discharged, I took him home with me. Someone had to look after him. Pain, bleeding, diarrhoea, the lot, it went on for months. He wouldn't let me call the professor, insisting we wait for the tablets to work and they did — eventually. It took six months before he could work a full day without an afternoon nap.

Inflammatory bowel conditions are cruel, the symptoms horrendous. Worse, they come and go for no reason. Chronic relapsing is the medical term for this torture. Just when you're getting better and think you might have beaten the bastard, back it comes, swooping into your life without warning, to wreak havoc. Just as inexplicably it swoops out again, leaving you to pick up the pieces and get on with what's left.

Effectively bedridden during the first six months of 2013, Andrew hung out on the net where he caught up with the future — our future. Bitcoin started the year under two hundred dollars. By December it had climbed to over a thousand dollars. More importantly, Andrew noticed that every day the volumes traded were increasing. We talked.

Rather he talked and I listened. He decided the best way to get into the game was to become a miner, the people who work the programme to process transactions earning new Bitcoin as payment for the work. I had nothing else to do, so yeah, I said, what the hell. By the end of the year, my apartment ran at a steady twenty-five degrees Celsius with the air conditioning on full. The neighbours threatened to complain to the landlord about the incessant humming of the cooling systems for the rigs, the computer hardware used to mine crypto, but their objections disappeared when Andrew paid them a year's rent in advance.

In the early days, being a miner and running a node was way more complex than it is now. These days the programmes can be downloaded from the net and they are updated automatically. Back then miners had to develop their own programmes. Andrew took to the business like the tech genius he was. Algorithms were his best friend.

I made the coffee. I made sure he slept, ate regularly and healthily. I bought the groceries. I made him exercise. I changed his sheets and did the washing. I made sure he took his meds on time. Vaultange was always his company. It was his vision, not mine. He made it work. He fronted it. Working every hour possible he reaped twenty-five new Bitcoin as a reward for every transaction he processed. He banked everything back into the business. I ran support. And was paid well for it. We were so busy I barely remember, the years 2014 through 2018. What I do remember was being happy.

It was all work and very little play, but the money. In four short years, Bitcoin, the little darling, climbed steadily in worth from several hundred dollars to twenty thousand dollars. US. Sure, it dived a month later in January 2018 to hit three thousand dollars. It was still worth ten times more than it had been four years earlier. Name me any other asset which does that tax-free?

After the third halving in 2016, Andrew stopped mining. Halving is the system Satoshi designed to limit the numbers of Bitcoin generated by the system so there will only ever be twenty-one million. Transactions are the source of new Bitcoin and the amount a miner earns per transaction halves every four years or after approximately two hundred thousand transactions. Cunning, because it builds scarcity and thus value into the model. With only twelve and half Bitcoin earnt per transaction, Andrew thought being a miner was no longer commercially viable. The information on the blockchain had grown exponentially and the computers required to store it had become prohibitively expensive. Add to the cost of upgrading rigs every few months, rising electricity prices, it was better to outsource transactions to contractors in faraway places. Andrew made more money charging commission to the clients clamouring for his services anyway.

Without the servers and rigs running to keep us warm, we had to buy winter clothes for the first time in four years. It also meant we didn't have to be onsite 24/7. There was life outside my flat. Andrew, who was now able to run the business from a laptop, moved into his penthouse apartment. I moved into a townhouse.

Then he got sick again and I took him back to hospital. He met Jess. And fell in love.

By then, Murray and the goons were regular nocturnal visitors.

SEVENTEEN

SILENCE. Buzzing. More buzzing. Prolonged buzzing. Jess opened her eyes. Thin beams of sunshine slanted across the bed through a crack in the curtains. The buzzing hadn't stopped. As she sucked in a lungful of air, Jess sat up. The sheet was clammy and cold on her body. Still the buzzing continued.

She grabbed the silk dressing gown she'd given Andrew for Christmas and pulled it on, tying it around her as she padded out to the foyer and pressed the button. Henry's face loomed large on the screen. He stepped back. She could see all of him. He was balancing a tray with coffees, a paper bag in one hand and his satchel in the other.

'Okay, okay,' she said pressing the release button. She leant against the wall and waited for the elevator to arrive.

'It's ten o'clock,' he said handing her a coffee as he walked past her. He dumped the paper bag on the table and his satchel on a chair. She yawned as she followed him still half asleep, but grateful for the promise of proper coffee.

Without another word, he popped the lid on his coffee, staring at her breasts over the rim of the cup as he drank.

Jess pulled the dressing gown tighter and folded her arms across her chest. 'Give me a few minutes,' she said. She went back to her bedroom and shut the door, shuddering at the look she'd seen in his eyes, muttering under her breath as she did up her bra, pulled on jeans and one of Andrew's old sweatshirts, the baggiest one she could find. A pee. A quick splash of cold water on her face, the brush through her hair and she was done.

She would have preferred to sit on the other side of the table, as far away from him as she could, but she needed to see the screens on the laptops he'd opened — one was his, the other Andrew's. She made do by moving her chair and leaning away, consoling herself there would be a time when he and his unholy cologne would no longer be in her life. She would be back at the hospital working in her own environment where she was the expert, who was used to people depending on her for advice. Having to depend on Henry did not sit well with Jess.

'Let's do this.' Lame, but it was all she could think of to say.

Henry pressed a key on Andrew's laptop and instantly the backend of the Vaultange site appeared. Damn. She'd forgotten to log out.

'How did you get in?' he asked.

'Usual way,' she said.

'Andrew told you his password? He must have really loved you.'

Jess drank her coffee. Not logging out properly, had been a mistake a beginner would make. Andrew would never have done that.

'Okay, so you've worked out what's happening?' Henry asked.

'Yes.' She stopped herself. 'No, not really.'

'What do you want to do?'

Jess picked up her satchel from the floor and took out the Excel spreadsheet and handed it to Henry. 'Can you explain this to me please?'

Henry flipped over the pages, then back again. 'These are Vaultange transactions for the third quarter of last year. They're from Andrew's computer. Where did you get them?'

'Ross gave them to me.'

'How did he get them?'

'No idea. Andrew must have given them to him. What do they mean?'

'See these columns, July, August September, all 2018.' Henry pointed at a line of numbers. 'And these are ID numbers. I am assuming client ID numbers.' He traced his finger under a row. 'Tracking across, you can see the date, deposits, commissions, the codes for different contractors the money was sent to — I know those — more commissions, transaction fees, conversion to cryptos, date received and different wallet codes.'

Now the numbers made sense. 'Wow, the commission fees are pretty big when they're added up.'

'We have to charge commission, or we wouldn't make any money. Andrew stopped mining at the last halving.'

'Mining is processing the transactions on the blockchain, right? Each transaction earns the miner new Bitcoin?'

'Correct. And the same as mining for gold, it's not cheap. The electricity to run the programmes costs a fortune. Did you know computers and the energy needed to run them contributes more to CO_2 emissions than all the air travel in the world?'

'Really?' Jess filed away that fact for another time. 'How do we find out which clients belong to which ID number?'

'There should be a file. Did you check the document folder last night?'

Jess shook her head. 'I didn't know what to look for. Hey, before we look for the client files, can we check the bank records?'

Henry keyed in the bank URL and then passwords. Jess watched taking a mental photograph, filing them away for later. An array of account numbers spilt down the screen, each with its own suffix but all under the account name, Vaultange. Henry opened one and pointed to lines of transactions. 'Strange,' he said. 'See this. It's a deposit account for investors. I put it on hold as soon you told me Andrew had died.' He scrolled down.

'Wow!' Jess totted up the amounts in her head and came to a large conclusion. 'Over three-quarters of a million, in the week before.'

'That's a day. Not a week.'

'So, what's wrong?'

'The balance isn't right. There should be four to five times that.

Andrew always waited until there was enough in the account to make it worthwhile before he sent the buy requests to contractors. That way he minimised fees and trading times. It's cheaper and quicker to bundle multiple transactions together into one big contract than to do them one by one.'

'So what are you saying?'

'Look,' he said scrolling to page three of the account and pointing at a figure. 'It's a bank to bank transfer for five hundred thousand, US.'

'What does that mean?'

Henry opened up the transaction details. 'It's got a SWIFT code. It's gone to an overseas bank.'

'Which one?'

'I'd need to check, but I think that's the number for the Caymans.'

The only thing Jess knew about the Cayman Islands was they were in the Caribbean and the banks there were used by rich people to hide their money. 'That's not good?'

'No, it isn't. Look at the date.'

Jess looked. It was the day before Andrew died. 'Where's the money now? Can you find out?' she asked.

'I can try, but it's a bit late.'

Jess's brain, tired from lack of sleep was working at half normal as she tried to make sense of what was in front of her. Five hundred thousand was a lot of money in any one's world. Clients deposited money to buy crypto, not to have it sent to an account in the Cayman Islands. 'We need to check the client IDs to see who made the deposits.'

'Andrew had spread sheets for that. He reconciled them with the bank statements twice a day. But I assume, not while he was away.'

'He didn't take his laptop out of his bag, but I wasn't with him every second of every day.'

'You surprise me,' Henry said, but he was smiling. 'The information is in here,' he said waving his hand over the laptop. 'The problem was he didn't trust the cloud. He had his own security system. Let's see.' He clicked the Excel icon and a list of file names appeared. A-F, F-H, et cetera. He clicked one and a spreadsheet of closely typed names and dates appeared. It looked identical to the printout Jess was holding. Then the screen went black. Henry didn't move.

'What's wrong?' Jess asked.

'Could be a flat battery. Where's the charger?'

'I don't have it. I think it's still at the resort.'

Henry leant back in the chair, staring at the laptop.

'What is it?' Jess asked.

'The power was 85%.'

'Meaning?'

'Meaning, it's not the power.'

'What then?'

Henry pushed his chair back, stood up with one hand on the top of his head and his other in a trouser pocket. He leant forward and tapped the on/off button. Nothing happened. 'If it's what I think ...'.

'Tell me.'

'Malware. I left the fucking thing connected.'

'What does that mean?'

'I didn't log off the net before I opened the file. As soon as I opened it, malware triggered by something, somewhere, someone, deleted the document. By the looks of this,' he said pointing at the blank screen. 'Everything else has gone as well.'

'Get it back.'

'I can't.'

'You have to. Vaultange is in there.'

'You don't think I know that?'

EIGHTEEN

'You haven't touched it?' Ross asked when Jess handed him the laptop.

'I did exactly what you said. See, I sealed it and wrote the date and time on the tape.'

'And you haven't found anything else?'

'Nothing. We searched the apartment from top to bottom,' Henry said. 'I would have expected something. It's as if the place has been cleaned out.'

Jess thought about the upended drawers, clothes tossed out of wardrobes, sofa cushions on the floor beside overturned chairs. They'd searched every inch and found nothing. Henry's list of what she had to look for had been extensive: old computers, discs, USBs, CDs, phones, laptops, notebooks, books, scraps of paper, anything which might hold records, passwords or keys.

As soon as the laptop went down and Henry blamed malware, Jess had insisted they call Ross. He was so quiet once she'd told him what happened, she had to check to make sure he was still listening. That was when he told her how to secure the laptop. It was evidence. 'For the police,' he said.

Part of her had been hoping he was going to laugh and say there was nothing to worry about, that Andrew had given him back-ups of everything for safe keeping and the paper print-out she had, was one of many such documents. But he didn't laugh or say that. He told them to search the apartment and bring anything they found along with the laptop to his office as soon as they could.

'You know what this means, don't you?' Ross was addressing the question to Henry.

'I've a fair idea.'

Jess tried not to sound as anxious as she felt. 'We've lost the client records, haven't we? But let's say, it's only for now. Andrew wasn't reckless. There'll be back-ups. There has to be. And we will find them.'

'I wish I had your faith,' Henry muttered.

Jess continued as if he hadn't spoken. 'We've got the bank records. We can use those. We've got emails, the website. We can identify the clients who deposited money. We contact them, explain what's happened. They'll have their own records. They'll know exactly how much cryptocurrency Vaultange was storing for them.'

'You're joking, right?' Henry said. He was pacing up and down at the back of Ross's office. 'Tell me you're joking.'

'I'm not,' Jess said. 'People must have records.'

'First,' Henry said, 'we have nothing to verify their records and prove they're telling the truth. How do we confirm who owns what? I mean really confirm it. People aren't honest and you're naïve if you think they are.' He stopped pacing. 'Second,' he said holding up two fingers. 'Depositing money doesn't automatically mean they bought crypto. If they did, we don't know which one, when, or at what price. That matters. We could guess I suppose. It'll be expensive doing the trace work, but it's your money. Third,' he said holding up three fingers. 'We have no proof whether clients stored their crypto on the exchange or if they took it away. If they took their keys offline but said they hadn't, we'd be none the wiser. Fourth. We have the contents of one and one only trading wallet. It holds a fraction of the assets. Fifth. Without the cold wallets, there are no assets. We can't pay anyone out anyway.'

Jess was afraid, but she had to ask, to get it right in her head. Many was the time in her medical training when asking what she feared was a stupid question, hadn't been at all. At other times her teachers had treated her with contempt for being so dim. She was used to it. 'Tell me again what a cold wallet is?'

Henry sneered, took a deep breath and walked her slowly through his answer. 'Cold wallets, offline storage, either on the website or in the hardware wallet. It's where Andrew kept the client keys to their particular piece of currency. All of them. More importantly, it's also where he kept the company keys. Without them we've got nothing and Vaultange can't legally trade. Something else you haven't thought of although I'm surprised you haven't, as you're a doctor.' Henry was layering his disdain. 'Some of the clients might not want to come forward with their neat little bundles of records. They might not want to be linked to Vaultange. There are privacy considerations which the law requires us to take into account.' Henry's face was red, his neck veins were bulging, he was angry.

Ross cleared his throat. 'Henry's right, but he doesn't go far enough.'

'Meaning?' Jess asked.

'Andrew's lap-top was corrupted. Someone has done this. On purpose. Files don't disappear without a reason. Someone doesn't want Vaultange restored. Why else would there be malware? Whoever did this may be waiting to see what we do next.'

No one spoke. Jess looked first at Henry, then at Ross.

'Now we call the police,' Ross said finally.

'And what do we tell the clients?'

'The truth,' Ross said pointedly. 'Today.'

'I have to tell them, don't I?'

'Who else? You're the owner,' Henry replied as he sat down in the chair next to hers.

Jess felt a burning in the back of her throat. She didn't have time to excuse herself. She only had time to stand up, rush from the room and run down the corridor to the women's bathroom. She pushed through the door, slammed into the middle stall, just as the morning's coffee erupted through her fingers and into the toilet bowl.

Afterwards, she slurped cold water from the tap to rinse the bitterness away. She spat and rinsed a few times then rubbed her face with a paper towel, its roughness, reminding her that this really was happening. There was no getting away from what she had to do. Andrew had left her the business. She had no choice but to cope. Adjusting her jeans, she rolled up the sleeves of the sweatshirt and checked the front for specks of vomit.

'You can do this,' she said to her reflection as she scraped her fingers through her hair settling it back behind her ears. Satisfied she looked okay, she opened the door. Voices at the end of the corridor stopped her on the threshold.

'Ross, even you have to admit, something isn't right.' It was Henry. 'She spent weeks with Andrew before the wedding, living with him 24/7. He barely had time to talk to me. I wasn't just his best mate, I worked for him. I'm the only person on this planet, who knows as much about Vaultange as he did. Or I used to.'

'What can I say?' Ross said.

'She had used his laptop. Before it went down. She said he told her the password, but he would never do that. So how did she open it? I wouldn't be surprised if it wasn't her who loaded the malware. And another thing, where are all his old phones and devices? Who took them?'

'Stop now before you say something you can't take back. Jess is my client. Not you.'

'I'll wait until the police get here. I'll have plenty to say to them.'

'I'd advise you to be quiet. A case can be made for you being an employee of the company and as such you have responsibilities, wild talk not being one of them. Their forensic people will sort this out. Things will become much clearer. Until then ....'.

Their voices faded as the men moved away.

Jess leant against the door. *So that's how the bastard wants to play it. So much for his so-called friendship.*

NINETEEN

WHEN SHE REACHED the lookout Jess pulled over, turned off the engine and got out of the car. In front of her the flat blue of the Tasman Sea merged indistinguishably into the sky at the horizon. Below was Piha Beach, divided not quite in the middle by Lion Rock, a huge outcrop of granite capped in green. Not a breath of wind, just afternoon sunshine, and birdsong. A perfect day. At last she was out of the city and away from the mess that was Vaultange.

The policewoman had been very polite. She asked questions, wrote down answers and took contact details. She put the laptop in a plastic evidence bag and sealed it before asking Jess and Ross to sign the label, so she could take it away. She explained she was only there to make initial contact. The Digital Tech Crime team (the DTC) who would be leading the investigation, were busy on another job.

Henry huffed and puffed and told the poor woman how millions of dollars were at stake and she needed to get the right people on to it now, today, or it would be too late. Her attempt to reassure him by repeating what she'd said but more slowly made things worse. Henry yelled at her. 'It's her they have to talk to,' he yelled pointing his finger at Jess. 'She owns the company not me.' The policewoman smiled quietly and thanked him for clarifying the matter. Jess watched her draw a big circle around her name, writing *owner* beside it, before snapping her notebook shut and thanking them for their time.

As she leant against the car with her arms folded, Jess shut her eyes and listened to the background buzz of bees on roadside flowers and the skylarks singing overhead. After spending the morning in Henry's toxic company, it felt good to be outside.

Was it only ten days ago, that Andrew had been alive? Ten days ago, his clients were sleeping peacefully in their beds, secure in their belief that their investments were safe. Ten days ago, she had been wondering what the chef was going to prepare for them to eat that night. Ten days ago, Henry would not have dared to speak to her the way he did after the policewoman left. To think, she had almost trusted him — almost.

She turned and reached inside the car, feeling for the clips which attached the hood to the windscreen. Automatic roof retractors hadn't been invented in 1964 when this particular MGB roadster had rolled off the production line. The clips were stiff, and she nearly broke a nail trying to undo them. The car, a gift from Andrew, had been a surprise.

'A present,' he announced proudly when it was delivered one Sunday morning outside the apartment building, a huge yellow bow taped to the bonnet. 'No particular reason other than I love you.' He stopped then with his hand over his mouth and sheepishly asked if she could drive, before admitting he had never learnt.

She wrapped her arms around his neck. 'Yes, I can drive. This is a joke though. It has to be. No one gives away a car,' she whispered.

When she realised he was serious, she shrieked with delight and as she jumped up and down, she told him over and over how much she loved him, totally oblivious to the stares from passers-by. He tried to look cool, but she could tell he was pleased. 'The apartment car parks are all taken,' he told her. 'So I've rented one downtown. It's not far and the details are in the glovebox. Now, are you going to stop screaming and take me for a drive?'

They spent a fabulous day following the coastal road around Auckland's eastern beaches with the top down, stopping first for an

Italian lunch in one of the restaurants looking across to the fountain in the park at Mission Bay. Back in the car, Jess navigated the tree-lined streets of St Heliers and around Tamaki Estuary to Buckland's Beach. 'No particular reason', she said when he asked why this was her destination. 'I've never been here before. Call it curiosity.' The flat crescent of the white sand, the half-grown Norfolk Pines dotted along the foreshore, families enjoying picnics, the taste of their ice-creams as they strolled arm in arm to the end of the bay — made a complete contrast to days spent staring at screens or at the hospital. It was as if the world away from work was putting on a display just for them, to remind them there were alternatives. They drove home making plans for their future, talking until they lapsed into companionable silence — only to find Henry waiting for them. Since then, she'd barely had cause to drive anywhere. Today, driving was the first thing she thought about after Henry's tirade.

Ross said they needed to write a statement for the website. 'The police can't be trusted to represent our interests. As soon as they put out a statement saying they're investigating Vaultange, we're screwed.'

When Jess had asked why they'd do that without checking with her first, he told her it was their way to get people to come forward. It's important as the owner that you set a precedent by explaining that the site will be down for a few days while everything is sorted out following the death of the founder. Sensible enough, she thought, then queried whether her name needed to be on the statement. 'I have my medical career to consider and I don't want the two worlds confused,' she said. 'When Vaultange is behind me, I want to be able to see patients and hold my head high. I don't want the Medical Council poking their nose in and asking questions about matters to do with public trust.'

Henry had gone ballistic. 'You can't pick and choose,' he said. 'The decision was made when Andrew left you Vaultange and don't tell me you didn't know. You knew, you conniving little bitch. Don't you dare hide behind your dainty medical career while this gets sorted out. It's your responsibility as the owner to sort this shit out. You have to front it. You'd be first in line to take the money if things were good.'

Jess had reeled back in shock when she heard this. Each statement so monstrously unfair it was impossible to rebut them. Ross had tried to calm Henry down, reaching out to him, pouring him a glass of water and suggesting he sit down, but Henry would not be soothed. Outside the office, people's shadows visible behind the frosted glass walls froze before slinking away.

Henry had towered over her, jabbing his finger inches from her face, his teeth bared, his eyes screwed to slits. 'Of course your fucking name has to be on the statement. If it fucks your medical career so be it. Clients needed to know who is in charge and it damn well isn't me.'

Ross took Henry out of the room at that point and she didn't see him again.

Not only were the clips on the roof hard to undo, but the fabric was stiff and didn't fold back easily. The end result wasn't neat, but it would do. With sweating hands she climbed back into the car and turned the key. Changing gears still took a bit of getting used to, but she was learning, enjoying the control it gave her as she negotiated the heavy, vehicle around the bends from the lookout to the bottom of the road and into Piha itself. She took it slowly, in no rush to get to where she was going. She had the rest of the day to herself. She turned up the music, the driving beat of The Killers blasting the last of the morning and Henry from her brain.

Jess slowed down and changed into neutral letting the car coast into a park opposite the Piha General Store. It was a week day and the beach, the streets behind it and the grassy park looked empty.

When Jess was ten, and before Bryan arrived to ruin her world, one of her mother's colleagues told her mother she was working too hard and needed a break. Her mother had snorted, saying she barely had enough money as it was, and certainly couldn't afford a holiday. The next day, her colleague gave Jess's mother the key to his family holiday house at Piha. It wasn't an expensive house. It had one bedroom, but the bed was comfortable and had a view through bi-fold doors on to a sandy lawn leading down to a creek and on to the beach. The kitchen and living room were one and there was an outdoor toilet. The week they spent there was Jess's happiest childhood memory.

Her mother was transformed. Jess remembered how young Marguerite looked after two days away from work, with her hair blowing free in the wind, and her face free from worry lines. Gone was the harried solo mother and in her place was a lively woman with a naughty grin. She remembered her mother's laugh as they joked about silly things, sillier things than usual. They ate when they felt like it. Different food which her mother had bought especially for the holiday: soft cheeses, prosciutto, French loaves, melon out of season. Her mother drank wine in the evenings raising her glass to toast the good health of her thoughtful colleague. She played music, pop during the day and soulful melodies at night which lulled Jess to sleep. Sometimes when Jess half woke, the music would still be playing, and her mother would be sitting in the doorway staring up at the stars.

On the first day, her mother brought out a bag of books from the library in town. In it were all the Harry Potter books J K Rowling had ever written and one other, for variety her mother said. It was *My Family and Other Animals* by Gerald Durrell. 'Harry Potter for adventure and Gerald and his family, to make you laugh,' she said.

It had been a school week and there were no kids to play with. The only people on the beach had grey hair, men in their wetsuits toting surfboards and women in bare feet walking dogs. She knew not to go swimming alone because her mother had told her terrible stories about sharks waiting behind the waves for the rips to deliver hapless fools into their hungry mouths. Jess promised she wouldn't so much as get her toes wet and her mother trusted her, letting her go off and explore, while she lay in the spring sunshine and read books.

Every afternoon, her mother would come and find her, and they would play together in the surf, running and screaming from the waves which occasionally caught one or the other, tumbling them under the foam, filling their noses with seawater, and their hair with dark sand which streamed out in the shower for days afterwards. Later, they'd walk up the beach to the store for ice creams, raspberry ripple double scoop for her mother, and hokey pokey, single scoop, chocolate dipped for Jess. They had to eat them quickly before they melted and rivers of creamy stickiness ran over their fingers, mingling with streaks of gritty sand.

Jess told her mother over and over again that she was the best mother in the world. They'd fallen on the bed laughing and giggling, before her mother gently swept her hair aside and held her face between her hands and told her how much she loved her. She told Jess she could do anything she liked with her life. That she could be anything she liked. 'Never, ever, doubt it. Never let anything get in your way and do whatever it takes to get to where you want to go.' Jess had never forgotten her mother's words.

In a soft, sing-song voice she told Jess how she was going to make sure all doors would be open to her. She was saving money so Jess could go to university because the teachers had told her how clever, and how gifted her daughter was. They'd recommended she be put into extension classes and her mother had said yes — of course — anything for my girl.

Jess turned off the engine and got out of the car. The sound of the sea thundering up the beach reminded her of going to sleep in her mother's arms during that magical week.

The shop had barely changed. It had the same sun-bleached signs for pies and Coke stuck to glass doors with yellowed sticky tape. A billboard advertised surfboards and lessons, the blue paint peeling on the cracked wood was just readable. She grabbed her handbag and went in hoping they still served cones and hadn't defaulted to ice creams on sticks. A buzzer rang as she crossed the threshold and a young man emerged from the back. His blond stringy hair, and his deep tan, attested to years in the sun. His shoulders were broad underneath a fawn t-shirt, printed on the front with a bleached sun above Aloha and faded palm trees.

'What can I getcha?' he asked as he wiped his hands on his board shorts.

The ice cream cabinet was exactly as she remembered. Mum's raspberry ripple was second from the right, in the front exactly where it had been years ago, the hokey pokey next to it. 'I'll have a single scoop hokey pokey, thanks. Do you still do chocolate dips?'

'Sure do,' he said taking the ice-cream scoop out of a jar of milky water.

'Great, that's what I'll have.' Jess wandered back to the counter while he scooped, jamming the hokey pokey into the cone until it cracked on one side. He looked up guiltily but dipped the ice cream into the cylinder of liquid chocolate anyway, then held it up as he waited for the drips to stop and the coating to set. 'Nice car,' he said nodding at the MG parked out front. 'They don't make them like that anymore. Costs a bit to run I bet. Goes through a bit of gas?'

She smiled, uncertain what to say in reply. Suddenly she didn't want to be here. She most certainly did not want to be noticed. He handed her the cone and told her the price. She tapped her card on the machine saying an automatic thanks as she headed for the door. He called after her.

'Declined.'

'What?'

'Your card. Try again?' She returned to the counter, keyed in a different account and waited.

'Phew,' she said trying not to feel too awkward when this time the payment was accepted. She had eaten half the ice cream before deciding it didn't taste as good as she remembered. The walk on the beach was no longer inviting. It had been a mistake to come here. She started the engine and driving slowly past a bin, Jess ditched the cone. With her foot flat to the floor, she drove back up the hill.

TWENTY

ON THE DRIVE back to the city, she wondered when the statement would be released. How much time did she have before her world changed again? Clients would be clamouring for answers — demanding their money. Vaultange's plea for patience would be given short shrift if Andrew's widow was seen flashing a huge diamond and driving a classic car. If a guy in an ice cream shop could leap to conclusions about her financial status, then the media and Andrew's clients would too. Jess had learnt early that people prefer to think the worst of their fellow human beings. Then, like a vulture circling over a carcass, they swoop in to mindlessly tear apart whatever they find. She needed to make herself as inconspicuous as possible. That meant stashing the car and her ring.

Having no money left in the joint account was another worry. Thanks to the Prof granting her unpaid leave, Jess had a job to go back to, but until then she had no income. Not while Vaultange was being sorted out. She had repaid her student loan before meeting Andrew but hadn't spent long enough in specialist practice to save for emergencies. Her insistence that she pay for her wedding dress meant she had depleted what savings she'd had.

'It's important that I do this,' she said when Andrew burst out laughing. 'I want to start our life together as a contributor. At the very least, I want to pay for my own dress. I don't need you to pay for everything.'

'I'm rich Jess. It's not a problem.'

'I know, and I bet you think I'm being stupid, but this is important to me.'

'Okay, if that's what you want,' he replied holding up his hands in a gesture of surrender. 'Now about that Lear jet I was thinking of buying ....'.

'Very funny,' she said. 'Don't make light of this Andrew. I'm serious. I don't need you to look after me. I'm with you because I love you.'

He stopped smiling, took her in his arms and kissed her lightly on each cheek, then softly on her mouth. 'I know.' It was all he said.

Jess pulled over to the hard shoulder and turned off the engine. With her hands on the steering wheel she sat in the car remembering the feel of his arms around her and the touch of his lips on hers. The road stretched in front of her, two lanes of faded black seal through a corridor of green trees. She wasn't ready to go back to town. Would she ever be? Idly she reached over, opened the glovebox, and took out the owner's manual and the logbook. As she flicked through the pages she saw the car had had two owners. The first, some guy from the South Island who had bought the car new. His entries in the logbook were meticulous and long, his care of the vehicle bordering on the obsessive. Then his entries stopped, suddenly there was nothing for two years. Had he died, got sick, gone missing, lost the use of his right hand? She let her imagination run wild, anything to delay having to go back. The second owner was Gordon Holdings. Gordon Holdings had been set up way back before they were engaged. Why hadn't Andrew told her? Did he think she wouldn't understand? Or had he kept it from her for a reason known only to him? Stupid, because it was here in black and white. She could have opened the glove box of her car at any time in their relationship and seen it. The logbook had been brought up to date. The car had been checked by a mechanic before purchase, the name of the garage was stamped over his signature. She closed the books and put them back in the glovebox, and as she did so, her fingers brushed against something hard. She had to undo her seatbelt to lean over and reach it. It was a USB stick. Ledger was printed on the side. It was exactly the same as the one Henry had given her. And which she remembered guiltily that no one, not even Ross had remembered to give to the policewoman. Henry's USB was still in her handbag. She stared at this new one, then whooped out loud. Partly with joy but mainly because of an overwhelming, all-encompassing feeling of relief.

You bloody idiot, Andrew. You, gorgeous, fabulous, bloody idiot. You didn't run off and leave me high and dry. This is the backup. It has to be. There was a trail she could follow after all. He would have put the stick in the car planning to come back and get it when they returned from their honeymoon. He would have known, if for some reason he couldn't retrieve it, then she would. She would be the only one to find it and she would know what to do. Simple.

She got out and searched the rest of the car, humming as she poked into every conceivable nook and cranny. Under the seat, under the dashboard and around the gear stick in the middle. She climbed into the back seat and checked everything. Tucked into the back of the driver's seat pocket was another USB, plain this time, the common type sold by tech shops. She was standing by the side of the car, staring at the sticks when a jeep pulled up beside her. 'Do you need help?' The man, bearded was wearing shorts and a loose shirt unbuttoned to the waist. 'I'm fine,' she said. 'Thank you for stopping though. I didn't think people did that anymore.' The good Samaritan smiled and drove off with a jaunty wave. *Life is good. Andrew hasn't abandoned me, and strangers take the trouble to stop and offer help.* Jess gave a little skip as she went around to the back of the car. She emptied the boot, unscrewed the spare tyre from its mounting, before she felt the recesses deep in the well. Next, she popped the bonnet and inspected the motor. Nothing looked out of place, the heavy lid dropping back with a thump. That was it. Two sticks. More than enough for her to hope the nightmare was nearly over.

She put the sticks in her handbag with Henry's one and checked her phone. Three missed calls, two voicemail messages, all from Henry— she deleted them with a tap on the screen. He could wait — a long time. She typed a query into the search engine and scrolled down the responses, selected one of the options, brought up the number and pressed *call now.*

'Drive in. Turn off everything. Lock the door and take the key,' instructed the manager of the storage facility. 'Make sure the payments are deposited monthly and that's all there is to it.'

She found the garage easily and the key was in the padlock as she had been told. The hardest part had been taking off her engagement ring and sliding it inside a small cut she made in the fabric on the underside of the passenger seat. Her only consolation was knowing Andrew would have understood. She heaved up the top, clicked the catches shut and locked the doors.

It was a twenty-minute walk to the nearest bus stop, where after a half-hour wait, she caught the bus back to town, getting out at Smith and Caughey's department store in the middle of Queen Street. Passengers from a cruise ship crowded the pavements, easily identified by their attire which consisted of comfortable sneakers and waterproof jackets worn open on this very warm day. Men and women, in couples and small groups, wandered aimlessly peering in shop windows but not venturing in to buy. It was a slow walk to the harbour, but now Jess had the sticks it didn't matter. She took her time, indulged in some window shopping and relaxed.

'Where the fuck have you been?' She was barely through the doors of the apartment building. Henry was standing in the lobby, with his arms folded across his chest, and the same angry look on his face that he'd had earlier that morning.

'You gave me a fright,' she said clasping her bag to her chest.

'I've been calling. Why aren't you answering your phone?'

'I needed time to think.'

'And ...?'

'I've thought.'

'And?'

'And it's none of your business,' she said suddenly tired of the man and whatever game he was playing. Keen to get upstairs and see what was on the USBs, she pressed the button for the elevator. The doors opened immediately. The last she saw of Henry was him opening his mouth to say something. By then it was too late. The elevator doors had closed.

TWENTY-ONE

THE NEXT MORNING, Jess opened her laptop to find hundreds of emails clogging the Vaultange inbox. Ross had agreed with Henry that a contact email address should be included in the press statement and it was — right below her name.

The story which accompanied the statement could only be described as sensational. Overwritten was too modest. *Crypto-entrepreneur's sudden death on honeymoon, beautiful doctor wife grieves, missing millions in cryptocurrency.* This was a story which would keep giving over days if not weeks — the frisson of links to international crime syndicates, the icing on the cake.

Most emails were polite, stating how sad the writers were to hear of Andrew's death. A few sent condolences. Without fail, every email asked how and when money or crypto would be returned. Some messages merely requested information, others made outright demands for the immediate return of funds, threatening legal action if compliance was delayed. Good luck with that she thought, resisting the urge to send the terms and conditions attached in a reply. More than a few messages were of the wacky, weird and downright obscene variety. One person suggested that because Jess was single again, she must be ready for another relationship. Photos of body parts were attached to aid her decision. Another suggested business investments now that she was a wealthy widow. She created a folder and moved the genuine messages into it, planning to answer these later. She blacklisted the addresses of the nuisance emails and deleted them. As soon as she finished, another dump of messages hit the Inbox. She groaned and was cursing Ross, Henry, the statement, cryptocurrency and the Internet, when her phone pinged. *Have coffee and cake. Carole.*

Reading the word cake reminded Jess she still hadn't bought food. In a hurry to open the USBs last night, she'd ordered Uber Eats, relieved when it wasn't Ahmed who arrived with the bags. She had been silly thinking he was following her. She understood that now. Hearing the elevator zooming up the shaft, Jess hurriedly squished the empty food containers and stuffed them down the chute.

'You weren't joking about the cake,' Jess said as she relieved Carole of a large box.

'I never joke about cake,' Carole replied as she put two coffees on the bench and after a short search, found plates, a knife and two forks. 'Carrot cake. I know how much you like the icing.' She cut two pieces, plated them, and handed one together with a fork to Jess. 'I saw the press statement.'

Jess looked up, her mouth full of cake and nodded. 'Uh huh.'

'I didn't let Dad see it.'

The cake was delicious. Perfect icing — sweet, sour and creamy. 'He'll have to sometime,' Jess as she took another bite.

'I know. But he was asleep when I left. He's been up most of the night. I heard him pacing up and down in his room.'

'You were awake then too,' Jess said as she looked at her friend. There were dark rings under Carole's eyes. She wasn't wearing her trademark red lipstick and her hair was loose rather than in its usual ponytail. 'I'm working as fast as I can.'

Carole didn't return her gaze. Instead, she focused on picking a hair off her plate where it had got stuck in the icing. 'I've never seen him like this,' she said quietly. 'Not even when Mum died. He blames himself. He says he doesn't understand why he did it. He keeps apologising for letting me down. It's hard, Jess. He's the guy who never let things get on top of him. Mum was the worrier, not him. I guess never having had a father you wouldn't know what it's like.'

Jess stopped mid-chew and slowly put her fork back on her plate. Was Carole being careless because she was tired, or was she trying to hurt Jess on purpose?

'He doesn't deserve this,' Carole said as she cut another thin slice of cake and tipped it on to her plate. 'He put up with Mum all those years. We both did. She wasn't an easy woman. Some days, when she was in one of her rants, we'd sneak out of the house, jump in the truck and drive to the back of the farm. It was easier to stay there all day than be around her.'

Jess hadn't heard this version of Carole's family life before. It was disappointing to hear her friend disrespect her mother, a woman who by all accounts had kept the farm running profitably so Carole could attend a private school in town, before travelling overseas.

'There isn't a kinder gentler man on the planet,' Carole said as a glob of icing bobbed up and down at the corner of her mouth. 'Look how nice he's been to you. Someone he hardly knows and yet he took the time to come to that ceremony of yours. And dinner. He's been the best father anyone could have. Now, when he has the chance to take it easy, he gets conned into a ridiculous investment.' Silence hung like a warning between them.

'As I mentioned before, I'm trying. So is Henry. And Ross,' Jess said eventually.

Carole hooked her hair back over her ears and stared at her. 'I have to say I'm disappointed in you Jess.'

'Excuse me?'

'We were supposed to be friends.'

'We are friends. What are you talking about?'

'You should have told me it was bad. The police are investigating Vaultange. The Digital Crime Unit or some such thing. It was on the radio as I was driving over.'

'For a minute I thought you were being serious,' Jess said then paused as she searched for words which weren't going to be misinterpreted. 'It's what they do, it's part of the process we have to go through, that's all. I was going to tell you, but I thought it could wait until I saw you next.'

'Were you? Because hearing a crime unit is involved doesn't sound like part of any process I know about. You could have told me when I arrived.'

'You haven't exactly given me a chance.'

'Tell me now then.'

Jess winced at the tone in Carole's voice and she hesitated unsure if she wanted to carry on with this conversation. Apparently, Jess was guilty no matter what she said or didn't say. Better to be open and upfront, she decided after a few moments for the sake of their friendship. 'Promise to keep this between us?'

Carole nodded.

'Yesterday, when we opened Andrew's computer, the client records disappeared. Henry says it's malware. Ross got the police involved. Long story short, they have the laptop. Their forensic team is working on it now.'

'But the records will be backed up. They have to be.'

'We haven't found any back-ups, not yet.'

'What if you can't?' Carole carefully lined up her fork to be in the exact middle of her plate.

'Ross has hired accountants, lawyers, and tech guys. The bank is going over their records. Everything that can be done is being done.'

Suddenly, Carole pushed her plate away, sending it skidding across the marble worktop, and with it the carefully placed fork which clattered into the sink. They both looked at it, then at each other. Jess watched Carole's face crumple in despair before she burst into tears.

'He's lost everything,' she said. 'Everything. You don't understand.'

Jess put her arm around Carole's shoulder only for her friend to angrily push her away. As she grabbed her bag, Carole looked at her with such venom, Jess reeled back.

'It will be okay Carole you have my word,' she said.

'I don't want your word. I want Johnny's money,' Carole said as she turned and left.

TWENTY-TWO

'SORRY YOU'VE HAD to wait Mr Turner,' said the larger of the two nurses as she closed the cover of the morphine pump and handed him the control. 'You're good to go.'

I pressed the button and started counting. At twelve, a wave of morphine washed through me. The pain in my left arm subsided to bearable as my body relaxed.

When I opened my eyes, the nurses were gone. I was left with white walls, no windows, no pictures, and a closed door.

'Whenever, you're ready? It was a male voice. 'In your own time.'

I lay back, trying to remember where I'd got to in the story before the operation robbed me of three days. Or was it two? No matter. I coughed and cleared my throat.

I admire her. Jess Cullinane. She's still Jess Gordon you know. Dr Jess Gordon. She hasn't changed her name. Not officially. No time. Andrew booked the tickets for their honeymoon before the ceremony and they left the day after. I bet she hasn't thought about it since. Why would she? When there are so many more important things to get that pretty little head around.

I had never picked Andrew for the marrying kind. Not in all the years I knew him. He didn't seem interested in women. He liked women, don't get me wrong. He wasn't gay. He went out. Had sex. Lots of short-term flings, but never anything which lasted longer than a few months, never anything serious. He just wasn't interested in women as people. He would smile and nod if they were speaking. But really listen? Hear and retain what a woman was saying, then interact and engage in two-way conversation? Not him. Not unless she was speaking code and/or sex.

I was blindsided when he told me he was in love. I had to check if he was kidding. He wasn't. He had a stupid look in his eyes, a dreamy — on a different planet look. How do I describe it? Charged up? Sparkly?

A doctor. He kept saying it over and over, as if he didn't believe it himself. She knows so little about computers and nothing about code or crypto. 'But Henry — she's *the one*,' he said making those silly quote marks in the air. 'Who knew love at first sight existed?' He kept asking me — me?

'First sight is good,' I said humouring him. 'What about *morning-after sight?*' I asked adding aerial quote marks to emphasise my point. 'Have you had sex yet?' He shook his head. 'No? Then wait with the love pronouncements until you do. You need to consider the possibility she's taken advantage of your weakened state to bat her eyelids and stroke your fevered brow to lure you into her womanly clutches. Maybe, when you feel better, you'll see it for what it is. When you're more in control of yourself.'

'Wait until you meet her,' he said.

So, I did. He hadn't told me how good-looking she was. I don't mean she's drop-dead-built-like-a-playboy-model, with the face of a goddess, gorgeous. She's not that good looking. *Handsome*, that's a better description. She's got good hair, shoulder-length, blonde and thick. Clear skin, bright eyes and great teeth. She's tall for a girl; the same height as Andrew, and she isn't afraid to wear heels. She has a great figure, a tiny waist and taut bum, but her tits are a bit small if I'm being honest. On reflection, I think her tits look small because of her broad shoulders, explained by her having been a competitive swimmer in her teens. She was talented from what I've read in the papers. She could have gone to the Games if events hadn't intervened.

Andrew never saw how men looked at her when they were together. Jess did. She could tell they were wondering why a woman like her was with a man like him. I noticed that about her as soon as we met — her awareness. But Jess ignored those men and focused on Andrew. Damn me, ten minutes in their company and she even convinced me she loved him as much as he adored her. He was always lucky. Now the bastard was lucky in love. Sickening, but kind of nice.

Jess moved into the apartment in December 2018. I moved out. I hadn't been living with him exactly, but I might as well have been because I spent so much time there. The spare room was called Henry's den. The townhouse was where I stored my clothes, my notebook and where I entertained women. Such as Pearl and Carole — never at the same time — more's the pity. Pearl might have gone for it, but Carole would have run a mile. It's not that we didn't have a good time, the few weeks we had were a revelation. The sex surprisingly good. It's more that we had a bond which transcended the physical. Carole was the first woman I had liked spending time with since Rachel. Which is saying a lot. And why I had to end it.

Vaultange was going gangbusters, when Jess moved in. We had more people wanting to become clients than we could accommodate in the outdated system Andrew still insisted on using. The two months he was in hospital had given me time to research an upgrade. I wrote a discussion paper for him, outlining best practice in light of the changing regulatory environment, but his heart wasn't in it. Not then. He skim-read it, nodded and said it sounded fine but told me he would sort things out properly in the New Year.

His spell in hospital had slowed things down but not much. I kept the exchange ticking over as best I could, but I couldn't trade. Not like him. Don't get me wrong, I know how to. I'm not an idiot, the new software being easier to understand helped. But, what he did … and how fast he did it … he was in a different league from mortal wanker-bankers like me. He was so quick. Andrew recognised patterns as they were forming and then backed himself to take positions few would dare to take. By the time the rest of the market caught on, he had made his money and got out.

That's the simple explanation. The other stuff, the super complicated bits, shuffling (mixing up individual stakes into one big pot), derivatives (selling off the shuffled stakes as different products), short runs, long runs, this currency (fiat and crypto), against that one, anonymity price loading, dark web trades — I could manage one or two given enough time. When he was well Andrew kept all the balls in the air, all of the time. While they were up there, he rearranged them to his advantage, adding another deal, or a follow-on trade and taking his cut before he moved on to the next deal. And the one after that. He had plans within plans, within plans and in the empty time between trades, he didn't play chess. Nah. Too simple. He played GO. He played it online, several boards at once. Fun fact — after the first two moves in chess there are 400 possible next moves. In GO there are 130,000 possibilities. He won more games than he lost. Think about it.

My niche was maintaining the backend of www.vaultange.com. I replied to the smaller clients when they sent anxious emails asking where their money was or wasn't. I'd explain why that day, week or month it was taking longer to process transactions. I explained to Joe Public that Bitcoin took a minimum of ten minutes per transaction because the proof of work was designed to take that long. Because that's the way Satoshi Nakamoto designed it, as a means to protect the integrity of the chain. I kept the banks happy, and when they weren't happy, I organised a Vaultange exit — stage left, *sans* bear. Shakespeare —The Winter's Tale. I'm not an idiot. I went to university.

The next bank would be primed and ready to go before Vaultange had outworn its welcome at the last one. Anti-money laundering legislation had gone through in 2009, and the regulations updated in 2017, but no one took much notice. It slowed us down for a bit. Vaultange was persona non grata with a couple of the big banks, but I always found one who would take our business. Morality in finance is only as good as the money you're willing to pay for it. The great recession of 2007 and 2008 taught us that.

My life was tracking along nicely in 2018. Thank you for asking. I'd cashed up a percentage of my holdings in December 2017, and I was richer than I ever dreamt I would or could be. I was earning a salary and a commission on each new customer I brought into the exchange. I had a friend I could trust. We worked well together and at times we went out and had fun together too. Was I still using the dark web? Maybe. If I was, I had learnt from my mistakes. Or I thought I had. Possibly I was a little too cocky.

It's when life is going well and you least expect it, that something comes along to shake things up. It's the puddle which is deeper than it looks on life's highway. It's the tax bill you never thought you'd have to pay, dropping innocently into your Inbox, when you've splashed out on the new boat you couldn't afford. It's the pimple on the chin of the supermodel which turns into a boil on catwalk day. In my case it was the knock on the door in the middle of the night — the early hours of the 27th of August 2018 to be exact. I was in bed having sex with an expensive woman whose only goal was to make me come and then come again.

The aforementioned Pearl was a professional. She was not only meeting but was exceeding the KPIs we'd established at the beginning of the evening. She had my hard dick in her mouth and was tonguing it slowly when there wasn't just a knock on the door — it was a goddamned battering ram. The door didn't stand a chance. Neither did Pearl.

Murray Chambers, as he introduced himself, and two goons sauntered into my bedroom. If you don't know Murray, he looks like a bald toad wearing false eyelashes. His goons? Taller versions of their boss but without the eyelashes. Now I'm a big guy. I know how to take care of myself. But even I could see there was little point in leaping out of bed in my naked state to take on these two. For one thing they were wearing clothes. For another, they were bigger than me. The real clincher was their baseball bats — retractable baseball bats. Murray told them to take Pearl next door and amuse themselves.

He wanted to have a chat with me and he didn't want to be overheard.

He sat on the edge of my bed saying nothing while we listened to Pearl's muffled screams from the other room. It wasn't the best night of my life, but it wasn't the worst either. When the screams deescalated to an occasional groan, Murray said what he'd come to say. He had a plan. I was to be part of it. I must have looked reluctant, because he called out. 'Boys.' The muffled screaming started again in earnest. I didn't need to hear more screams to look interested.

It turned out Murray was already a Vaultange client. He was running multiple accounts under different names. Small ones so no one would mistake him as a big investor. He liked the anonymity. He needed it because he was putting dirty money in and getting nice clean money out. Okay as far as it went, but it was boring. Predictable. Murray wanted more. He didn't like feeling he was just another passive cryptocurrency holder. He wanted to wash his money, dry it and then fluff it into something much bigger. He wanted me to help him. He'd considered asking Andrew, but he didn't trust Andrew not to get clever.

'People like Andrew can't help themselves,' he said. 'They believe it is their mission in life to break the rules. They take it as a personal challenge. You, Henry, you're not the sort to get clever. You understand the system. You're the middle bear.'

I looked puzzled.

He sighed.

'Did no one read to you when you were a kid? It so important. Parents have to read to kids otherwise how are the kids going to know things when they grow up? *Goldilocks and the Three Bears?*' He bounced on the mattress to emphasise his point. 'You're the middle bear. You're not too smart and you're not too dumb. You, Henry Turner, are just right for what I have in mind.' He leant over and patted the top of my head — once, twice, and harder — a third time. Then he told me what had brought me to his attention and why he thought that would make me help him. Next he gilded the lily. 'You understand, Henry, that when I say I'll kill you and your pal Andrew if you don't do exactly as I ask, that I mean it.'

I did. 'Okay,' I squeaked. My mouth was dry. I licked my lips, but it made no difference. I swallowed. 'What do you want me to do?'

'I'll be in touch — later. Until then, this is between us. You are not to breathe a word to Andrew. I don't want him attempting any genius mastermind payback,' Murray said as he stood up and zipped up his puffer jacket. Now he looked like a fat black toad. 'I'm glad we had this little chat.' He made his way to the door and turned. 'We've reached an agreement, haven't we?'

I nodded.

'Good.' He cocked his bald head to one side listening to the silence in the other room. 'I think the boys are finished. Tell the girl thanks for keeping them entertained.'

Murray left then and was followed by his goons who hastily put their shitty dicks back into their pants.

Naturally, Pearl was upset. As I was when I saw what they'd done to her. Smart girl though. She hadn't put up a fight. She wasn't going to be able to work for a couple of months. That much was obvious. I reckoned it would take that long for the bones in her hand to heal. The bruises, they'd only last a few weeks. Max. They hadn't touched her face thank goodness. She still had her teeth. Her poor lovely talented tongue; however, had almost been ripped right off the floor of her mouth and there was blood all over my sofa. She couldn't speak. Not clearly and not without spitting blood, but I knew she was grateful that I dropped her off at the hospital. And happy to take the money I gave her. It would get her through her enforced holiday. Before she got out of the car, she motioned for my phone and deleted her contact details. She gave it back to me with a shrug. Fair enough I thought as I watched her limp through the door to the emergency department. I had my own shit to ponder.

TWENTY-THREE

'MURRAY AND HIS GOONS. It could be the name of a rock band. *Florence and the Machine; Smokey and the Bandits; Mumford and Sons.* I didn't hear from him again for a month. Now that I knew what to look for, I watched as he poured money into the exchange, always from a different identity and from multiple locations. Over one ten-day period he routed nearly a million US dollars a day through the exchange, each deposit, under the ten thousand dollar threshold which automatically triggers the bank watchdogs. That amount of money couldn't help but draw attention and it took a lot of talking to convince the bank it was legitimate. I sent word to Murray to dial it back which thankfully he did.

Andrew was delighted. Why wouldn't he be? The exchange earns commission on both sides of a deal. Occasionally when the mood took him, and if Jess was working late, Andrew managed the larger transactions himself, the mined Bitcoin a token for his efforts. Keeping his hand in, mattered far more to him than twelve and a half Bitcoin. Andrew showed no curiosity about the amount of money or where it was coming from. It was of no interest to him. Andrew was a rabid libertarian who believed in the supreme right of any man, to do whatever he wanted when he wanted, with his money and his property. He believed the state owed him nothing and he owed the owed the state even less. His belief in the supremacy of the individual, was one reason he kept Vaultange small — so as not to draw attention to himself. He was not going to explain himself, his actions or those of his clients, to anyone — ever. Which was also why he loved cryptocurrency. Because it's private. It's private from governments, from banking institutions, from the markets. Offline cryptocurrency has the same cachet as a bearer bond. Think about it. A dollar bill is a bearer bond. Whoever has it in their wallet owns it and can use it, (or not) however they choose, when they choose and secretly, (or not) if that is how they choose to make the transaction. Cryptocurrency is the digital expression of a bearer bond. Unless you physically possess the keys, you own zip. If an individual does not have the correct key to that particular cryptocurrency there is no ownership. It stays on the blockchain unclaimed — unable to be traced.

He loved it for another reason. Crypto can cross borders with impunity. You can take the keys to tens of millions of dollars wherever you go, and no one will be any the wiser. Those random numbers on the piece of paper in your pocket mean nothing to anyone else. There are no exchange rates, no government limits, no currency trading officials poking their noses into matters which don't concern them. No explanations. No justifications. No tracks.

Cryptocurrency's big problem is that it's new. And that the banks have done their best to discredit it. Commentators paid by vested interests warn people that governments will join together to outlaw cryptocurrency and make it worthless overnight. Andrew laughed like a hyena when he heard that trope for the first time. 'Talk about driving something underground and sending value stratospheric,' he said. 'Bring it on,' he yelled at one old fart. He was mystified that people would believe every government in the world would ever join together to do anything.

'Remember the Internet,' he used to tell wary clients, 'and how long that took to change the world. It developed in the late fifties and early sixties, and only a few scientists had access to it. It wasn't until 1991 that it became available to the general public and it took another ten years before the net was ubiquitous, disrupting communication as we knew it. Look how quickly Bitcoin has been taken up in comparison,' he'd tell them. 'Ten years after Satoshi invented it there were 890 million separate transactions.' By the time Andrew had finished his pitch, the client would be begging him to take their money.

Murray, too, preferred privacy. It was good for his laundry business. What he didn't like was the volatility. When he started buying in January 2018, he congratulated himself on getting a bargain. He's a fat little toad, and he thought he'd been smart. The price dropped through February, March, and April. Unable to admit he might have been wrong, Murray doubled down. In June the price dropped again. Tense and impatient he came to see me in August. A week later he told me what he wanted me to do.

Another month passed. Bitcoin dived in September. By November it was bumping around the low six thousand mark. Even I was getting worried the bankers were right about it being a dud. It sleazed along the bottom of the pond going as low as US$3294 in early December. That was after Jess moved in. That was when Andrew was happy. His mind wasn't on Vaultange.

Two weeks before Christmas, Murray and his goons arrived at my townhouse at their usual hour to wish me the compliments of the season, minus the Christmas spirit.

I'd put a new lock on the door. I wished I hadn't because it splintered the wood when they burst through it.

'This relationship of Andrew's. It presents a whole new opportunity.' He was sitting companionably on the edge of my bed — the bed where I was lying — naked and vulnerable. 'He'll be concentrating on the little woman and not the business.'

'Tell me,' he said, his voice sounding more gossipier than threatening. 'Is she for real? Or is she with him for the money? Because the way I see it, she's out of his league. A girl like that, a doctor and a looker, she could do better.'

I assured him they were in love and that a date had been set for their wedding in the New Year. Murray nodded. As a Catholic he didn't approve of people living in sin.

'Perfect,' he said rubbing his hands.

Murray had a new plan. He was tired of waiting for the market to come up. He told me what he wanted, and how things were going to run. He was talking a huge amount of money, the contents of the Vaultange wallets to be exact. An impressive amount. Until December, I'd assumed Murray was a small-town, medium-risk-kind-of guy. To pull off what he was suggesting would catapult him into the big, big league. Not least because of who he was planning to steal from.

'I can't do this without you,' he said. 'Your first job is to make absolutely certain your boss leaves the country on his honeymoon. I want him out of the picture. A few days, a couple of weeks would be better. Think you can manage that?'

'Do I have a choice?'

'No.'

'What do I get for helping you?'

Murray would have asked the same question in my position but that didn't mean he liked me asking it. 'You'll be taken care of,' was all he said. An answer which in my opinion did not contain seasonable tidings of good will. But hey. Retractable baseball bats, being retractable baseball bats … what could I say?

TWENTY-FOUR

JESS CONTINUED to work at the hospital until the week before Christmas. She'd leave the apartment before I arrived and would get home after I left. Some nights when there was an emergency she'd have to go back in, other nights she had meetings and lectures to attend. Andrew was getting tetchy about how hard she was working and how tired she was when she got home. She never complained, but she couldn't hide her exhaustion. It was obvious in the fine lines around her eyes and the way her shoulders drooped before we finished dinner. I told him it would be easier dating a nurse — they had fixed hours. He snarled and said he wasn't in love with a nurse.

On the plus side, Jess being away meant I had Andrew to myself during the day. It was almost back to what it was like before she stole him from me — almost but not quite. His genius was still distracted. Vaultange no longer occupied his thoughts from sunup to sundown. The company, as Murray predicted, was no longer his only concern as it had been for the last five years. Worst of all, I was no longer the only person in his life who shared his thoughts, his wild ideas and his equally outrageous plans for the future. I was no longer important to Andrew and I didn't like it — it hurt — it hurt a lot.

Did that make it easier for me to do what Murray asked? I don't know. Honestly, I tried to think of a way out, but I always arrived at the same bloody dead end. The end where one or both of us ended up maimed, deceased or both. I didn't care about me. I had to protect Andrew. I had to follow the plan. When it was done — when Murray had taken the money and was gone, I would confess. I would throw myself on Andrew's mercy. I figured that after all we had been through together, he would understand. Mostly, he would be grateful I'd kept him alive. He would thank me. He would tell me I had no choice and that I had done the right thing. He would forgive me and together, like all the king's horses and all the king's men, we would put Vaultange back together again. Other exchanges had survived being raided — we would too. We were best mates. We had each other's backs. Andrew would know what to do. It would work out. I wouldn't lose him after all.

The week before Christmas Jess started her leave. She had six weeks off work, leave which she was owed because she hadn't taken a holiday, not a proper one, in years. She wanted the time to shop, to organise the wedding and to go on her honeymoon. For the first week, she planned to chill at home. Which meant she was in the apartment all day — every fucking day, doing some half-assed cleaning —a cleaning service came with the apartment for chrissakes. If she wasn't cleaning, she was sitting on the sofa, reading. Listening more like. I started communicating with Andrew by email, even though we were sitting next to each other. He didn't say anything. He knew how I was feeling. He emailed back. The apartment was so quiet, just the tapping of keyboards to show there was any work being done. There was none of the usual banter between mates. Jess killed it.

Before she descended like a thick cloud on our relationship, we enjoyed ourselves. We made each other laugh. I mean the side-splitting, tummy-aching, eye-watering type of laughter, which you remember forever, and which makes you laugh all over again, whenever you remember it. We stayed friends, because of that laughter. I got him. He got me, and nothing was off the table if you could make a joke out of it.

Andrew was a funny guy, but his sense of humour could be

problematic. Not everyone understood when he was making fun of a situation and not the person. Okay, often it was the person. That's why he got in so much trouble at school. He would riff too long about the wrong person at the wrong time and he'd end up headfirst in the nearest rubbish bin. One time, some arse, cling-filmed the little guy to the goal posts on the rugby field. It was four hours before one of the teachers looked out of the window and realised there was a boy under all that plastic.

In the years B J — before Jess, when I was looking after him, I learnt to cook. I had to make sure he ate well, so he didn't get sick again and leave me because I had no future without him.

Occasionally, we would make a night of it, hit the bars on the waterfront and pick up women. Most evenings; however, because we'd be working late into the night, I'd cook dinner. He'd take a break and watch me. I perfected several impressions — Julia Child, Marco Pierre White, Gordon Ramsey and Andrew's particular favourite Jamie Oliver. Each one was courtesy of the You Tube *University of Advanced Studies in Impersonation.* I'd mimic their accents, their posturing and facial expressions as I prepared the *dish du jour.* He'd pretend to interview me and ask the sorts of questions everyone wants to ask a celebrity chef, but no one dares. Staying in character was the easy part. Reigning in my imagination to give socially acceptable replies was more of a challenge. Especially after a few wines.

Jess can't boil an egg, let alone cook a meal. Carole told me she'd done all the cooking while they were living together. It was easier than trying to swallow the food-in-a-jar meals Jess served up. If the four of us (me and Carole, her and Andrew) weren't trying out the latest restaurant, Jess ordered in. His gut seemed to cope. I'm sure the new medication helped, but it didn't stop me worrying.

We also stayed friends because he was loyal. A most attractive trait in a person, a trait I have never claimed to possess. He never forgot what I did for him and he repaid the favour many times over. I thought he trusted me. At least I assumed he did. Right up until I found out otherwise.

Thankfully, after a couple of days off work, Jess found the pool and went there in the mornings to swim for an hour. That restored some of the time Andrew and I spent together. We could talk business aloud, undistracted by her presence.

When Andrew gave Jess a credit card with her name on it, she took up shopping. It beats me how one woman can buy so much and then go shopping again the next day and the day after that. Granted she had excellent taste and granted not everything she bought was for her. She cleared out Andrew's wardrobe. No more nineties rock t-shirts and genuinely worn-out jeans. In came quality 100% organic cotton t-shirts, designer jeans, shorts, hoodies and jackets, caps and beanies, sneakers and brogues, boat-shoes and flip-flops. The *costume du jour, chaque jour.*

I was surprised how much he liked it, how much he revelled in his new clothes. He preened and primped in front of the mirror like a teenage girl. I could only watch from the side lines as he adored her more and more each day. I have to admit that if a woman loved me as much as she appeared to love him, I'd be strutting my stuff like a peacock too. She was good for him. He was happy. I stepped back — reluctantly.

TWENTY-FIVE

SEVEN BUSINESS CARDS were lined up on the table in the glass-walled conference room at Martin Derbyshire. The table, black and rectangular, was easily able to seat ten people on either side and two people at each end, with elbow room. High-backed, black-webbed office chairs on wheels had been set out at appropriate intervals along each side and at one end nearest the door. In the middle of the table, a multidirectional microphone with cords leading off it, sat over a round hole. At the far end, stood an interactive whiteboard which doubled as a screen for presentations. The room was typical of conference rooms everywhere — functional and lacking in soul.

The card from Ronald Barton the managing partner at Barton Barlow, the financial advisory firm employed on Jess's behalf by Ross was a courtesy because she had met Ron before. The rest of the cards belonged to people she hadn't met. In order, they were from the police, the Digital Tech Crimes Unit, the bank (Investigations Department), the Serious Fraud Agency (Digital Crime Division), the Financial Marketing Regulatory Body and the Inland Revenue Department. Every card except one belonged to a man. The exception was the card from the police. That belonged to one, Detective Sergeant Sarah Parker. She was wearing a black long-sleeved shirt over black office trousers, and black ankle boots. Her dark curly hair framing a face devoid of make-up made her look older than she was. When the men introduced themselves, they shook Jess's hand, met her eye and smiled pleasantly. DS Parker seemed barely able to look at her, her handshake was weak, and she certainly didn't smile. The woman seemed indifferent to the point of hostility. Why? What could Jess have done to offend her? Jess's confidence, after the morning's encounter with Carole, was already shaken. This reaction from a perfect stranger didn't help. It became worse when she observed how well Parker interacted with the others, appearing for all intents and purposes as a smart, no bullshit woman ready to get on with the business at hand.

Ross and Ronald, had suggested the meeting, thinking it would be a good idea, *to get everyone together, so we can all see where we're at.* The call at six a.m. informing her she was to be there at one p.m. had felt more like an order, as was his *suggestion* she bring Andrew's death certificate — the real one not a copy. 'Oh,' Ross added, 'and don't forget Henry's hard wallet.'

Ross called the meeting to order then introduced himself and Jess. Like Parker, Jess was wearing trousers and a shirt. Unlike Parker, her trousers were beige, and tapered to the ankle. Her shirt was fitting, silk and in a brightly patterned pink with a bow tied loosely over her breasts. Jess hadn't bothered with full make-up, the mascara and light lipstick were enough to highlight her complexion and give some colour to her face.

Immediately after the introductions Ross handed the meeting over to Ronald Barton. He was cut from the same establishment fabric as Ross. Thick grey hair combed straight back over his head, a beaky nose and thin lips, he wore a pin-striped suit which included a waistcoat in the same material. He and Ross had gone to the same boarding school, belonged to the same clubs (Remuera Golf Club and the Northern Club) and married women from similar backgrounds as their own. The only substantial difference Jess could perceive between the two men was one had chosen the legal profession and the other, finance.

Ronald's dry but very informative power-point presentation left no one in any doubt that there were significant funds missing from the Vaultange bank accounts. It was galling when Ronald looked at Henry, and not Jess, for confirmation, but what did she expect. Henry was a man. His last slide was headed *Customer Records*, below which there was a cartoon of a stick of dynamite exploding with *Malware Attack* written in bright-red letters on the stick. No one laughed. Ronald coughed and resumed his seat.

Ross spoke next. 'Dr Cullinane is as shocked by these disclosures as everyone here. She inherited Vaultange after Andrew's tragic death two weeks ago. While in no way responsible, she has assured me, she will do everything possible to remedy the situation. Ronald and Henry are also available to her, as am I.'

'When did Mr Cullinane write his will?' It was Guy Harding from the Serious Fraud Office. Jess identified him from the photo on his card. His voice was soft, quiet but commanding and she noticed the others in the room stiffened when he spoke. Glasses, average build, reasonably good looking, short dark hair, Guy Harding looked ordinary, the sort of man who could blend into any crowd.

'There is a dated copy in the bundle of documents in front of you,' Ross said. 'Mr Cullinane had me draw up his new will ten days before leaving on his honeymoon.'

'I'd like to see the original death certificate,' Sarah Parker said.

Jess took the document out of her handbag and gave it to Ross who checked it before passing it down the table to the detective.

'I'm sorry for your loss,' Parker said with all the feeling of an automaton. 'Where is your husband buried Dr Cullinane?'

'He isn't. He was cremated over there. I brought his ashes home. They're in a box, at my apartment.'

The detective licked her top lip and placed the certificate flat on the table in front of her.

'Is that a problem? He told me he preferred cremation to burial. I didn't see any reason to bring him home to do it. His doctor arranged it for me.'

'You were married less than a week and yet you knew that he

preferred cremation?' The question came from Paul Weaver an IRD employee. Overweight, the underarms of his pale yellow shirt were rimmed with sweat. He moved uneasily in his chair when he saw people frowning. Jess couldn't understand what it had to do with him and was about to reply when Ross interrupted her.

'I'd like to remind you my client is here voluntarily. She brought the death certificate signed by her late husband's surgeon. I'll have copies made and sent to each of you. I believe she also has the cremation certificate,' he turned to her and raised his eyebrows. Jess nodded. She reached in her handbag again and handed it to him. 'We are here this afternoon to determine what we need to do to move forward — to protect the interests of Vaultange customers. Let's stick to the agreed agenda, shall we?'

Jess let out a small sigh. No matter how much Ross cost, he was worth every penny. As soon as Ross had spoken the man from the IRD found something interesting to look at on his phone.

Ronald cleared his throat. 'I understand you're conducting a forensic examination of Mr Cullinane's laptop.' He had directed his comment to the person from the DTC unit at the other end of the table. 'How's that was getting on?'

'Too soon to say,' Adam Heath replied. He was by far the youngest person in the room but what he lacked in years he made up for with confidence.

'Let's hope it leads to something. The bank is working through the accounts. Is that correct?' The man from the bank put down his pen and smiled. 'We'll liaise with you when we know more.' Ronald directed his next question to Henry. 'Can you confirm the laptop is the only place you know of where Andrew kept client records?'

'Yes.'

Jess cleared her throat. 'I found these,' she said putting the USBs on the table.

Henry sat bolt upright. 'We looked everywhere. Where did you find them?'

'In a pocket in his backpack.' She hadn't been planning to lie. She was surprised how easily it slipped out. 'He must have taken them with him. I found them when I was unpacking his stuff. I hope they'll have the information we need.'

Ross picked up the sticks, turned them over in his hands and passed them to Ronald.

'Well done,' Ronald said, making eye contact with Jess for the first time. 'Well done,' he repeated smiling at her.

'I'd like to be there when you open them. I presume the DTC will be involved,' Parker said.

'Fine with me. Open invitation to you all,' Ronald said. 'Ross, Jess, okay with you?'

'Of course,' Jess said and Ross nodded.

The atmosphere in the room changed. Comradery replaced the earlier wariness and suspicion. 'Hopefully, if we find what we need, we can put this investigation out of its misery,' Guy said. His hopeful optimism seemed to be shared by one and all. The man from the IRD was the first to leave, quickly followed by the man from the bank and Guy Harding. Ross and Ronald left together, joking about golf handicaps and saying they should set up a game as soon as this business was behind them. Henry left with a curt goodbye, adding he would call Jess later.

Only Sarah Parker stayed behind, slowly sorting her papers until it was just her and Jess in the room. She snapped shut the clips on her briefcase and swung it off the table. As she walked out, she stopped beside Jess and leant down. 'I know who you really are,' she said.

TWENTY-SIX

THE WALK back to the apartment took Jess through town where the summer sales were in full swing. Women loaded down with shopping bags ducked past her as she wandered along High Street indifferent to the bargains on offer. *I know who you really are.* The words echoed in her head. Jess would have been more surprised if Parker hadn't known who she was. The woman had the entire police database at her disposal. Any detective worth her salt would have done a background check and found Jess's file. Not that it would have revealed much. Her case went before the youth court and as such the file would be sealed. She doubted Parker, a detective sergeant, would have the authority required to access her file in its entirety.

Jess's years in care homes had brought her into contact with a whole range of people, some good, some bad and a few like Parker — bullies. The only child of a protective parent, Jess had been shocked at what passed for normal behaviour in these places. On her first day she was confronted by a full-on brawl caused when one girl accused another of taking her friend. The shrieking violence stopped when staff waded into the melee of bloody, flailing limbs to haul the culprits out by their hair. Jess, who was barely in the door, watched as calm was quickly restored, and everyone carried on as if nothing had happened.

After that she kept to herself. Girls would make approaches, asking her to join their groups in return for a veneer of friendship and a guarantee of protection. She resisted. Instead, she waited, observing how each place worked, who was at the top and who was at the bottom, who were the conduits and who were the circuit breakers in the system. It didn't take long before she was able to identify those to be wary of, and those it was safe to be around, those she could trust to behave predictably and those who flared into incandescent rage with minimal, if any, provocation.

The bullies fell into the predictable category. They couldn't help themselves. Like sharks circling a school of fish, they waited for the outliers, the weak, and then they would strike. Hard and fast, doing as much damage as they could before swimming away. As Parker had done this morning. Purposely waiting until the end of the meeting, she had attacked when no one else was around and then she had left. What was she hoping to achieve? Jess had no idea.

Jess smiled at the unnecessary melodrama Parker had injected into her statement. 'I know who you really are.' Boo hoo. Was Jess supposed to be scared? Of what? Of being exposed by a policewoman sworn to uphold the law of the land, such as name suppression for instance? It was laughable. Not that Jess had laughed. She had played the silly game. She had looked suitably startled and afraid, noting the sadistic satisfaction in Parker's tight smile. Who did it remind her of? Yes. That was who, the creepy husband at her very last care home. She had discovered his peephole in the bathroom on her second day. Later that night, when everyone was asleep, she accessed the files on his computer, deleted her own photos from the day before, and sent the images of the naked girls in his care, to the police and social services. Just for fun she copied them to his mistress, who his wife knew nothing about. The couple were removed by the police the next day. When creepy-husband's wife found about the mistress, she not only showed the police where more explicit videos were kept but led them to the secret room where they had been made. By the time the couple came to trial, Jess was long gone. It was then that her phone rang.

'Johnny's had a heart attack,' Carole said.

'You're kidding.'

'Why would I kid about something like that?'

She heard the panic mixed with anger in Carole's voice. 'Where are you? What can I do?'

'They've put a stent in. We got home an hour ago.'

'I'm on my way. Do you need anything?'

'You don't have to come. There's nothing you can do.'

'I can make tea. I'm good at that. I'll see you soon.'

TWENTY-SEVEN

'REMEMBER TO GIVE ME A FIVE,' Ahmed said as he pulled alongside the curb outside Carole's house. If she hadn't been in a hurry to see Johnny, she wouldn't have got into the car. She would have called the police. But she hesitated. On what grounds? What could she report him for? Responding to her request for a ride? Meanwhile Johnny and Carole needed her. Perhaps, it was a coincidence. He worked the CBD. He said. This was his patch. Lots of people took rides with him. Not just her. He said. In the end, expediency won out and she got in the car. Damned if she'd give him a five though. Jess told him not to wait, adding that he better not be there when she wanted to go home, or she would call the police and report him — for stalking her. She slammed the door as hard as she could, hoping she'd made her point.

Carole was at the front door as soon as Jess walked through the gate. They hugged and Carole put one finger to her lips and ushered her towards the kitchen.

'How is he?' Jess whispered.

'Tired, but okay,' Carole replied as she sat on the sofa. Jess moved dirty dishes aside to fill the kettle in the sink. Ants crawled over plates encrusted with dried food. Pots and frying pans littered the stove top and the bench. After searching for clean mugs and finding none, Jess washed two from the pile. When she looked up, Carole was curled on her side, snuggled into the back of the sofa, fast asleep. She rinsed away the ants, stacked the plates in the dishwasher and turned it on, then she turned her attention to the pots and pans, slipping them into a sink of hot soapy water before she started scrubbing. The benches were wiped down, clean pots were put away and the kettle had boiled twice. Carole hadn't moved.

Jess tip-toed down the hall to check on Johnny and found him tucked up in bed in her old room. He too was asleep and so she clicked the door shut and tip-toed back to the kitchen to make a cup of tea. She had just opened the fridge to get milk when Carole stirred and woke up.

'What happened? Is Dad okay?'

'He's fine. I just checked on him; he's asleep. Tea or coffee?'

'Tea would be grand.' Carole rubbed her eyes and sat up.

Jess made the tea and tipped some biscuits she'd found at the back of a cupboard on to a plate. 'Eat,' she ordered. Carole wolfed down the biscuits and asked for more. After taking one for herself, Jess passed her the rest of the packet.

'I was at work,' Carole said between sips of tea. 'I got called to the emergency department. The old guy from next door was with him. Isn't it awful? I don't know his name and we've been neighbours for years.'

'Bert. His name is Bert.'

'They were supposed to go for a walk and when Dad didn't show, the old guy peered in the window and saw him on the floor. Thankfully he dialled 111. By the time he got to the hospital, he'd come around. He looked awful. He went straight to the cath lab and two hours later they put in a stent. His recordings overnight were stable. They discharged him this morning. To be honest it happened so fast, it's all a bit of a blur. He's got to rest for a couple of days, but that's it. An outpatient appointment in a month. I keep thinking there's been a mistake and they sent him home too early.' Carole looked at Jess, seeking reassurance.

'Standard procedure always feels difficult when it's your relative. Thank goodness for Bert.'

'Totally.' Carole heaved a sigh. 'I haven't got my head around it yet. Bet Dad hasn't either.' Neither spoke for several minutes.

'I guess,' Carole said at length. 'I guess nothing. I don't know. I mean, he had a heart attack and could have died, but he didn't. The cardiologist said he'll be fine. Lucky we got to the catheter study straight away, blah blah. Lucky we could put the stent in and open up his blood vessels again, blah, blah. All the stuff they say to make you feel better. But I don't. Feel better I mean. I can't help thinking what I would do if he died. I'm not ready to be alone. He's all I've got.'

Carole didn't stop talking. She didn't notice Jess start to speak then stop. She talked about her fear and how she had sat up all night watching the line on the monitor, listening to the beeps of her father's heart, holding his hand, praying he would live and be okay. 'I know he's my father. I know he's old. I know he's going to die before me. I just don't want it to be now. I'm not strong like you, Jess. I can't turn off my emotions. You've taken Andrew's death in your stride and carried on regardless. I couldn't do that. Not, if anything happened to Dad.'

Jess wanted to take her friend by the shoulders and shake her until she apologised. She wanted to yell at her, that she wasn't strong, that she wasn't carrying on regardless, that she missed Andrew every day and grieved for him deep, deep, deep inside her very being. She wanted to scream that she hadn't been ready for the man she loved to die and leave her alone. She wanted to rage at Carole for her thoughtlessness, her downright stupidity and for the pressure Carole had put on her to sort out Vaultange, a pressure born of greed and her father's recklessness. She said none of it.

'He'll be fine,' Jess said. 'Stents work miracles. Johnny will be up and around in no time, bossing you about, driving you nuts.'

'Yeah, he will, won't he?' Carole got up and put her mug on the bench. 'Sorry Jess. I'm all over the place. Look at me. Still in my uniform.'

There was a yell from the other room. 'Who does someone have to pay to get a cup of tea around here? I'm as dry as a dingo's what's it.'

'You go,' Jess said as she stood up. 'I'll make the tea. How does he have it?'

'White with one sugar. On second thoughts make that white, no sugar.' She disappeared and while Jess was making the tea, she could hear them murmuring together in the bedroom. It was a cosy sound. The sound of a family.

As she walked down the hall with Johnny's tea and what was left of the packet of biscuits, their voices changed. Johnny, becoming more insistent, Carole trying to soothe. When she pushed open the bedroom door with her foot the conversation stopped.

'You're a sight for sore eyes,' Jess said as she put down the tray on the table beside the bed. 'You've been getting up to all sorts.'

'Trying to, Girlie,' he replied grimacing as he pushed himself up against the stack of pillows. His hair, in need of a wash, stuck up at the front and was flat at the back. A day's grey stubble smudged the contours of his face, highlighting the lines around his mouth. Johnny looked old.

'Careful Dad,' Carole said pointing at the top of his right leg under the duvet.

He lifted the duvet and looked down. 'That's a big bruise, no wonder it hurts. Is that where they did it? My heart's up here, not down there?'

'Very funny.' Carole passed him the mug. 'Drink your tea.'

'First things first. I need to ask Jess about my money.'

'No, you don't,' Carole said. 'You need to rest and get better. Everything else can wait.'

'Call yourself a nurse. The doctor said to get up and get moving. He specifically said not to lie around like an invalid.'

'I was there too, remember,' Carole said. 'His exact words were to rest today and get up tomorrow.'

Jess who was standing halfway between the bed and the door was unsure whether to stay or go. The last week had made her painfully aware she wasn't considered family and she didn't want to intrude.

Johnny decided for her when he brushed away his daughter's hand and leant towards her.

'Is it all gone?' he asked. 'Tell me, I can take it.'

'I'm not sure. I can't tell you one way or the other. Not yet.'

Carole rescued the mug before tea spilt on to the duvet then turned on Jess. 'Really? Now? He's just had a stent. You could have lied?'

'He deserves the truth.'

'Not right now he doesn't.'

'Yes. Right now, he does,' Johnny insisted. 'Tell me.'

'Don't you dare,' Carole hissed.

'Stop it,' Johnny said. 'And listen. It's your money too.'

He put on a brave face, but Jess could tell he was hurting as she told him what she knew. There was no point making excuses or giving involved explanations about where the money might be. She didn't know. She said so. Johnny could spot bullshit from a mile away. She knew better than to make things sound better than they were. Andrew had put the money in a safe place where hackers couldn't get it. Now, no one else could get it either. She told him that unless it was found, all the while assuring him the best people were looking, then his money was gone — forever.

'Ghost money,' Johnny said as his voice cracked.

Carole sat on the bed beside her father, one hand over her mouth, one arm wrapped around her body, rocking backwards and forwards as Jess apologised for the twentieth time. When there was nothing more to say — she said so. Carole didn't move. Neither did Johnny. Carole didn't get up to see her out. She stayed on the bed, holding her father's hand. She didn't look at Jess, didn't even call out bye, as Jess closed the door behind her.

TWENTY-EIGHT

As Jess walked to the end of the road she wondered what they would do. Carole owned the house outright with no mortgage, and she had a good job. She loved her father. She would take care of him. That was a given. Johnny was too old to make a new start. Carole would keep working and support them both. Her dreams of travelling and living overseas were effectively over.

For the first time, Jess was angry — with Andrew. Deeply, furiously angry. Taking Johnny's money had been a dumb thing to do. Mixing business with friendship? Why? And why had he taken all of it, every last cent? Unless the answers were on the USBs, then everything Johnny had in the world was most likely gone.

Why hadn't she realised what Andrew was capable of doing? Money mattered more than people. He hadn't hidden it, but she had been blinded by love and hadn't seen it. Or worse, she had seen it and ignored it because the people affected were faceless clients, people she didn't know or care about. When she pushed Andrew to tell her about the company, he'd brushed her off, giving simple answers to complex questions. Sometimes he would shut his laptop, lean over, kiss her, say he loved her, and change the subject.

So total was her love for him that she had thought it better to let it go. There'd be time later when she could find out the truth. She kicked herself for playing along, convincing herself that he was a good man, an honourable man, the man she assumed him to be and the man she had fallen in love with. Dammit, she'd relaxed her guard just when alarm bells should have been ringing.

When she crossed a busy road without thinking or looking, a cyclist slowed in the nick of time and avoided a collision. He yelled and gave her the finger as he wobbled to rebalance his bike. Barely noticing, not caring where she was going, Jess walked on.

Andrew had swept her off her feet with his promises of eternal love and happiness, assurances he would make a home for her and their children. After being alone for so long, it felt good to be looked after. He promised her their life would be worry-free and glorious once everything was settled, he would set up a fund. She could do the research she'd always wanted to do. They would travel, have children, live in exotic locations, buy a yacht and sail the Med, the Atlantic, anywhere she liked. Nothing was off the table. It was all too wonderful for words. Too wonderful to be real. Yet, she had believed it.

Jess stopped walking and shook her head. After everything she'd been through, why had she been so gullible? So childish? So desperate to embrace the fairy tale with open arms? Why did she not know deep down that no one lives the life Andrew had dangled in front of her? No one.

The next intersection was much busier, and noisier than the quiet suburban streets she'd crossed already. The signs for turn-offs to Western Springs were more frequent. Cars and trucks sped past, their drivers focused on vehicles, not lone pedestrians. Unfamiliar street names followed one after the other as she carried on walking in the evening gloom. The threatening clouds arrived, blocking the last of the sunshine. A chill descended. She shivered and wrapped her light cardigan around her body just before she admitted she was lost. She took out her phone and tapped the Uber App. A car was five minutes away. She dropped her phone back in her bag and huddled in her own embrace. Right on time, a light blue Mazda slowed, did a U-turn and pulled up beside her — unbelievable.

'Ahmed?' She looked in the window. 'I told you. I'm calling the police.'

'You're not where you said you'd be and neither am I,' he said as if that settled the matter.

'You saw my name. You knew it was me.'

'Okay, okay … I'm here now. You want to wait for another car. Fine. I'll go. Ten dollars cancellation fee. If not, get in.'

Jess wanted to tell him to go, but she wasn't dressed for the weather and she was cold. She got in. His brown eyes met hers in the rear vision mirror as she put on her seat belt. She looked away, huddling against the door.

'You're following me,' she said once they were moving. His eyes flicked up to the mirror, narrowing for a moment, before looking away. He said nothing and turned up the radio. When they reached the apartment, he stared straight ahead as she got out, driving away before she had time to shut the door.

The person at the police call centre took down her details and assured her that an officer would be in touch as soon as one was available. 'No actual crime has been committed, has it?' the operator asked. Jess had to concede that was true. 'He's an Uber driver, so have you spoken to their head office and made a complaint?' When Jess admitted she hadn't, the woman sighed loudly and suggested this might be a good place to start. 'As far as the police are concerned, an Uber was requested, it arrived and took you to your destination. It may be a while before we get back to you,' said the operator. Feeling stupid, Jess ended the call.

TWENTY-NINE

THE NEXT MORNING Vaultange featured again in banner headlines on news sites not only in New Zealand but overseas. Below the headlines were photos of Jess at her graduation and one from a med school end of year dinner. In the graduation photo, she looked the wide-eyed innocent beaming with achievement. The other photo dispelled any innocence that was in the first one. Bleary eyed, Jess was holding a glass of wine on an angle and blowing a kiss to the photographer. Her classmates had been edited out and it looked as if she was on her own and drunk — messy drunk. She hadn't been. She'd been putting on a show to keep up with the others. Too late now. Regrettably perception is reality, she remembered. Hopefully, the *good friend* who'd supplied the photograph would go straight to hell.

Is this Doctor the Key to Bitcoin Millions? Following this headline was a timeline of her relationship with Andrew, no doubt supplied by the same *good friend* from the hospital. In a box to the side of the page was a story about the date and *mysterious* circumstances of his death. Details and facts were sparse, but were more than compensated for by innuendo, every sly statement reflecting badly on one person and one person only — Dr Jess Cullinane née Gordon. On other sites, articles were more generic, less personalised, but equally alarming if you read between the lines. *Is Cryptocurrency for Real? Why invest in Bitcoin? Some say it's digital gold because it can be kept from the predations of government and is thus a hedge against currency collapse such as has occurred in Venezuela or Argentina. Others call it a giant Ponzi scheme waiting to fall over, bankrupting those late to the Ponzi party. Buying in 2011, when Bitcoin was valued at US$30, holding for six years and selling in December 2017, when the value had risen to US$20,000 would usually make a convert out of the most dubious. However, if you bought in December 2017, only to see the value decimated two months later, you might not be as bullish.*

The security of cryptocurrency is a huge issue. Online theft is real and ever present. Mt Gox, the Japan based exchange, which in 2014 handled 70% of worldwide Bitcoin transactions, was hacked and 850,000 Bitcoin valued at four hundred and fifty million dollars disappeared overnight. Untraced and untraceable to this day.

Modern exchanges say they have learnt from these mistakes and are working with regulators to safeguard investments. Regulators though have been slow to respond to this new world because of a combination of lack of expertise, funds and patchy government responses.

Sophisticated thieves will always circumvent security systems given time and opportunity. Criminals go largely unpunished, because no individual or country has jurisdiction over the Internet. Difficulties tracing stolen Bitcoin on blockchains adds to the complexity of the problem, as has growth in the system. In 2012, there were one million Bitcoin in circulation. In 2019 — seventeen million.

Vaultange, the exchange built from nothing by Andrew Cullinane, once had a solid reputation in the tech community. Over the last week, sources close to the company report discrepancies in banking and record-keeping — issues which the authorities are investigating.

Jess sipped her coffee. It was cold, but she swallowed it anyway. She stared at the screen unsure what to do. Until the forensics people cracked the passwords and opened the wallets, she was powerless. She could send pacifying messages to the clients who had contacted her, but that was all she could do. Without the files she couldn't ratify any claims and she couldn't pay people with money she didn't have.

But she did have another company. The properties in Gordon

Holdings were valuable and they needed her attention, Ross had said so. Seven houses in five countries. Too many houses for one person. If Ross could get more information about them, she could decide which ones to keep and which ones to sell. The money might go part of the way to refunding clients. Ross wasn't available when she called, so she spoke instead to one of his juniors, asking that detailed inspections be commissioned on each house. The junior said Ross was tied up for the rest of the day but promised to pass on her instructions.

As she drummed her fingernails on the bench Jess decided idleness was overrated. She preferred to be busy. She needed her mind to be challenged in order to feel alive. Relaxation was for holidays — short holidays. Maybe she could return to work, while she was waiting for the experts to sort out Vaultange. Her colleagues would be pleased to have her back on the call roster even if only temporarily. She called the Prof, but his phone went straight to voicemail. A tinge of jealousy reared its green head that these people could be occupied with their work, while she sat in the apartment, idle. She left a message saying she was available to fill in for a few days and to call her back as soon as possible.

Outside grey clouds were bundling up the harbour from the west bringing with them more rain for the plants on the balcony. It was supposed to have been one of the driest summers since records began, but the last two days of gloomy rain had put paid to the forecast. She turned up the heating, then turned it down again and went to find something warm to put on instead.

She needed food. The prospect of going to a crowded supermarket did not appeal, even as a way to fill in time. Instead, she ordered groceries online, enough to keep her from starving to death and pressed the tab for an express delivery. The order would arrive within the hour. Not enough time to spend answering emails and too much time to sit and do nothing. Exercise. That's what she needed.

She hadn't been for a swim since getting back from her honeymoon. Her swimming costume was still sandy from her last day on the beach. Once she shook the sand out in the shower, she got changed and put on a robe, before riding the elevator down to the basement. A woman was swimming laps when Jess pushed open the heavy glass door. Another regular, they'd spoken a few times in passing. The woman had made a point of welcoming her to the building, suggesting they meet for coffee, which they still hadn't done. Andrew had pretended to be miffed when she told him, none of the other residents having spoken to him much less suggested coffee.

What was her name? Anne? Angela? It didn't matter, she'd wing it, if necessary. She met so many people as patients, she often forgot their names after they left her care. Those who wanted to be remembered, reminded her. Those who didn't seemed relieved she had no idea who they were. She dropped her robe on a chair, rinsed her goggles in the pool and put them on. As she stood at one end of the pool, she wiggled her arms and legs to loosen up, then dived in, settling into an easy crawl.

Annie. That was it. Annie immediately stopped mid-lap, swam over to the side and hauled herself out of the water. With her back to Jess, she bundled her towel around her, and headed for the changing room, slapping a trail of wet footprints across the tiles. Jess stopped, treading water and stared at Annie's departing back. She almost said something, but hey, maybe the woman needed to pee. No matter. With the pool to herself she could focus on swimming without having to worry about keeping pace or getting in anyone's way at the turn. She adjusted her goggles, kicked off the bottom and struck out to continue the fifty laps she planned to swim, hitting the lap counter at each end before her tumble turn. Sliding through the water felt so good after yesterday. She would call Carole later to see if she'd been forgiven for telling the truth. The rhythm of the strokes, the feel of her body slicing through the water revitalised her and she thought about what she was going to do.

Two nights ago, she had plugged the plain USB into her laptop. A dialog box had come up — one entry appeared, marked Vault Files. When she clicked on it, another dialogue box requesting a ten-digit password zoomed into view blocking any further progress. She googled the brand name written on the side of the USB and read the operating instructions to see if there were any shortcuts she could use to override the system. As she expected there were none. With further research she learnt it was technically possible to go into the back of a stick but as someone in the chatroom advised, *it was not an easy hack.* The last thing Jess wanted to do was jeopardise any attempts by the forensic experts to access the data. The second last thing she wanted to do, was have them discover she'd tried to open it. Reluctantly she unplugged it.

She didn't even try to open the *Ledger.* Not after studying the tutorial on how to use the Nano S. Anyway she didn't have the right cable to connect the stick to her laptop, and she had no idea what the eight number PIN might be let alone the random twenty-four-word recovery phrase. Holding the sticks in her hands, knowing they more than likely held the information she needed to open the wallets, had felt both eerily futuristic and immensely frustrating. Such small repositories of such important secrets.

Her fervent hope was the forensic team would open them. Sooner rather than later. But if all the experts in the world couldn't open them? What then? The answers were in the palm of her hand, but they might as well be in a black hole in the next galaxy if the passwords weren't found.

Jess's hand hit the end of the pool. She tumbled awkwardly, water flushing her sinuses and stinging the back of her throat. Ignoring the pain, she straightened out and pushed on, finding her rhythm again easily.

Having grown up as an only child who preferred reading and swimming to making friends, Jess hadn't been exposed to boys. Not until she was sent to the care homes. They had been a revelation. Boys were so different, not only in appearance, but in the way they thought and what they thought about, the dumb ones anyway. The bright ones were more like her. They kept to themselves, observed others and thought ahead, strategizing to get what they wanted. The bright ones had a reason for everything they did, even though that reason might not always be obvious.

Andrew didn't leave the sticks in the apartment. He didn't give them to Ross to put in the safe at the firm. Both sensible options. Or maybe, thinking about it, only one. She remembered something he'd said as the plane was taking off. 'How long will Henry wait before he snoops through our stuff?' It had taken a few moments before Jess realized he wasn't joking. 'Eeuw,' she'd said.

Andrew shrugged. 'Nothing we can do. Don't think about it, think about us, what we're going to be doing.' The flight attendant arrived and refilled their champagne glasses. 'To us,' Andrew said clinking his glass against hers.

'To us,' she'd replied.

Andrew had left the sticks in the car for a reason. A car which no one else knew about and which was parked anonymously in a building in the city. Only two people would ever find the sticks and understand their significance. Andrew hadn't come back. Planning for that eventuality, he had therefore meant for her to find them — only her. By extension, he must have left the passwords and PINs for her as well — somewhere.

Fifty on the lap counter. She checked the time and guessed she had another ten minutes before the groceries would arrive, so she sprinted twenty laps, finishing her swim short of breath but energised. It felt good to push past set goals. It made her feel stronger, in control. She pulled herself up the ladder, picked up her robe and walked into the changing room to shower off the chlorine before going upstairs.

Written in red lipstick across the mirror in the changing room was the word, KILLER. Each letter a straight, hard, punch to her chest, knocking the wind from her lungs. The only person here while she'd been swimming was Annie. Which didn't make sense. Theoretically, as if logic could calm her beating heart, the writing could have been there all day, it could have been written about someone else, by anyone. It could have nothing to do with her. She couldn't look away. It was meant for her. Huge letters written with such fury, small chunks of lipstick were stuck, suspended on the glass, more lumps had broken off and dotted the hand basin below. She had to get rid of it.

Wads of wet toilet paper made it worse. All she succeeded in doing was smearing the letters across more of the mirror. KILLER was still readable. Without the proper solvent, she couldn't wipe it away. She looked from the soggy mess of paper in her hand to the mirror, refusing to allow herself the luxury of tears. After all this time, her feelings hadn't gone away. They had merely been hibernating. Grief, shame, disgust, horror, guilt, they were all there as fresh as the day her mother had died.

Outside, she heard the door open. Fighting an overwhelming urge to break cover and escape, she rubbed the mirror hopelessly one last time and flushed the paper down the loo. She didn't want to be caught red-handed and be associated with this obscenity. She had to get out. She had to run. She couldn't bear the puzzled questions, the hesitation and doubt, before realisation dawned and a look closed her out. She wrapped a towel around her head and put on her robe, pulling it tightly around her with the collar up. With her head tucked down she walked purposefully around the edge of the pool, into the foyer and straight to the elevator.

Thankfully, the new arrival had been a man who was busily removing his watch, peeling off his track pants and getting ready for his swim, and he took no notice of her as she walked past. When would the next woman use the changing room? When did the cleaners come? The elevator doors closed. It was over. Not her problem.

Back in the apartment, with the hot shower raining down her back, the red letters flashed in her mind like a neon sign in the darkness and were still there as she dried her hair. KILLER. Annie wrote that? Annie? Nice, we-must-have-coffee Annie?

The groceries arrived, and with them distraction. She put a pot of water on the stove, dotted the surface with olive oil and added salt ready for a packet of home-made spinach ravioli. Annie? Nice, Annie wasn't so nice after all. How did she know? The court file was sealed. Her name had been changed. She wasn't Jessica Davidson anymore and she sure as hell didn't look like her fifteen-year-old self, the kid who was hustled in and out of a closed court with a blanket over her head. The only photos, which made it to the press, had come from Bryan, her loving stepfather, and they were already two years out of date back then.

Jess was a woman now. She was taller, she had breasts and hips. She had changed the colour of her hair, she was blonde, not dark. She wore make-up. She had gone to medical school and become a doctor. She wasn't Jessica Davidson anymore. That girl had died on the bed with her mother. She was Dr Jess Cullinane. Previously Dr Jess Gordon.

Who else knew? If Annie knew, then … she could rule out Andrew and the investigator. Ross knew. He had to, but he was bound by law as well as his ethical principles to say nothing. Assuming Parker's cryptic comment referred to her conviction, Jess had to believe she would not be stupid and reveal what she knew. Parker would not be so dumb as to risk her career. At the same time, an anonymous tip off, a letter sent from a well-wisher. Parker was more than capable of mean-girl behaviour.

Henry Turner. It could be him. But why tell Annie? And why now?

The ravioli had been tumbling on the surface of the boiling water for too long, the pasta slowly disintegrating in the bubbles when she turned off the element. She drained the water and tipped her meal into a bowl. At that moment her phone rang. Carole. Not the right time. She pressed send to message. Jess had missed nine calls, three from Carole, four from Ross, and two from numbers she didn't recognise. She couldn't bear the thought of talking to anyone. Not Carole. Not Ross. No one. Steam rose from the bowl as she speared a piece of ravioli with her fork only to have it fall apart and drop back in pieces. She wasn't hungry after all. She crept into her bedroom, got into bed, pulled the duvet over her head and shut her eyes.

THIRTY

Jess woke to her phone ringing. It was Carole. Jess's heart sank, but she answered it anyway. She had been hoping it would be Ross with news of the properties. She'd been awake half the night, planning how to sell them so she could pay Johnny back.

'Can I come over? We need to talk,' Carole said.

Half an hour later, Carole was filling the kettle when Jess emerged from her room, wearing one of the sundresses she had taken on honeymoon and never worn. Carole didn't look up.

'How's Johnny?' Jess asked as she perched on a stool.

'Better. Thank you,' Carole replied. The kettle boiled and she poured water over the coffee and replaced the lid. 'That guy from next door is with him, the one who's name I can't remember.'

'Bert,' Jess said.

'Whatever.'

'What's wrong? What have I done now?'

Carole pushed the plunger down too hard. Hot coffee spilt over the top and on to the bench. She filled the cups regardless took one, leaving the other for Jess to retrieve from the puddle.

'Is it still the money—'

'It's not the money. Not everything is about money,' Carole snapped.

What then? Because something is going on—'

Carole put down her cup and took her phone out of her pocket. She tapped the screen until she found what she was looking for and handed the phone to Jess. Is that you? Are you the Jessica Davidson they're talking about? The fifteen-year-old girl who killed her mother?'

Jess tried to speak but no words came out.

'It is you.'

'I'm supposed to have name suppression. These people have broken the law,' she said and as soon as she heard her words she realised how self-serving and pathetic she sounded.

'In New Zealand. The rest of the world doesn't care about our name suppression laws. They put up whatever they like. By now the whole country knows that the fifteen-year-old girl who killed her mother, goes away on honeymoon ten years later and then her husband dies mysteriously, leaving her all his money.'

'He was sick. And you fucking know it.'

'He looked perfectly healthy the last time I saw him. Just saying.' Carole got up walked over and stood in front of the window and stared out.

'You think I killed him? You think I could do that?'

Carole shook her head. 'I don't know. I don't know you, do I? Not after reading this. I looked after Mum when she had cancer. I know what it's like, how awful it gets, but I couldn't kill her? I could never have done that. I could never be that cold. Call yourself a doctor? No wonder you got over Andrew so quickly.'

'You bitch,' Jess said as she stood up. 'What if I told you the stuff in the papers is wrong. I could tell you the truth, but you'd never understand. Doctors and nurses aren't Gods. There is no God. No one should get to say how a person has to live or how they die. Johnny said your mother had a *good death*, that her pain medication worked, and she drifted off with you and him beside her. Lucky her. Not everyone has that option. I refuse to have you or anyone else judge me. And yet here you are, the sanctimonious nurse doing exactly that when you don't even know what really happened.'

'I know you were convicted of manslaughter. I know you kept it from the medical school.'

'They would never have let me in otherwise,' Jess yelled. 'Of course, I didn't tell them. What happened then has nothing to do with now.'

Carole turned to face her. 'You can't be serious. Everyone knows. Do you really think you'll be welcomed back to the hospital with open arms? Patients won't trust you. The staff won't trust you. I'm not sure if I trust you and I'm your friend.'

'Are you? Because it sure doesn't sound like it.' Jess picked up Carole's bag and handed it to her. 'It's best you leave — now.'

That's all you have to say. No explanation, nothing.'

'You've made it perfectly clear you already know what happened. Nothing I say will make the slightest bit of difference.'

Jess walked to the elevator and pressed the down button. Carole followed and got in the lift. Jess turned her back as the doors were closing. She didn't want Carole to see her crying.

THIRTY-ONE

'You've got surgery at two, Mr Turner. Are you sure you want to continue?'

'I'd rather get it over with,' I replied.

'All right. Start when you're ready,' said the voice. The light dimmed. The white walls faded, the bed was the only thing visible in the room. I pressed the button on the morphine pump and counted to twelve. At sixteen seconds I started speaking.

I defy anyone to look good peering over a balcony, seven floors above the ground but Jess Cullinane managed it. Correction. She didn't look good, she looked … tempting. Tousled hair, sleepy eyes, breasts akimbo under the thin silk kimono. She looked like morning should look and the photo went viral. Courtesy of a great camera rather than a great photographer. The Nikon D40 with megapixels to spare, fitted with a 400 mm lens did the grunt work. A monkey could have taken that shot. A monkey who knew where she lived. A monkey with his camera mounted on a tripod, aimed at the balcony, his finger on the shutter button. A monkey who knew she was home. I tipped the monkey off. We split the fee fifty/fifty. I didn't rip him off. He got the name credit. Beneath the photo and above the headline: *Doctor Killed Mother. New Husband Dies on Honeymoon.*

That photo ran on every national and most international news sites. It was the lead on CNN and BBC for the next twenty-four hours, and was only bumped off when Trump fired his latest team member. Someone would have taken the shot sooner or later. Why not my guy? What was wrong with it. Jess looked natural. She wasn't naked. Sure she was hurt by the exposure. But is that my problem?

She was still furious when she arrived at Ross's office two days after the photo was posted. I was there. She stormed in, wearing that same sweatshirt of Andrew's she wears everyday along with the same baggy sweatpants, trainers, a baseball cap and dark glasses. Puleese. A disguise? She could do better than that.

Ross and I were enjoying a quiet beer at the end of a long and arduous day. Two guys shooting the breeze, we'd been left carrying the Vaultange can after Jess went to ground. We'd been fielding questions from the media, the police, the bank, in fact, all the teams attached to the inquiry. It had been a stressful day and we needed a few moments to decompress. We needed peace and quiet.

Ronald, the accountant and his firm's auditors had sent through the previous three quarters' bank statements ten minutes before we cracked open the cold ones.

'News we need like a hole in the head,' Ross said when he read the attached memo.

'Wasn't it them who signed off the accounts in the first place? Now they come at us guns blazing,' I said. I was feeling justifiably indignant. 'They should have picked up the discrepancies earlier when they were auditing the books. That's what they were paid to do. They can hardly plead innocence now.' I took a long drink from the bottle, almost emptying it. 'Vaultange has to lodge a formal complaint with their regulatory body.' Ross winced and looked up at the ceiling. I swear he was counting slowly to himself.

Anyway Ross notified the cops as soon as we got the news. We were waiting to hear what they wanted us to do next. It was the calm before the storm. The staff had left for the day including his secretary.

Sick kid or some such problem. Why women work when they have kids beats me. I've never met a working mother yet who didn't expect some form of special treatment, when their kid either got sick or there was a school concert or some other kid-thing requiring a maternal presence. Who pays for this namby-pamby parenting? Not them. The employer. The clients. Me. That's who. The people smart enough not to have kids. My point is, no one was there to stop Jess when she charged through reception and slammed open the door to Ross's office, stopping on the threshold when she saw us. I expected yelling, abuse, hysterical screaming, then more abuse, but she didn't do any of that. What she did was worse. She took off her dark glasses, and her cap, and stepped forward. 'Some bastard leaked my file. Who do you think that shithole of a person might be?' she said quietly and then she glared at me.

Stuck for words, I turned to Ross. It was him she'd come to see, it was his office, his shit show.

'I would be hauled in front of the Law Society's disciplinary panel if I broke client confidentiality,' Ross said, his voice weary after our long day. 'And before you say anything, I can assure you no one at the firm knew the file even existed. It wasn't Henry, so stop giving him the evil eye. Andrew gave me specific instructions Henry was not to see the file or even know of its existence. Instructions which I followed.'

Another dagger in my heart. I know now how Caesar felt. All the years, when Andrew and I were as thick as thieves. The years when we shared everything. We lived together, we ate together, we worked and partied together. Those years, our friendship, what I had done for him. It meant nothing after she arrived.

Jess sat down in the chair beside me, shaking her head at Ross's offer of a beer. 'It had to be someone. Maybe the private investigator?'

'The investigator? I can vouch for him. Solid as a rock. He's worked for me for years with no problems in that regard whatsoever.'

'You're sure your staff weren't poking around?'

'The file was sealed when it was handed to me. I handed it, still sealed, to Andrew. No one at the firm knew about it. He read it and handed it back to me. I kept it in my personal safe.'

I've always admired the way Ross can defuse a tricky situation. It's not what he says, it's the way he says it — calmly with a hint of firmness to indicate client nonsense will not be tolerated. Add the aura of legalese, a dash of trustworthiness and a pinch of age and even the iratest person becomes putty in his hands.

'From what you told me, you have every right to be angry,' Ross said soothingly. 'And regrettably Annie has taken the matter up with the body corporate. Not the details you understand. She doesn't want to be prosecuted for contempt, but she's said enough for the body corp to ask your landlord to review your lease. Not great. Especially after today.'

She jerked her head up. 'Please. Not more bad news.'

'I was about to call. You've saved me a job by coming in.'

See how good he is. Jess is doing him the favour.

'Ronald has found more discrepancies in the bank accounts which go back over the previous three quarters.'

'I didn't meet Andrew until November. No one can accuse me.'

'I never thought for a moment it was you. But I am officially advising you to stay silent on the matter. You can't say a thing,' Ross said firmly and slowly enough for his advice to sink in. 'Not until the investigation has been completed."

'You're kidding. Right?'

'I wish I was.'

'In the meantime, my photo gets plastered over the Internet, and some woman I barely know, is spreading rumours which could get me evicted. Millions of dollars are missing and I'm the one they're blaming. Me! I'm the reason clients can't get their money out of Vaultange,' she said, the tone in her voice rising to pre-tears — nine out of ten on the female emotional scale. 'To top off what has been the most horrific month of my life, I not only can't go back to work; I might never be able to work as a doctor again. What patient is going to trust a doctor convicted of manslaughter? The Medical Council will be typing their *please explain* letter as we speak.'

I almost felt sorry for her.

'Someone is setting me up Ross,' she said. I don't know who or why, but I'll find out. And when I do, I'm bloody well going first to the police and second the media. I don't give a damn whether the investigation is over or not.'

THIRTY-TWO

THE INVESTIGATION into Jess was Carole's fault. I would never have stirred up that nest of hornets but for her. Unlike Jess, Carole likes to talk. When she wasn't talking about her father or the professor, she proved to be a veritable mine of information about Jess. The recent Jess — she knew nothing about the past Jess. She delighted in telling the story of how they came to live together. Jess was a shy young doctor still living in hospital accommodation. Carole's flatmate had moved out. One evening when the ward was quiet, and they were in the staffroom drinking tea, Carole had suggested Jess come and live with her. 'Jess didn't think about,' Carole said. 'She agreed immediately. It made me wonder if anyone had ever asked her to share a flat before.'

Jess arrived with a small suitcase of clothes and a larger suitcase containing her books and computer. Nothing else. No family photographs or personal mementoes. Carole thought it a bit strange but soon forgot about it because Jess was so easy to live with. Her big exams were coming up and when she wasn't at the hospital, she was at home in her room, studying. She did her share of the chores, keeping the house clean and tidy and paid her bills on time. Carole did the cooking. Jess did the washing up. Sometimes they'd catch up, but

Carole did the talking, telling Jess about her life, her parents and growing up on the farm. Jess said very little. Jess had no stories of her own, no family. 'When you think about it,' Carole said rolling over to look at me. 'It is a bit weird isn't it. What sort of person has no family?'

It was weird. So weird, the next morning at the café, I asked Andrew how much he knew about Jess's background. 'Not much,' he said after thinking about it. It didn't take a rocket scientist to figure out what he would do next. Andrew was in love, he wasn't a fool. He asked Ross to run a background check.

The investigation was straightforward. I bribed the right people at the courts and the files (yes all of them) magically appeared in the investigator's inbox with a BCC to mine.

Tracking down the stepfather was more difficult. Along with the proceeds of the sale from the family home, the mother's insurance policy and the money from Jess's education fund, Bryan Randell had high-tailed it to Australia. Once there, the bastard lived the life of Riley. He had expensive tastes and before long he'd spent the lot on drugs and fast cars. The week before Christmas 2018, I found him in a homeless shelter for ex-addicts. He was suffering from an advanced case of destitution. Not only was he broke, but he was sporting a rip-roaring case of Hepatitis C. Couldn't have happened to a nicer man. Thin, jaundiced and desperate, he was a pathetic remnant of his former self which wasn't saying much. No hospital would take him and he couldn't pay for the medication he needed to save his life. Enter Henry Turner.

For the right price, Bryan told me what really happened to Jess's mother. It wasn't a pretty story but I wrote it down word for word, made him sign his statement at the bottom and had the shelter supervisor witness our signatures. Then I put him on a plane. Bryan thought he was going home to have his Hep C treated and walk his stepdaughter down the aisle. He'd done the decent thing and told the truth. He was redeemed. I told him I had arranged for a nurse to meet him at the airport. Murray likes dressing up and was only too happy to welcome home the prodigal Kiwi. Nothing more to be said.

The private investigator had already submitted his report when I got back. Lazy bastard. Andrew had read it. Not that you'd know. He carried on as before. The fifteen-year-old Jessica Davidson's manslaughter conviction, apparently making no difference to his feelings for her — none. I was relieved. The wedding had to go ahead. Murray would have had him killed in a tragic accident otherwise. We were in so deep by then, there was no Plan B.

Yes, you're right. I could have gone to the police and confessed all. I could have ratted Murray out. I could have disappeared off the face of the earth hoping the gang wouldn't find out I was the man responsible for the losses. I could have thrown myself on the mercy of the law and Andrew. I could have taken my chances, but I didn't. I was his best man. I gave the speech at the wedding and the next day I drove them to the airport and waved them off. 'Don't worry about Vaultange,' I told him. 'It's in safe hands.'

When I got home, I found out my best friend had changed the passwords to the Vaultange cold wallets.

That night when Murray arrived for a progress report, I thought he knew, he was so twitchy. I held my nerve and bluffed it out. Thank Christ, because he didn't know what Andrew had done. He just didn't want anything to cock up things at the last minute. He had the feeling he was being watched, he said, but it was only a feeling. He had no proof. Regardless, he'd stopped using phones and computers. Even cipher phones were too risky he said. 'Can't be too careful,' was his new motto. He meant it. Before we got down to business he had one of his goons sweep the room for bugs. The place was clean. That didn't stop him turning on the radio and insisting we form a huddle to hear each other's whispered updates. I wouldn't have minded, but it was late at night and Murray hadn't cleaned his teeth since that morning. I had nothing to tell him. He'd paid in all the money and was waiting for me to do my bit. Which I hadn't done. Because I couldn't. 'Yet,' I said. 'Yet,' I repeated, twisting sideways to keep him from grabbing my balls. 'It would be dumb to mistime the next part,' I told him. 'Let Andrew and Jess get settled into the resort first. I want them to relax. I want him to get used to not checking in. We have one chance to get this right.' He snorted when I reminded him patience is a virtue.

'You know,' he said draping his weighty arms across my shoulders, linking his sausage fingers behind my head. We were so close it was difficult not to stare at his eyelashes. They really are amazing. The deepest black and much thicker when you're a few inches away from them. He pulled me even closer, puffing his stale breath into my mouth.

'You know,' he repeated.

A line of sweat rolled down one side of my face. I kept perfectly still. The boys flanking him were playing statues. No movement, not even the bat of an eyelid, as they waited for him to speak.

'I've been lucky. Some people are,' he said as he leant back, his hands gripping my shoulders, his thumbs digging into my collarbones. 'I'm lucky. I get what I want — always. Do you believe in luck?'

'Can't say I do. I believe we make our own luck.'

He let me go and walked over to the window, his eyelashes curled in thick silhouette against the street light outside my house.

'I'm a patient man. I've let you call the shots. When you said to wait, I waited. I'm still waiting because you said that it's the right thing to do. But not now. Now we have a problem.'

How did he know? How could he know? He couldn't, I'm the only one who knows and I haven't said anything.

Murray continued. 'My clients need their money. All of it. Now. There's a big shipment coming in from a new supplier. A cash sale. It's earlier than we planned, but I have no choice. I'm under pressure. A pressure I told them, I'd share with you, my partner.'

Partner? What the fuck? Telling the gang I was his partner wasn't in the plan. I'd made that very clear when I agreed to co-operate.

'All of it? Now?' I tried to keep the panic out of my voice.

'Correct.'

'Are you mad?' I said. 'It's impossible to move that much all at once without drawing the attention of the authorities. I have to divvy it up and run it through multiple exchanges over days or better, weeks, to disguise what I'm doing. If the authorities get wind of it, they'll shut us down, and I'll end up in jail and no one will get a cent.'

I was buying time. I had to. Revealing I could no longer access the wallets would result in much pain and suffering. I certainly couldn't tell him about the ten million Andrew had advanced himself to pay for the properties. I value breathing too much.

'You can't change the plan this late in the day, Murray. Not now,' I said. 'Explain it to them. A couple of weeks. It's the best I can do. In the meantime take out a bank loan, do something. You have to delay them or the last six months will have been a complete and total waste of time.' My voice was steadier now, I sounded convincing.

Murray nodded at the taller of his boys. I didn't see his fist move, he was that quick. The bastard punched me in the stomach so hard, I was lifted up and off my feet before crumpling on to the floor, gasping for breath which wouldn't come. I swear the second goon took a run up before kicking me not once but three times. Rapid fire, steel-capped work boots straight to the gut.

Murray, courteous as always, waited for me to stop groaning. 'You're wrong Henry. The plan has changed. Now you be a good boy and get me out of this shithole.' He didn't wait for an answer. He didn't look down. He stepped over me on his way out with his boys following.

THIRTY-THREE

WHAT THE FUCK was I supposed to do? Was I afraid? Yes. Was I terrified? Yes. Was I really, really terrified? Yes. Could I do anything? No. As I lay there curled up on the floor I thought how much simpler this would have been if Jess and Andrew had never got married. Better still, if they'd never met. I should have sabotaged their relationship back at the very beginning and then I wouldn't be in this mess.

Andrew used to take my advice. He used to listen to me. Jess was the sole reason he stopped. If she hadn't been around I know I would have told him about Murray. Andrew would have known what to do and we could have carried on as before. It was her fault I was in this mess. She had turned him into a patsy — her patsy.

When Jess said he had to get a suit, just like that, he got a suit to wear to the wedding. He'd never worn a suit in his life. She also made him visit his mother. She even asked me to go with them. I thought why not. I was hanging around. I don't think she thought I'd say yes.

I liked visiting his mother. I did it often. His mother didn't care. She was living in the past. She remembered the conversations from her childhood and reeled those off to whoever was in the vicinity.

Even if they weren't. Her nurses didn't speak much English so her chatter didn't bother them. They would nod and smile, humming as they washed her down after changing her clothes for the tenth time that day. I'd talk to her about what I'd been doing. She nodded and smiled, and at the end of the afternoon she asked me who I was and how long I'd been there. It felt good to talk to someone who didn't judge, who didn't remember what you'd said and hold it against you later. The nurses assumed I was her son, I went back so often. So that day, when the three of us walked down the corridor to her room, one of them called out, 'Mrs Cullinane, your son is back.'

Jess looked at Andrew and he shrugged as if to say the nurses were as bonkers as the patients. But she figured it out. She told me I was a kind man. She actually said that. Kind? She has no idea. Andrew poked me in the ribs when he saw me blushing. Anyway, I poked him back, he pushed me and I pushed him through the door to her room. He stumbled, and almost fell on top of his mother. She put up her hands to save herself, wrapping her arms around him, holding him tight. Like a fly caught in a spider's web, he panicked. He struggled and broke free, standing up and glaring at her, his nose wrinkled in disgust. She looked so confused. Lost. She had no idea who the man snarling at her was. I was about to say something, but it was Jess who saved the day, taking the old lady's hand and stroking the wrinkly skin. Soon everyone was all smiles.

'Andrew and I are getting married,' Jess said.

The old lady cleared her throat. 'I have a son called Andrew,' she said. 'He's overseas.'

He got restless then. You would think, having been a patient himself, he would be more understanding, sympathetic even. Nope. He wanted to leave, and moved towards the door. A tear ran down the old lady's cheek, but he was already gone. He didn't see her raise her hand and wave and he didn't see Jess hug her. He didn't hear Jess tell her about the wedding or that they would come back to see her when they returned from their honeymoon. For a moment the old lady's eyes cleared. She smiled at Jess, the most wonderfully radiant smile, then it disappeared. She said she needed the nurse and we should go. I gave her a kiss before I left. The next time I saw her was at the memorial service.

THIRTY-FOUR

THE NEXT THING that happened was also Jess's fault. One morning, Andrew and I were having coffee; it was the week before the wedding. We were hunkered down in the café — together like the old days. Pete was pleased to see us, judging by the constant stream of coffees he brought. No sooner had we finished one, than another, the crema an exceptional rich reddish-brown, arrived and the old cup and saucer were whisked away. Did I mention the apple Danishes? Fresh from the oven, hot, buttery flaky pastry stuffed full of cinnamon flavoured baked apple. Pete only uses Granny Smiths. The perfect baking apple, always tart and tangy on the tongue. The sun was shining, the sea smelt salty and clean, the joggers were running along the waterfront, the boats were bobbing gently at their moorings. You get the picture.

Andrew asked if I was making progress with the bank. He needed to know before he left on his honeymoon. Had they agreed to keep the trading account open for the next three months and at what cost? I told him the good news. 'We're locked in for six months at a reasonable interest rate. The bad news is the account fees.'

'Easy. We'll pass those on as commission. We've had some big orders lately.' Andrew was staring at the yachts, not at me. 'In this last quarter of 2018 we've doubled our transactions for the whole of 2017.

Different bank accounts, different IDs but large amounts.' He turned away from the marina to face me. 'Know anything?'

Sweat rolled down the inside of my t-shirt. I was pleased I was wearing a loose hoody over the top so he couldn't see. 'Word's getting around. People see Bitcoin as a safe haven.'

'It's time to get out,' he said turning back to the boats. 'Not everything, but a good chunk.'

I almost swallowed my tongue. For fuck's sake what did he mean get out?

I was already hurting because he spent so much time with Jess and not with me, but I was getting used to it. I was coping with the emptiness when he wasn't around as long as we had times when we could be alone together. Like it was in the old days before Jess. I didn't make a fuss. I accepted that he loved her. This was new. By saying it's time to get out, was that his way of saying goodbye? Was he going to take his *good chunk* and abandon me? Leave me and the business behind, for her?

'What's a good chunk,' I asked quietly. 'And why now?' I really wanted to scream at him. I'm not important now you have her. Is that it? After all I've done for you? I washed your fucking underpants for fucking years and you tell me you're getting out, now, like this. I said nothing. I stared at the boats too. They can be very calming. It's not as if I could stop him leaving. He could do whatever he liked. It was his money. His company. He controlled the wallets, the trades, he could do anything he liked. Why was he telling me? I didn't need to know and he didn't need my permission. He could empty the exchange of every last crypto-asset and I wouldn't be any the wiser. Our arrangement, which kept things on a business footing, meant I got paid regardless. I'd be okay. Financially at least. I'd been stashing away a percentage of everything I earnt. Not all of it in crypto. I wasn't destitute, but I could be richer. The money didn't matter. I'd be fine — without him. What I'm trying to say is I realised when I was staring at the boats that I didn't need him. It was me doing him the favour by staying. Not the other way around. Memories of other people leaving me concertinaed one on top of the other — gate-crashing my pity party. I'd coped then. I'd cope now. I was used to being left. Abandoned. Tossed aside. Sure it hurt, but I'd get over it.

Did he know what he was doing then? I don't know. Did he care? Again I don't know. Part of me hoped he did, but part of me had always hoped he'd be nicer to his mother.

Enough of the cry-baby stuff. You can't disappoint the disappointed. That's how I felt looking at the boats. Then I felt grateful. Knowing how he really felt about me made it so much easier to do what I had to do next. 'It's your company,' I said when he didn't answer my question. 'You can do whatever you like with it.'

'I know,' he replied.

He meant it. He said getting married changed things. He wanted children. She wasn't keen, but he was and sooner rather than later. In case his health crapped out. He'd worked nonstop for years. He was tired. Seeing Jess walk into shops and plunk down real money for stuff that made her happy, had made him understand that life was for living and money was for spending. Having it sitting in wallets under lock, key and password, was no fun. It was strange he hadn't realised that before, he said. That's when he thanked me for making him take time off to go away on a honeymoon. He hadn't realised until he booked the resort how much he was looking forward to the break from Vaultange so he could (get this) *rethink his priorities.*

I was still screaming inside. What the fuck? I nodded and steepled my fingers in front of my lips in meaningful contemplation while inside my heart was ripping its way out of my chest, making like the monster in *Alien*. I like to think that on the outside I appeared zen-like, whatever the fuck zen-like is.

I had to do some quick thinking to keep the plan on track. So I said the first thing which came to mind. Take money out. Sure. Buy property. The rest came gushing out. I was making it up as I went along. It sounded so brilliant, even I was getting excited. Quality pieces which hold their value. Two — no three — more. Get it done before you leave. Overseas properties gets the money out of the country and into something liquid. Yeah, I told him, don't buy in New Zealand. Everyone will know it's you. You won't get any peace.

Overseas, no one cares if you settle with crypto. I offered to organise it. You decide where you want them. Just don't tell Jess. You've seen how picky she is with clothes, the last thing we need is for her to come over all *House and Garden* and veto perfectly good investments because she doesn't like the curtains. When I'm on a roll, I'm on a roll. I waited while he mulled over the idea or appeared to. Said he'd been thinking the same thing and had done some research. He'd email me the details later and could I go ahead and finalise the purchases. He suggested Gordon Holdings, be the purchaser. Smart I said when he told me the shares were all in her name. That way the houses belong to her, not you, but you're married to her. Andrew was ahead of me on that too.

THIRTY-FIVE

'Dr Cullinane, are you certain your husband is dead?'

Jess reared backwards. 'Of course, I'm certain. Why would you ask?'

'You made sure he was dead, how exactly?'

DS Parker sat on the other side of the table unmoving, uncaring and expecting an answer. Ross reached across and covered Jess's hand with his. 'You know better than that, detective,' he said. 'Give us both some credit.' He turned to Jess, forcing her to look at him and not the policewoman. It helped. 'Detective Parker,' he said slowly, all the while maintaining eye contact with Jess, 'is in her inimitable way asking whether you saw Andrew's body after he died. That's what you meant, isn't it, detective?'

'Correct.'

They were in one of the interview rooms at the Central Police Station. Formica table, plastic chairs, a door with a reinforced glass window inset into the top third. Scuffed black and white speckled linoleum covered the floor and extended half-way up the walls. Jess and Ross sat on one side of the table facing Parker and behind her was a darkened window which in some light could pass for a mirror. A recording machine, sat on its own table to the side, its on-light shining green. The room smelt of cleaning products and Detective Parker's deodorant.

It was early. Eight a.m., and so far it had been a shit of a morning. Jess had been woken by her phone pinging with a text from Carole, asking her to call. Jess, who was in no fit state to talk to Carole, deleted the text. Then her phone rang. It was Parker. She asked if Jess could come to the station, in the next half an hour if possible.

'Bring your lawyer,' Parker added before hanging up. Jess called Ross, who suggested she wait at the back of her building and he'd drive by and collect her. He had Gordon Holdings matters to discuss. In the car, he quickly caught her up on developments, telling her he had hired agents in the different countries to visit and photograph the properties. He expected to hear back any day. Slow progress to be sure, but it was something.

'Why does Parker want to meet?' she asked.

'I guess they want to bring us up to date with the investigation,' he said. 'I expect the others will be there too. Nothing to worry about.'

'Funny way to ask. Calling early in the morning and giving us half an hour to get there.'

'I don't think DS Parker is exactly blessed with social graces,' Ross replied. 'Odd woman. Strangely repellent.'

'I didn't want to say anything, but I'm glad you think so too.'

They were pulling into the curb beside the entrance to the station and he had been reassuring her that there was nothing sinister about the detective's methods when they saw the scrum of reporters waiting outside. Men mainly, with cameras and microphones draped about their person. Someone spotted Jess, pointed at her and in no time the car was surrounded. Jess, head down with her hands over her face leant forward into the dashboard as they yelled questions through the windows. 'How did your husband really die?' 'What are you going to do with the money?' 'Why didn't the hospital know about your conviction?' Flashes popped — lenses zoomed. There were so many people trying to get at her that the car rocked from side to side. Ross hit the horn again and again, at the same time as he drove slowly forward. The mob didn't budge until a couple of officers emerged from the station and took control, clearing a route and indicating that Ross should drive around the back of the station. When they reached the safety of the parking area, tall gates clanged shut behind them. Another policeman held open a side door and they ran inside to relative peace and quiet.

After dusting themselves off, they were led down a corridor, through another set of doors, and down more corridors to an interview room where they waited — and waited. No one came. Ross smiled ruefully and shook his head.

'She knew we were coming. The policeman who let us in would have told her we were here,' Jess said after another five minutes had passed.

Ross was about to reply when Detective Parker arrived, looking fresh and alert, and holding a cup of coffee. She didn't apologise or explain. She walked over to the recording machine, turned it on and then sat down. Ross and Jess sat down then too. Matter-of-factly Parker stated for the record, the day, date and time, introduced who was present and launched straight into her questions.

'You did see his body,' she asked again.

'I didn't want to see his body. I was on my honeymoon. I'm a doctor, I know what a dead person looks like. I didn't want to see Andrew like that. I wanted to remember him as I knew him — alive. His surgeon told me that he'd died. That was enough.'

'You saw him later then? Before the cremation?'

'No. I didn't. I told you. I wanted happy memories. God knows I had few enough of those in the short time we had together.'

'Which brings me back to my first question, Mrs, sorry Dr Cullinane. How can you be sure he was really dead?'

'What else would he be?' she yelled before she turned to Ross. 'What's this about? I thought we were here to talk about progress with Vaultange?'

'My client has a point, detective,' Ross said. 'We've come this morning at short notice, I might add, expecting an update. We didn't come to re-litigate Andrew's death. You've seen the death certificate.

You've got copies of that and the cremation certificate. Surely they're sufficient?'

'You would think so, wouldn't you? My problem is the surgeon who signed the certificates is unavailable. The medical director of the hospital tells me he's on sabbatical. Planned a while ago apparently. Gone to one of the outer islands where there's no cell phone reception, or even, unbelievable in this day and age, any Internet. He's away for three months, which means,' she paused. 'I haven't been able to have the certificates verified. There's that word ... verified. Loose ends, minor details, normally these are easily settled. But in this case, it's proving harder than I thought.' Detective Parker, with her hands resting on the table, looked at Jess. Jess stared back.

It was Ross who broke the silence. 'Is there anything else? Because if not ...?'.

'No. Thought I'd ask before the others got here, that's all.' She crumpled her empty coffee cup in one hand and threw it at the rubbish bin. It missed and bounced off the rim and on to the floor. When there was a knock on the door, she got up and dropped the cup in the bin.

Two men Jess recognised from the meeting in Ross's office walked in. As there were no spare chairs, one man left and came back carrying a stack of white plastic ones with no arms. He proceeded to set them around the table.

'Sorry we were late,' said the man from the Digital Tech Crime Unit. Jess couldn't remember his name and she was grateful when both men gave her their cards again. The one she couldn't remember was Adam Heath, and the other was Guy Harding from the Serious Fraud Office, a lawyer according to the letters beneath his name. Before they had a chance to say more than pleasantries, Ronald Barton arrived looked ruffled but pleased.

'That crowd out the front are a bit rough,' he said smoothing his hair back into place. 'Demanded to know if I knew you Jess. But never mind; rugby skills; they never go away. Shoulder down and barrelled straight through,' he said beaming with delight as he squeezed into the chair next to Ross. Jess sat very still, staring at a point above Sarah

Parker's head, while everyone settled. Adam opened his laptop on his knee and tapped a few keys. 'I gather DS Parker, has been filling you in on progress,' he said.

Jess was about to protest when Ross intervened.

'Probably best if you go over it again. Catch Ronald up.'

'I think I know most of it,' Ronald said.

'Right.' Adam joggled his legs to stop his laptop slipping to the floor catching it just in time. 'It will be helpful if I summarise the situation. While he rattled through a summary of Vaultange's obligations to its clients as set out in the terms and conditions on the website, Jess shut her eyes. He made it seem so straightforward but she knew from the emails that most clients had not understood what they agreed to when they had signed up. These were the inexperienced investors Adam referred to and they were only now starting to understand they had no comeback against Vaultange. Dismayed and humiliated by their own naivety, their anger, fed by the media, was being directed straight at Jess.

Adam continued. 'Unfortunately, Mr Cullinane made no provision for anyone to access Vaultange files and wallets, in the event of his incapacity or death.' He let silence emphasise his last statement before he carried on. 'Dr Cullinane inherited the company in a will made ten days prior to the wedding — three weeks before his death. At the same time properties purchased overseas were put into a company whose sole shareholder is Dr Cullinane. We have no evidence to link either the assets used to purchase the properties or the properties themselves, to Vaultange assets. Because we can't open the wallets. However, the search for a link continues.'

Jess felt three pairs of eyes bore into her from the other side of the table.

'We think Mr Cullinane used a hard wallet to store the Vaultange crypto-assets. Unusual when there is so much money at stake, but as Mr Turner explained, he and Mr Cullinane were planning to revamp the systems at Vaultange and bring them up to date after he returned from his honeymoon. The loss of client files has not helped the situation and we can't rule out the possibility Mr Cullinane himself embedded the malware. Possibly as a security feature as he was legally entitled to do.'

Jess opened her mouth to speak, but out of the corner of her eye, glimpsed Ross shake his head. She remained silent.

'My guess, for what it's worth, is that Andrew was so used to his own systems and processes, he'd forgotten it was there,' Ronald said.

'It's possible,' Adam said and was echoed by Guy. Jess saw disbelief flash across Parker's face.

'The forensic team say the laptop is munted — a technical term apparently. We can't do anything with it. Which brings me to the USBs you brought in, Dr Cullinane. The good news is we have managed to access some client information from the plain drive.'

'Fantastic,' Jess said and sat up straighter. 'At last.'

'It's slow, but we're endeavouring to match clients with bank transactions. Unfortunately, the records stop in September 2018 and we know a lot of money has been transacted since then,' Guy Harding added. He was sweating profusely in the small room grown stuffy with too many people sitting too closely together. Parker got up and opened the door, leaving it ajar. Guy pulled out an ironed handkerchief cleaned his glasses, then mopped his brow before fanning himself with it.

'How much are we talking?' Ross asked.

'Thirty-seven million — US dollars,' Ronald said.

'But there was only $176,000 in the hot wallet,' Jess said.

'Mr Turner thinks the system might have been hacked while you were away. However, without the data, we can't know for sure,' Guy said. 'We can only make assumptions.'

'Hacked? You mean someone broke into Vaultange? How?' Jess asked.

'The cold wallet was offline, but hackers have a way of finding gaps in the system given enough time. Once they're in it's like an open book. They access the passwords, the keys and the wallets and before you know it the assets are gone.'

'If they can get in, why can't you?' Jess asked.

'Good question,' Guy replied. 'One, it takes time. Two, it's expensive in terms of money and expertise. And three, the hackers change the passwords and install their own security, more malware normally, before exiting. We have to tread very carefully in order not to set anything off and even then, there are no guarantees. Everything about this case points to bad actors, taking advantage of Mr Cullinane's absence.'

Jess sagged back in her chair. How was she going to tell Johnny? 'What about the other USB?' she asked. 'The ledger thing-a-me. The Nano S.'

'Without the seed words, it's useless,' Guy said. 'We need twenty-four random words in the correct order. They could be anywhere. And judging by your husband's unusual approach to security, I mean anywhere. You've searched everywhere, and you're sure you don't have them?'

'No, and I've looked. He wouldn't have left them lying around. He would have put them somewhere unusual. I'll keep looking,' she promised. 'Have you asked the manufacturers? They must have a way of opening the stick. They made it.'

'If only,' Adam replied. 'We've contacted them but we're not optimistic.'

'So, what's next?' Ross asked.

'I've got a team on its way to the States,' Ronald said. 'If we can access the offshore servers with a view to tracking down the earlier transactions, hopefully we can build a database of the contractors who processed them. If we get to them quickly enough and if they cooperate, we might be able to track recent trades.'

'That's a lot of *ifs*. What if, they don't cooperate?' Ross said.

Guy and Adam started to speak at the same time, but Guy stopped and let Adam take the floor.

'We think they will. Or the ones we can find, will. The FBI is helping us as of this morning.'

Jess gulped. *Serious Fraud, Digital Tech Crime and now the FBI. How had her life got to this?* 'I thought we were looking for lost passwords to files and wallets. Why is the FBI involved?'

'They have expertise we don't. It's such a new field, tracking cryptocurrency. Out of our league, I'm afraid,' Adam said. 'Sarah, do you want to add anything?'

Jess braced herself, especially when she saw Parker flick a sideways glance at her colleagues, but the detective shook her head. The men started gathering their papers and putting away laptops. Ronald asked Adam if he could have a word outside about another matter. Ross left the room chatting to Guy about a charity dinner they were attending later in the week. Parker got up and turned off the recording machine.

'Is it you who's spreading the rumours about me?' Jess asked.

'Hardly rumours,' Parker said. 'But me spread them? No.'

'Do you expect me to believe you?'

'You can believe what you like. It's against the law to break name suppression,' she said. 'But if people want to do their own research, I can't stop them. You were lucky. Convicted of manslaughter and sentenced to three years in a youth facility, for what you did? It's unconscionable. And ten years later — your husband turns up dead and you inherit his millions. You might have fooled the others with that grieving-widow, poor-me act. Me? I'm not convinced.'

'You dislike me, don't you?'

Sarah rolled her eyes. 'There's a stench to this business with Vaultange, a stench that wasn't there until you arrived on the scene.'

Jess's felt her face burn. She felt as if she was twelve years old and had been told off by the teacher in front of the whole class. She tried to think of something to say, but the detective had already called a constable to come and escort her and Ross from the station.

THIRTY-SIX

As THE STATION doors slid open Ross put his arm around the young woman, whose head was covered with a large jacket, and ushered her down the steps. The press rose as one like a swarm of bees and surrounded the couple, with camera's high above their heads, and shutters clicking. The same questions regarding missing millions and dead husbands were yelled again. Passers-by stopped on the other side of the street to gawp. Reporters fell into step beside them, shoving microphones at the woman, demanding answers, photos, anything to get a reaction. While Ross and his receptionist drew the pack away from the station, Jess watched from the back of the foyer. He held the door to the taxi open and the woman got in, bent forward and put her head against the front seat, while he jumped into the front seat and slammed the door.

It had been Ross's idea to get Petra to act as a decoy so Jess could leave later, when the fuss had died down. The taxi pulled away from the curb and the mob bereft of its prey, dispersed. With her baseball cap low over her face Jess walked down the same steps before breaking into a run as soon as she hit the street. As she rounded the corner, she looked back. No one was following her. She slowed down and crossed the road to a café.

'A large flat white, please,' she said to the man behind the counter. The only staff member, it was just as well the place was empty. It was one of those hole-in-the-wall cafes — two tables, six chairs, a coffee machine dominated the narrow counter, next to a jar of crumbly biscotti. Scenes of Venice featured on one wall, the Grand Canyon on the other. In a seat facing the door with her back to the wall, she waited for her coffee to arrive. It took five minutes before the barista/waiter plonked the cup and saucer on the greasy table. A newspaper lay with the sections messed up on a chair beside her. She pulled out the front page and she spread it in front of her. The photo of her peering over the balcony looked back at her. But it was the headline underneath it which made her gasp. *Vaultange Hacked. Millions Missing.*

Mr Henry Turner, ex-assistant to Andrew Cullinane, the recently deceased owner and CEO of Vaultange, has speculated the exchange was hacked while Mr Cullinane was out of the country. Mr Turner stated it is possible that hackers had taken advantage of a lack of oversight occurring while the CEO was absent in order to access company wallets. The NZ Police have released the following statement: Police are actively considering the possibility of unauthorised transaction activity at the Auckland-based crypto-currency exchange, Vaultange. There is potentially a significant amount of crypto-currency involved. All the relevant agencies in New Zealand and overseas have been notified and are taking the matter very seriously. Police are talking to those involved to develop an understanding of what may have occurred. Specialist staff are being deployed with some urgency after recognition of the speed required to follow up any possible breach in data systems. Police emphasise they are not yet in a position to say how much cryptocurrency is involved and owing to the fast-moving and fluid situation, are unable to be specific about details at this stage. Digital forensic investigations are underway. It is not possible to put a timeframe on how long these investigations might take. The priority is to identify the missing funds for Vaultange customers. Having done so, we will do what we can to recover these. We ask that Vaultange clients make a copy of their investment records and provide these to the company website as soon as possible. Police are aware of speculation both in the national and international online community about what could have occurred. It is not possible at this stage to draw any conclusions. Investigations are ongoing and Vaultange management are cooperating fully. Further updates will be available in the next few days.

Where the hell did Henry fucking Turner get off talking to the press? Unauthorised transaction activity does not translate to hacked and he should know that. All the *Johnny's* out there will be thinking their money's been stolen. The police statement helped, but not enough to rectify the damage Henry had done. She drained the last of the coffee and replaced her cup in the saucer with a thump. Where is the journalistic excellence, this paper boasts about? No one checked the story with her — the owner of the exchange.

Jess stared out of the window at the people walking by, wrapped up in their lives, seemingly without a care in the world. What she wouldn't give to be one of them, worrying about what to cook for dinner, or which movie to go to. Which holiday to book or whose turn was it to pick up the kids from school?

She tilted the cup sideways and watched the dribble at the bottom pool in the crevice as she considered whether to order another cup. Sick of her own company, she wasn't ready to go back the apartment. The barista made her decision for her when he appeared from behind the curtain leading to the back, rubbing his hands on his apron, startled to see that she was still there. He came over and took her cup. 'Finished with the paper?' he asked.

She nodded and got up to leave. She was at the door when through the window she saw a light blue Mazda. Leaning against it was Ahmed.

THIRTY-SEVEN

THERE WAS NO BACK EXIT. She asked. With no choice she emerged blinking in the noon day sun. Ahmed stood up, smiled and opened the back door.

'I'm calling the police,' she said loudly so passers-by couldn't help but hear. Most hurried on, not wanting to get involved but one or two turned to look, one man even slowed. 'Are you all right Miss?' She nodded because by now Ahmed had his hands held high and was backing towards the driver's door. The man walked up the street slowly, turning back once to check she was safe.

'The crowd outside the police station,' Ahmed said waiting until the passer-by was out of range, 'I watched how you got away. Very clever. I thought you might need a lift home, so I followed you.'

'You were outside the station? You've been waiting ... how dare you—'

'You don't remember me, do you?'

'Are you trying to be funny?' Jess asked.

'From the hospital — two years ago. You were my mother's doctor.'

His reference to a life which seemed so long ago, caught her off guard. That life belonged to a different person. She hesitated, lowered her phone and studied his face. There had been so many patients. She couldn't honestly say she remembered him or his mother. His surname, on his Uber ID. Prakash, that did ring a bell now she thought about it.

She was back in the emergency department, but it wasn't two years ago. More like eighteen months. October 2017. She remembered it because it was Diwali. His mother was forty-seven, and plump; her long-dark hair was streaked with white, and tied in a plait which lay limply over one shoulder and across her chest. Her sari had been damp with sweat, the crimson fabric contrasting dramatically against the white hospital sheets. Her skirt lay open across her belly when Jess pulled back the curtain of the cubicle. Jess introduced herself and apologised for not seeing her earlier. It had been a busy shift, and as Mrs Prakash's vital signs were stable when she arrived, she hadn't been considered urgent.

A spasm of pain had flashed across the woman's face. She stopped groaning and lay rigid on the bed, her eyes staring wildly at the ceiling, her fist in her mouth stifling a groan. Jess waited for the pain to go away. Grey and drenched in sweat Mrs Prakash acknowledged Jess by raising her hand off the bed, then she closed her eyes and let herself breathe out. Three people were standing around her. They looked frightened, but there was no time for Jess to do anything other than nod in their direction as she examined the woman's abdomen. Something was seriously wrong and Jess swung into action. It took five minutes for the ultrasound machine to arrive and in those five minutes Jess inserted an IV line, took blood for analysis and paged the vascular surgical team to come to the emergency department. The ultrasound confirmed her diagnosis. If Mrs Prakash didn't get to theatre before her aorta ruptured, she would die.

Things moved even more quickly after the surgical team arrived and took over the case. Jess had last seen Mrs Prakash being pushed hurriedly through the doors at the end of the corridor, her trolley laden with IV lines and beeping machines. Three people followed behind, as confused as they were terrified by what was happening. She tried to picture their faces now, but she had paid them no attention, her focus had been on the woman, not the people with her.

A couple of days later, Jess heard the surgeon had got to the aneurysm in time. Mrs Prakash was doing well and was grateful to be alive. Good to know. Jess had thought no more about it. Saving lives was her job. It was what she had trained to do. Maybe it didn't happen so dramatically every day, but it happened often enough for her not to dwell on it. She had forgotten all about Mrs Prakash — until now.

'You saved my mother's life. The surgeon told us after the operation. 'Without Dr Gordon's quick diagnosis, your mother would be dead.' His words. We tried to thank you, but you had moved to a different part of the hospital and no one would tell us where. I recognised you the first time I picked you up at the airport. I wanted to say something then, but you looked so sad.'

Jess looked across the roof of the car into his brown eyes. Ahmed held her gaze. In truth it was a relief to be with someone who remembered her as she had been once — a doctor who tried and often succeeded in doing good for others. Someone who people trusted, whose actions weren't being interrogated for evidence of a crime.

'Okay,' she said. 'I know you don't mean any harm and I'm pleased your mother is better.' She glanced at him. 'Is she still alive and well?'

'My mother is so well she has gone back to Pakistan to see her family. I messaged her about you. She was happy I was finally able to thank you in person for what you did.'

'I'm pleased Ahmed, but ...' she hesitated then blurted out, 'you're following me. It's creepy.'

Before he could reply his phone beeped and he leant inside the car and picked it up. 'Headquarters want to know why I haven't moved,' he said. 'I have to go. I'm sorry.' He paused. 'I can see how it looks. I won't bother you again.'

'I'm glad you understand.' She turned and walked away as he got into the car. When she reached the corner at the end of the block, she heard footsteps running towards her. A hand grabbed her arm, and pulled her around. It was Ahmed, he was out of breath and puffing.

'You have to be careful, Dr Gordon.'

Jess raised her eyebrows. 'What are you talking about?'

'I overheard two men. I picked them up outside your building, the day after I brought you home. They were not saying nice things. One of them is a tall man. You know him. I saw you talking to him one day in the foyer.'

It could only be Henry. 'The other man? What did he look like?'

'Bald, ugly. Strange eyes. Thick eyelashes. When he caught me staring at him in the mirror, he swore at me … not nice words. One star — he gave me. The boss wasn't happy. His name is Murray I think.'

Ahmed had described the man she remembered from Andrew's memorial service. The man who had stood at the back, studying her as she spoke, and who left without speaking to anyone —no wait — he said something to Henry. She remembered now, because Henry suddenly went very pale.

'What were they saying?' Jess asked.

'It was not nice. A man does not repeat such words to a woman. Afterwards, I read about you online. You need to know that these men mean to harm you. That's why I have been following you Dr Gordon. To keep you safe. You saved my mother's life. I can maybe save yours in return.'

THIRTY-EIGHT

'Murray Chambers. Does that name mean anything to you?' Guy Harding had called asking if he could meet with her. 'Very informal,' he had assured her. 'Off the record. A heads up.'

She hesitated. She had just walked in the door with every intention of going for a swim to clear her head after the morning's revelations.

'A few minutes. I'll come to you, if that's easier. Would now, suit?' he'd said sensing her reluctance.

'Will I need a lawyer?'

'Goodness me no,' he'd said laughing. 'This is strictly off the record. Some things I thought you should be aware of, that's all.'

Jess could tell from the tone in his voice that he wasn't going to give up, so she agreed. She hadn't expected him to launch straight into the conversation with the name of the man Ahmed had just warned her about. Turning away from Guy she filled the kettle and busied herself getting mugs out of the cupboard.

'Murray Chambers?' he repeated, prompting her.

'Don't know him,' she said. Not a lie as such. More of a sidestep. Jess looked at the kettle wondering why it wasn't making any noise and realised she had forgotten to switch it on.

'Henry hasn't mentioned him? Or Andrew?'

'No, but I'm not sure I would remember if they had. Tea or coffee?'

'Tea, black is fine. The weaker the better.'

Jess made his tea and passed it to him. She had decided against a hot drink.

'We believe Murray Chambers is laundering money for a local gang.'

'Okay. Not sure what that's got to do with me.'

Guy looked at her, his eyes blue behind his glasses.

'Oh, you mean,' Jess said not enjoying the silence. 'Laundering money ... has he got something to do with Vaultange?'

'I didn't say that.'

'What are you saying then?'

'Only this, Murray is an ex-tax accountant. A good one. He was a partner in one of the big firms until he got greedy and helped himself to client funds. He was found out, which was inevitable. Give credit where it's due though, he was clever. It took a year to get the evidence together, before the other partners could confront him. They hushed it up, no court case, instant dismissal that sort of thing, but he can no longer practice. Barred from legitimate work, he offered his services to one of the gangs. I can't tell you how we know that, but we do. It was a small job. He did it well. More importantly he was discrete. Yada-yada. More work followed. Right now, we're watching him, seeing where he takes us.' Guy stopped talking and looked at Jess. 'You realise this is confidential information.'

'I promise not to tell a soul. On my Hippocratic Oath.'

He nodded. 'Murray knows his stuff. He has international connections in all the overseas centres — St Kitts, Cyprus and of course London. He's worked for this outfit for three years now. Steady income, bonus plan, protection if he needs it, respect for jobs well done. He should be happy. But men like him are never satisfied. Murray decided there was money to be made in crypto. Using gang money, he did well cashing out in December 2017 — more by good luck than any smarts on his part. What's interesting is that he didn't tell his clients how he was able to give them back their money, not only clean but with a handsome bonus. And that was after he'd kept most of the profits for himself. His clients were so pleased they gave him all their business.'

Jess was starting to feel uneasy. Guy was revealing a lot of very sensitive information, stuff she wasn't supposed to know. With no Ross here to protect her interests she didn't like where the informal heads-up was going.

'Our source tells us Murray went dark three weeks ago,' Guy continued oblivious to her discomfort.

'Okay so you can't find him. What's this got to do with me? I don't know the man.'

'I suggest you watch out for him.'

'Why would I need to do that?' she asked.

'We think, actually we know, he put gang money into Vaultange.'

'And ...'.

'And ... he can't get it back. My guess is he hasn't told the gang. He's waiting to see what happens.'

'My God, that's awful. What does he look like?'

'Average height, bald, your basic comic book thug except for his eyelashes. They stand out.'

'There was a man like that at Andrew's memorial service. He stood at the back and left early. I remember his eyelashes.'

'That would make sense.'

Jess had the impression he already knew what she'd just told him.

'We don't know where he is. You need to be careful.'

'Me? Why?'

Guy carefully rubbed his eye with one finger behind his glasses.

'Ever heard of the 501s,' he asked.

'Should I have?'

'They've been in the papers recently. I thought you might have read about them.'

'I haven't.'

Guy finished his tea and took a deep breath. 'For a long time local gangs, a couple of families, controlled organised crime in New Zealand. They kept things rolling along without much aggro until 2014.'

'What happened then?'

'A member of the Hell's Angels motorcycle gang was bludgeoned to death with a bollard, in public, on the main concourse of Terminal 3, Sydney Airport to be exact. The bludgeoning, by rival gang members, was witnessed by families, children, and law-abiding airport staff.'

'That's horrible.'

'Indeed. The Australian Government set up a task force to drive the gangs out of existence, or at the very least to make life very inconvenient for them. They applied the good character definition in section 501 of their residency act and before long, New Zealand citizens not smart enough to have taken out Australian citizenship when they were young, innocent, or hadn't yet been caught, were assessed and found wanting. Men mostly. They didn't need to have been convicted of a crime to fail the test; they only had to be deemed as *not very nice*. They were rounded up for deportation, kept in detention centres for unspecified amounts of time and sent back to a country they knew nothing about. A country that didn't want them.'

'Our government? Surely they appealed?'

'They did. The Australians wanted rid of them and the law was on their side. Naturally this came as a shock to the high-ranking, New Zealand-born members of the biggest gangs — the brains behind most of the organised crime on the East Coast of Australia. These bosses brought their international contacts, primarily with the Chinese and the Mexican drug cartels to New Zealand and their foot soldiers brought a new level of brutality not seen before in our fair land.'

'You don't work for the Serious Fraud Office, do you?'

'My card says I do,' he replied evenly.

Jess rolled her eyes.

'I'm nearly done. To say the locals were unprepared is an understatement. Gang culture changed overnight. Guns and knives, torture and contract killings, replaced baseball bats, fist fights and dumb luck. Drunken brawls and macho posturing were out. Professionalism, including the digital encryption of communications nationally and internationally, was in. Our population has a surprising appetite for drugs. Some would say astounding considering the price to the consumer. Drugs of every variety flooded in. Economics did the rest. It wasn't long before the extra supply led to a price war. People were killed. The police who'd been monitoring developments with every resource at their disposal went after the leaders, locking them up and confiscating bundles of cash, drugs, gold-plated Harley Davidsons, flash cars and boats.'

Jess looked up. 'Now I know. I've read about the gold-plated Harleys.'

'Indeed. The criminals had too much money. Seeing their toys loaded on to police trucks and hauled away was a bitter pill to swallow. Enter Murray Chambers. He started by channelling it through offshore companies which then invested in properties and shares. Clean legitimate money. Everyone was happy, but Murray got greedy. That's where Vaultange comes in.'

'You can't know that for sure.'

'Can't we?' Guy got off the stool, dusted off the front of his trousers even though they were clean, and did up the button on his suit jacket.

'You need client records, and the passwords to prove Vaultange was involved. Everything we can't find. I'm not a lawyer, but I know that much.'

Guy smiled. 'As I said, I came here today to give you an informal heads-up. I've done that. Murray Chambers. Watch out for him. He's desperate. You know what desperate men can be like.'

'No, I don't. I haven't met many desperate criminals on the run from a syndicate of vicious Australian drug lords in business with the Mexican cartels before. Certainly not at the hospital where I work. You'll have to forgive my ignorance.'

Guy chuckled. 'Thanks for seeing me so quickly. Oh, and for the tea.' He started walking towards the elevator.

'That's it?' Jess asked as she followed him. 'You're not going to offer me any protection from this Murray person?'

'Sorry, the resources of the Serious Fraud Office don't stretch that far. I shouldn't have come, the others told me not to. I thought you deserved to know, that's all.'

THIRTY-NINE

THERE WAS no one at reception. And no response when Jess tinged the bell next to the handwritten sign: *Green Trees Retirement Home: Ring Bell if No One at Reception.* Five minutes passed and she tinged the bell again. Nothing. The doors leading off the reception area were locked. From somewhere deep inside the building she could hear murmuring, then further away a trolley rattling towards its destination. She took out her phone.

'Green Trees Retirement Village, Julie speaking. How may I help you?' the operator asked dragging out the o syllable.

'Good morning. I'm at reception in the advanced care wing. There's no one here.'

'I'm sorry, our receptionist is sick today. Have you rung the bell?'

Jess resisted the urge to poke out her tongue at the phone. 'I have. Twice.'

'Oh dear, I'm sorry. Who did you say you were visiting?' Julie didn't wait for a reply. 'Let me call the ward. Someone will let you in when they're free. Is that all I can do for you today?' The ay syllable was sing-song-long.

'Thank you. You've been very helpful.'

'Thank you for calling the Green Trees Retirement Village.'

When one of the doors promptly opened Jess doubted it had anything to do with Julie. A small woman in a green uniform backed through pulling a wheelchair behind her. Jess rushed across to hold the door and the woman smiled her gratitude as she spun the chair free, then lined it up to exit through the automatic doors leading outside. The occupant of the wheelchair who was slumped under a blanket, hadn't moved.

'Look Mrs Wilkinson, sunshine,' the nurse said cheerfully in accented English. 'Fresh air.' The doors swished open. 'Elbows in,' the nurse called out. With a final heave to gather momentum, nurse, wheelchair and occupant, exited the building, swerved to the right, took off down the ramp and disappeared from view.

Jess ducked through the door she had been left holding open. At the far end of the corridor a nurse carrying a tray, stopped and squinted at her. Jess smiled, waved and pointed to the door of a room. The nurse hesitated, then nodded and disappeared.

Jess knew how retirement homes worked. Geriatrics had been part of the medical curriculum. Overworked nurses, many with minimal English, in the country on work visas, did what they could for high-needs patients with a sympathy Jess had never been able to muster. To Jess the destructive impact of age on the human body was both repulsive and fascinating. On the one hand the pathology was intriguing, but on the other, medical interventions to stave off the inevitable decline seemed futile and a waste of resources better spent on the young. She had been relieved when her six-month run had ended and she could leave the medical care of the elderly to others who weren't so conflicted.

The Green Trees advanced care ward was typical of such facilities with its scuffed beige-yellow walls, handrails and patterned carpet splodged with anonymous and random stains. Doors opened off both sides of the wide hall, revealing identically decorated rooms containing a single hospital bed and the standard wipe-clean armchair. A jug of water, a lidded plastic cup (with straw) and the occasional family photograph in a cheap frame stood on nightstands. Thin old bodies either lay on beds or sat sagged in chairs paying no attention to the wall-mounted televisions, where pictures flickered, with the sound on mute, and the remotes out of reach. Most rooms had windows, but these stayed closed, draughts being the curse of the old. The rooms on one side had a view, their windows looking out on to rose beds flush with colourful blooms. The rooms on the other side overlooked the visitor's car park, empty at this hour of the day. The omnipresent smell of vegetables boiled to gummy softness intermingled with the aroma of decline, and had no means of escape in this hermetically sealed environment.

Jess tried to breathe through her mouth. It didn't help. Her thoughts were with Mrs Wilkinson who she hoped was enjoying the fresh air. Jess was halfway down the corridor when she recognised Andrew's mother. Sitting in her armchair, with a white sheet across her lap, she was staring at the blank wall above her bed. A glittering diamond brooch held her dark cardigan together at her neck. In response to Jess calling her name, her mother-in-law slowly turned her head to see who was there, and reminded Jess of an ancient turtle she had seen at a zoo.

'I'm Jess Cullinane, Andrew's wife. Your daughter-in-law,' Jess said kneeling down beside her chair.

'I know who you are dear,' the old woman replied. 'You've been to see me before.'

Surprised she had remembered, Jess smiled. 'I have, with Andrew.'

'My son,' Mrs Cullinane said as she nodded. 'He's overseas.'

What was she supposed to say? No. He's not overseas. Your son died a month ago. Remember you came to his memorial service. Judging by the misty look in her mother-in-law's eyes, there was no point in reiterating the facts. It would only cause confusion. And if she did understand that she would never see her son again, pain. Better to leave it.

'He came to see me before he left. He gave me this.' The old lady lifted up the brooch so Jess could see it. The large stones twinkled against her cardigan. She crooked her finger. Jess leant forward.

'Don't tell anyone,' the old lady whispered. 'It's real.' She sat back with secret satisfaction etched in the lines of her smile.

She looked so happy Jess had to return her smile. The only precious gem she had ever owned was the four-carat diamond engagement ring stashed in her car for safe keeping. Jess couldn't tell if the brooch was real or not, but she doubted it. She remembered how shocked she had been to learn how much her ring had cost and how she tried to get Andrew to exchange it for something more modest. Something she could wear without feeling embarrassed when she saw patients. He wouldn't hear of it, insisting she keep it as a token of his love. 'A forty-thousand-dollar diamond is some token,' she'd said. When she asked if he could really afford it, he had laughed for a long time. 'If you're that uncomfortable, tell everyone it's a fake. They won't know the difference. But whatever you do, don't lose it.'

The stones in the old lady's brooch looked to be the same size and brightness as the stones in her engagement ring. There were eleven of them set in the shape of a rose. If they were real, Jess estimated the brooch would be worth nearly a quarter of a million dollars. That was impossible. No one gives something that valuable to an old lady living in a rest home, not even Andrew. Stories of staff appropriating items from their less aware patients were common. Who would be so reckless?

'It's magnificent,' Jess said with a smile. 'Andrew was a very generous man.'

'Is a generous man, dear.' Her mother-in-law covered one hand with the other in her lap and leant closer. 'It's really yours. He said you'd come and see me. And that I was to give it to you,' she whispered.

His mother sounded so lucid Jess was surprised. She was more coherent than when she had talked to her previously. But then, dementia had such mysterious effects on the brain. It could present differently in the same person on different days. It is well known that dementia causes memory loss and confusion, but equally it causes delusions, some quite complex. These can vary from the mundane to the grandiose and by their nature are almost always convincing if the listener doesn't check collateral information. She decided it would do no harm to play along and let the old lady believe Andrew had visited and entrusted her with a priceless piece of jewellery.

'It looks lovely on you. It suits you. I think you should keep it,' Jess said. Her knees were aching with the strain of kneeling and she stood up and looked around. 'Is there anything you need Mrs Cullinane? Anything I can get you?'

'Like what dear?'

'Toiletries, a new nightdress? Food?'

'Andrew brought me everything I need last week. Before he went,' she replied.

For a moment, Jess wished she could draw on the comfort of her mother-in-law's delusion. If only Andrew had visited a week ago. There was no doubting how happy the old lady looked. Long may she stay that way.

The room might be dull, but it was clean and tidy. Jess checked the water in the jug. A slice of fresh lemon floated on top, a nice touch. The bedlinen had been changed and the bed was comfortable. In the bathroom everything was in order. No mouldy walls or horrible smells. New bottles of expensive shampoo and conditioner were stacked on the shelf in the wheelchair friendly shower and there was a full bottle of Chanel perfume beside the basin. She made a mental note to check the prices for mark-up on these items on the monthly invoice. It wasn't that she minded someone purchasing these on the old lady's behalf. The trust was well endowed. There was; however, no point in squandering money unnecessarily.

A nurse poked her head in the door to ask if Mrs Cullinane and her visitor would like a cup of tea.

'No thank you. I was just leaving,' Jess said. 'I'll come and see you again soon,' she said turning back to the old lady.

'I'm sorry, I didn't catch your name,' the nurse said as she stood in the doorway, effectively blocking Jess's exit.

'Jess Cullinane. I'm Mrs Cullinane's daughter-in-law.'

'How nice. Your husband was here last week. It's white tea, isn't it, Mrs Cullinane?' she said turning back to pour tea from a large pot on the trolley. She added the milk and carried the cup and saucer into the room and put them on the small table beside the chair. 'You can manage without a straw, can't you? Don't let it get cold.'

Jess followed the nurse out of the room. 'Who did you say was here last week?' she asked.

'Mrs Cullinane's son. She's only got one son,' the nurse said as she pushed the trolley to the next room where she stopped outside the door. 'I didn't see him.'

Jess grabbed her arm turning her around to face her. 'Who did see him? This is important.'

The nurse pulled away from Jess's grasp and stepped behind the tea trolley rubbing her arm at the same time. 'I don't know.'

'When? What day?'

The nurse looked at her strangely. 'I'll get the manager to call you.'

'Is your manager here now?'

'It's her day off. She'll be back tomorrow.' She straightened up still rubbing her arm. 'I think you should go.'

Grabbing her had been a mistake. Jess had scared her. Wary and suspicious, she would tell her nothing. Jess pulled on her jacket, waved to her mother-in law, smiled at the nurse who ignored her and left.

FORTY

IT WAS A GOOD WEDDING. As far as weddings go. The bride looked beautiful. The groom was chilled. Carole refused to look at me much less talk to me no matter what I did or said. When I told her, I was going to Australia, she asked if she could come with me. I said no. I said I was meeting someone there. The discussion grew heated and you can guess the rest. A pity because she was a nice lady. Dignified. Polite too considering.

The happy couple left the next day, which was when I found out Andrew had changed the PIN and the seed words. Not for the hot wallet — for the important one, the cold wallet holding between thirty and forty million in Bitcoin and assorted cryptos. Anyway that's roughly how much was there last time I looked. Fucked! The plan was fucked.

I messaged him. He didn't reply. I tried to email the resort, but you needed a special passcode to get through their security and I didn't have it. Sophie their travel agent laughed at me when I asked her for it. Such a bitch.

The next time I saw Murray, a week after his goon kicked me so hard I peed blood for two days I told him the banks were getting suspicious and had put a hold notice on the Vaultange accounts until Andrew got back. I told him I didn't want the clients to find out, which is why I'd kept the website open. That lie saved my life — for a few more days.

It wasn't long before Murray really started yanking my chain. He ordered me to use other banks. I told him I couldn't without Andrew there to co-sign the documents. And I said I didn't want to alert our bank. 'The banks collude because they hate crypto,' I said. 'Crypto challenges their business model. The banks work with governments and tax departments to drive crypto out of existence. It's world-wide, not just New Zealand. They've formed a secret cartel. Big business and governments are plotting to destroy what they can't tax, profit from, or control, I told him. Hold the line,' I said.

Murray, bless his stone-cold heart, being an ex-tax accountant knew I was right. What paranoid capitalist, neo-libertarian, fascist with a conspiracy fetish and gang connections wouldn't believe me? He knew what the banks were capable of. He didn't trust them any more than I did and so another day passed. And another. He wasn't happy. Murray, the same as Andrew did, believes he has an inalienable right to be free and do whatever the hell he wants. Other people follow the rules, but not him.

It was the day after my last meeting with Murray that I got the phone call from Jess. Andrew Cullinane was dead. Jess heartbroken, shocked, traumatised, was coming home with his ashes in a box. Andrew had abandoned me as I knew he would.

Murray needed to assess the authenticity of the grieving widow for himself which is why he came to the service. Jess did me proud. Convinced by the silent tears of a broken woman, the woman who now owned the exchange, Murray said he'd keep the guys off my back for a couple of weeks — one fortnight. After that the widow better not get in his way. He didn't stay for the food.

Two weeks, better than nothing but not much. With the plan blown to smithereens I was having to re-group and re-strategize — fast. I'll admit Andrew's will was a blow. To live and work side by side with someone all those years, and to be passed over like yesterday's cold takeaways, was hurtful on so many levels. I could rationalise a temporary change in PIN and passwords as a prudent business move while he was out of the country. But to be left out of his will? That made me question our friendship. It made me question a lot about my life.

FORTY-ONE

WITH PARENTS LIKE MINE, hating the police was my genetic default setting. Programmed into my DNA and nurtured in the bosom of my dysfunctional family, overt antipathy for the cops was normal. The police returned it in full — to a kid.

Sure, Mum and Dad supplemented their benefit income with a side-line in drug dealing. Sure, they were bad parents. That was still no reason for the police to kick in the front door of our latest decrepit rental in Mangere at two o'clock in the morning. They could have knocked. Why trash the house when if they'd asked nicely, I would happily have shown them where Mum kept the stash? My parents were nothing but human refuse. Me and my siblings we were the spawn of that refuse.

To request an informal meeting with DS Parker was therefore one of the more difficult things I ever had to do. I'd never volunteered to have anything to do with the police in my life before. Thankfully, she didn't keep me waiting. She did keep the door of the interview room open and from the way she sat side on in her chair, knees crossed, barely able to look me in the eye, I knew she'd read my file. She was polite.

'Why did you tell the journalists Vaultange had been hacked?' she asked before I had even sat down.

'I didn't. I said it could have been hacked.'

A smirk escaped the corners of her mouth. Parker wasn't a bad looking woman. A few years older than me, curly dark hair, small nose and green eyes. If she'd bothered to use make-up, she could have been passably attractive. Judging by her clothes, battered leather jacket, black turtleneck jersey, black jeans and boots, she didn't care much about her appearance or the opinion of others.

'Vaultange customers, hundreds, have called the station, panicking, wanting information and demanding we find those responsible.'

'I'm sure you said everything that can be done will be done.'

'That's not the point and you know it. If you hadn't gone to the press with essentially a baseless and unproven speculation, we wouldn't need to spend time we don't have sorting out the mess you created.'

'That's not fair,' I said. 'You don't know. The cold wallet could have been hacked.'

'You don't know either and that's the point. The assets could still be there. You have deliberately stirred things up. Why would you do that?'

'It was me who asked for this meeting, I didn't come here to be told off like a small child. If you'll excuse me, I have another appointment to go to.' I stood up, forcing her to look up at me. I could see the hairs in her nostrils, her deviated septum.

'Sit down,' she said.

I stayed standing. Waiting for her to say please. When she did, I sat down.

'I don't suppose you know Annie Winter?'

'Never heard of her.'

'She knows you,' Parker said. 'She said you had coffee together.'

'That Annie. The one in Andrew's building. Yes, sorry I do know her. Is that her last name? Winter you say.'

The bitch was toying with me. She knew I'd told that stuck up cow about Jess.

'Does the name Stacey Allen ring a bell?'

'The reporter? Yes, I know her. We dated, two years ago or was it three?'

'Interesting.' Parker was nodding now.

I nodded too. I said nothing. I'd fed the hacking story to Stacey on the condition she didn't reveal her source. I trusted her. She wouldn't let me down. Parker was fishing. I twiddled my thumbs and waited.

'How much do you know about Dr Cullinane?' she asked finally.

'Dr Gordon,' I said. 'She hasn't changed her name. Not yet.' Parker waved her hand for me to go on. 'Not much. She met Andrew when he was a patient in the hospital. He wasn't her patient which I'm told makes it all right. They got married. She's an orphan, no family. Now we know why.'

Parker looked at her hands and waited. I hate that technique. The one where the interviewer says nothing knowing the interviewee will feel so uncomfortable, they will rush in and fill the silence. I hate it, so I know how to use it.

'At some point in time,' I said slowly as if I had only just remembered, 'I heard her say her stepfather lived in Australia. Bryan I think she said.'

Parker picked up her pen and started writing. 'Did she say where or if she was in contact with him?'

'She didn't. From the way she spoke she was in no hurry to find out. I was surprised because Jess hardly ever talks about herself. I suppose that's why I remembered.' I watched as she wrote Australia under his name and underlined both, before turning to a fresh page.

'Tell me again what happened when you opened Andrew's laptop,' Parker said. 'From the beginning.'

I settled in my chair. 'Jess and I arranged to meet the day after the service. We needed to get the exchange running again. She didn't know what to do and asked me to help. It was the least I could do in the circumstances.'

'And generous,' Parker said. 'Your partner left the business to her, a business you helped found. You weren't angry?'

'Of course I was angry. I was furious. But what could I do? My concern was for the clients.' I paused. 'I know this sounds corny, but Andrew was my best friend. I knew he would have wanted me to help her.'

'You're right, it does sound corny. Go on. What happened?'

'I could tell Jess had already opened it. I'm not sure how.'

'Did she tell you that?'

'She didn't need to. It fired up straightaway.'

'Do you know what she did or how long she was on it for?'

'No. Your forensic people could tell you that.'

'Go on.'

'It was fine, until we opened the Excel file. Then, it closed down — blank screen, nothing.'

'What did you do?'

'I was stunned. Horrified. The data was gone. I tried to bring it back until I realised that could make things worse. So, I left it and told Jess to call Ross. He said he'd call your lot.'

'What did she say when you told her it was serious? The first thing she said. Her exact words?'

'She swore, then she said, someone doesn't want us to see the files.'

'Really? Most people, would think there was a fault with the computer, like a flat battery, or that it wasn't plugged in, that you'd pressed the wrong key? The common reasons why programmes drop out, or don't load properly.'

'I see what you're getting at,' I said slowly. I waited. To give Parker time to join the dots.

'Did you know about the USBs before Jess handed them in?' she asked.

'No. I'd never seen them before. Jess and I searched the apartment. We didn't find anything.'

'You searched the apartment together?'

'Yes, we divided up the rooms and turned the place upside down. Didn't find a thing.'

'So, you didn't see what Jess might have found and vice versa?'

'I hadn't thought of that. But you're right. I didn't find anything. I can't say for sure if Jess did or didn't.'

She looked past me, at whoever was stationed behind the darkened window at the back of the room. Naturally, I had assumed the interview was being monitored as soon as I saw the layout. It would have been unprofessional otherwise and never, not for a minute, did I doubt Parker's professionalism.

'Thanks for your help, Mr Turner,' she said getting to her feet.

Was that it? Obviously. I stood up too.

'I'll be in touch,' she said.

I put out my hand, but she ignored it standing to one side to let me pass in front of her. Another cop met me at the door and escorted me from the station.

FORTY-TWO

I RETURNED to the townhouse once, after my meeting with Parker. She hadn't exactly put me at ease. The whole purpose of my going there was to dump Jess in it. I didn't want the police finding my computer. You understand why.

Remember the cop with the broken nose? The bastard had been Murray's neighbour back in the day. A backyard barbecue, too many beers late at night, two men one-upping each other with tall tales wild and true, and my name came up along with all the tawdry details. Before he threatened to kill us, Murray had threatened to tell Andrew about my hobby. You think he already knew? Sure, he'd paid for my lawyer, but he was too busy and too far away to bother with the specifics of the charges against me. He had no idea what I'd done. I wanted to keep it that way.

That first night when Murray broke down my door, I had a secure job at Vaultange, an income, a place to live, girls, money, you name it. I was living the dream. Even better, I had someone I cared about. Even more amazing he cared about me in return. I was happy. I didn't want it to blow up in my face. Andrew might have understood. He might not have cared. He might have said he believed in the right to privacy. I couldn't take the risk. I was ashamed. It was easier to help Murray.

Then Andrew met Jess and Murray sniffed opportunity. He already had motive. I was the means. You know the rest. Andrew fell in love and married Jess. Andrew went away. Before he left, he changed the codes to the wallets. The cold wallets I was going to hack in his absence and make it look like an outside job. Was Andrew being security conscious, or did he suspect something? I was surprised. Annoyed. Angry. But I didn't panic. Not then. Andrew died. Then I panicked. Murray panicked. I don't like my chances when Murray panics. I had to buy time until I could figure a way out of the mess. Jess was to blame for everything. That much is clear. I saw no reason not to tell others what she'd done. She could take the heat, not me. I think Parker bought it. Murray certainly did. He told the gang who already had their noses out of joint. Without the cash to pay for the goods, the big shipment had to be diverted to Australia. It wasn't the money, or the lost profits on the consignment which made them angry, it was being seen as an unreliable supplier in a highly competitive market. Not only that, but they had lost face with the cartel. The gang weren't bothered with apportioning blame, they blamed everyone. Me, Andrew, Murray and Jess. They put the word out on all of us.

Murray and his goons went to ground. So, did I once I'd tidied away my computer. Being in hiding was no help. I could feel them watching me, following my every move. Sooner or later, they'd come for me. If the gang didn't get me first.

FORTY-THREE

JESS OPENED her eyes and focused on her surroundings. Damp sheets wrapped around bare legs, her clothes scattered across the floor, a mug of cold herb tea on the bedside table — all testimony to her restless night — and sunshine. Too much and too bright. Annoyed that she hadn't closed the curtains before collapsing into bed, she groaned and rolled away from the smell of cold cranberries, away from the brightness, and buried her head in the pillow where Andrew's head should have been. He should be here, warm, breathing, smiling in his sleep when she touched him, his arms holding her safe. All she wanted to do was to go back to sleep and not wake up.

Damn his mother. How could she have seen Andrew? He was dead. He died in Fiji. She had carried his ashes home, and they were in the box beside the bed, the box she reached out and touched now. But someone had brought the old lady toiletries and perfume. And someone had given her a brooch and told her to give it to Jess. These facts were indisputable. A man had visited her and either he'd told people he was Andrew, or the staff had made a mistake, and assumed it was him. Either way, it was hard to take these explanations seriously when his mother had only recently attended her son's memorial service in the company of a staff member. Maybe the notice of Andrew's death had not been as widely circulated as it should have been, and the nurse yesterday didn't know. Maybe she was new. Maybe the blame for the mix-up started and stopped with her. The toiletries could be explained. The brooch less so. Jess looked at her phone. Seven-thirty. No self-respecting manager would be at work yet. She put the call at the top of her to-do list, ahead of worrying about Murray Chambers, ahead of the meeting in Ross's office and ahead of calling Carole. But not ahead of calling the Prof to talk about when she could come back to work.

Not since being sent to the care home, had Jess had so little control over her life. Those years of being told where to sleep, where and what to eat, where to live and where to go, had dragged by. Day after day of conforming, watching injustice pile on injustice and saying nothing, had been how she had coped then. Silence, keeping her head down, fitting in and doing what she was told. Silence. And being too smart to get caught. Not marked as a troublemaker meant she had been left alone and given the time and space to read and study — until she could escape — which she did. In the time and manner of her choosing Jess resumed control of her life, fiercely guarding her freedom until Andrew wooed it away from her.

Now her life was not just in tatters, it was under threat. Henry and his leaks to the press had all but destroyed her reputation. Hence the need to talk to the Prof. A friend as much as her mentor, she trusted his counsel. He would help her. He would back her up, as not only trustworthy, but as an asset to the profession. He could rehabilitate her. He had to or the last fifteen years had been for nothing.

She was less concerned about Murray Chambers. Mainly, because there was nothing she could do about him. She wasn't going to search him out. If he wanted to find her, he would. It was simple. If and when he found her, he'd understand she had nothing to tell him. She'd deal with what came next, when the situation arose. Worrying about it served no purpose.

When she heard her phone vibrating on the counter in the kitchen she hoped it was Ross with news of the properties. Knowing she could sell them and pay Johnny back was the one positive among a sea of negatives, yet it was still not enough to motivate her to get out of bed. She listened as the phone rumbled against the marble, waiting for the call to end. No follow-up ping, no message. Ross probably wanted to tell her the good news in person.

Sooner or later, she would have to get out of bed and sort out her problems. She had to be at Martin Derbyshire at ten. Hiding was no more a solution than running away. She groaned, rolled over and off the bed, landing on the floor with a bump hard enough to hurt.

Once she was showered, dressed, and the coffee made, Jess checked her phone again. There were missed calls from Henry, Carole, Ross, Carole again and Ross. No messages. No texts. Nothing from Green Trees. And no reply to her call to the Prof that she'd made yesterday.

FORTY-FOUR

THE MEETING WAS in full swing when Jess pushed open the door to the boardroom. Lee Smith from the bank was at the front — ginger haired and freckled he suited his Irish accent. He was talking through his power point presentation when he saw her and stopped mid-sentence.

'Sorry I'm late everybody.' Jess walked around the table to the chair next to Ross and sat down. They were all there, Parker, the accountants, Adam Heath, Guy Harding, Lee Smith plus two people she hadn't met. No one looked as though they'd had any sleep since their last meeting, stubble and red eyes, the norm rather than the exception — apart from Henry. Freshly shaved and wearing a snow-white shirt and jaunty pink and green paisley tie, he smiled at her so broadly, so openly, she couldn't help but smile back before she caught herself. Maybe it was because he was the only friendly face in the room.

Ross saved the day by welcoming her matter-of-factly then telling Lee to carry on.

A screen had been set up at the far end of the table, a stenographer was sitting off to one side. Water jugs and glasses sat at regular intervals along the table, as did small bowls of cellophane-wrapped peppermints. The light on the central microphone was green.

Lee drank from his water glass and placed it back on the table, away from his laptop. 'We decided it would be best if I started with everything I have in chronological order,' he explained for Jess's benefit, his eyes on the screen and not on her. He tapped a button and the presentation came back to life. 'These are the transactions in the Vaultange current or trading account opened eighteen months ago by Mr Turner on instructions from Mr Cullinane.' The red dot of the laser pointer zoomed up and down the columns. 'In total eight million dollars.' He tapped another button. By the time the red dot reached the bottom of the next column, the balance, which should have been $8,000,000, had been whittled away to $176,000. 'Efforts to trace the missing $7,824,000 have led us to conclude that it has been split up and sent to different overseas accounts. Hard to find, especially so long after the event. In the worldwide scheme of things, because it's only a small amount of money there has not been a lot of co-operation.'

'Can you confirm the bank's insurance company will make good the loss?' Ross asked.

Lee flushed red under his freckles as he considered his reply. 'Naturally, we hope to find the money, but if we don't then, yes, insurance will cover the loss.' He sat down and closed his laptop.

'And the AML team at the bank are aware of the irregularities in the account?' Ross asked.

Lee shifted in his chair. 'They are.' He replied as he reached over for a peppermint, popped the wrapper and put the sweet in his mouth.

'AML team?' Jess whispered.

Ross put his hand in front of his mouth. 'Anti-Money Laundering. Banks are supposed to pick up this sort of thing early.'

Money laundering. Guy had told her that was what Murray had been doing for the consortium. Guy didn't look up, his face steady and unmoving as the conversation proceeded.

Parker stood up next. She had spent time on her presentation. Instead of figures, she displayed a diagram in which arrows fired off in different directions from a number of blank squares. 'This,' she said, waggling the pointer in a circle around an empty square, is the trading account. The words *trading account* obligingly zoomed in, with whishing sound effects, and inhabited the box. At that point Jess switched off. The arrows and boxes were all over the place. Parker must have spent hours on her little display, and it meant nothing. The money was still missing. The client records were still missing. And the passwords to the cold wallet were still missing. Vaultange was fucked and all the power point presentations in the world weren't going to change that. Jess wished she hadn't come.

'Without the client records which we think were on Mr Cullinane's laptop, we can't track down who owns anything,' Guy Harding said. 'One of the contractors in Russia who processed the transactions told us Mr Cullinane bundled everything together at his end, sent it over for processing then unbundled it when he got the crypto back presumably to assign the correct amounts to the different clients. A less than optimal system in this day and age. Some, but not all clients have supplied us with their records.' He sipped from his glass of water. 'As far as we can tell there should be US$9 million in different cryptos attributable to these clients and held offline in the Vaultange cold wallet.'

Guy sat down and Ronald Barton stood up. 'As Mr Harding states, not all clients have come forward. An additional thirty-seven million in deposits remains unclaimed. This was deposited from overseas accounts, which interestingly have all been closed, most in the first week of February.'

Jess shook her head as the words sank in. Vaultange, the company she owned was a crime scene. Seven and a bit million would likely be covered by insurance — the rest was as good as gone. Johnny's face, pale against the pillows, flashed across her mind.

Ronald adjusted his tie and continued. 'We now know complaints about Vaultange were being made to the regulatory authorities as far back as the beginning of last year, but other than sending emails requesting a response, nothing was done.' Ronald sat down and tidied the papers in front of him into a neat pile. The stenographer stopped typing.

Jess pinched the soft flesh at the base of her thumb as the import of what she'd heard sank in. This had happened while she and Andrew were enjoying themselves on their desert island. He had to have known there was a shitstorm waiting for him when he got back. She put up her hand to ask a question. Ross pulled it down and leant towards her. 'Say nothing,' he whispered.

'I knew Andrew,' Henry said breaking the silence. 'He was a careful guy. He would definitely have kept back-ups.' He paused. 'Jess?'

One by one, the people in the room turned to look at her. 'I … I've looked. We both looked. You looked too Henry. We searched the apartment together and we found nothing—'

'Where did you say the USB drives were again?' Parker's voice cut through Jess's protestations.

'They were in Andrew's backpack. The manager of the resort packed it and sent it on after Andrew died. They were at the bottom of a side pocket.' Jess fixed eyes with Parker just as her phone rang. Damn she hadn't turned it off. She had to fumble in her bag to find it, the cheery tune filling the awkward silence until she did — Carole.

She tapped the screen, *Can't talk now, leave a message*, and turned it off. 'Sorry.'

'That doesn't make sense. Why would Andrew take the back-ups away when he could have left them with Ross or me?' Henry blustered. The others murmured. They could see his point.

'You'd have to ask him,' Jess said. 'Until I found them, I didn't know they existed much less that he'd brought them on our honeymoon. I assumed he would have left anything like that with you, Henry. You worked together. You were left in charge. He trusted you.' Jess paused. 'Didn't he?'

'Seems he didn't.' Henry stared at her. 'Not after you came along anyway.'

Ross raised one hand. 'This isn't taking us anywhere. I suggest we take a break to gather our thoughts. I know our stenographer would like a rest. Ten minutes, everybody.'

Ignoring the protests, he stood up, pulled Jess to her feet beside him, before, with his hand on her back, he guided her out of the room and into his office, shutting the door firmly behind him.

FORTY-FIVE

'Don't you see, that's exactly what they want,' Ross said as soon as they were alone. 'They want dissension. They want someone to lose their temper and blurt things out that they shouldn't. They'll have someone to blame then. It's better for them if they can implicate one of you. Preferably both. This is an expensive and complex investigation. I'm guessing they don't have the time or the resources to see it through properly. Henry and you blaming each other, takes the pressure right off them. They can put out a press release stating there are irregularities at Vaultange, but there is insufficient evidence to proceed with charges. Their honour and reputations are saved. They make a strategic withdrawal and hey presto, they leave it to your creditors to take civil actions.' What he was saying made sense. Ross really did have her interests at heart.

'Well, I'm not going to stay quiet and have Henry make me the scapegoat.'

'Granted that's exactly what he was trying to do. Think. Is he succeeding? Or is he making himself appear not only foolish but guilty? Everyone knows the Andrew-Jess timeline. They know you're a doctor. Not a crypto wizard, whereas Henry had access to the whole shebang. Stay quiet. Let him hang himself. If you try and back him into a corner, who knows what he'll say.'

Jess sighed. 'I see what you're saying. But what about the other thing? He's been leaking stuff to the press. I know it was him.'

'You're referring to your mother's death—'

'They're implying I killed my mother so I must have killed Andrew, ergo, I took the money,' she said by way of interruption.

'That's a long bow to draw without evidence. It was a long time ago and there's been water under the bridge since then. Don't let them use it to bait you. If they see they've hit a nerve, they'll think there's something to it and they'll go after you — the police, Henry, the clients, all of them. They'll stop at nothing to bring you down. That's why you have to stay quiet and let me do the talking.'

Jess bit her bottom lip and nodded.

'Ready to go back?'

She nodded again and they returned to the boardroom.

'Moving on to the issue of the cold wallets,' Parker said as she took the floor. 'I'm going to ask my colleague, Toby, from the DTCU to speak.'

'*Kia ora katoa*,' he said, puffing as if he'd just finished a run. Toby looked as if he should have been in school, not working for a crime unit. His face was baby-bottom smooth, he was wearing Harry Potter glasses and his suit was too big for him. He bent forward and tapped the keys on his laptop. A diagram appeared on the screen. 'We know Mr Cullinane transferred the client's private keys into the Vaultange cold wallet which he kept on the hardware wallet — this.' He held up the *Ledger* Nano S. 'Mr Turner confirms this. This was developed and manufactured in France. Offline, it's more secure than Fort Knox.' He picked up the stick and tossed it from hand to hand much as a baseball player would toss a ball. 'The cold wallet is most likely in here.' He tossed the USB into the air and caught it overhand, as if he was catching a fly. 'There are two things we need to open it. The first is the eight-digit PIN number, and the second is a list of twenty-four seed words in the correct order. Not all twenty-four are needed every time you open it. That,' he laughed, 'would be painful. To prevent someone just *having a go,* entering PINs and words at random to see if they work, the manufacturer installed a mission impossible type self-destruct code. Three attempts and if the correct PIN and correct words haven't been entered, then *poof.* Not actually smoke but as good as. The stick is rendered inoperable. It's useless.'

'Which means the keys to the cryptos stay in the cloud?' Lee asked.

'Correct,' Toby replied.

'And no one can access them?'

'On this particular Nano S, no, they can't.'

'Not even the people who make them?' Lee asked.

'Not even them,' Toby confirmed.

There was a moment's silence.

'How many times have you tried?' Ronald asked.

'None. I connected it to my laptop and ran the programme to see if it's operational. It is. Without the PIN and seed words I see no point in ruining any future chances there might be to access the wallets and thus, the keys.'

'What happens if the person who knows the seed words and the PIN loses the USB? What then?' Ross asked.

'The stick is replaceable. The PIN and seed words are not. Get another stick, connect it to the net via the programme, enter the PIN and seed words, *Et voila!* Open Sesame.'

'There's no guarantee that even if we can access the cold wallet that the crypto will be there. They could have been moved, or used already and we wouldn't know,' Parker said.

'Top of the class.' Toby pointed the stick directly at her.

'Trades could be happening as we sit here?'

'Correct.'

'You've identified some of the contractors. Why not ask them to go back to their trades — identify the keys and track them forward from there? I've read there are blockchain analysts who can do this.' Jess asked.

Ronald broke the silence which greeted her suggestion. 'Inquiries along those lines have been made in the US, but without more information, I'm not optimistic. The companies you're talking about are not only new, they're expensive and for this amount, thirty-seven million or thereabouts I don't know if they would be interested. They also need transactions to follow. Bitcoin is currently trading at three to four thousand dollars. It's cheap, there's no incentive to sell until the price goes up. Why would anyone attract attention for such a return? I could be wrong, but it's not likely,' he added smiling. 'However, as we have so little to go on, we can follow up your suggestion and see what turns up.'

'Or they could be lost forever,' Toby said as he sat down and put the USB stick on the table in front of him.

'In the meantime, I suggest we put out another statement. The police and Vaultange. Clients need to be kept informed of progress,' Ross said.

'Our comms team will draft something and send it over for your approval.'

After murmurs of agreement the meeting ended with a closing of folders and scuffing of chairs on carpet.

Henry left quickly, without saying a word.

FORTY-SIX

'WELL DONE,' Ross said when they were back in his office. 'You presented well, you came across as genuine and believable which has brought us time. Who knows what Ronald's team will turn up? The essential thing to do now is to calm the clients and let them know we're working hard to find their money.'

'Even though we're not likely to find out anything? Isn't that giving false hope?'

'That's not the point. Realistically, most know their money is gone. People who buy crypto and leave their keys on an exchange know the risks, and if they didn't, they do now. It's not the first time it's happened and sadly it won't be the last. *Caveat emptor.*' He opened a drawer in his desk and pulled out a bottle of whisky and two glasses. 'Want a drink?' Without waiting for her reply, he splashed a measure into each glass and handed Jess one. He drank his in one gulp and topped up his glass again. Jess took the smallest sip and winced as the harsh liquid hit the back of her throat.

'You, the owner along with the police have to be seen to be going through due process. That's all we can do. Once the fuss dies down, we, and you can get back to normal.'

'Whatever normal is,' Jess said. Nothing about the last month had been normal. She looked at the golden liquid in her glass and wondered what a future normal might be. She still hadn't heard from the Prof despite leaving several messages with his secretary before coming to the meeting.

'Admittedly it'll take a while. You're the best story they've had so far this year.' He turned the screen on his computer towards her. *How did Andrew Cullinane die and why?*

Fuck, fuck, and fuck.

Ross tapped a key. *Young Doctor to Crypto-Millionaire. Where's the Money?*

'They're not going to give up, are they?' Jess said.

'No.' He refilled his glass and drank again. Jess hoped he wasn't going to go for a fourth. She needed him clear-headed.

'I've been thinking. They say attack is the best form of defence. I think I should give an interview. Simon Abercrombie or Rachel Childs? Which one?'

'Neither. Stay away. It's better to ride it out. Say nothing. They'll get sick of flogging a dead horse and move on.'

'But when? It's getting worse not better. I have to defend myself and stop them writing these terrible things about me. It was like this after Mum died. It was horrible. The lies, the way they made me look as if I was a murderer. This time, I want to tell my story, my way. I've narrowed it down to Rachel or Simon. Which one?'

Ross pulled his tie out from his collar and undid his top button. 'Think about it. Once you contact either of them there's no going back.'

'There's no going back anyway. Which one?'

'Either would be fine.' Ross sighed. 'Simon is a member at the golf club. I haven't had much to do with him, but he seems okay. And it would look better if the interviewer was a man.'

'Why?'

'If you're going to do this and it seems … anyway you want people to hear the truth, not feel sorry for you. A woman interviewer can't be seen to go easy on you, the sisterhood and all that. So, she does the opposite and …'.

'You haven't seen Rachel Childs in action, have you? But I get what you're saying. Simon would be better. Will you ask him?'

'If you're sure.'

'I am. By the way, what's happening with the properties? Have you got the reports I asked for yet?'

'I'm assured they'll be ready any day, but you're right, it's taking longer than it should. I'll give the agencies a hurry-up and let you know.'

'Thanks.' She got up to leave. Ross skirted around the desk and walked her to the elevator. Just as the doors were closing he put out his foot to stop them and handed her an envelope.

'Sorry,' he said. 'The partners insist. They say I'm spending too much time on your case and they're the ones having to make it up to the other clients.' He took his foot away and the doors closed.

Jess knew what was in the envelope. She wasn't ready to see how much she owed in legal fees, so she stuffed it in her bag, took out her phone and turned it on. Ping, Ping, Ping. Messages filled her inbox. All from Carole.

Thankfully, the foyer was empty when she got to the ground floor, but she wasn't prepared to risk being spotted and bailed up by a member of the public, so she found a back entrance which opened on to an empty service alley behind the Aotea Centre. Standing in a narrow shaft of sunshine, she called Carole.

'Dad died this morning,' Carole said before she started crying.

Jess leant against the building, sliding down to her haunches while she listened to Carole sobbing. She thought about Johnny's smile, his voice, the way he said *Girlie,* his laughter. All gone.

'I should have called you back,' she said. 'I'm sorry.'

'It wouldn't have made any difference.'

'I'll come now.'

'Please don't.'

'You shouldn't be alone.'

'I'm not alone. David's here.'

'The Prof— that David?'

'He came as soon as I called. I'm fine. You do what you have to. I know you're busy.'

'I'll come tomorrow then. I'll bring lunch.'

'Honestly, there's no need. I'm fine.'

'You don't want to see me?'

'I need a break Jess. From you and the mess surrounding you.' Carole's voice faded for a moment. 'Dad was worried. About you, Vaultange — all of it. It was all he talked about. You promised you'd help, but he never heard back …'.

Jess listened to Carole breathing. 'At least let me come to his funeral.'

'It's on Wednesday, I'll text you the details,' Carole said after a long silence.

FORTY-SEVEN

EVER SEEN A WHIPPED PUPPY? That was Jess at Johnny's funeral. The church hall we adjourned to after the service was packed with mourners from all walks of life. What can I say, he was a popular guy. Jess stood alone in the crowd, no one spoke to her, least of all Carole. Jess did her best to remain composed. She'd dressed for confidence. Tailored coat, matching dress and court shoes, her hair freshly trimmed, the other women looked like drudges in comparison — until she took off her dark glasses and you saw her eyes. Red rimmed from crying, dark rings — a picture of misery. She hadn't looked that bad when Andrew died. I guess it was all catching up with her.

Carole resembled someone who had been hollowed out from the inside and nothing had been put back to fill the space. Losing a parent? I don't get it — the crying, the metaphorical rending of garments palaver. I guess her parents were different to mine.

Jess was surprised to see me there. I was surprised to see me there. I shouldn't have gone, given my need to keep a low profile, but Carole asked me to go. She said she needed me. I guess that thing we had was more important than I thought — to her anyway. Yeah, and I liked her old man. Top bloke, salt of the earth, one of nature's gentlemen. We often shared a beer while we waited for Carole to get home from work. He told me about farming, and I told him about crypto. I'm not sure who was the biggest liar. Johnny could more than hold his own in the banter stakes — his work stories were pure gold. Seventy-six and still with a twinkle in his eye. You could tell he'd been a lad once, before he had to knuckle down to married life. He talked about the things he wished he'd done when he was younger. The experiences he would never get back. He wanted to make up for lost time. The farm was off his hands. He was a free man. He'd done what all old guys do after seeing that movie, the one starring Jack Nicholson and Morgan Freeman — he had drawn up a bucket list. He wanted to make sure Carole would be okay financially before he went off jaunting — jaunting — get that — seventy-six — ready to jaunt.

The only tricky conversation we ever had, was when he asked about my intentions towards his daughter. I couldn't lie to the bloke, so I told the truth. He'd thought as much. We were good. 'She had a great fiancé a few years back. But she chose her career. It broke her mother's heart. She's too much like me — stubborn,' he said.

Then he asked me how to buy Bitcoin. I gave him the spiel I give to all the punters, then checked how much he wanted to invest. 'The lot — the whole bloody lot.' His exact words. I bet you thought it was Andrew who'd reeled in Johnny's four million. That's what Carole thinks. She'll never forgive Andrew for duping her father out of his money and for some reason she's got it into her head that Jess knew and didn't tell her. 'A true friend would have said something,' she said. Carole blames herself for bringing a viper into the family nest. She tells people Andrew and Jess inveigled their way into Johnny's head, spinning a load of lies about getting rich then suckered him into betting the lot. She even thinks Jess told her father to keep it a secret from his daughter.

Johnny wasn't stupid. He understood the risks. Damn me if that wasn't the attraction in the first place. Johnny was a natural born risk-taker. He was a spinner at the roulette wheel of life. He googled the USD Bitcoin graph, and as Murray did he too saw the highs, but he conveniently ignored the lows. I tried to explain volatility to him, but he didn't want to listen. Crypto was the fastest way he could provide for Carole and have enough left over to go jaunting guilt-free into the sunset of his life. Each Bitcoin another cobblestone on his yellow brick road. He practically forced his money on me.

When Andrew died taking every last trace of Vaultange assets with him into the furnace, Johnny got very anxious. I ignored his calls. There was no point in my telling him the same-old, same-old, over again. It wouldn't make either of us feel better. I couldn't tell him anything that wasn't in the papers. I texted, saying that Carole and I were over. It was a bit awkward to meet now, but when the time was right, yada yada, yada, I'd be back in touch. I'd added not to worry and that it would all work out. How was I to know he'd take it so hard? His heart couldn't bear the weight of his guilt and sadness, Carole said at the service. She didn't say it aloud, not there, but I knew as far as she was concerned, Andrew and Jess had as good as killed her father.

So, there we all were, at Johnny's after-match function. Your basic bog standard suburban church hall, double doors at the front, serving area to the side and a stage at the back whose curtains had seen better days. His farming mates had driven into the city in their mud-caked utes to pay their last respects. Foreigners in their own land, faces battered by the elements, these men spoke a language not heard in the city. They dressed differently too, for the weather and not to impress. A few got up and reeled off entertaining yarns about Johnny's general farming ineptitude. Made people laugh. Lifted the mood — for a moment.

Carole asked me to be a pallbearer. Hard, when you're a good six inches taller than the other blokes, but we managed. We carried the old bugger out to the hearse, then it was off to tea and sandwiches in the hall. Johnny would have been horrified there was no booze. Carole's decision. Smacked of self-punishment. She could have laid on a few bottles of whisky. She was playing the victim. 'Never thought I'd have to give Dad a pauper's send off,' she told people, before muttering under her breath about theft and hacking and disappearing millions sending her father to an early grave.

Jess heard what Carole was saying. She couldn't help it. The men of the land stood with their backs to the wall, their arms folded across barrel chests and stared at her, their upper lips curled in contempt for what she'd done to one of theirs. She stood her ground. Gotta' admire her. The whole time she was struggling to keep her dignity as she searched the gathering for a friendly face. I didn't look away quickly enough when she spotted me, her eyes suddenly alight with fury as she started across the room towards me. I turned to find the nearest exit. It was blocked. Murray was standing in the doorway, and his goons were standing behind him. Murray crooked his finger.

FORTY-EIGHT

IT WAS a funeral with grieving friends and distant relatives, sandwiches in one hand, cups of tea in the other. It wasn't as if I could make a fuss. I put my hands in my pockets and stared Murray down, and shook my head — once. He stayed where he was — by the door. He nodded. His goons left his side, pushed through the crowd quietly excusing themselves, their eyes never leaving me as they executed a classic pincer move to circle in behind me. Something hard jabbed my back. 'Nice to see you again. The boss wants a word,' one of them whispered The hard thing jabbed me again in my left kidney. It hurt. I stepped forward, one foot in front of the other — slowly. I was relying on them to stay close behind me. I needed them to be touching me as we progressed as one unit across the room, people moved aside, puzzled glances followed us.

I waited until we were standing in front of Murray before I flicked the caps off the needles I had prepared earlier. Palming two syringes, I took my hands out of my pockets. Murray must have thought I was going to shake his hand and raised his in response, sneering at me as he did. He saw the surprise on his goon's faces as I thrust backwards, and the needles pierced trousers — then skin — then muscle. I pressed the plungers — hard.

Wildnil is one hundred times more potent than your basic fentanyl. As are all drugs, it's available on the dark web, delivery syringes included in the price. Primarily wildnil is used to sedate large animals, elephants, grizzly bears and the like. At the right dose it will keep a full-grown grizzly knocked out for between twenty and twenty-five minutes. It's not the safest drug for humans. It works the same as it does for bears but more so, respiratory depression being common and sadly a lethal side effect. I might have over-estimated how much the goons weighed when I was calculating the dose, because they dropped like boulders off a cliff. Time enough for me to grab Murray, twirl him around and shove him on top of the men piled behind me. Time enough for me to yell, 'Call an Ambulance' as I ran out of the door around the back of St Luke's Church through the graveyard, bypassing trees and houses to reach the intersection of Atawhai Lane and St Luke's Road where I jumped into the taxi, which I had stationed there for just that moment. I had been expecting Murray and planned accordingly. What I hadn't expected was Jess getting in the back of my taxi, before the driver had pulled away from the kerb.

'Can I drop you anywhere?' I asked sarcastically. Her reply was pre-empted by the wailing of an ambulance travelling at full speed in the opposite direction.

'We need to talk,' she said.

'Okay, but not here. No disrespect,' I said to the driver.

'None taken,' he replied keeping his eyes on the road ahead. 'Where to?'

'Your call Jess. I insist we drop you off first.'

'The apartment will be fine,' she said cool as a cucumber.

I gave the driver the address and handed him an extra twenty when we pulled up half an hour later. 'No need to tell anyone where you dropped us.' As he took the twenty, he saluted.

The apartment was dim and airless when we got out of the elevator. I must have wrinkled my nose, because Jess turned on me, like a cornered cat.

'It's like this because I have to keep the windows closed and the curtains drawn to stop people taking photos. Someone told them where I lived.'

'Don't look at me. It was common knowledge this was Andrew's apartment.' I yanked at my tie and undid the top button of my shirt. 'Can we turn on the air-con?'

'Costs too much. I got the lawyer's bill this week. Sit down.' She pointed to a chair

and sat opposite me.

'No drink?'

She ignored me. 'What did you do to those men?'

'Tranquilliser darts. They'll be okay when the paramedics give them the antidote.'

'What if they don't?'

'Not so good.'

'You don't care, do you?'

'Considering what they were planning to do to me, no, I don't.'

'Don't you think it's time you told me what's going on?'

I almost did. I almost told her everything. Why not? Things couldn't get any worse and I was exhausted. I'd been hiding out in a shitty motel, eating shitty food, not getting any shitty sleep. Part of me wanted to dump the whole sorry business on the table and leave it to her to sort out. Part of me wanted her to listen, to tell me it wasn't my fault and that she was sorry for taking Andrew. I wanted her to tell me she understood. Part of me wanted her to help me. The other part of me, the realistic part, told me what a total fuck-up I was and that it was too late. We were both doomed. That part told me, it was every man or woman for themselves and to get out — now. That was the part I listened to — I left.

FORTY-NINE

I SPENT the night in the sauna next to Jess's precious swimming pool. I figured no one would look for me there and I was right. I wasn't disturbed. Not the best night's sleep I've ever had, but it wasn't the worst. A hot shower and plenty of clean towels helped make me feel human the next morning.

I was sitting on the bench in the changing rooms, a towel draped over my head and another wrapped around my waist, looking as if I'd just come out of the sauna when a middle-aged dude, my height swaggered in wearing an oversized Burberry. The coat looked vintage and he wore it with the belt looped and knotted at the back, wanker style. He muttered the usual pleasantries as he shrugged off the coat. I grunted from under the towel. Wrapped up in his morning ritual, he took no notice of me. After checking the time on his overly bulky watch, and undoing his laces, he slipped off his shoes and socks, and took off his suit, hanging it carefully on a hanger, his trousers folded neatly across the bar, the jacket on top. Fair enough, it was a nice suit. His shirt and tie went on to another hanger. Modestly, he turned his back, dropped his under-daks inadvertently presenting a flash of clenched buttock before he hurriedly pulled on his swimming trunks. He exited, whistling and swinging his goggles in one hand.

When I heard the regular slap-slap of hands carving through water, I checked the wallet in his jacket pocket. Driver's licence, money, credit cards. Bingo. I took the money and his bus card, both untraceable. In his satchel, I found a sandwich (ham) and a MacBook. The tie was not to my taste, but the suit fitted fine. As did his Burberry trench. Clothes indeed maketh the new man. I was out of there, leaving sandwich crumbs in my wake like a modern-day Hansel.

Pearl tried to shut her door as soon as she saw me, but my foot was in the way. It had taken an hour of bus and train rides, looping back a couple of times to check for tails, before I arrived at her workman's cottage located in the shadow of One Tree Hill, an extinct volcano, in the centre of town. The swimmer, whose driver's licence revealed he was Errol Parsons, had been most useful. I'm as environmentally aware as the next man, but using public transport when you're on the run had never occurred to me before. It turned out to be an inspired choice. Easy to see who's around, who gets on the same ride at the same time, who's furtively checking shop windows at bus stops. Much better than a taxi and because the buses are electric, I had done my bit for global warming.

I was feeling suitably virtuous when I stuck my size eleven shoe over Pearl's threshold. 'I've got nowhere else to go,' I said as she rammed the door repeatedly against my foot.

'Fuck off, or I'll call the cops.'

I dangled a hundred-dollar bill in the gap. The door ramming stopped. I dangled another hundred. The money melted the gold in Pearl's heart, and she opened the door. I ducked in. She slammed it shut.

'This is nice,' I said inspecting the joint. 'You've done well.'

What looked like a nineteenth-century wooden cottage on the outside was a fully modernised, sleek, white, Scandinavian redo on the inside. Timber floorboards had been polished to a honeyed patina and ran the length of the open-plan, living-dining area which extended to a landscaped garden surrounded on all sides by a high-brick wall. A kitchen was tucked into one side of the living room. The door to the master bedroom was next to the kitchen. There was a good-sized bathroom beside that. Simple but elegant and beautifully furnished with expensive European pieces.

'Your hair looks different,' I said.

'It's not,' she replied.

I looked at her again. She was right. On a good day she could have passed for a young Liza Minnelli. The movie star — she was in Cabaret. I don't know if she's still alive but she had a great voice. Pearl looked just like her, short dark hair, big eyes made bigger with eyeliner and big lips. Instead of fishnet tights and high heels like Liza always wore, she was wearing jeans, a t-shirt and Birkenstocks. Mother earth meets pre-war German artiste.

I checked every inch of that house. I didn't want to be surprised by a partner or housemate popping back from wherever with period pain or a migraine. One toothbrush, and the king-sized bed had a dent on one side of the mattress. I emerged from the bathroom, to find the bitch with her phone, thumbs flying, texting. I dived across the sofa and batted it from her hand. It landed on the floor, the screen cracking on impact.

'Work, I was texting work, to tell them I won't be in today,' she screamed.

I retrieved the phone and read the text. She was telling the truth.

'How much trouble are you in?' she asked.

I shrugged.

'That much.' It wasn't a question.

'Same blokes?'

'Yup.'

'You came to me after what they did? You're a fucking arsehole.' The fear in her voice was justifiable. I knew what they'd done to her. We both knew what they would do to her. I should have done the decent thing and left, but I had nowhere else to go. So, I lied. 'I'm working on the basis that they don't know where I am.'

'They'll find out. People like that always do.'

She had a point, which wasn't in my best interest to concede to.

Not aloud anyway. I used the oldest trick in the book. Distraction. 'Any food? I'm starving.'

She opened her mouth to speak, but unable to find the words, gave up, staring at me instead with dead eyes. I almost relented and left her to her new life of anonymity — almost — but no. My fear trumped hers. I walked into the kitchen and took eggs, milk and bread out of the refrigerator. 'Scrambled or poached?' I asked.

'Scrambled. Then you go.'

'A few days, that's all I need. To sort stuff out online. Can I use your laptop?'

Pearl smiled, not a happy smile, but a rueful, resigned smile. She knew I wouldn't leave without a fight. She went to the front door and slid internal bolts closed, top and bottom. Next, she locked the doors to the garden and closed the blinds. I heard her bolt windows in the bathroom and bedroom. We were locked in, and for both our sakes I hoped the world and Murray's goons were locked out.

I cracked the eggs into the pan, added milk and over a low heat, stirred gently adding a pinch of salt as they started to gel. The toaster popped just as Pearl came out of her bedroom carrying three baseball bats. The eggs were nearly ready. I plated the toast, watching as she put a bat by each door, front and back. She pushed the third one behind the cushions on her sofa.

'Butter or margarine?' I asked, seeing both in the refrigerator.

'Butter. High cholesterol is the least of my worries.'

FIFTY

EXACTLY ONE HOUR after Henry left, Parker arrived. Jess was surprised it took her so long. 'So, this is how the one per cent live,' she said settling into the same chair Henry had so recently vacated. 'Impressive.'

'Isn't it? Nothing like the care homes I lived in as a teenager.'

The detective ignored the reference, flipping pages in her notebook until she found what she was looking for. 'You were seen leaving the funeral after two men were assaulted. You were running after Henry Turner and you got into a taxi with him,' she said.

Jess waited.

'He's wanted for questioning regarding the assaults. Do you know where he is?'

Jess looked down at her nails and then up at the detective.

'Well?'

'No.'

'You're sure? Because if you do know where he is and you don't tell me you'll be charged as an accessory to attempted murder and aiding a fugitive. If you're convicted, you'll go to prison.'

'I don't know where he is.'

Parker leant forward in her seat. 'You left with him.'

'I followed him. There's a difference,' Jess said placing her hands on the table. 'I was never with him. I needed to ask him about the money.'

'And?'

'He wasn't in the mood to talk. How are the men by the way?'

'They'll live. A doctor and Carole did CPR until the paramedics arrived. You saw what happened?'

'From the other side of the room.'

'You followed Henry instead of helping?'

'Carole and the Prof were there. I knew they'd cope. Henry had been avoiding me, not answering my calls.'

The detective undid her top button. 'It's very hot in here,' she said fluffing her shirt out from the waistband of her trousers. 'Do you think you could open the windows, or turn on the air con?'

Jess didn't move. 'Really? I've grown used to having everything closed — the paparazzi ...'.

Parker shut her eyes and sighed. 'Okay. Why do you think he attacked those men?'

'I assume it's something to with the short guy — the one with the eyelashes.'

'Murray Chambers. That's the eyelash man's name. White collar crim involved with some bad people.'

It was unusual for Parker to be so forthcoming. Clumsy. *If only the bloody woman would pack up her stupid notebook and leave.* She must realise Jess wasn't going to say anything without her lawyer present.

'Do you know Murray Chambers?'

Startled, Jess asked her to repeat the question.

Parker was fanning herself with her notebook, sweat beads visible on her top lip. 'Do you know Murray Chambers?'

'Never heard of him,' Jess replied. Parker seemed to accept her denial, which means Guy Harding hadn't told her he had been to see her.

'Henry didn't say anything in the taxi?'

'He wasn't happy that I followed him. We came here because he had nowhere else to go. He didn't stay long — a few minutes. He left an hour ago. I don't know where he went and I don't want to know.'

'So, you won't mind if I look around?'

'Do you have a search warrant?'

'I don't.' Parker inched forward in the chair unpeeling her trousers from her legs with two fingers, and flapping her arms when she stood up; the smell of deodorant mingled with perspiration joined the air between them. 'I can get one and come back if that's what you'd prefer.'

Suddenly Jess was sick of playing games. 'No. Look around. I've got nothing to hide.' She wanted it over, the detective off her back and gone. 'Fill your boots, look anywhere you goddamned like.' Jess waited, resisting the urge to open the windows and wash the place with fresh air as she listened to drawers and cupboards opening and closing in empty rooms.

'None of this looks good for you,' Parker said when she returned.

'When you say *this*, what are you referring to exactly?'

'Everything. Your husband dying so mysteriously and so quickly, Vaultange, the missing wallets, the empty bank accounts. Henry doing a runner after trying to kill two men. And you. Right behind him, sharing a car, him coming back to your place before he disappears.'

'We've been over this. I let you search the apartment. I've answered your questions and I'm tired. Anything else and I want to have my lawyer present.' Jess picked up Parker's bag and notebook from the table and handed them to her. The same height, they stood face to face. Parker was the first to look away.

The elevator doors were closing when Parker called out. 'You know more about your husband's death than you're letting on. Don't think you're going to get away with it.' The doors closed. Jess watched the numbers count down to the basement.

FIFTY-ONE

EXACTLY FIVE HOURS after Jess took one of Andrew's sleeping tablets she opened her eyes. She didn't remember dreaming. She didn't remember sleeping, but she felt better, more like her old self. For the first time in weeks she was looking forward to the day ahead. Parker, Henry, Guy, Carole, even Johnny — all of them had been dictating the agenda for too long. Today she was going to take back control of her life. She was no longer a teenager, she was a grown woman, and it was time she acted like one.

Jess almost marched out of the bathroom, she felt so positive about what she was going to do. First on her agenda was a meeting with the Prof whether he liked it or not. Then she needed to make things right with Carole because a future without her friend was a very bleak prospect indeed. She would talk with her face to face and try to get her to listen. If she couldn't convince her best friend she was innocent, how could she expect to convince anyone else.

Ahmed was yawning when she yanked open the door and climbed into the Mazda. Judging by the smell and the stubble on his chin, he'd spent the night in the car outside the main entrance to her building. Any self-respecting criminal would have spotted him and his blue Mazda a mile away and used the back entrance if they had wanted to get to her. Nevertheless, it was nice to know someone in the world was looking out for her, no matter how inefficiently.

'Take me to the hospital please,' she said. 'Then go home and get some sleep. You look exhausted.'

'I'm fine,' Ahmed said as he stifled another yawn. He rubbed his face, turned the key, then just missed a pedestrian as he pulled out into the morning traffic.

'On medical grounds alone, you shouldn't be driving. I'm more at risk from you falling asleep at the wheel than I am from being attacked.'

He glanced in the rear-vision mirror and their eyes met, his questioning, hers reassuring. He turned up the radio and drove.

Surprised to see her, the professor's secretary Janice, efficient and fifty, got up and quickly shut the door to his office. Back at her desk she fumbled in the diary beside her keyboard, and finding the correct page made a show of looking for Jess's name in the appointment section.

'Did the professor ask you to come in this morning Dr Gordon because he hasn't told me? He's busy all day, I'm afraid.'

'It's Dr Cullinane now. And no, he didn't ask to see me. I've been asking to see him and since I haven't heard from him I thought I'd pop in on the off chance. I know he does his writing in the morning and I was hoping he could spare a few minutes.' Without waiting for a reply, Jess moved quickly to his door, opened it, walked in, and shut it behind her in Janice's startled face.

'Jess, how nice to see you,' he said looking up from his desk. The Prof was one of those men who gets better looking with age. The extra weight filling out his face, the sleek haircut, designer glasses, the gym three times a week. No wonder he was popular with the female staff. As he stood up, he pointed to the chair in front of his desk. 'Do sit down.' He made a show of looking at his watch. 'I haven't got much time, as Janice will no doubt have mentioned. Zoom meeting in five. You know how it is.'

'I'll be brief. We can talk about what happened yesterday another time. I want to know when I can come back to work? There's nothing for me to do at Vaultange. It's silly for the others to have to work double shifts, when I could be back on the wards. I've left messages but ...'

'The Medical Council hasn't been in touch?'

'About what?'

'Come on. You're not stupid. You know how the system works.'

'No one has contacted me about anything.'

'They should have.' He looked at his watch again. 'I really do have a Zoom meeting.'

'In five minutes.'

He took a deep breath and leant forward with both arms on his desk. 'The hospital has lodged a formal complaint. This means your licence to practice has been suspended pending a hearing of the Professional Conduct Committee. You need to contact your medical defence solicitor and take advice.'

She had been half-expecting it, but to hear it like this from him of all people was a shock. For a moment she thought he might relent and talk to her as a human being, but that moment passed. It was obvious from his demeanour that no quarter would be given for her transgressions no matter how long ago they had occurred or what the reasons for them might be. He re-positioned his laptop in front of him and started writing.

Silence fell. He didn't get up and see her out. Outside, she asked Janice to look out for any mail addressed to her and to forward it on. Janice grudgingly pushed a piece of paper across her desk and asked Jess to write down her details. Jess's normally even handwriting looked as shaky as she felt. It took all of her self-control not to cry. Embarrassed, Janice managed a curt goodbye then returned to her task of setting up the Zoom meeting.

Jess banged on Carole's front door until she opened it. It took her another five minutes of fast talking before Carole would let her in and even then, she kept Jess standing in the hall, the door wide open behind her. Jess told her about her mother and Bryan. She explained why she had run after Henry and over and over she said how sorry she was. Finally, when she ran out of things to say she stopped.

With her arms crossed, and her head down, Carole was silent.

'The point is,' she said just as Jess was about to give up and leave. 'It's too late. We spent two years living in each other's pockets and you said nothing all that time. I thought we were friends.'

'We were.' Jess stopped and corrected herself. 'We are friends.'

'Really? When all this time, you've been living a lie? I can't tell you what it did to Johnny. He was distraught. He gave up. He just gave up.'

'I should have told you. But I honestly thought it was behind me. I'd blocked it out. I thought I would never have to think about it again. No one believed me after it happened, no matter what I said. They believed Bryan. He was the one who was crying. I couldn't cry, I kept hoping Mum would come back. I gave up trying to explain. Let people think the worst of Jessica Davidson, she's not me, I thought. And when they changed my name and I became Jess Gordon, it was as though I was a new person. I didn't have to explain anything to anybody.'

'I'm sorry. I'd like to believe you. But I can't because I don't trust you.'

'I did not kill Andrew. I did not steal from Vaultange. At least believe that. I am trying to find out what happened. So are the police, the accountants, the banks. It's costing a fortune. There is money, not a lot, but I promise I'll use whatever the lawyers don't take, and I will pay you back.'

Carole looked down and stubbed her toe on the edge of the rug.

'Look at me Carole,' Jess pleaded. 'You're my only friend in the world.'

Carole bent down and plucked a loose strand of wool from the rug.

'I suppose I can't blame you for what Andrew did.'

Jess breathed out slowly. It wasn't much, but that one sentence was better than nothing. It gave her hope that maybe, just maybe their friendship could be salvaged. It would never be the same. How could it be? But if Carole stayed in her life, right now that would be enough.

FIFTY-TWO

MINDY WATSON, MBA (Hons), Director, Green Trees Retirement Village Inc. said the sign on the door. Jess knocked and waited. A few moments later the door opened. Mindy Watson was younger than Jess had expected. With short dark hair, glasses, a pale complexion, and sharp features, she was slim and suited the simple long-sleeve dress and white Vejas sneakers she was wearing. Jess reserved judgement on the ear studs.

'Dr Cullinane. I've been hoping you would drop by. I recognise you from your photo. You look better in person,' she said with a smile. 'Come in and take a seat.' Mindy indicated one of the two armchairs facing each other across a low table at the far end of her large office.

'My predecessor's taste, not mine,' Mindy said by way of explaining the beige carpet, gold mirrors and flower-patterned upholstery on over-stuffed chairs. A mahogany desk resplendent with two antique lamps sat stolidly in a bay window draped floor to ceiling with fine net curtains. Mindy's phone and laptop looked small and out of place on the dark-wooden surface. 'I moved in a month ago and it's taken that long to get everything organised, but this old-lady shit goes tomorrow. I can't wait. It's driving me nuts. Come back in a week. I guarantee you won't recognise the place. Now ... can I get you something to drink, tea, coffee?' she said.

'Thank you, no,' Jess said taking the chair closest to the door.

Mindy sat down opposite her and crossed her legs. 'It's good to meet Mrs Cullinane's trustee in person. You visited yesterday and she recognised you I hear?'

'She did. We've only met twice before. A surprise because I understand she has advanced dementia.'

'She does. At least that's what her old GP diagnosed her with ten years ago. He's retired and she has a new doctor now. A younger man, as I'm sure you know.'

Jess felt instantly guilty. As her mother-in-law's trustee she should have known about the changeover, but she didn't.

'Her new GP thinks the cognitive decline has been caused by the excessive amounts of tranquillisers prescribed by her previous doctor. He's recommended reducing the dose over three months, and so far, fingers crossed, it seems to be helping. She's more with it. You saw for yourself yesterday.'

Jess nodded.

'Even better, she's starting to look after herself. For example, she had the catheter taken out a week ago and has been fully continent ever since. A godsend for everyone. Do you know how many old ladies die of urinary tract infections caused by catheters?' She stopped and put her hand to her mouth. 'Silly me. You're a physician, of course, you know.'

Jess smiled. 'That's wonderful. Truly, but there's another matter ...'.

'You're wondering about Andrew's visit. What can I tell you? Our ward receptionist has been away. She usually keeps a record of visitors. I'm not making excuses, just setting the scene. Mrs Cullinane told me her son had visited when we asked about the toiletries in her bathroom. That's also when she showed me the brooch. I questioned the staff, of course, and none of them remembered her having such a brooch before.'

'Assuming someone did visit her and give her these items, surely someone must have seen something.'

'That's the problem. The receptionist was away, and the CCTVs aren't working. They haven't worked for six months, something the board only recently discovered. One of the reasons I've been brought in. To bring everything up to compliance. The new system has been ordered, but it takes time.'

'So, no one saw him?'

'No.'

'Let me get this clear. This is the most expensive facility of its kind in Auckland. Staff have left without being replaced and your CCTV has not been operational for months. People can wander in at will and have contact with vulnerable residents and no one is any the wiser, certainly not the people entrusted with their care.'

Mindy sat forward, her back straight, her shoulders squared. 'As I've already said, the board is aware there have been lapses in our normally high standards. I have been tasked to correct these regrettable lapses. I can understand your distress—'

'I don't think you could possibly understand my distress, Ms Watson. 'While in the care of this over-priced facility my mother-in-law has been sedated into stupidity for years, which has resulted in her estrangement from Andrew, her only son. Her son, my husband is dead. She went to his memorial service accompanied by a member of your staff who let the contents of her catheter bag spill all over the floor, by the way.'

Mindy started to speak but Jess held up her hand.

'No, let me finish, because here's the kicker, she now believes her son visited her a week ago. Someone did, but despite her being in a supposedly secure ward, your staff have no record or knowledge of when exactly this visit took place or who it actually was. My husband died on our honeymoon, so I am reasonably certain it could not have been him.'

Mindy got up and walked over to the desk, opened a drawer and took out a form which she handed to Jess. 'This is a complaint form. Please complete it and send it back to me and I'll put your concerns to the next board meeting.'

'Is that it? Is that all you have to say?'

'Other than informing you of the situation as it stands, you have my heart felt apologies for any distress caused. An apology which I will put formally in writing.' Mindy, her hands clasped in front of her, walked over to the door and opened it.

'I nearly forgot,' Mindy said as Jess was about to get up. 'You have to take the brooch. We can't keep it on the premises.' She pulled open another drawer from which she retrieved a small blue box and handed it to Jess who opened it. Inside was the brooch nestled against a black velvet lining.

'Let her keep it. For obvious reasons, I don't want it.'

'Mrs Cullinane was given two brooches. She was told to give this one to you. Your mother-in-law has the copy — the fake. You've seen for yourself how much pleasure it gives her. This one is the real deal. I had it checked. It's too valuable to keep on the premises. Our insurance policy doesn't allow it.'

Jess dropped the box as if it was poison. It clattered on to the desk, bounced off and landed on the carpet at her feet. She stared at it. Mindy picked it up and put it on the desk. 'You'll need to sign this form to say you've received it,' she said pushing a sheet of paper towards Jess.

'I don't want it,' Jess said. She could feel pins and needles starting in her fingers and around her lips, a sure sign she was over-breathing, panicking. Mindy produced a pen and put it in her hand and Jess found herself scrawling her signature on the paper without reading what it said. Mindy handed her the box again and this time Jess held on to it. She felt herself guided out of the room, out of reception and into the noon day sunshine. A car pulled up and Mindy opened the back door. Jess got in. Ahmed was driving, their eyes met in the rear vision mirror and he smiled. The door slammed shut. At the end of the driveway, Jess turned to look back. Mindy was gone.

FIFTY-THREE

TWO WEEKS later and the day before the interview Jess asked Ahmed to drive her to the storage facility. She needed to reassure herself the car and engagement ring were still there. She still had no job, no income. The glacial pace the Medical Council called due process, meant it was unlikely she would be able return to work in the foreseeable future. As yet there was no word about the properties and her financial situation was growing more dire by the day. Ross's invoice hadn't been paid and she noticed he was taking longer to return her calls. Also unpaid, Ronald was similarly less than forthcoming when she contacted him. The lease on the apartment was up for renewal and unless she found money quickly, she would have to let it go. Once she could have relied on Carole to take her in, but their friendship remained tenuous at best. The only person truly on her side was Ahmed. He wanted nothing from her. He alone looked out for her.

'My mother said to tell you, she is well,' he said after they settled into a steady pace on the Western Motorway. 'She is enjoying her visit with her family very much.'

'That's good to know. Give her my regards, won't you.'

'She will be happy to know she is in your thoughts.'

Jess shifted forward, leaning against the seat belt across her chest. 'Have you seen those men again? Henry and the other one?'

'I haven't. Not for a long time.'

'Perhaps they have gone away, and you don't need to keep such a close eye on me. I feel guilty you've lost business because of me.'

Ahmed glanced up to meet her eyes in the rear vision mirror. 'Don't give it another thought. I am happy to help you. But maybe you're right about them going away. Maybe they've forgotten about you.'

'Go back to your normal job. I'll be fine. You've done more than enough. I'm grateful — truly.'

'If you're sure?'

'I am.' Jess patted his shoulder, sat back and closed her eyes. She had been rehearsing what she was going to say tomorrow. It would be such a relief to finally be able to put her side of what happened at Vaultange. Murray Chambers, if he was still around, along with the rest of the country, would understand she'd done nothing wrong and therefore had nothing to hide. He was smart. He'd figure out there'd be no point in coming after her. Henry had done his best to incriminate her, but after tomorrow even Murray would see his efforts for what they really were. Distractions and deflections to take the blame off himself. She almost felt sorry for Henry, should Murray ever find him.

As for the brooch. She took the box out of her handbag and opened it. The stones glinted in the daylight mocking her with their richness. It had to have been Henry who visited her mother-in-law. He made no secret of the fact that he visited her many times when Andrew was alive. It would have been easy to make the old lady believe he was her son. Getting to know how the facility worked on his many visits would have helped too. She guessed he knew the CCTV wasn't working. With the receptionist away and knowing ward routines he would have plotted his visit during a time when staffing levels were low. It was the only logical explanation.

The only part which didn't fit, was the brooch. Why leave it with Mrs Cullinane and insist she give it to Jess? She had no answer, not yet anyway. The possibility of him planting it on her and telling the police, came to mind. As did all sorts of other possibilities, none of them pleasant. Until she knew what he was up to, she decided it best to stash the brooch, along with her engagement ring, in the car where no one, not the police, not Guy and his crew and definitely not Henry, would find it.

FIFTY-FOUR

THE TELEVISION INTERVIEW with Simon Abercrombie went better than Jess expected. Ross had put them in touch as promised. 'Not your average reporter only after sensational soundbites, Simon is intelligent and well respected in his field. His sole motivation is to get to the truth,' Ross had said. With Jess being the one who suggested him in the first place, she was amused to see how much Ross subsequently bought into the idea of the interview.

Simon proved to be all of the above. Objective and fair, he was no patsy. He dug deep into Jess's background or his team had, and he wasn't afraid to ask hard but brief questions about the circumstances of Marguerite's death. Jess provided clear and precise answers detailing what happened and why, without any self-serving, over-justifications. Thankfully, Simon accepted her version, and with respect for her feelings ended that part of the interview quickly. Jess was particularly grateful he hadn't dwelt on the time she had spent in care and how this had affected her. He'd told her he preferred to leave misery journalism to others. What Simon did explore in detail, was Andrew. Their time together and Vaultange. Jess spoke without interruption unaware he had asked for the camera to focus tightly on her face. The tone of the interview changed. Simon leant forward, listening intently to everything she had to say. He was open to her grief and then to her explanations. 'Regretfully the passwords to the cold wallet have gone to the grave with Andrew,' she told him. 'There's nothing I can do to bring them back. I want to put things right for as many people as possible but with no access to the crypto-assets, how can I?'

Viewers feedback was immediate and mostly positive. There were a couple of short matter-of-fact articles on news sites the following day, her manner and her explanations seemingly reassuring to previously doubting reporters. Besides, by now Vaultange was old news. The facts were the facts. No one could say any more. Life goes on. Wildfires in Nelson, and the search for the arsonists who had lit them had replaced Vaultange as the news of the day.

FIFTY-FIVE

JESS HAD HEARD nothing from Henry after he left her apartment on the day of the funeral. Errol Parsons from apartment 2B reported his clothes had been stolen from the swimming pool changing rooms the following day. Henry was assumed to be the culprit. He had disappeared. It was if he had magicked himself out of the mess he had created.

The official enquiry continued, but nothing was found. No client records, no crypto keys, no trace of the missing millions despite exhaustive overseas searches. The Nano S hadn't revealed its contents, and nothing came of the attempt to track keys through the contractors. The blockchain had moved on. The bank's insurers handed over eighty per cent of the amount stolen in full and final settlement, keen to put a quiet end to their part in the whole sorry saga. It was a huge relief when she checked the Vaultange account one morning and found six million dollars had been deposited overnight. Ross and Ronald were even more relieved because their partners were growing restless about the unpaid invoices.

While many clients had come forward with records of transactions for verification, most were sanguine about their chances of getting their money back. With no choice but to wait for the company's liquidation, something which Ronald and Ross both advised Jess was the most appropriate step to take, clients stopped emailing her. Vaultange was over. It was heart-breaking knowing so many people were going to lose so much, but she had to accept it.

After Simon Abercrombie's interview, the press too moved on. Jess was able to go about her day-to-day existence without fear of being accosted by disgruntled creditors. Her routine was getting back to normal albeit without employment. She and Carole met for lunch or coffee when Carole's hospital roster allowed. Their relationship had survived — just.

Jess went swimming most mornings when she knew Annie Winter would be at work. She had started using the gym and taken up running. Sometimes she would see Ahmed in the distance, he'd wave, and she'd wave back. She was getting used to different drivers whenever she called an Uber.

Lonely evenings were spent learning everything she could about cryptocurrency. This proved to be more interesting than Jess had thought possible. And so much more interesting than the documents her medical defence lawyer sent her to review prior to the first hearing before the disciplinary tribunal.

Her desire to develop competency in basic crypto-skills soon became a quest to know as much as she could about Andrew's world and how it worked. She listened to regular podcasts such as *What Bitcoin Did* when she was running or at the gym. The seventeen episodes explaining the basics of Bitcoin were particularly helpful. She subscribed to online magazines and websites and followed the trades of almost one hundred different alt-currencies marvelling not only at the creativity and skill of their developers but their optimism. Innately logical, Jess easily followed complex dealings on different exchanges, learning and growing in expertise with each passing day. What she didn't have was any money to finance her own trades. So, she made do, setting up a virtual portfolio which she played with over different time periods, some historical, some based on her predictions for the future. She joined chat groups, initially staying in the background as she read what others said as they tested ideas and theories. As time passed and her confidence grew, she started contributing, gratified when people not only agreed with her but endorsed her approach. One member of the chat group, Inigo a man or woman, she had no idea which, although easily the brightest mind in the group, seemed particularly interested in what she was thinking and they spent many hours discussing the more esoteric aspects of cryptocurrency and economics.

It was April, the autumn days noticeably shorter and cooler, when one morning as she was returning from a run around Mission Bay, she received a brisk text from Ross telling her to come into the office asap.

'The properties don't exist,' Ross said before she'd sat down. 'The Gordon Holding properties don't exist.'

Jess, still slightly out of breath having been shown into his office as soon as she arrived, wasn't sure she was hearing correctly. 'Don't be silly, there are photos, title deeds, sale and purchase agreements. You showed them to me.'

'Forgeries. All of them.'

'That's impossible. Your firm did the conveyancing. You dealt with the overseas agents.'

Ross pushed his glasses back to the bridge of his nose. 'No, we didn't. We were given the sale and purchase documents after the deals had gone through. I had already set up Gordon Holdings. Andrew used it to make the purchases.'

'But your staff checked the title deeds. They can't be fake.'

'That's why it's been so slow. The title deeds are real, the land is real. The land exists, the houses don't.'

'You're sure?'

'Why do you think it's taken so long to get the information you requested back in January? The police, the authorities, the fraud office, for God's sake. They got their counterparts overseas to check the agents were telling the truth about new valuations, otherwise we wouldn't have known. They found bare land. The houses, swimming pools, tennis courts, don't exist.' He tossed a bundle of photographs across his desk at her.

She tidied them into a pile on her lap. The first photo was of a white villa supposedly in the South of France — Provence to be more exact. It was surrounded on all sides by wide verandas, a pool, an all-weather tennis court and a cabana at the back of the main house. Nestled into a hillside overlooking the surrounding countryside, where villages dotted hilltops, set high above endless acres of vineyards, it looked fantastic. The next photo showed exactly the same hills and vineyards, the same hillside, but the site was bare apart from survey pegs just visible among the grass and rocks. No house.

She looked at Ross.

'Photoshop,' he said, his voice flat.

'You're kidding me.'

'Not only the photos — the deeds, the sale and purchase agreements, the estate agents' documentation, the government stamps verifying the sale, the bank records, the owner, the interior shots. You name it, they're all forgeries. Good ones, very, very good ones, but forgeries nevertheless.'

Jess turned over the next pair of photographs and glanced at Ross.

'Fake,' he said.

'I liked this one.'

The bare land is worth diddly fucking, excuse my language, squat.' He rocked back in his chair, his white tummy skin flashing at her between bulging shirt buttons.

'If Gordon Holdings is broke, that means there's no money to pay Carole back,' she said eventually.

You'll get something for the land, but I doubt there'll be much left after fees.'

'What do the police say?'

'What can they say? Gordon Holdings is a private company. It's a private matter. Fraud, certainly, money laundering most likely, but finding those responsible won't be easy. These are not simple countries to do business in.'

'Who did this?'

'Who do you think Jess? He got the documentation together and said he knew about buying offshore. He said it would save money if he did it. Andrew okayed the purchases and I signed them off. Because Andrew was happy, I didn't think to check.'

'Who are you talking about?' Jess asked, but she realised as she said the words, she already knew who he was talking about.

'Henry,' Ross said.

FIFTY-SIX

JESS WALKED BACK to the apartment in a dream, her mind struggling to grasp the complexity of Henry's deviousness. The totality of his betrayal was simultaneously stunning, and deeply insulting to everyone he had worked with in the last five years. As Ross made the call to Guy Harding to formally report the fraud, she had barely been able to contain her anger. How dare he? How dare he use, first Andrew, and then her to cover up his crimes? How dare he destroy her life? If he could lie about the properties, he could steal from the bank accounts. She had no doubts now that he had emptied the cold wallets while he was at it. She had never liked him. She certainly hadn't trusted him. To know that she'd been right was no consolation. Why Andrew hadn't seen what Henry was really like, remained a mystery. She felt sick remembering him at their wedding, standing beside Andrew, his best man for chrissakes. He spoke at the lunch afterwards. All the while, he was perpetrating this gigantic rip-off. Oh God! The memorial service. Outwardly mourning his friend, he must have been delighted by Andrew's death. The hypocrisy, the crocodile tears, the flattering speech, all tactics to delay the discovery of what he'd done behind his friend's back. Doubling over, Jess dry-retched into the gutter, the bitter taste of bile clinging to her tongue when she stood up again.

He'd listened so self-righteously as Ross explained Gordon Holdings to her, all the while knowing the properties were worthless. He had as good as accused her of being a gold digger while all along it was him, he was the thief — a cold calculating thieving traitorous bastard of the first order.

'Mrs Cullinane?'

Jess looked up surprised to find she had nearly walked past her building. DS Parker was standing outside, waiting for her. A sunny day, it was nevertheless cool in the wind, but not as cool as the conditions Parker had apparently dressed for. A thick jersey, black jeans wrinkling at the ankle over scuffed Doc Martins, and a calf-length wool coat completed her ensemble. Jess, still in her running gear instantly felt lighter and freer in comparison.

'I need to have a chat. Do you mind if I come up?'

'Maybe another time. It hasn't been a good day.' She swiped her card and pushed open the heavy glass door to her building.

Parker followed her into the lobby. 'It won't take a minute.'

'Then it can wait until tomorrow,' Jess said tersely as she pressed the call button for the elevator. 'I want to get out of my sweaty clothes,' Jess added, yet Parker didn't move. What was taking so long? The numbers above the doors counted down, six, five, four. Four stayed on, then three, then dammit, four again. Annoyed at being stuck with Parker, Jess pummelled the call button with the heel of her hand.

'About your husband—' Parker said.

'Stop! I am not talking to you, about my husband or anyone else without my lawyer present. Look around. Is he here? Can you see him? Is he hiding behind that pot plant perhaps? No? I am now formally asking you to leave my property.'

Parker snapped her notebook shut. 'We still haven't been able to verify your husband's death certificate.'

Jess looked up. Thank goodness the numbers were counting down towards her.

'Bryan ... your stepfather has disappeared. I thought you should know.'

Jess turned, her arms at her sides, her fists clenched. 'Why? Why do you think I should know?' Jess moved towards her and Parker had to step back.

'He was living in a night shelter for ex-drug addicts in Sydney until December 2018,' Parker stuttered. 'Then suddenly he was able afford a ticket to New Zealand. He told everyone he was going home to see his daughter. Australian immigration confirmed he got on the plane. Immigration at this end processed his arrival, but he hasn't been seen since. The only person who could be described as his daughter is you.'

'I was never his daughter,' Jess snarled. 'Now piss off.' The elevator stopped on the first floor and seemed to be taking an age to start moving again. She was about to take the stairs when it arrived. The doors opened. Parker put her hand in the way to stop them from closing. Bar smacking the detective's hand out of the way and being arrested for assaulting a police officer there was nothing Jess could do. She was stuck.

'First your mother, then your husband and now your stepfather...', Parker said, standing so close Jess could smell stale coffee on her breath.

Jess shook her head and stepped around Parker and into the elevator. 'Why are you doing this? Why are you hounding me?'

'It's my job. And I don't believe you're as innocent as you claim.' Parker removed her hand and stepped back.

FIFTY-SEVEN

'Where was I?' I asked.

'You were at Pearl's house,' said the voice, female this time.

I smiled beneath closed eyes. 'How long have I been here?' I asked.

'If it matters. Not long enough for your arm to heal.'

'Where was I?'

'Probably best if you slow down on the morphine Mr Turner. You were at Pearl's house.'

After a few weeks we'd settled into our own version of happy families. Pearl went off to work every morning and came home at the same time every evening. She brought food, wine, and the necessities of life — for me — her secret. She even bought me warm clothes as autumn replaced summer. During the day, I mostly stayed in bed with the blinds drawn and the windows and doors bolted. I watched TV or slept. Slept mostly. It made the days go faster. I set the alarm to ring an hour before Pearl came home. I'd leap up and into the shower. A quick shave, a splash of cologne on both me and the sheets before I made the bed. I put on clothes that I laundered myself. The house was easy to keep clean. Neither of us made much mess, but what there was

I tidied away before she walked in the door. We were remarkably content with the way things had worked out, after the fraught start.

I hadn't meant to stay as long as I did, but I had nowhere else to go. After Jess's interview with Simon takes-it-up-the-arse Abercrombie, my role in the Vaultange affair didn't look good. Even Pearl could tell I was in trouble. So much for me blaming Jess. That plan died a death in her interview. She'd come out of it looking quite the innocent. Untrue. But I was in no position to prove otherwise. Not with Murray and the whole goddamned Auckland underworld looking for me.

Why hadn't Murray tracked down Pearl? Probably because Pearl was no longer Pearl. She was a respectable early childcare teacher, named Margaret McFarlane, with a new hair colour, a new nose and no boobs, the silicon having been sucked out of the old ones. Margaret McFarlane was Pearl's real name. It suited her. Margaret was boring, dreary and stayed out of sight. Easy to do in a city of one and a half million respectable dull people just like her.

I lay low for weeks. I got used to it. It's not hard to do in a comfortable home, with tasty food and enjoyable sex when we could be bothered. It's such a pity when good things reach their inevitable conclusion. Bad things too sometimes.

By the middle of April my friend Bitcoin had increased sixty-seven per cent on January's price. That's a hike from $3,400 to $5,000 in less than six weeks and it was still going up. 2019 was proving to be a much better year than 2018. The trough had bottomed out, the tide was in my favour and it was time to saddle up, leave my self-imposed exile and get out of Dodge with my ill-gotten gains.

It was the school holidays. Pearl was home during the day so I had no excuse for staying in bed. I worked away on her laptop, while she watched movie after movie on Netflix, all romcoms — all with happy endings. The consummate hostess she used ear buds, so the house was quiet apart from the occasional creak as the wood in the walls and floorboards expanded then contracted with the change in temperature outside.

One particular evening, at five o'clock; it was nearly dark, and I was done. The markets were bullish — bells, tinsel, trumpet calls, the whole nine yards of bullish. Damn me if gold (the shiny stuff) wasn't also on the up, its trajectory against the USD not as steep as Bitcoin but pleasing enough. Gold reinforced Bitcoin, both enjoying their positions as go-to currencies. Why were they up? I don't know. I didn't care. My investments were bearing fruit.

The miners must have smelt my desperation to cash out because they racked up the commission to take me to the head of the queue. In no position to argue, I paid. Transaction processing speeds had slowed to almost twelve minutes and I didn't want to spend any longer than I had to in the full glare of the network. The transactions were quick and dirty and the less attention they drew, the better. I didn't want my private keys exposed to unnecessary scrutiny. If you pay enough then transaction times fall away to the ten-minute mark leaving other punters too preoccupied with their own business to take much notice. You gotta love commerce.

I leant back in my chair, arms above my head stretching the day's tension out of my shoulders. It felt good to be alive. No, it felt fucking marvellous to be alive. I glanced over at Pearl to see if she was feeling as happy as I was. She was asleep on the sofa. *When Harry Met Sally* was playing noiselessly on the giant screen on one wall — it was the orgasm scene. It had been a week since we'd last had sex. Meg Ryan's mouth was open — wet as she licked her lips. My cock perked up in my pants straining for release. I tip-toed over to Pearl, undid my fly, and released myself from the confines of my boxers and brushed her lips, slowly with the tip — just the tip of my cock. No reaction so I parted her lips with one finger and pushed, feeling the wetness.

The baseball bat caught me in the back of my knees and I collapsed forward on to the empty sofa where Pearl had just been lying. Thank Christ I rolled as I fell. She was standing over me, legs apart, looking for all the world as if she was planning to hit a home run. I raised my arm to fend off the blow she aimed at my head. She brought the bat down with all her might and the bones in my forearm snapped. I screamed. Thank God I did because the noise brought Pearl out of her zombie-trance. The second swing of the bat stopped an inch from my left eye. She looked at me and shook her head.

'Dick!' She didn't say the word, she spat it, contempt carried in two articulated consonants. After dropping the bat over the back of the sofa, she walked into the kitchen and poured herself a glass of red wine. She watched me over the rim as she drank it without stopping.

I peeled back my sleeve. The bruise which was forming was thick and purple mid-way between my wrist and elbow. I whimpered as I ran my hand over the swelling. It hurt. When I looked at her for consolation, all I got was disgust. My poor penis, once a rampant lion, but now forgotten, dangled limply in front of my open fly. With my good hand I tucked myself in and tried lamely to zip up. Not easy one-handed, but I could tell it was either that, or I leave the damn thing out there.

'First aid kit?'

'Bathroom cupboard.' She stayed behind the counter and poured herself another glass of red.

'I'm sorry. I was out of line.'

'Ya think?' She knocked back the wine. 'Get yourself sorted, then fuck off before I break your other arm.'

I could take a hint. Thank God I'm right-handed. My left arm throbbed mercilessly, pain like flaming arrows was shooting from my elbow to the tips of my fingers. In the bathroom, I made a reasonable job of wrapping a bandage around the lump. I fashioned a rough sling from another bandage and let that take the weight of my arm — the relief. Pearl had a cabinet full of pills, some legal, some not. I took the legal ones, swallowing a handful, washing them down with water slurped from the tap. Once I'd stood up, I checked my reflection. Unshaven, pale and a little shaky, I didn't look too bad considering. Still handsome. A quick pee, a tidy up and my work here was done.

Having only one good hand and the other in severe pain makes it hard to aim at that tiny little hole in the toilet. As for keeping the stream, straight and true ... it's fair to say, I didn't. It was too difficult peeing, with one arm in a sling. The piss went all over the floor and up the walls. I didn't clean it up. I was annoyed, and I had just completed a revenge pee. Pearl had taken to me with a baseball bat, when a simple, *no*, or *please stop* would have sufficed. I'm not an animal. I would have done as she asked. If she'd asked. I washed, ran my good hand through my hair, pocketed the pain pills and adjusted my pants and shirt as best I could.

Pearl was standing by the kitchen counter when I emerged. The wine bottle was empty, and she was opening a second. I collected Errol's coat and pulled it on to my good arm, struggling to flick it around my other shoulder.

'I'll be off then. Thanks for the use of your place. By the way, I transferred money into your account earlier as a show of my appreciation.'

She was drunk. Her eyes unfocused, she looked confused and I felt sorry for her.

'How did I get your account number? You may well ask. Your laptop is an open book. God help you if it ever gets stolen. Two words for you — password management.'

'Thanks,' she replied slurring her ssses. 'Sorry. About your arm. Self-defence classes.'

'Who with? The SAS?'

'Close,' she said. 'After that time at your apartment, I had to do something.' She came over and unbolted the front door, holding it open for me. I liked Pearl. When I think back, waking her up with my cock in her face was not the smartest thing to have done. 'Yeah, I'm sorry too,' I said. 'Should have been more gentlemanly.'

'Go straight across the road, there's an alleyway between the two houses opposite. It'll take you down the next couple of blocks to the edge of the park. After that, I don't want to know.'

I was barely down the steps when I heard the bolts being slid inside the door. I was on the street when I heard her roar of disgust — she'd found the mess in the bathroom.

FIFTY-EIGHT

As I FOUGHT the pain in my arm, I hurried down the alleyway with the aim of making it to the nearby park where I could hole up and plan my escape across town. One Tree Hill is primarily parkland, and it's closed to traffic at night making it safe from prying eyes in passing cars. Thank goodness the medication kicked in as I scurried across the busy road, or I don't think I would have made it. The pain was still there, but it was bearable. I could breathe more easily again.

Bucolic is the word which springs to mind when describing the park on warm summer days. Acres of green grass where sheep graze among demarcated picnic areas for humans, where the citizens of Auckland and tourists enjoy walks and cycle ways. An oasis of nature in the suburban desert on sunny summer days. On a wet cold April evening it was miserable. Muddy and slippery underfoot, it was a place to hide — nothing more. I knew where I had to be and the time I had to be there, but how to get there from here? I hadn't worked that out. I guess the baseball bat to my legs and the pain caused by the ends of bone grating across each other was affecting my thinking. Discombobulated. That's the word.

I knew I had to get off the streets as quickly as possible. A tall, heavily built man walking alone on a busy street cradling his left arm in his right, is bound to draw attention. People are curious. They have long memories when properly incentivised. The police may have stopped looking for me, but I was dead certain Murray and the gang hadn't. There are enough meth users in Auckland who would do anything to get a free spot from their dealers. Dealers who had been alerted to look out for me.

Pearl would have made the call. Any sane person would do the same, if only in the interests of self-protection and hopefully a wad of cash. She'd been in their sights since that night in my flat. She didn't know how long she could hide behind Margaret McFarlane. She needed insurance — I was it.

In ten minutes, I had reached the park, clambered over a stone wall and crouched down behind it, my back propped against volcanic rock. It was a different world on this side of the wall. For one thing it had sheep. Lots of sheep. Sheep don't like rain any more than the next mammal. Like me they had found the only shelter available — the lee side of the wall. I wedged myself between two big ones who swung their heads around nervously to inspect me for teeth and weapons. When no threat was detected, they went back to thinking whatever sheep think about, which I suspect is not that much. Me on the other hand. I had a lot to think about. The cold was making the pain worse and scenes of me dying pathetically from hypothermia flashed in front of my eyes. I'd had broken bones before. Rugby. I was younger then and I don't remember the pain being as bad. I couldn't believe how much it hurt when I eased my arm out of my makeshift sling, and tried to put it into the sleeve. I leant against the wall when I'd finished and almost cried.

It was then that a Peanuts cartoon came to mind. *It always rains on the unloved.* That's me, I thought — unloved — alone — in pain — abandoned. The story of my life. Isn't that the truth? Okay, I did cry. A tear did dribble down one cheek and plop on to Errol's coat. One tear — no more. With both my arms in sleeves, I was able to wrap the trench tightly around me and as my body warmed up inside my Burberry cocoon, I tried to think.

Damn it, I should have smashed the fucking laptop. I'd wiped as much as I could, but not enough — not enough. Any techie worth their salt, could, given enough time, recover what I'd done. Acid, a hammer, spilt coffee, all or one of the above, would have worked. Instead, typical me, all I could think about was a blow job. Fucking Meg Ryan. I reckoned I had twelve hours, twenty-four max, before they found me. Focus. All I had to do was get to the ship. Leave the sheep, the park, the city, the country behind. That, I had planned. The ship was waiting for me. Arranged weeks ago, it was due to sail at high tide, eight-forty p.m. tonight. I checked the watch in my pocket — Pearl's watch, the one her mother gave her for her 21st birthday. The one she left in her bathroom cupboard, with *Happy 21st Love Mum* engraved on the back. I'd nicked it when I was in the bathroom. Hey, I didn't have a phone. Six-twenty-six p.m. I had two hours to get from the sheep to the ship. Less than that if you took in getting past security and customs. The port was ten kilometres away. In the good old days when I was younger and fitter, I could have jogged it in under an hour. In the good old days when I was wearing trainers and not office brogues, and a hoodie, not a trench coat. In the good old days when I didn't have a fucking broken arm. No phone meant no Uber. Not that I'd trust them anyway. Taxi? They still existed, but I had no money. Luckily the bus card was in one of the pockets and it still had money on it.

Climbing over the wall back to the pavement was difficult. There being a longer drop on the street side. I almost broke a tooth I was clenching my jaw so hard. Once I was over I lifted my left arm carefully with my right and tucked my hand into the pocket. Not as secure as the sling, but less obvious, and it would have to do. There was a bus stop at the end of the road. I headed for that, taking care to walk as normally as possible cursing Pearl and her self-defence fucking classes every time my left leg bore my weight and jarred the bone ends. A bus pulled up, but it was too far away. Passengers got off and it swooped into the rain before I could reach it. Just as well. Because that was when I saw the car parked behind where the bus had just been. A sedan, dark with two men sitting inside, smoking —

waiting — watching. I carried on walking. The crowd of passengers who'd got off the bus came towards me, encircled me and without missing a step, I turned one-eighty and walked with them, taking comfort in the safety of numbers. The only problem — I was walking away from the port — away from the safety of the departing ship.

FIFTY-NINE

'The operation went well Mr Turner. The surgeon is pleased.'

I looked down at the array of bolts and screws poking out of my arm like a giant Meccano set.

'I look like a cyborg.'

'It's temporary — until the bones heal. Another day and you can get up and start moving around.'

'I can leave the room?'

'No.'

'Oh.'

'The machine's running. Start whenever you're ready.'

By the time I reached Quay Street, I was colder, wetter and in more pain than I had ever experienced in my life. I'm no wimp, but the pain was getting to me. It was excruciating. I know, a real man wouldn't complain. Richie McCaw captained the All Blacks to World Cup victory in 2011 with two broken bones in his foot. I tried reminding myself of his stoicism, but it didn't help. My arm was throbbing, pulsing waves riding a searing, gut-clenching wave to surge down to the ends of my fingers which felt as though they were being ripped off in a vice. To cap off the misery, I was starving and the smell of warm, spicy food wafting into my nostrils from the nearby Asian food outlets didn't help. Four scrambled eggs eaten ten hours earlier are not sufficient to maintain the energy levels of someone my size. I needed food, lots of food, protein preferably, but I had no cash, no card and even less time.

I stumbled across the street in the dark, dodging in and out of cars and trucks, hugging my arm against my body. I had to find the fastest and least obvious route to the container terminal on Ferguson Wharf. I had arranged to meet my contact by the crane nearest the road at eight p.m. Pearl's watch showed seven-forty-three p.m. and counting.

In front of me was a bloody great wire fence topped with huge loops of razor wire. A sign with restricted access written in big red letters on a white background was clipped to the wire. A road led into the port and a young bloke manned the booth at the entrance. He looked unsure when I approached on foot, most people were entering the area in vehicles. I gave him points for politeness but not for speed, when he greeted me with the obligatory *kia ora* and asked for my ID.

'Undercover cop mate,' I said. 'Need to get to a meet-up asap.'

'On foot?'

'Too right, less suspicious.'

He looked doubtful but didn't ask me to move on. Instead he asked again for ID.

'I'm undercover, I don't carry ID for obvious reasons. Are you going to let me through or not? Because if you don't then I'll have to report you for obstruction.' I looked pointedly at his name badge. 'Nigel Howard.'

Nigel was young. He wasn't stupid. 'Let me call central police and check. Name there?'

'DS Sarah Parker,' I said praying she wouldn't answer her phone. He kept his eye on me, as he asked to speak to Sarah. 'She's not on duty,' he said, covering the mouthpiece.

'Yeah well. I can't help that. Get them to page her. Tell them to hurry.'

Nigel hung up. A line of cars and trucks had backed up at the gate and some of the drivers were even more impatient than me. Arms were being waved out of windows and horns were being honked.

'What's your name,' he asked.

'Guy Harding,' I replied without a moment's hesitation.

Nigel wrote it down. 'Go on,' he said waving the first car forward. I ducked under the barrier arm. It was nearly seven-fifty p.m. I broke into a lurching jog, not sure where I was supposed to be going. As I looked up, the red lights at the top of the cranes loomed over a building so I changed course and headed towards them. Four minutes. Surely the contact would wait. What if he didn't? I couldn't take the risk and broke into a proper run, swearing every time my arm hit the edge of the pocket, sweating as I forced myself to keep going, too afraid the ship would leave without me. In my mind I saw it pulling away from its moorings in a surge of white water, front and rear, as the tugs towed it towards the shipping lane to begin its journey to Singapore and freedom.

Seven-fifty-two p.m. I leant against the steel leg of a crane and would have vomited if there had been any food in my stomach. I dry-retched and gagged, then retched again.

A man stepped out from under the shadow of the gangway. He beckoned, walking slowly towards me in the darkness, hat drawn over his face in the rain. I stopped retching, pulled myself upright and walked towards him. Relief flooded every fibre, every muscle every inch of my body and suddenly the pain was not so bad. Suddenly I had hope. We met in the middle. Underneath the crane, I saw his face, his eyelashes — it was Murray.

'You know the rest,' I said. Silence. I called out. 'Hello? Is anybody there?'

'Thank you, Mr Turner,' said the voice. 'You've been very helpful. One of us will be in touch next week. In the meantime, remember you're here for your own protection. Relax. Let the doctors do their work.'

I looked at the white walls as I listened to the silence. I pressed the button on my morphine pump and counted to twelve. At twenty, I shut my eyes.

SIXTY

It was when the leasing agent called to arrange a time to show a prospective tenant around the apartment that Jess knew she wasn't ready to leave. Leaving meant relinquishing her life with Andrew. Despite knowing more about him and despite how her feelings had changed, she couldn't let go of what they'd had together. Not yet. Not until she had something and somewhere to go to. She needed to work out what she was going to do before she left the place where she had been happy for such a short time.

When she called Ross to ask him how she could extend the lease, he suggested she take a small stipend from the insurance pay out, enough to fund her through the next three months. Hopefully by then, he said, she would know if the Medical Council was going to reinstate her practising certificate. Initially she'd been reluctant to take the money, which should have gone to creditors, but thinking through her position she tucked her conscience into a corner and accepted his offer — as a loan. She planned to pay it back once she was working again. Ross reassured her there was no hurry.

If it wasn't for DS Parker continuing to hound her, life would have been tolerable. But the woman wouldn't back off, seemingly determined to keep her in legal limbo. Jess hated the word closure. It was so over-used, so trite, but it was what she needed if she was to *move on* to use another over-used phrase.

Parker had been poking her nose into places she didn't belong, dredging up Marguerite's old work colleagues, old neighbours, interviewing the Prof, talking to the Medical Council and calling on contacts in Australia to dredge up information about Bryan. It wouldn't have been so bad if she kept her progress, such as it was, to herself, but Parker was a sharer. She insisted on calling Jess at regular intervals to inform her of any new information even after Jess had specifically requested that all communication go through Ross. Jess never knew what would land in her Inbox from one moment to the next. The uncertainty and unpredictability kept her in a constant state of low-level anxiety. Just as Parker no doubted hoped it would.

It was the end of April, and Parker had still not found any evidence to either discredit the death certificate or a link from Jess to Bryan, yet she continued to insinuate to anyone who would listen that it was only a matter of time before she did. When Jess found out Parker's repeated calls to the Medical Council had unsettled them to such an extent that her first hearing before the disciplinary tribunal had been postponed for three months, she was furious. The woman was intolerable.

'What can I do Ross? She's making my life a misery.'

'Find the surgeon who signed that certificate. Get it verified. That's one thing out of the way. The private detective could do some digging about Bryan for you. Give her irrefutable evidence then legally she has to leave you alone.'

Jess went back to the apartment and started her search. Phone calls to the hospital in Fiji put her in touch with the surgeon's receptionist who informed her politely that she had already told the detective he was on an island setting up a new clinic. He had extended his stay by three months, and no, there was no Internet. When Jess expressed surprise that there was no way of contacting him, his receptionist, Mrs Santu expressed surprise she would think that. Because, of course, there was a way to contact him. Fiji was a developed country not a backwater. The receptionist went on to say how surprised she was that the detective had ended her call so abruptly without asking about other means of contact.

'It was as if, she didn't want to know,' Mrs Santu said warming to the conversation. 'This is the number of his sat phone.' She reeled it off and Jess wrote it down. 'As I told Simon, he's contactable in the early evenings after ward rounds are over for the day.'

'Simon?' Jess asked. 'That isn't the same Simon who is the manager at the resort.'

'The very same,' Mrs Santu said her delight at being able to impart this information audible in her merry tone. 'They're old friends. I thought you knew. Your husband, Simon and Mr McDonald. They lived together in Vietnam, ten years ago. They called themselves *the Three Musketeers*. You know what young men are like at that age.'

Jess said she did know what they were like. Mrs Santu laughed and asked if there was anything more she could do for her.

'No, nothing more. You've been a great help. Thank you.'

Jess ended the call with Walter Scott's words, ringing in her mind. *Oh what a tangled web we weave, when first we practice to deceive.* Exactly whose web was being woven, that was the problem. Parker's? Andrew's? Henry's? Whose ever it was, she was sick of it. Everywhere she turned there was another complication, another twist. She wanted to return to the simplicity of medicine and be done with these people.

In the meantime, knowing she could neutralise Parker on one count was enough. Tempting though it was to immediately phone Simon and confront him, she needed time to think through what it was she wanted to ask him. *The Three Musketeers.* Seriously?

It was the beginning of May when Jess returned from her swim to a message from Parker requesting her presence at the station. She needed Jess to verify several documents, and was suggesting they meet at one p.m. the following day.

Jess showered, dressed and made coffee. She ate her breakfast and spent the next two hours checking her crypto positions. The chat group was busy. Inigo had gone long on Ether and people were wondering why. Wait and see was their answer. Inigo liked being mysterious. The discussion which followed was mostly gossip, but it was happy gossip considering Bitcoin had surged thirty per cent in value in recent weeks. Someone speculated the increase in value was because of one trade in April, when an investor traded 500,000 tether for 122 Bitcoin. More orders followed and boosted the price. Nothing unusual, Inigo said. They explained the original trade had occurred in a period of low liquidity and the stimulatory effects had lasted. After so much time studying the market, Jess understood what they were talking about. Whoever Inigo was, she thought, they were right. The group then turned to talk of one whale who'd moved over $212 million Bitcoin, unusual, but what was really amazing, the transaction had cost just $3.93 in fees. Try doing that with fiat currency.

The morning over, Jess called Ross to check the private investigator's report had been received and that Ross was available to go with her to the station, not at one p.m. but at five p.m. On receipt of his confirmation, she emailed Parker and advised her when the meeting would take place.

Parker met them at the front door, wearing the same black jeans, jersey and boots she always wore. She'd had a haircut, which Jess said suited her. Parker shrugged but she seemed pleased with the compliment. Nothing in the interview room had changed other than the temperature which had gone from chilly to freezing. Huddled around the table, Ross and Jess made polite conversation as they waited for the room to warm up. It took five minutes, but finally the temperature had risen sufficiently for them to get on with the business at hand. Parker launched into her usual diatribe about not having the death certificate verified.

'Before you traverse the same old ground I have something which will help,' Jess said.

Parker looked up from the papers. 'You do?'

Ross took out the original death certificate and lay it flat on the table facing the detective.

Jess had already emailed Tim McDonald on his sat phone to make sure he was standing by. Fiji is an hour behind New Zealand, which meant he was at the tail end of his four o'clock ward round, but he agreed to take the call. She dialled the number and after a few rings, he answered.

With the phone on speaker, Ross informed Tim who was in the room and asked him to formally state his full name, qualifications and his position at the hospital at the time of Andrew's death. That done, he asked Tim to give a quick rundown of where he was and what he was doing now. He described the hospital he was building in the Lau Island group and how it would bring up-to-date services for the first time to a population of ten thousand people scattered over sixty islands north of Fiji, only thirty of which were inhabited.

Parker sniffed as Ross asked the next question. 'Do you remember treating Andrew Cullinane?'

'I do,' Mr McDonald replied. 'I—'

Ross stopped him. 'Please just answer the questions as asked Mr McDonald. You operated on Mr Cullinane. He died and you signed his death certificate.'

'I did.'

'And you confirm that for DS Parker of the New Zealand Police who is sitting here beside me.'

'I do. I signed Andrew Cullinane's death certificate.'

'Thank you, Mr McDonald. Detective, do you have any questions?'

Parker sniffed, louder this time. 'It's DS Parker speaking Mr McDonald, can you restate the cause of death for me please?'

'From memory, it was either bowel perforation causing sepsis or sepsis resulting from bowel perforation. Either will do.' With her finger, Parker followed the words on the certificate next to cause of death. His first version was the correct one.

'Thank you for your time. We'll let you get back to your patients.'

'Right then,' the surgeon said. He was about to say something else, but Jess quickly ended the call. Parker, her lips pressed tightly together, refolded the death certificate and handed it back to Ross.

'I can provide you with a copy of the conversation if you need it. I recorded it. Two people went on a honeymoon and only one came back — me. I did not kill my husband DS Parker. He died as a result of fatal complications from his pre-existing bowel condition.'

'Noted and accepted. I'll inform the coroner's office,' Parker replied quietly. 'There's still the matter of your stepfather,' she added clearly unwilling to give up.

Ross took a manilla folder out of his briefcase and put it on the table. 'This is a legal statement, duly sworn in my presence. It is from a flight attendant on Flight ANZ 102. He states he offloaded Jess's stepfather in a wheelchair on arrival in Auckland on that date.' Ross opened the folder, turned it around to face Parker and pointed to a date on the first page. 'He states he accompanied Mr Randall through immigration and customs, before delivering him into the care of a private nurse. His description of the nurse is here.' Ross pointed to a paragraph at the bottom of the page. 'Short, stocky, bald. Unremarkable in other words except,' Ross paused for dramatic effect. Jess stifled a smile knowing what was coming next. 'For his prominent eyelashes. A description which does not fit my client, but which does fit—'

'Murray Chambers,' Parker said as she sat silently chewing her bottom lip. 'Why would Murray Chambers be meeting Bryan Randall?'

'You'll have to ask him,' Jess replied.

'Henry Turner knows him,' said Parker said with her elbows on the table, hands woven together her thumbs flicking against each other. 'It's strange, isn't it? You, finding this attendant when all my enquiries led to a dead end.' She looked up at Jess who returned her stare.

'That's exactly what we have been thinking detective, in fact, I will be putting our concerns about this investigation to your superiors. In the meantime, I have the attendant's contact details if you would like to interview him yourself,' Ross added. 'That done,' Ross said as he fastened his briefcase and stood up. 'I have another appointment.'

'Of course.' Parker got up and opened the door to call a constable. She stepped back to let Ross and Jess out of the room. 'Thank you for your assistance, Mr Martin. It's so helpful to get these matters cleared up so comprehensively.' Ross was half-way down the corridor when Parker handed Jess an envelope. 'For you,' she said and shut the door.

SIXTY-ONE

WITH NO UMBRELLA, no coat, and only a light jacket between her and the elements, Jess cursed Auckland's weather. Four seasons in one day — the song was right. It had been a nice day when she walked up the slight rise to the station on College Hill. No longer. She stopped in front of the station doors and peered out into the street. Rain was pelting down and getting heavier with each passing minute.

'You can wait over there, miss,' a friendly voice said. 'You know what Auckland's like. This'll be gone in ten minutes.' An elderly man was sitting at a desk where neat piles of *Neighbourhood Watch* pamphlets were displayed. He was wearing a name badge identifying him as Paul Manford — community volunteer. He pointed to a line of plastic chairs set back in an alcove. 'Better than getting wet,' he added seeing her reluctance.

'Thank you,' she said. With nothing else to do, and nowhere to be, it made sense to sit down while she waited. Curious to see what was in the envelope she peeled it open. One page, grimy and frayed at the fold-lines; it looked as if it'd been torn from an exercise book. It was the type used by school students which would have had a soft cover and the paper stapled at the centre to hold it together. At the bottom of the page were three signatures. Bryan Randall and Henry Turner and a name she couldn't decipher. The date — 15th December 2018. With shaking hands, Jess stumbled through the bad grammar and Bryan's awful spelling, and forced herself to read each word slowly. She didn't want to miss anything.

Marguerite said, she wanted it. Before she couldn't speak, "Don't let me suffer. Promise. Jess can't see me like that." After that I stayed away. I couldn't look. She was disgusting. Do you know what it's like to kill someone? Even if they beg you to do it? It's hard. I stayed at garage. The nurses were with her and Jess. What could I do? I'd only get in the way. Marguerite didn't care. What would happen if I got caught. Her precious daughter was more important. I don't know why she married me. One morning I needed clothes. The nurse had left and the new one was late. Jess was asleep in a chair beside her mother. Marguerite opened her eyes. Stared at me. Really stared. Then gurgling, choking and crying. Too much crap. So I did it. The sound, I couldn't hear that. I put the pillow over her face. I pushed harder and harder and it stopped. Jess woke up and pushed me, she pushed me across the room. Strong, so hard I hit the door. She rushed back, and was lifting the pillow off her face. The nurse arrived. I said, "I caught her, I'll call 911." I left. Marguerite was gone. Left her with her precious Jess. Didn't see her. Didn't want to. I deserved that money. Payment for what I went through. Jess didn't say a word. Fuck knows why. Got out as quick as. Came here, to work with the Holden team for free at Bathurst. Did a few days. They said not to come back. Not my fault, they didn't give me a fair go. Met Chelsea. We got on. Bought her a car. She pissed off so I hooked up with Lisa. Bought her a car too. A Ford not a fucking Holden. Lisa was into coke. Got me on it. Better than the brown. That's all. Here I am. Not proud of myself, but that's how it goes.

'Are you all right miss?' The old man asked. White-haired, he was wearing a cardigan with pockets over a checked shirt buttoned up to the neck and baggy pants. He had left his desk and was bending over her, offering his handkerchief. 'Here, take this. Come on, don't cry. It all works out in the end. Usually for the better.'

'I don't think so,' Jess said grateful for the kindness as well as the handkerchief. Lately …'.

'You've got your whole life in front of you, a pretty young girl like you. Whatever this is, it won't last. It never does.'

'I hope you're right,' she said, blowing her nose. She held out the handkerchief, but Paul shook his head.

'Keep it. I've got a stack in the drawer. My wife thinks real ones are better for mopping up tears.'

Jess smiled. 'You must have a nice wife.'

'I do, but like all good things, I had to wait to find her.' When he sensed she had recovered, he patted her on one shoulder and walked back to his desk and sat down.

Jess folded the pages and put them back in the envelope. Paul was right. She should be laughing not crying. This was the closure she had been searching for. When the Medical Council saw what Bryan had said, they would have to reinstate her practising certificate and she could go back to work. Not with the Prof, not after he had turned his back on her when she needed him most but somewhere new, where she could make a fresh start. This was good news. Good news which reminded her of how much she missed her mother.

At the door she turned and said thank you to Mr Manford. The rain was still bucketing down, muddy water swirled along the gutters of Gudgeon Street and backed up over drains, pooling across the road. At the bottom of the steps she pulled her jacket up and over her head. After looking both ways she turned right towards town and home. As she ran along the pavement, skipping over puddles, she couldn't keep the smile off her face.

By the time she reached the corner of Hargreaves and Gudgeon, her jacket was soaked and water streamed down her bare legs into her shoes. As she took shelter in a doorway, her teeth chattering with cold, she tried to figure out the fastest way home. A car drove past sending a fan of water high in the air on to the pavement. It just missed her. No blue Mazda in sight. Where was Ahmed when she needed him?

A silver sedan pulled to a stop at the curb, the passenger window open. Someone called her name and she crouched down to see who it was. The inside of the car was in shadow and she couldn't make out any faces. Whoever it was, called again, more urgently this time. She had taken a step towards the car to get a better look when she felt a figure move behind her. He pinned her arms against her body and clamped a huge hand over her mouth forcing her head against his chest. She tried to bite him, but his grip was too tight, and she couldn't open her mouth wide enough. As she screamed through his fingers she was carried the few steps to the car and shoved forward face down on to the back seat. A thick blanket was thrown on top of her, before she could lift her head. Hands held her down and something hard and round was jammed into her skull behind her ear. For a moment all she could think about was how she'd dropped her laptop out of her bag and how the rain would ruin it. A stupid thought; she was about to die and she was worried about a cheap laptop. She had to get out of the car before it started moving. She tried to bring her knees underneath her to get leverage against the seat and kick out behind her, but before she could, she was pushed off the seat and into the foot well. Her face hit the floor, her teeth piercing her bottom lip.

'Keep fucking still,' hissed a man.

She screamed and kicked the door, all the while scrabbling forward, reaching up for the door handle. The man whacked her hand away, then punched her on the back of the head so hard bright lights shot across her vision. Still, she struggled to rear up, to get her head to the window where someone might see her and hear her calls for help. The man swore, whacked her again and grabbed her arm through the thick blanket and viciously twisted it up behind her, ramming it between her shoulder blades as high as it would go. As she gasped with pain, Jess felt as if she would never breathe again. His grip on her wrist tightened, each fraction of movement triggering another excruciating surge of agony. Jess stopped resisting. There was nothing she could do. No one was coming to help.

Face down in the back of the car, she had no idea how long the journey took. The man let go of her arm, but only after he positioned his feet which were clad in heavy boots on her body, stomping on her if she moved. If she raised her head, he slapped it down, not once but twice, laughing as he hit her the second time. She lay still then, counting the seconds and the cars driving past, torturing herself with the knowledge their drivers were oblivious to what was happening. No one spoke. The blanket was rank with the smell of animals. Horses? Dogs? Cats? Urine definitely.

When her head tipped forward, it meant they were turning off the motorway, but in which direction, she had no idea. Minutes passed. The car slowed to a stop, its engine running. She heard the driver's side window go down. Cold air sucked against her bare wet legs. The driver called out. A metal gate rolled back. The car bumped forward. The rain on the car roof stopped, followed by the engine.

The man in the back climbed out, moaning about how stiff his legs were, petulantly stating he was going to drive next time. Someone laughed and called him a girl. Next time? Every part of her body was numb with pain. Her tongue probed the cut on the inside of her bottom lip, tasting the iron in her blood. The door opened behind her. Hands gripped her ankles and pulled her backwards out of the car, her wet skirt riding up underneath the blanket. Manhandled upright she was propped against the side of the car with the blanket over her head.

All Jess could see were her feet and a stained dusty concrete floor. A door opened near to her. Another hand, another push. Her feet caught and she pitched forward into space. Gravity took over and she landed heavily on the floor. The door slammed shut. A key turned in a lock. She tugged off the blanket desperate to see. Nothing except intense eye clogging darkness. She waited for her eyes to adjust. It made no difference, there was no light.

She was lying next to someone — warm and breathing. She reached over, her fingers feeling the body for clues. A suit, shirt, trousers. Cologne mixed with sweat. She whisked her hand away and stared into the darkness. The smell — it could only be Henry. She shook him and he groaned. As she shook him harder, he groaned again, but otherwise he didn't stir.

On her knees she reached out her arms trying to get a feel for where they were. One hand hit a wall, the other nothing. Still on her knees she inched forward, then sideways and backwards and finally having determined they were in a small room, she got to her feet and as she straightened up, she hit her head on the ceiling with a bump. It was a cupboard, not a room.

As she groped in the dark she leant over Henry, this time shaking him impatiently and whispered furiously. 'Henry, it's Jess.' No response. Employing an old doctor's trick, she knuckled the bone behind his ear. Henry moaned, flinched at the pain, his breathing changed to grunting as he finally came to.

'What the fuck?' he croaked his breath foul. 'Jess?'

'Yes, now listen. I'm moving this way.' She took his hand and pointed it. 'You move that way, away from me, then we can sit sideways and not have to touch.' He didn't object. Groggy, and holding his breath he struggled to follow her instructions, wriggling on to one side and moving his bulk away from her. Now side by side in the darkness, their knees were jammed under their chins. Uncomfortably warm after being so cold in the car, Jess felt steam rising from her clothes on to her face.

'Fuck, fuck, fuck ...', Henry yelled, drawing out the last syllable.

'What?'

'My arm's broken. It hurts like fuck when I move.'

'How did that happen?'

'Pearl hit me. With a bat. Long story. Any professional advice?'

'Don't move.'

'Call that professional.'

'I'll look at it in a minute, okay. How long have you been here?'

'Not long. As you can tell by the pristine environment, I haven't had to ablute.'

'Who's outside?'

He moved, his foot thudding against the wall. 'Murray Chambers or the gang who employed him. Take your pick. There's no reason anyone else would want us. They think we know the passwords.'

Jess gripped her wrists in front of her ankles hugging her knees even more tightly into her chest and rocked back against the wall. 'You know what they are. Tell him.'

'I don't know them.'

'I don't believe you. You're a liar. Tell him.'

'I. Don't. Know. Them. I keep trying to tell you, Andrew changed the passwords before he left.'

'It's over Henry. Stop now. You've hurt too many people. Give up and tell them what they want to know.'

'Did you get hit in the head when they grabbed you? Listen to me Jess. Andrew changed the passwords before he left.'

'Is money that important to you? I don't get it. I really don't. I also don't get why you had to involve his mother.'

'His mother?'

'You saw her. Last week. You pretended to be Andrew. She thinks he's alive.'

'She's got dementia.'

'She's better.'

Henry groaned. 'People with dementia don't get better. You're a doctor, you of all people should know that.'

He was right. Damn it. She should have asked to see her mother-in-law's medical records instead of taking Mindy at her word. People with dementia don't get better. But, then if she hadn't had dementia in the first place, as Mindy implied, then she would get better.

'Park the dementia for now okay. I'll check it later.'

Henry snorted. 'You're serious aren't you?'

'Someone visited her Henry, because they gave her a diamond brooch to pass on to me. It couldn't be anyone else but you. Admit it.'

'Why the hell would I ask her to give you a diamond brooch? You know me, or you think you do. Would I give away something valuable or would I keep it myself?'

He had a point. 'Forget it,' she muttered. 'It's the passwords which matter. Tell these creeps what they are so we can get out of here.'

Henry heaved a sigh. 'Andrew changed the passwords. I don't know what they are.' He paused. 'And if you think Murray is going to let us go, you're dumber than I thought.'

Neither spoke. Jess shivered and hugged her knees more tightly than before making herself as small as she possibly could. When that didn't work, she focused on the sound of the rain on the roof outside.

'Another thing,' she said.

'Of course, there is.'

'Bryan killed Mum. You knew that and you didn't tell Andrew. You let him read that awful report and believe what it said about me.'

'Who told you?'

'DS Parker gave me that pathetic statement you made him sign. Remember. Before you put him on the plane to Murray.'

'I knew she'd search my apartment. So predictable.'

Jess swivelled around and kicked the dark where she estimated he might be. Her foot connected because he yelled and told her to fuck off back to her half of the cupboard.

'Where's Bryan?'

'What do you care?'

'I don't. Where is he?'

'How the fuck should I know? Ask Murray. He'll be delighted to tell you the gory details.'

'Don't you feel anything for what you do to people? You stole from your best friend. From clients you knew. You set me up to take the blame and you've made an old lady think her son is still alive.'

'You're wrong on all counts. I did not steal from Andrew. He stole from me.'

Jess wanted to punch him she was so angry. Instead, she hammered on the door, beating it over and over until her fist hurt, puffing when she'd finished. 'You can't seriously expect me to believe you.'

'I tried to steal from him. True. Did I steal from him? Not true.'

'What about the properties? Ross said you bought them.'

'So?'

'They're fakes.'

'They can't be. I saw the photos, the deeds. I went through an agent.'

'Liar. You faked the documents, the deeds, probably even the agent to launder Murray's dirty money.'

'Andrew found the properties. He supplied the documentation. He told me to buy them.'

'Fuck you!'

Henry shifted position, sucking air between his teeth as he did so. She could tell by the bitter smell of his breath that he had turned to face her. She buried her nose between her knees and breathed through her mouth. His hand groped for her shoulder and gripped it, forcing her to look up.

'It was my idea, sure. He said he wanted out of the company, he wanted to cash up. He'd met you. He wanted a different life. Your fault, like everything else that happened. I was stunned. I couldn't believe he would do that. Leave me, for you. Sure, I was furious. Sure, I hated you. I still do. You've ruined everything. I asked him to wait until the market improved, but he said he didn't want to wait.' Henry sniffed, then let out a sob. 'He would have discovered what I was doing with Murray if he'd opened the books. I couldn't let him do that. You're right, I suggested the properties. To stall him, until I could put things right. He agreed so quickly I was surprised. But it was Andrew who provided the documentation. He practically ordered me to buy those particular ones and to pay a premium to secure the deals. It was Andrew who arranged payment from Vaultange — not me.'

'You're a liar. A liar who blames his dead friend instead of manning up and admitting what you've done. You're despicable. You know that.' Huddling into the corner, Jess turned away, preferring the company of the wall.

'Andrew changed the passwords.'

'I'm trying to sleep.'

'I reckon he did it at the airport.'

Jess sighed. 'If he did and it's a big if, he had a reason. He didn't trust you. And he was right as it turned out.'

'But why then? I've been trying to figure that out. There are two possibilities. Either he knew about Murray and me, or he had a scheme of his own going. Have you thought about that?'

'If he had a scheme of his own, why would he change the passwords? Andrew could access the wallets any time he liked.'

'Any time? Are you sure? He couldn't do it anytime, no. Not if he wanted to gut the Vaultange wallets and get away with it. Think it through Jess. Maybe—'

Jess kicked him again, harder and this time she connected with his broken arm. Henry howled in pain. Jess leaned closer. 'Now will you be quiet!

SIXTY-TWO

JESS ESTIMATED she had been asleep for an hour at the most when the door opened. She woke as she fell out, landing on the concrete curled stiffly on her side, her eyes watering as they adjusted to the light. Two men on either side of her hauled her upright, sending blood coursing into her feet, the fierceness of the resulting tingling almost making her cry out. Unable to support her weight she was half-dragged, half-carried to the other side of the space and pushed into a chair. A roll of duct tape was produced, and while one man wrapped it around her chest and the back of the chair, the other did the same with her arms and legs.

By now her eyes had adjusted to the gloom and she became aware she was in an old factory. The machinery was gone, rusty chains hung from beams around the walls, and the few high windows were grimed with years of dust and cobwebs. An old wooden work bench had been set up in front of her, with three mismatched stools arranged along one side.

'Please, please, don't do this,' Henry begged as he was dragged and dumped in the chair beside her. His suit, freshly stained at the crutch, was ripped in places and he was barefoot. Jess recognised one of men from the funeral. He kicked Henry's legs out from under him to make him sit, and with a grim face taped Henry to the chair in the same manner as Jess, ignoring Henry's screams when he slammed the broken arm on to the arm rest and taped it. She couldn't look. Listening to his whimpering was bad enough. If she wanted to survive, Jess couldn't allow herself to be infected by his fear. She had to stay in her own reality, she had to stay calm. Three men took up positions behind the bench. The man from the funeral was dressed in black, tall and muscle bound, the light reflecting from his shaved head, above dead eyes. He said nothing. His two companions were smaller. They were less sure of themselves, edging away from him, their hands held nervously in front of their bodies, their eyes fixed on a spot above Henry's head. If she could get rid of the funeral guy, she was pretty sure, the others would run.

Before she had time to think of a plan, Murray Chambers emerged from the gloom at the back of the factory. The three men stood to attention and stared straight ahead as they listened to his approaching footsteps. Murray was as short as she remembered and he was still stocky, but he'd lost weight by the look of his clothes which were hanging loosely on his frame. He walked straight across to Henry, bending over him, speaking so quietly Jess had to strain to hear what he was saying. Even then she didn't hear every word, but she didn't need to. Murray wanted the PIN and the passwords.

After the first hammer blow to Henry's broken arm, Jess vomited, spewing the contents of her stomach down the front of her damp clothes. Henry's scream was a sound she would hear for the rest of her life. The two little guys looked at each other, their eyes dark and round as they shifted from foot to foot. With tears running down her face Jess yelled at Henry. 'Tell him, just tell him for chrissakes.' Henry, his lips bared in front of gritted teeth, shook his head. 'I told you. I don't know.'

Murray hit the arm again. Harder, the hammer bouncing up on impact with the arm rest. Henry's eyes bulged, in their sockets, spittle hung from his open mouth as he made the sound of hell. Jess had nothing left to vomit.

'Tell me the PIN,' Murray said quietly. The rain had stopped and Henry's moans were the only sound echoing off the factory walls.

'He changed it. I don't know.' Murray held the hammer to Henry's mouth and gently tapped his teeth. He swung backwards then forwards, stopping an inch in front of his mouth. Laughing, Murray pivoted on his left heel and walked the few steps to stand in front of Jess.

'First the PIN number, Jess, then the seed words. What are they?'

Jess couldn't believe how reasonable he sounded. It was as if he was asking for directions with every expectation of receiving a civil answer. She shook her head. Murray turned his back. The man from the funeral stepped into the gap. He was holding the hammer. Jess saw it and glanced up at Murray. His head moved a fraction of an inch.

When the man from the funeral pulverised the tip of Jess's left little finger with one blow, Jess screamed. Her scream, high-pitched and long, echoed around the building smothering every other sound. She screamed again and again, barely drawing breath as tears ran down her face. When she stopped, it was Murray who picked up the hammer and asked her the question again. 'The PIN? What did Andrew change it to? You were with him. You know what it is.'

'I don't. I don't know it. I swear.' She begged and pleaded over and over again. He raised the hammer above her right hand, halting midway with his swing. Jess peed then, the urine pooling on the floor under the chair. Murray stepped over it and asked her again. 'Tell me the PIN Jess. Tell me what it is. You know it, you were with him, what is the PIN.'

'I told you, I don't know. I don't know.'

The man from the funeral moved in front of Murray.

'Jess. Think. Please.' Henry was talking. 'Andrew wouldn't tell you the actual numbers, okay? Did he have a word he used for you, a pet name? Something which reminded him of you.'

Through her tears, Jess looked at the mash of blood and bone, all that was left of her finger. She was in so much pain, how could she bear any more, how would she cope if Murray carried on smashing her fingers one by one until her hands were useless? How would she return to medicine without functioning fingers? She remembered Andrew's fingers, his hands, his face, his lovely face, his voice was telling her how brave she was, how much he loved her, how he loved her kind eyes. Over and over, he had told her she had kind eyes and she had believed him — she had believed him. Because she loved him.

'Kind eyes,' she said.

'Kind eyes,' Henry repeated as he worked it out. 'Eight letters Murray. Assign a number to a letter. K is 11, defaults to 1, I is 9, N is 14 or 4 ....'

Murray was faster. 'The password. It's 1, 9, 4, 4, 5, 3, 5—'

'Nine, the last number is nine. 1.9.4.4.5.3.5.9.' Jess looked up. Guy Harding was standing next to Murray.

The man from the funeral, the nervy sidekicks, all gone. Guy put his arm around Murray's shoulder. The hammer slid to the floor, landing with an empty clang on the stained concrete.

SIXTY-THREE

JESS LOOKED up from the book she was reading and saw DS Parker's
face on the evening news — again. Parker was at a press conference in
front of a roomful of reporters, answering their questions with non-
committal replies. She'd had a makeover. Gone were the black jeans
and jersey, replaced by a smart-red suit over a silk-patterned shirt.
She was even wearing make-up. Groomed, confident and in control,
Parker was a different woman. Jess turned off the TV. The mysterious
disappearance of Bryan Randall and the arrest of his murderer had
been the leading news story for three days. Every time she turned on
the TV, she saw Parker looking serious but feminine. The police
hierarchy had swung the full might of their PR machine in behind her
and she was positively glowing with the attention. Murray Chambers
had been charged with Bryan's murder and was on remand in prison,
awaiting trial. No mention was made of his role laundering money for
the gangs, or his association by proxy with Vaultange. From her
hospital bed Jess had to conclude the highest echelons in law
enforcement, for reasons known only to themselves, had decreed this
side of Chamber's story was to be kept hidden. For how long was
anyone's guess.

Jess looked at the gap where her finger should have been. Murray's face as he brought the hammer down flashed in front of her. If he lived long enough to appear in court, his murder conviction would be the least of his worries. The gang believed Murray had stolen thirty-seven million dollars from them. Sooner or later, whenever they damn well pleased, in fact, they would take their revenge. She didn't feel sorry for him, but the knowledge brought her no comfort.

It had been a long week. She would have more sympathy for her patients in future, now that she knew first-hand how exhausting and relentless pain could be, draining you of the will to live. From stopping sleep to making every movement something to be anticipated and managed, she was grateful not only for the medication but for the care and attention of the nursing staff. Being in a private room meant she didn't have to deal with other people's noises and smells, their inane conversation or their visitors sneaking looks and whispering about her. She could concentrate on getting better.

Guy Harding had arranged her treatment. So he should, thought Jess. How long had he been outside the factory, listening to Henry's screams, then her own? Doing nothing because he said it was police procedure to wait for back-up. Having her admitted to the Mercy Ascot under an assumed name was his way of saying sorry for his lack of action. 'The false name is so the press won't find you,' Guy assured her when she questioned him. 'Or the gangs.' She banished the thought of what they would do to her, if they found her, from her mind and concentrated on getting better.

Auckland's top hand surgeon had been waiting when she arrived by ambulance at the entrance. She was taken straight to X-ray and from there to surgery where her finger was deemed beyond repair and had to be amputated at the knuckle.

The nurse had just been and taken off her bandage and she was staring at the new shape of her hand when Guy walked into her room — without knocking and sat down.

'That's a long and complicated story — your Henry is telling my associates.'

'He's not my Henry.'

It was if she hadn't spoken. 'He exonerates you completely, you'll be relieved to know.'

'So he should. I've done nothing wrong, nothing to deserve this,' Jess said as she held up her hand. It felt heavy and weird, as if her finger was still there poking the air next to the others. 'How is he?'

'He's still got his arm if that's what you're asking. I can't say for how long, but everything that can be done is being done. On the other matters, he's been very helpful.'

That was all she needed to know. She didn't want anything more to do with the man. Better to flex her fingers and tap into her pain as a distraction. Better to focus on Guy and what he'd come to tell her. He was here for a reason. She knew by now, Guy Harding didn't make social calls.

'You got the PIN right by the way,' he said. 'But without the seed words, it's not much use.' He looked at Jess. She looked back.

'The money's gone,' she said.

'For now.' Guy got up and walked over to the window which looked out on to a line of poplar trees planted between the hospital grounds and the house next door, their leaves brown and golden against the grey sky. He plunged his hands deep into his trouser pockets and rocked backwards on his heels. 'Our sources tell us the gang considers the matter closed. The man responsible for the losses has been found. He will be dealt with. Respect and order will be restored. Lessons have been learnt and the same mistakes won't be made again.'

'That's it?' she asked. 'The gangs are happy. All's right with the world?'

'I didn't say that.' Guy was annoyed. 'This is a very complicated investigation, and it's still playing out. However, you'll be relieved to know your role in it is over.'

'My role? What did I do?'

'You led us to Murray.' Seeing the puzzlement on her face he continued. 'After Andrew's death, Murray thought you and Henry were in cahoots against him. It was only a matter of time before he wanted to talk to you in person.'

'You used me as bait to lure him out.' Jess shifted in her bed, pain flashing the length of her absent finger.

'You were monitored throughout. How do you think we found you?'

'Ahmed,' she said. After everything she'd been through, it was hard to feel grateful for the brown eyes in the rear vision mirror.

'Ahmed sends his best wishes.'

'I didn't treat his mother?'

'Yes, you did, that part was true. It's just that he's not an Uber driver. That part we made up.'

Jess shook her head. 'What happens now? To me I mean?'

'You get better and you go home. We won't need to meet again.'

Why did this sound like an order?

'If I were you, I'd leave the country. The Medical Council is not inclined to look favourably upon someone who lied to get into medical school, no matter how well that person might have done subsequently. Not to mention the now very public conviction for manslaughter which still stands. You know what a conservative bunch doctors are. And how they fight like cornered rats to protect the reputation of the profession. Or so my sources tell me. Patients should be able to trust their doctors not to knock them off when things get a bit tough. A pity because from what I've heard, you were good at your job.'

'But you've got Bryan's statement. Give it to them.'

'What statement?'

'Parker gave it to me. It was in my bag.'

'Did she indeed?'

'I had it at the factory. My guess it's either in the car or in the cupboard where they kept us.'

'It's a crime scene Jess. We've searched the place from top to bottom. We found no statement.' Guy was too busy picking dirt from under a nail to look at her.

SIXTY-FOUR

'You know the rest,' I said. 'You saw what he did to me.' Silence. 'How long do I have to stay here?' I called out to the room. 'What's going to happen to me? I've kept my side of the bargain. I've told you all I know.' Silence. 'Is anybody there? Hello? Hello?' Silence.

I eased myself out of bed, lifting my arm carefully so as not to catch the metal brackets on the sheets. As I stood upright for the first time in weeks it took a few moments leaning against the bed for the dizziness to pass. When I felt my way along the wall to the door, I half expected it to be locked. The handle turned easily. I pushed it open, unsure what would be on the other side — more white — more doors — no windows. I felt a draught on my legs, bare under the hospital gown. I was almost at the end of the corridor when a door opened and a middle-aged nurse bustled towards me.

'Mr Turner, going for a walk? It's about time. The doctors will be pleased to see you up and about. Can I help you back to your room? You must be exhausted.'

I was surprised to find she was right, I was exhausted. I let her take my good arm and help me back to my room.

'Where am I?' I asked.

'You're in hospital.'

'But which hospital?'

'Come now, let's get you settled. It's time for your medication.' She took a container out of the pocket on her uniform and shook out two tablets which she handed to me along with a glass of water. 'These will help with the pain.'

'My pain is better. Please tell me where I am.'

'You're in your room at the hospital,' she said firmly this time. 'That's all you need to know for the time being. I'll ask Mr Harding to come and see you. He'll explain everything.'

SIXTY-FIVE

THE WEEK in hospital working with the physiotherapist gave Jess time to come to terms with her new reality. Guy was right. With no prospect of her career being rehabilitated, no husband and no company, there was nothing to keep her in the country. There were too many memories in Auckland, too many triggers. Still lurking in the shadows was the gang. Guy said they were operating as before. Business had never been better. Sure, they had Murray once the authorities were finished with him, but she had no guarantee they would not come looking for her. She was still the public face of Vaultange. She had to get away.

Ross and Ronald were more than capable of overseeing the liquidation of Vaultange plus they could contact her by email if necessary. The insurance money would take care of their fees and there would be some left over to make partial repayments to the more deserving clients, those who could prove genuine hardship. The fickleness of the justice system after her mother's death had shown Jess that what was legal was not always fair. Ross assured her the right people would get what was owed to them. The rest, the gamblers and speculators, would have learnt their lessons and moved on.

She transferred ownership of Gordon Holdings to Carole. The

properties weren't worth four million, but the land had some value. She asked Ross to wait until she'd left the country before informing Carole of the arrangement. That was all she could do. She didn't want to see Carole again. She didn't want to explain the loss of her finger. More importantly, Jess was done with apologising.

The people who would lose most from Vaultange's demise were the criminals. Jess didn't care. Just as they didn't care about the victims of their crimes. The amount lost was a drop in the bucket and easily recouped. Murray's capture meant they saved face. Maybe that was all they wanted. Jess wasn't going to stick around and find out.

The week before her departure, Jess took the car for a last drive out to Piha. Wrapped up warmly, with her scarf around her face, she drove out to the coast with the top down. She filed away the smell of the bush, wet with winter rain, the birdsong and the clear sky above with memories of her mother to retrieve later if she should ever become homesick. The dark-sandy beach pounded by waves was empty, the weather too cold even for the hardiest of surfers. The store was closed, the houses scattered on the steep hillsides, shuttered. She turned the car around and drove back. There was nothing for her — here.

The car made fifty thousand dollars at auction. The brooch, three hundred and twenty thousand, not as much as it was worth but enough. Jess thought long and hard about selling her engagement ring. It meant losing her link with Andrew, but when she put it on it looked silly with no little finger to hold it in place. It easily reached her reserve price of forty thousand dollars. Able to repay the advance from Ross, Jess had enough money left over to start her new life.

She bought first class tickets to Athens where she would catch a plane to Corfu. She wanted to feel warm every day, swim in the ocean and enjoy the relaxed island life she had read about when she was a child. With the money left over, she bought Bitcoin at US$5323.

It was early June before she was ready to go. Her worldly possessions were packed into her trusty suitcase, the file was safely stashed in her carry-on luggage, as she did a last circuit of the apartment. There had been happy times here and she was grateful for the memories. Jess pressed the ground floor button one final time. The Uber driver had been waiting long enough.

Somewhere over the Indian Ocean, Jess woke up. Several hours into the flight from Auckland, unable to get to sleep, she'd taken one of Andrew's sleeping tablets. Still groggy and with a bitter taste in her mouth she padded unsteadily to the bathroom, washed and brushed her teeth and changed into summer clothes. The temperature in Athens was twenty-eight degrees and she didn't want to be sweating in winter clothes on her arrival. Back in her seat, feeling human again, Jess pressed the call button. The attendant arrived with a smile and Jess asked for champagne. As she sipped from her glass, she took the file out of her bag. Everything was as exactly as it was when Ross had given it to her. Memorising the contents, she had replayed it in her mind many times since; twenty-four pages detailing the findings of the investigation into her past. Back then she had noticed the irregularity on each page but had dismissed these as mistakes by a punctuation-ignorant author. It was after Henry explained how a Nano S worked, that the mistakes had made sense. The author hadn't made them — they had been added. On the first page, the word *family* had unnecessary quotation marks. On the third page, either side of *house* there were inexplicable hyphens. Twenty-four seed words embedded in order on twenty-four numbered pages.

Andrew had entrusted the file to Ross to keep in safe storage while they were away. The same as the sticks in the car, he had anticipated that if he was not around to recover them, Jess would be. He had risked everything assuming she would pass the sticks on to the authorities, but he knew she would keep the file to herself. Jess smiled and sipped her champagne. What a distraction those sticks had proved to be. Sending the investigation down a blind alley to nowhere, wasting valuable time and testing the patience of all involved.

It was the next part of his plan which was a masterstroke. And a gamble. How much he would have enjoyed wondering what she would do with the file? Would she understand its significance? Would she keep it? Or destroy it? To know the answer to that, Andrew had to know her.

Their last month together hadn't been his building their relationship so much as a psychological assessment. When Henry said it was Andrew who had bought the properties, Andrew who had transacted the deals using crypto taken from the exchange, she hadn't wanted to believe him. But why would he lie? He had been as shocked as she had been when he found out the properties were fake. Then, when they were about to be questioned by Murray, he knew they were never going to get out of there alive. Why not tell Murray what he wanted to know and spare himself the pain? Every conversation Andrew had with her was so he could work out how she thought. In every regard except her childhood, Jess was an open book with the ability to rationalise and make complex decisions. Anything to do with her childhood and she shut down. As he'd predicted, she had kept the file. Not only had she kept it, but she had hidden it, guarding it fiercely from prying eyes. Her guilt, her shame, her fear, the file held it all. But it was more than that. It was a tangible connection to her past, with her mother. Andrew had bet his company that Jess would carry the file with her forever. Andrew the master strategist had played her — brilliantly.

When the flight attendant appeared and refilled her glass, beads of bubbles fizzed randomly to the surface of the wine.

'I'd like to change my booking, before we land if possible,' Jess said.

'Certainly, what did you have in mind?'

'Instead of flying straight to Athens today I'd like to break the journey and spend a day in Qatar City.'

'One day? Would you like me to organise accommodation and a car?'

'Yes. That would be very helpful.' She sipped her second glass of champagne, smiling as she stared out of the window.

SIXTY-SIX

'THESE WALLS ARE DRIVING me nuts Guy. The doc told me I needed your permission to leave, so ...?'.

'You're not worried?'

'A little, but I'll take my chances. Once I get rid of this thing.' I lifted my arm off the bed.

'Ah. We're in the middle of an operation. Murray has been helpful, in exchange for us keeping him in solitary. He's opened up several lines of inquiry that we didn't have before which we are pursuing, but it'll take time.'

'How long?'

'Six months, maybe a year.'

'I'm not Murray. I have my rights. Either you charge me with a crime, or you have to let me go.'

'I wish it were that simple.'

'It is that simple. I'd like to see a lawyer — today.'

'This is a hospital, not a jail. You're receiving treatment, you're not technically in custody. No can do re the lawyer I'm afraid.'

'If it was truly a hospital, I would be able to get up and walk out that door and no one would stop me.'

Guy walked to the end of the room, turned and leant against the white wall. He sighed. 'If I could be sure you would never breathe a word of this to anyone then maybe, just maybe we could come to an arrangement.'

I screwed up my eyes. 'A word about what?'

'Andrew, Vaultange, the whole shebang. Never speak about it again. As far as the press is concerned it's over. The DTCU doesn't want it brought up, nor do the banks. Forget you even heard of cryptocurrency. Andrew Cullinane was just some guy you met once at school. That's all — end of.'

I looked down at my arm. There was a gap between skin and bone where once I'd had muscle — now there was nothing where once I'd had strength. The skin grafts covered the defect, but the tissue underneath was gone forever. With no sensation and no grip what use was my hand except as a dead weight on the end of my arm?

'You want me to forget Andrew. Forget five years of my life? Is that what you're asking?'

'Sounds about right. I don't want you telling a soul — ever. You've got money put away. Don't get greedy and you can keep it. In fact, I'd be willing to help you cash up before you go into witness protection. How does that sound?'

'Witness protection? Where exactly?'

'I couldn't possibly say, but you'll be safe.'

'Why do I get the feeling you're not just talking about the gang.'

'As I said earlier this is a complex operation, we have new leads.'

'How do you know I have money put aside?'

'Andrew told us. Before he left ....'

I lay back on my pillows and smiled. 'Andrew knew, didn't he?'

Guy walked slowly to the door, opened it and turned around. 'Andrew who? I don't believe you know anyone by that name. Or do you?'

'I knew an Andrew at school, but I haven't seen him in years. My mistake. You're right. I thought we were talking about someone else entirely.'

SIXTY-SEVEN

THE HOUSE WAS EXACTLY as it appeared on the website. At the end of a short road suited more to donkeys than cars it had been built of local stone three hundred years before on much older foundations. Situated on a rocky promontory between Kalami Bay and Chouchoulio Beach on the northern coast of Corfu, it was small and private. Double wooden doors opened to a small courtyard, the living room, kitchen and bedroom with en-suite, opened off that. A terrace encircled the house, and at one end of this steps led over rocks to a jetty and tiny private beach. It was all she required.

Not interested in cooking, Jess ate her one meal of the day at the local tavern in the evenings. Being among tourists, even if she didn't understand what most were saying, helped her to feel less lonely while she waited.

A week after her arrival, everything was in place. It was Saturday the 29th of June 2019. She was ready. The extra wide monitor had been installed in the living room and the software uploaded. She positioned the file under the keyboard, after smoothing a corner which had been bent in transit. Two champagne flutes and an ice bucket sat waiting on the bench beside the refrigerator which was stocked with a half dozen bottles of Krug. The bedlinen in the master bedroom had been upgraded to the finest Egyptian cotton. Flowers from the markets in Corfu city arranged in huge bunches around the house scented the summer air. Food from the taverna, cooked lobsters and salads and freshly baked breads, laid out on platters and covered in clingfilm were in the refrigerator. The maids had completed their final clean.

Jess showered and blow-dried her hair. No longer blonde, she had been to the stylist in Qatar and reverted to her original dark colour. It suited her, bestowing dignity without detracting from her beauty. The stylist suggested that her wardrobe could do with a similar makeover and referred her to boutique in a nearby mall. Never in her wildest dreams had Jess ever thought she would spend so much on clothes. But she had. Why not? Looking at herself in the mirror, it had been worth it. She looked amazing — irresistible, in fact.

Her phone pinged a text. 'On the way.'

Jess checked that the monitor was running, picked up her bag and put on her sunglasses before walking down the steps to the boat waiting at the jetty.

SIXTY-EIGHT

CAN a heart leap in your chest? Can a stomach literally get tied in knots? At the sight of Andrew getting out of the car at the entrance to the taverna, Jess's did both. A little thinner, bearded, and dressed in clothes she'd bought him, she would have recognised her husband anywhere — even from this distance. As she focused her binoculars, she studied the lines on his face, every minute wrinkle, exploring the face she knew so well for clues as to what he was thinking. If only he would take off his sunglasses and she could see his eyes. He walked around to the back of the car and took out his bag, then stepped aside so the driver could make a tight turn and drive back up the hill. He stood for a moment inspecting his surroundings, the narrow road between scrubby trees on the hillside behind the bay, the boats at anchor, people on the beach, then he picked up his bag and approached one of the waiters to ask for directions. She saw the waiter point towards the house before Andrew put his hand above his eyes to see where he was supposed to go. She was studying him so intently she could almost hear the wheels of his suitcase rumbling down the stone path to the door.

Hacking the camera on the monitor had been simple. Jess put down her binoculars and opened her laptop. She watched the front door open. He called her name and the sound of his voice almost made her cry out.

Andrew was breathing heavily as he hauled his suitcase over the threshold and shut the door behind him. He took off his glasses and she saw the eager expectation in his eyes as he surveyed the room. He called again and when there was no response he went to the bedroom, noting first her clothes in the wardrobe, then the fresh linen on the bed. He peered inside her suitcase, left open on the luggage rack, and felt the damp towels, bringing one up to his face to smell it. She saw him smile.

In the kitchen he opened the refrigerator and took out a bottle of champagne and read the label before putting it back. He smiled properly then — the smile which had always made her want him — even now.

Once he'd walked through the doors on to the terrace, she saw him bend over the balustrade, searching the sea, the jetty, and the beach in quick succession. He stopped then, his hands in his pockets, a man in silhouette standing in contemplation in front of a house.

He noticed the file as soon as he went back inside. He pulled up a chair and sat down, his face so close to the monitor, Jess wanted to reach out and touch him. His brow wrinkled, then the lines above his nose deepening as he flicked through the pages quickly at first, then again. Slowly this time, running his fingers over every word marked with parentheses, or commas or hyphens or any of the other random punctuation marks Jess had seen fit to insert after her third glass of champagne.

The pages dropped to the floor. He opened his mouth, then closed it again. He started to type and stopped, unable to believe what she'd done. His phone rang in his pocket.

'Jess?' His voice was uncertain.

'Andrew.'

He looked at the camera and shook his head. The silence between them grew longer, neither willing to be the first one to speak. 'What have you done?' he asked eventually.

'I could ask you the same thing.'

I'm guessing you've already worked it out.'

'Clever Andrew. Which Musketeer were you by the way? I've been picking Aramis.'

'Right now I feel like Pathos.'

'Porthos? Oh. I get it. Very good.'

'Where are you?'

'I'm not ready to tell you.'

'I came back for you.'

'Did you Andrew? Or did you come back for the file? That's what I can't work out. You, Simon, Tim. You made me believe you were dead.'

'I had to. I found out what Henry and Murray were planning. It was the only way to save everything I had worked for. Who would believe I wasn't involved when the crypto disappeared? I'd only just met the love of my life and I didn't want to spend the next ten years in prison.'

How did you get the others to do it?'

'They're my friends. They'd do anything for me.' The laugh that followed sounded bitter. 'I paid them — up front. You've worked out the properties in Gordon Holdings have no value, I presume. The money went to them. Tim has his new hospital, Simon bought the resort.'

Hearing him confirm her suspicions, didn't help.

'Where are you Jess? Please tell me. I did this for you. For us.'

'Murray tortured Henry and me, Andrew. Your best friend, and your wife. Johnny is dead and Carole thinks I'm responsible. I can't practice medicine. Everything I worked for is gone.'

'I'm here. I came back for you. I'm sorry about your finger. I am. When Guy told me I was sick thinking about what you went through. I swear I'll make it up to you. For the rest of our lives, I'll make it up to you.'

'Guy?'

Jess hung up.

Guy had been part of this all along. She saw it now. From the beginning. It had to be Guy who told Andrew about Henry and

Murray. From inside the investigation, he'd been able to watch Jess for any sign she knew more than she should. He had waited outside the factory listening to their screams, not because he was waiting for back-up, but because he wanted to hear what they had to say. Guy had taken Bryan's statement, destroying it along with any hope of her being able to return to medicine. He had suggested there was nothing for her, and that she leave the country. Using his contacts, he had tracked her to the isolated house at the end of an isthmus on a Greek Island. That's how Andrew found her so quickly.

He picked up on the first ring. 'Jess?'

'What's happened to Henry? What did Guy do to him?'

'He's safe as long as he stays quiet. I made sure he'd be okay. He was my friend.'

'I'm sure he's very grateful.'

'Sarcasm Jess?'

'I sold the cold wallet last week.'

'Not all of it?'

'All of it.'

'You're joking. You have to be. That was my money. My Bitcoin. No one, not even you would be that stupid.'

Jess listened to the sound of his breathing, now harsh and fast. He started to speak and stopped. She waited.

'Jess?'

'Yes.'

'You know what you've done? You know you've ruined everything. What we had, what we were going to have — it's gone. You know that don't you.'

Jess had heard enough. She hung up. One of the stewards filled her glass. She told him to let the captain know she was ready to leave. The anchor chain clunked link by link against the hull, the yacht swinging free in the tide as the noise of the engine grumbled in reverse to get purchase in the water. Two men hoisted the sails, the material slapping in the breeze until they caught the wind, the boat heeling slightly as it moved out into the channel. Jess raised her glass and took a sip. She was getting used to champagne.

Three days before on the 26th of June 2019 to be precise, Jessica Davidson had opened the Vaultange cold wallets. One week earlier, Mark Zuckerberg of Facebook fame announced he was setting up a new cryptocurrency. It would be called Libra and it was to be backed by a range of currencies. People would be able to use it to buy goods online anywhere in the world. It was the announcement the community had been waiting for. Inigo and the others in her chat group were over the moon. Cryptocurrency was here to stay.

Jess sold Bitcoin at US$12,000. From the gang's initial investment of thirty-seven million dollars, she harvested one hundred and thirty-two million dollars. Fully funded, the Marguerite Davidson Memorial Foundation for the study of Immunological Disorders, would just be the beginning. She had plans, big plans for how she was going to put the money to good use.

Jessica Davidson stood at the stern of the yacht and raised her binoculars. She focused on the man standing on the terrace of a house she had left behind. As the distance between them grew, the man got smaller and smaller until he disappeared altogether. She put down her binoculars and went inside.

The End

ABOUT THE AUTHOR

Rosy Fenwicke is a full time writer living in Martinborough, New Zealand. In 2004 she edited, *In Practice: the Lives of New Zealand Women Doctors in the 21st Century*. This was published by Random House. Since then she has self-published three novels to good reviews — *Death Actually*, and *Hot Flush* and *No Sweat*, the first books in the *Euphemia Sage Chronicles*.

Rosy writes a monthly blog and newsletter to keep her Reader's Group up to date with news, special offers and general bits and pieces. You can read her blog and join her Reader's Group at www. rosyfenwickeauthor.com

She can also be found on Facebook at https://www. facebook.com/rosyfenwickeauthor

ALSO BY ROSY FENWICKE

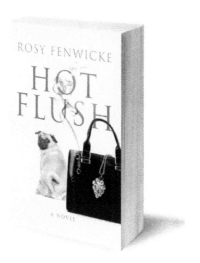

Hot Flush: Book One in the *Euphemia Sage Chronicles*

She's never backed down from a challenge. But nothing could have prepared her for her super-powered change of life.

"I absolutely loved this book. Who of us, that is, women of a certain age, would not love to develop super powers with menopause, other than being able to start sweating at the drop of a hat. The characters were engaging, the story captivating, and it kept me reading to find out what was going to happen next. I am looking forward to the next book." Patricia: 5 Stars: Goodreads

"I read this from cover to cover in one sitting and am eagerly awaiting Euphemia's next adventures". Michele: Goodreads 5 Stars.

Available at all good New Zealand bookshops and online.

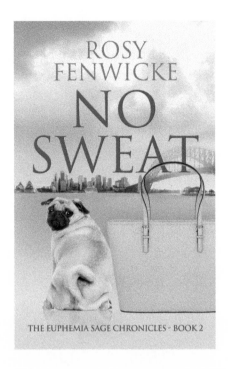

No Sweat: Book Two in the *Euphemia Sage Chronicles*

Tracked by a pesky journalist, opportunities for developing her powers are scarce. Her family and friends are mystified, and she can't explain.

Book Two of the *Euphemia Sage Chronicles* follows the fast-paced twists and turns we have come to expect from our favourite post-menopausal super heroine to reach an action-packed and satisfying conclusion.

> *"I enjoyed hot flush but really enjoyed 'No Sweat'. It was a great read and the chapters flew by. It was disappointing to finish as I wanted more. So can't wait for Euphemia's next challenges in the next book."5 Star Review.*

Available at all good New Zealand bookshops and online.

Box set of *Euphemia Sage Chronicles* also available (online only)

Death Actually

It's the middle of winter and Queenstown, a resort town in New Zealand, is full of skiers. Betty has just died and Elka needs surgery. Kate, a talented young chef is back from London and won't get out of bed. Nick feels guilty delivering fast food to an ex-champion skier, bitter about the injury which robbed her of glory. There is a movie star in town who, won't listen to advice and Maggie can't seem to put a foot right with the new doctor in town.

Review: The Reader: *NZ Booksellers Blog: 'The author has gently moulded the strands of the story together with humour and it moves along at a brisk pace with some very satisfactory outcomes from the twists and turns she created among the characters ... The underlining theme highlights strength, reliance and hope while looking to the future.'*

Review: Wardini Books: 'Death Actually is a light and lovely read; a love story with a healthy dose of comedy, an engaging cast and multiple plot lines. It's full of life (and death) and infiltrated my emotions enough to make me cry at the end. Definitely worth a read.'

Available at all good New Zealand bookshops and online.

ACKNOWLEDGMENTS

This work would not have been possible without the support and advice of Josie whose patience astounds me. I am proud to be your mother. Thanks also to Barbara Henderson, who provided the first appraisal and sent me back to the drawing board. To Barbara Unkovic thank you for your meticulous editing. Felicity and Judy — my early readers, I don't know what I would do without your support.

Thank you again to the amazing Elena for her cover design. Her work can be found at: https://99designs.com/profiles/l1graphics

And thank you to Martin Taylor at Digital Strategies for guiding this book into production.

Ganglands, by Jared Savage provided invaluable information about gangs in New Zealand and the impact of the '501s' on crime.

Information about Bitcoin and cryptocurrency is plentiful but not always easy to understand. No one knows who Satoshi Nakamoto is or was. I refer interested readers to https://bitcoin.org/bitcoin.pdf — the paper which started the Bitcoin revolution.

Grateful thanks for making the journey to understanding Bitcoin easier go to Peter McCormack and his podcast 'What Bitcoin Did'. I can highly recommend his series —*Beginner's Guide to Bitcoin.*

I recommend his bi-weekly podcasts to all those setting out to learn

about the meaning of money, the economies of nations and how cryptocurrency fits into the new world.
https://www.whatbitcoindid.com
For information about Quadriga, interested readers can access the Ontario Securities Commission Report:
https://www.osc.gov.on.ca/quadrigacxreport
Cold Wallet is a work of fiction. Anyone considering investing in cryptocurrency would be advised to take heed of the following statement.

"April 14 2020: Quadriga CX: A review by Staff of the Ontario Securities Commission: "Financial innovation has always been critical to the health of our economy and the competitiveness of our capital markets ... It is equally critical that investors have confidence to access new technologies and platforms that drive this innovation and competition. To that end, the investing public should be aware that using crypto asset trading platforms carries risks and that many crypto asset trading platforms are not registered and have taken the position that they are not required to register with securities regulators. Anyone considering entrusting assets to a crypto asset trading platform should take steps to learn about the platform's operations and approach to risk management prior to using it. This may not be possible with the current level of disclosure offered by some platforms."

If you would like to read more books by Rosy Fenwicke go to www.rosyfenwickeauthor.com

GLOSSARY

Allbirds: Shoes. https://www.allbirds.co.nz

Alt-coins: Altcoins are the other cryptocurrencies launched after the success of Bitcoin. The term "altcoins" refers to all cryptocurrencies other than Bitcoin. As of early 2020, there were more than 5,000 cryptocurrencies by some estimates. www.investopedia.com/terms

AML or Anti-Money Laundering: Anti-money laundering (AML) refers to the laws, regulations and procedures intended to prevent criminals from disguising illegally obtained funds as legitimate income. www.investopedia.com/terms

Bitcoin: a type of digital currency in which a record of transactions is maintained and new units of currency are generated by the computational solution of mathematical problems, and which operates independently of a central bank. www./languages.oup.com/google-dictionary-en

Bitcoin Halving: A Bitcoin halving event is when the reward for mining Bitcoin transactions is cut in half. This event also cuts in half Bitcoin's inflation rate and the rate at which new Bitcoins enter circulation. www.investopedia.com/bitcoin-halving

Blockchain: Blockchain is a shared, immutable ledger that facilitates the process of recording transactions and tracking assets in a business network. www.ibm.com/au-en/blockchain

Catheter Study: Cardiac catheterization is a procedure used to diagnose and treat certain cardiovascular conditions. During cardiac catheterization, a long thin tube called a catheter is inserted in an artery or vein in your groin, neck or arm and threaded through your blood vessels to your heart. www.mayoclinic.org/tests-procedures/cardiac-catheterization/about

Cold Wallet: A cold wallet is a wallet which is completely offline and used for storing cryptocurrencies. www.cryptoticker.io

Crema: a layer of creamy tan froth that forms on the top of freshly made espresso www.merriam-webster.com/dictionary/crema

Cryptocurrency: a digital currency in which transactions are verified and records maintained by a decentralized system using cryptography, rather than by a centralized authority. www.investopedia.com/terms/

Decentralised Ledger: A distributed ledger is a database that is synchronized and accessible across different sites and geographies by multiple participants. ... A distributed ledger can be described as a ledger of any transactions or contracts maintained in decentralized form across different locations and people. www.investopedia.com

Fiat: Fiat money is a government-issued currency that isn't backed by a commodity such as gold. Fiat money gives central banks greater control over the economy because they can control how much money is printed. Most modern paper currencies, such as the U.S. dollar, are fiat currencies. www.investopedia.com

Halving/ Halvening: see above.

Hardware Wallet: A hardware wallet is a special type of bitcoin wallet which stores the user's private keys in a secure hardware device. www.en.bitcoin.it/wiki/Hardware_wallet

Hot Wallet: A hot wallet is a tool that allows a cryptocurrency owner to receive and send tokens. Unlike traditional currencies, there are no dedicated banks or physical wallets that can be used to keep cryptocurrency holdings secure. www.investopedia.com

Private Key: A private key in the context of Bitcoin is a secret number that allows bitcoins to be spent. Every Bitcoin wallet contains one or more private keys, which are saved in the wallet file. ... Because the private key is the "ticket" that allows someone to spend bitcoins, it is important that these are kept secret and safe.

Public Key: A bitcoin public key is another large number but allows bitcoin to be locked and received. It's called a public key because it is meant to be shared publicly and enables you to receive funds.

Miner: Mining involves Blockchain miners who add bitcoin transaction data to Bitcoin's global public ledger of past transactions. In the ledgers, blocks are secured by Blockchain miners and are connected to each other forming a chain. ... In the same manner, a lot of computing power is consumed in the process of mining bitcoins. www.intellipaat.com/blog/tutorial/blockchain-tutorial

Mining: Bitcoin mining is the process of creating new bitcoin by solving a computational puzzle. Bitcoin mining is necessary to maintain the ledger of transactions upon which bitcoin is based. Miners have become very sophisticated over the last several years using complex machinery to speed up mining operations. www.investopedia.com

Mining Rig. Rig: A mining rig is a computer system used for mining bitcoins. The rig might be a dedicated miner where it was procured, built and operated specifically for mining or it could otherwise be a computer that fills other needs, such as performing as a gaming system, and is used to mine only on a part-time basis. www.en.bitcoin.it/wiki/Mining_rig

Node: A server or storage device which stores the entire Blockchain and runs a Bitcoin client software that peruses all transaction data and the Blockchain to check if they conform to Bitcoin protocol. www.blog.unocoin.com/bitcoin-miners-vs-bitcoin-nodes

Satoshi Nakamoto : the name used by the presumed pseudonymous person or persons who developed bitcoin, authored the bitcoin white paper, and created and deployed bitcoin's original reference implementation. As part of the implementation, Nakamoto also devised the first blockchain database. In the process, Nakamoto was the first to solve the double-spending problem for digital currency using a peer-to-peer network. Nakamoto was active in the development of bitcoin up until December 2010. Many people have claimed, or have been claimed, to be Satoshi Nakamoto. www.wikipedia.org/wiki/Satoshi_Nakamoto

Satoshi or Sats: "Sats" is short for Satoshis, the smallest unit of Bitcoin (BTC). One Satoshi (sat) is equal to 0.00000001 BTC (one hundred millionth of a Bitcoin). In other words, there are 100,000,000 satoshis in a Bitcoin. www.cryptocurrencyfacts.com/what-are-sats

Whale: A bitcoin whale is a term that refers to individuals or entities that hold large amounts of bitcoin , according to Investopedia. There are around 1,000 individuals who own 40% of the market.

Lightning Source UK Ltd.
Milton Keynes UK
UKHW010932180821
389055UK00001B/27